Bartholomew

Fair

MORE BY THIS AUTHOR

The Anniversary
The Travellers
A Running Tide
The Testament of Mariam
Flood
The Secret World of Christoval Alvarez
The Enterprise of England
The Portuguese Affair

Praise for Ann Swinfen's Novels

'an absorbing and intricate tapestry of family history and private memories ... warm, generous, healing and hopeful'
VICTORIA GLENDINNING

'I very much admired the pace of the story. The changes of place and time and the echoes and repetitions – things lost and found, and meetings and partings'
PENELOPE FITZGERALD

'I enjoyed this serious, scrupulous novel ... a novel of character ... [and] a suspense story in which present and past mysteries are gradually explained'
JESSICA MANN, *Sunday Telegraph*

'The author ... has written a powerful new tale of passion and heartbreak ... What a marvellous storyteller Ann Swinfen is – she has a wonderful ear for dialogue and she brings her characters vividly to life.'
Publishing News

'Her writing ...[paints] an amazingly detailed and vibrant picture of flesh and blood human beings, not only the symbols many of them have become...but real and believable and understandable.'
HELEN BROWN, *Courier and Advertiser*

'She writes with passion and the book, her fourth, is shot through with brilliant description and scholarship...[it] is a timely reminder of the harsh realities, and the daily humiliations, of the Roman occupation of First Century Israel. You can almost smell the dust and blood.'
PETER RHODES, *Express and Star*

Bartholomew

Fair

Ann Swinfen

Shakenoak Press

For

Tanya & Mark

Chapter One

I stood before the door of my home and stared at the unknown woman who was sweeping the steps. My dog Rikki pressed himself again my leg and whined softly as I laid my hand on the matted fur of his head.

'Is Dr Alvarez at home?' I asked her, trying to keep the panic out of my voice.

The woman stopped her sweeping and stared at me. Then she leaned on her broom and frowned. 'Are you his son? We were told his son had sailed on the Portugal venture.'

'Aye,' I said cautiously. Something was wrong. Where was Joan? This woman did not look like a servant.

'I am his son, Christoval Alvarez.' I frowned in my turn, suddenly full of mistrust. There was no Inquisition here. Surely my father was safe in London. Why was he not coming out to greet me?

'Where is he?' I demanded harshly. 'Where is Dr Alvarez?'

'You had better come inside,' she said.

She turned her back on me and I stepped after her into the kitchen. Rikki tried to follow, but she pushed him away with her broom and closed the door on him.

'Where is Dr Alvarez?' I repeated. Despite my attempt to keep my voice steady, I could hear that it shook a little.

'Dr Alvarez?' She propped her broom against the wall and faced me, her hands on her hips. There was something defiant in her face. 'Dr Alvarez has been dead these two months and more.'

1

A cry of pain burst from my lips. *Damn you, Dom Antonio! Damn you, Ruy Lopez, and all your schemes! May you rot in Hell!*

I swayed and clutched at the doorpost, as the world turned black. For a moment I thought I was back at the door of my grandfather's *solar*. Was I fated always to come too late? I knew my father had been declining fast when I left, but it was barely three months since we had sailed from London. He had seemed tired and confused, but not seriously ill. If I had not been carried off on that fatally flawed expedition by Ruy Lopez, at least I would have been here to hold my father's hand in his last moments, to help him turn his face to the wall in the traditional way, to say over him the *kaddish*, the prayers of farewell to the dead.

I am not sure how long I stood there in silence, staring down at the battered toes of my boots. I could not meet the woman's eye, in case I gave my feelings away. But I would need to assert who I was, so that I could reclaim my property. At last I lifted my head. Her expression had softened and she was looking at me not unkindly.

'So you are his son? You have returned from the Portugal venture?'

I nodded mutely. I must think. What was this woman doing here? Would the hospital allow me to continue in my post, if I was no longer working with my father?

'You are . . . ?' I asked tentatively.

'Mistress Temperley,' she said. 'Come.'

She waved me further into the kitchen and I looked around. Some of our furniture remained, but my father's fine carved chair was gone, and the hanging cupboard which held our medicines, and the press under the window where my father kept his precious books of Arabic medicine. In the far corner, near the door to the parlour, a baby was asleep in a cradle.

'You are living here?'

'My husband, Dr Temperley, is a physician. The governors of St Bartholomew's have appointed him, these six weeks gone, to take your father's place. They have given us this house and I

2

have been setting it in order, for it was in a fine pickle when we arrived!'

I sat down on a bench by the table, uninvited.

'Joan always kept the house sweet,' I said defensively.

'Was Joan your maid? She was long gone. When your father put all his money in the venture and the creditors came calling, she took another post, out at Barnes.'

'She had been paid in advance for the whole year till next March,' I said bitterly, 'on Lady Day, as she has been these seven years.'

So my father had died alone and uncared for.

The woman shrugged. 'A maid needs a mistress to keep her in order. My own girl would not dare do such a thing, or I would drag her back by her ear.'

'Where are all our goods? The medical equipment, the books, the medicines?'

I stared about me in horror. 'My lute? The recorders? Books of music?'

'Seized and sold by your creditors. My husband bought some of your things. Some furniture, the retorts and alembics. He thought he would buy the books as well, until he saw they were full of heathenish magical symbols.'

'Arabic,' I said dully. 'They were Arabic medical texts, the most precious and advanced in the world.'

It had taken my father nearly a lifetime to collect a library of Arabic medical books. We had lost them, along with everything else, in Coimbra, save for the four Dr Gomez had been able to salvage. Since we had come to London, he had spent little on clothes or food, but slowly and painstakingly, by searching the bookstalls in Paul's Churchyard, he had rebuilt his collection. My Arabic was still poor, but I had been trying to work my way through them before I went away.

'I had clothes,' I said. 'In my room upstairs. Three books of my own.'

She shook her head. 'All taken.'

She might as well have spoken it aloud, the next conclusion, for it hung in the air between us: I was destitute.

'I worked as my father's assistant in the hospital,' I said. 'I must go there and ask about resuming my duties.'

The woman gave me a look which was pitying but firm.

'My husband has his own assistant, his younger brother, who has just completed his studies in medicine at Oxford. There are no places left at the hospital.'

There was no more to say. A boy I had seen earlier in the street came clattering down the stairs, demanding that his mother help him tie his points. She turned away, forgetting me at once. I let myself out of my father's door and stood at a loss in Duck Lane amongst the familiar Smithfield dung and rubbish. Rikki was sitting amongst the blown straw in the gutter, looking at me anxiously. A young girl, carrying a market basket filled with vegetables and meat, stepped round me and went into the house. This must be the obedient maid. The sight of food awakened my hunger again, and I thought, somewhat bitterly, that the woman might have offered me a meal before turning me out of my home to wander the streets.

It was too much to comprehend at once. I felt overwhelmed. My grief for my father was tangled up in all this catalogue of disaster. I had no home, no profession, no money, and no possessions. I did not even have a whole suit of clothes to wear. For a long time I simply stood there, not knowing what to do. Then the hunger in my belly prompted me. I would think and plan better if I had something to eat.

With a whistle to Rikki, I walked the short distance to Pie Corner and used a ha'penny of Dr Nuñez's money to buy a hot pie from one of the shops which make them fresh from the meat corralled at Smithfield and slaughtered at the Shambles. This was no ordinary, with tables and chairs, instead I sat on the stone doorstep with the pie cupped in my hands, licking every drop of gravy that dripped on to my fingers and sharing the pie with Rikki. From the eagerness with which he gobbled down his portion I suspected that he had not eaten for a long time.

As usual, there were beggars and paupers in the street. As the saying goes, they were eating a meal of steam. Certainly the smell of the hot pies would bring the water to your mouth, but how cruel it must be when you knew that was the only taste of pie you would get. I wondered how long it would be before I joined those beggars. When one sidled up, looking for a handout, I hardened my heart and shook my head.

'I have nothing to spare,' I said. 'I am just returned from the Portugal expedition, and I have nothing.'

They were words that would become familiar to everyone in England in the next weeks.

The beggar glowered at me and aimed a kick at Rikki, but when I sprang to my feet and laid my hand on my sword, he ran off.

The food gave me some strength and I knew that the first thing I must do was to find somewhere to live, or at least to lay my head for that night. My journey back from Plymouth had used all but a handful of the coin Dr Nuñez had given me, so I could not possibly afford to stay at an inn, even one of the meaner sort. It was already late afternoon. Though it was July and the days were long, I must find somewhere before nightfall, for it would not be safe on the streets.

We knew very few of our neighbours, for my father had always kept somewhat to himself here, near the hospital. His friends were all in that other part of London, near the Tower and Aldgate, where most of our community lived, apart from those secondhand clothes dealers north of Bishopsgate, and the Lopez family in Wood Street.

Sara! I thought. Surely Sara Lopez would take me in, just as she had done all those years ago when we first arrived in London and I was a motherless waif of twelve. I had already started to make my way to Wood Street, with Rikki padding quietly at my heels, in fact had reached the corner of Newgate Street and Aldersgate Street, when my feet slowed of their own accord, and stopped.

Ruy Lopez would be home by now. He had set out for London with Dom Antonio even before I left Plymouth, both of them anxious to distance themselves as quickly and as far as possible from the angry creditors who awaited them at every turn of the street there in the town. I did not want to seek shelter with Sara if Ruy was at home. And if Ruy was there, Sara would have learned how disastrous the Portuguese expedition had been for her husband, and for her father Dunstan Añes, who had also invested heavily in it. I did not suppose Ruy would be ruined. He was far too crafty for that, far too careful to protect himself. He would have money invested elsewhere, in spices piled up in warehouses, in property, probably in precious gems and coin of the realm judiciously concealed in some safe hiding place. But even if he was not financially ruined, his reputation would have plummeted. What would the Queen say to him, who had been persuaded to invest four times her original stake, on the promise of rich rewards? What would Sir Francis Walsingham say, who had been promised defeat for the Spanish and their expulsion from Portugal? What would the Privy Council say, who had backed the venture and Dom Antonio's claim to the Portuguese throne? No, the Lopez house in Wood Street was no place for me to seek sanctuary.

Dr Nuñez? He had become almost a second father to me. No, he would still be in Plymouth. Unlike the other two, he had remained behind to try to set in motion some sort of compensation for the investors. Besides, he had looked so ill and tired before I started back to London that I could not take my troubles to him.

I stood there in the street, shaking off peddlers who tried to sell me hot codlings, spectacles, and shrimps. A man went by with his basket, calling out to maidservants to bring out any food scraps for the starving prisoners in the City's prisons. That spurred me on to get away from Smithfield and the hospital. It might be that my father's creditors had not been able to realise enough from our possessions to write off our debts. I might find myself taken up for debt and thrown in the Marshalsea with the debtors and Catholic priests.

The Marshalsea, I thought. *Simon!*

It was natural for me to think first of the motherly Sara, and of Dr Nuñez who had been so kind to me, but Simon Hetherington would help me. Someone of my own age, on whom I need not feel so dependent. Simon and I had first met when he summoned me to care for a prisoner at the Marshalsea, but that was a long time ago now, three and a half years. I would need to look for him amongst the players at the Theatre, north of the City, beyond Bishopsgate and near Finsbury Fields.

I began to hurry along Cheapside. If I could find Simon, surely he would let me sleep on the floor of his lodgings, for a night or two, until I found somewhere of my own. I had a moment's doubt about sharing a man's lodging, alone, but shrugged it off. I had spent the last three months on the ship *Victory* and in the army camp, living amongst men unmolested, by keeping to my cubbyhole on board ship and sleeping beside my horse on the long overland trek. During the fearful return voyage from Portugal, I doubt whether any member of our company would have noticed or cared, had my secret been suspected, we were all too concerned with merely staying alive. Simon had known me all the three years since we first met and believed me to be a young man like himself. Sometimes we make too much of what others see when they look at us. Simon would expect to see a youth, so he would see a youth. There would be no harm in it. I could not lose my reputation, for I had none to lose.

At Bishopsgate Street I headed north out of the City. I had to choose between the Theatre to the north, in Shoreditch, and the Rose, to the south of the river, in Southwark, but I thought Simon usually played the Theatre. Last winter he had had one engagement at the Rose, but that was Philip Henslowe's playhouse, where Simon had been on loan. Simon belonged to James Burbage's company, formerly the Earl of Leicester's Men, but since the Earl's death they were under Lord Strange's patronage. Burbage's men played at the Theatre and the Curtain, both beyond the north wall of the City, so I chose to go north.

I stopped at the Curtain as I passed, and asked for him, but they shook their heads. They knew nothing of his whereabouts. At the Theatre the crowd was just pouring out of the playhouse. I saw by the playbills blowing about in the gutter that they had been watching a play called *The Two Gentlemen of Verona*, said to be by someone called Will Shakespeare, a name I hadn't heard Simon mention. Here, at least, Simon was known, but I had made the wrong choice. The man sweeping out the galleried benches, and pocketing the odd coin dropped by playgoers, paused briefly.

7

'Simon Hetherington? Nay, he's been playing the Rose in Southwark all this summer. That's where you'll find him.'

Discouraged, I turned my back and started on the mile back to the City. I would then have to make my way across town to the river, over the Bridge, and walk along Bankside to the Rose. I stopped long enough to gather up some of the scattered playbills and stuff them into the bottom of my boots, to pad my feet a little, for I was hobbling like an old nag. Rikki, who looked as tired as I felt, plodded along behind me.

By the time I finally I reached the Rose, the playgoers were long away, the theatre closed up, and no one about. I sat down on the step and laid my head on my folded arms. I nearly cried with tiredness and the pain in my feet, but some instinct told me I must not give way, not yet at least. I could go to the Marshalsea. If the same keeper was on duty, the man Arthur that Simon knew, perhaps he could help me. Simon might be lodging again with Arthur's sister, if he was now working in a playhouse south of the river. I was so tired I must have dozed, and was woken by someone shaking my shoulder.

'Are you ill, young man?'

It was a kindly-looking woman of middle age, with strong arms showing below rolled-up sleeves and a vast apron of dazzling white tied around her comfortable waist. At her feet was a large buck-basket, containing brightly-coloured clothes, all neatly folded. I scrambled to my feet, rubbing the sleep out of my eyes.

'I'm seeking Simon Hetherington,' I said, 'one of the actors.'

'You come along with me,' she said. 'Take one handle of the basket. 'Tis much easier with two.'

'Are these costumes for the playhouse?' I asked, as we hoisted it between us. It was heavy, and I was surprised she had been able to lift it on her own.

'Aye, I wash for them. They care for these costumes better than they do for their own clothes, but I suppose they cost more.'

She led me round to a tiny cottage, not much more than a lean-to shed, on the other side of the playhouse, where the door was answered by a bent old man who kept watch on the Rose at night. He looked nervously at Rikki, who was a big dog, but seemed reassured when Rikki lay down despondently, his chin on his paws.

'Simon Hetherington?' he said, in answer to my question. 'Why, he's in the Low Countries this summer. He finished his time here with Master Henslowe and now Master Burbage has sent a travelling company to entertain the English garrisons over there, and then to tour the country. It's mostly the young fellows who have gone, and Simon amongst them. They'll not be back in London until the autumn.'

Chapter Two

$\mathcal{I}$ could indeed have wept, then. I had not realised how much I had counted on finding Simon and unloading my cares on him. If Simon would not return to London until the autumn, another two or three months at the very least, then I was truly bereft. Why I felt his loss suddenly and so deeply, I did not stop to ask myself.

The washerwoman and the watchman both looked at me with kind concern. The man pressed on me a glass of cheap ale, which I drank gladly, though it was bitter and caught in my throat, but I would not linger.

'It is getting dark,' I said, 'and the gate to the Bridge will be closed soon. I must go back to the City.'

The woman glanced briefly at my tattered stockings and the pitiful state of my boots, through which my grubby toes poked all too obviously.

'You can bide the night with me, my duck,' she said. ''Tis but a step away, past the bear garden.'

I shook my head and tried to smile, for it was a generous offer to make to a stranger, and one so clearly poor and desperate as I was.

'You are very kind, mistress, but I have friends in the City. I can reach their house before dark if I hurry. I thank you both for your goodness.'

I managed a better smile this time, taking them both in, and turned on my heel before my resolution failed. Rikki, who had been lying exhausted on the watchman's floor, hauled himself to his feet with a sigh.

I could not spare any of my precious pennies to take a boat across the river, but I must return to the City. Despite my wretched state, I part loped, part ran to reach the gate before it was closed. I would have to go to Sara in Wood Street after all, despite my reluctance to come anywhere near Ruy Lopez ever again. Gasping, my feet bleeding, I reached the Bridge just as the guards were swinging the first half of the gates closed and I slipped through the gap, Rikki clinging to my heels.

In the middle of the Bridge, I found suddenly that I could not go on. I crouched in a dark corner beside one of the houses and wrapped my arms around myself, for I had begun to shake. My father! He was dead. The reality of my loss suddenly loomed before me, impossible to shut out. For the last seven years we had clung to each other, the rest of our family lost. Never again would we work together, easing some patient's pain, or exchanging smiles when a sick man rose from his bed and took his first tottering steps. Never again would we sit by candlelight in the evenings, reading or playing music, on either side of the fire. Never again would I feel his hand on my head, saying a blessing over me before I went to bed. I laid my forehead against the damp bricks of the house and longed to howl like a lost child, for now I was truly alone in the world. Rikki pressed against me, shivering and whining. When I took my hands from my face and put an arm around him, he licked my wet cheek, as if to reassure me that I was not, after all, quite alone.

It was dark, summer dark with a large moon rising through racing rain clouds, when I knocked at last on the Lopezes' door. A maid opened it, Dorcas, a middle-aged woman I had known for years. She raised her candle-lantern the better to see and did not at first recognise me, tattered vagrant as I seemed to be. She frowned, then her frown changed to a look of sheer incredulity. Behind her Sara rushed forward with an inarticulate cry and put her arms around me.

'Oh, Kit! Are you safe? Ruy wasn't sure . . .'

I suppressed the urge to say that Ruy had not cared two farthings whether I had survived the voyage, nor had he offered me any help to reach London, as Dr Nuñez had done. In

Plymouth Ruy had ignored me totally. As Dorcas vanished into the back premises of the house, I could no longer suppress the sob which burst from me.

'My father,' I said. 'My father.' I need not hold back my tears before Sara, for she was my only woman friend and one of the very few people who knew my true identity.

She nodded and patted my cheek.

'I know, my dear. I'm afraid I heard nothing of your father's illness until it was too late.'

'Joan had abandoned him.' The words caught in my throat. 'He died alone and uncared for.' I was fuelled by anger as well as sorrow. 'They have taken everything. His creditors. Even my clothes. There are strangers living in our house, and strangers have taken our positions at the hospital. I have lost everything. I don't know what to do.'

My voice trembled like a child's. Had there been anyone to witness us then, I think my disguise would have been torn to shreds. I had no strength to play the man.

Sara took me by the arm and made no objection as the dog followed me into the house. Soon I was sitting with her in her private parlour, set apart from the large room where visitors were received and Ruy transacted his business. There was a small summer fire on the hearth, for although it was July it had turned wet and windy as dusk fell. I realised suddenly that the shoulders of my torn doublet were sodden. Rikki stretched out before the fire and a thin vapour began to rise from his damp fur.

Haltingly, for I was almost too tired to speak, I told Sara all that had happened that day. Before I was finished, one of the men servants had brought wine and food, which I ate without tasting, feeding half of it to Rikki, who gulped down every scrap, watching warily from the corner of his eye. He must have had to fight for every mouthful he had scavenged during these last weeks.

Sara reached across and took my hand.

'I had heard of your father's death, Kit, but only a week or more after it happened. Things have been . . . somewhat difficult, ever since the first despatches came in to my father from his fellow merchants in Spain and Portugal, that all was not well with

12

the expedition. We offered up prayers for your father. But I knew nothing about his creditors taking away all your goods. Ruy should never have pressed him to invest in Dom Antonio's Portuguese adventure. Well enough for City merchants with gold to gamble and little to miss if the venture failed. But not for a man like your father, who lost all he possessed so short a time ago, and had to start again from nothing, like a young man who has his life all before him. I cannot forgive Ruy for that!'

I pressed her hand, but could not speak. I, too, could not forgive Ruy.

She poured me more wine. I saw that she looked tired and worried. Everyone I knew seemed exhausted after this dreadful voyage, even those who had remained behind.

'Ruy?' I said. 'Has he lost a great deal?'

'He made Dom Antonio a loan of £4,000, against repayment when he was restored to his throne. Ruy is determined to have it back, and is this moment writing to the Privy Council, apologising for the failure and seeking the return of his investment.'

'But does the Dom have any money?'

'No. But there was some treasure taken, was there not?'

'Very little. And that will go to the Queen, I've no doubt. Anything that's left will find its way into Drake's pockets, I'd wager.'

'Walsingham refuses to speak to Ruy,' she said, getting up and pacing about the room, picking up her embroidery and wandering about with it in her hand, then throwing it down again.

'Walsingham will not speak to him,' she repeated. 'The Queen is outraged. The Privy Councillors want their own investments paid back. And his monopoly of aniseed and sumach imports is due for renewal. If he loses that we shall be worse off still. And he *will* lose it. They are bound to punish him. There is little they can do to Dom Antonio, save keep him in England as a pawn in the game with Spain, so they will punish Ruy in his place.'

I said nothing, but my face must have given away my feelings.

'Oh, I know, Kit.' She sat down with a sigh. 'Ruy is as much to blame as Dom Antonio, but he has had such dreams of returning to Portugal in glory! They are not my dreams, nor my children's.'

'It was not entirely their fault that the expedition failed,' I said. 'If Norreys had kept the soldiers in order in Plymouth, so that the provisions were not consumed, we would have sailed straight to Lisbon and taken the Spanish by surprise. And if Drake had not been more intent on attacking treasure ships and seizing booty than on the purpose of our mission, it might have succeeded even at the last. But Drake lied and betrayed us all.'

'It will do us no good, my dear,' she said, 'going over what might have been. Ruy is composing his letter of policy, in Italian if you please, to impress the Council – and telling them that I am ill, which I am not, in order to gain their sympathy – but you and I must decide what *you* should do. You will live here, of course. The house is more than large enough. And we must have new clothes made for you.'

She looked at me thoughtfully. 'How long do you intend to continue with this masquerade, Kit? You cannot live all the rest of your life as a man.'

I looked at her, startled. 'But I cannot give it up! How can I give it up? Now, of all times, when I have lost my father's protection!'

'You could live quietly concealed here, until your hair is longer. It has already grown while you have been away. That will change your appearance. Then we could bring you out in woman's attire, and say you are my cousin, newly come from Portugal.'

For a moment I was tempted. To give up my secret life and become a girl again, no longer afraid at any moment that someone would discover me, as my enemy Robert Poley had done. Poley himself would have no more power over me. Or would he? No, I could not do it.

'I should be recognised,' I said. 'Of that, I am sure. Walsingham. Despite his age, he has a keen eye. He would know me. Phelippes. I have shared an office with him for years. Harriot, my former tutor. We have had our heads together over so many mathematical problems. Day after day. That fellow, Marlowe, who has written plays for Simon's company. He has already as good as threatened mc, and he hates anyone with Jewish blood. There's an agent in Walsingham's service, Robert Poley . . . If it became known that I had lived in London seven years, disguised as a boy – they count it a crime of heresy, because it flaunts the divine hierarchy, a woman daring to pose as a man. I should be condemned to die at the stake.'

'Deuteronomy,' she murmured, ' "an abomination in the sight of the Lord". But you must realise, Kit, as you grow older, it will become more difficult to pass yourself off as a man. A girl of twelve can easily be assumed to be a boy, as you were. But a woman of thirty? Where will your beard be then?'

'Not all men of thirty wear beards!' I said, trying to make a jest of it. 'Besides, I am not yet twenty, not until come next Twelfth Night. Many young men in their twenties have no more than a wisp of a beard.'

I leaned forward and took her hand again. 'Besides, Sara, I am penniless. I must earn my living. As a man I can work, as a physician or as an agent for Walsingham. As a woman I can do nothing.'

'We will look after you.'

'No, Sara,' I said gently. 'You have five children of your own to care for and establish in the world. Ruy has lost heavily in this venture and probably will not recover his investment. He may lose his monopoly. If the Queen is angry enough, he may lose his greatest patient. Let me stay here a little while, until I find work. And I will gladly let you buy me new clothes, for I cannot present myself for work looking like a beggar. But let it be doublet, breeches, and hose, not bodice and kirtle.'

At last she agreed, and we made our way to bed. As I reached the foot of the stairs, following Sara with my candle, I saw that the light still shone under Ruy's door, where no doubt he was chewing the end of his quill and turning out his fine flourishes of Italian to appease a hostile Privy Council.

Sara found me a night shift of her own to sleep in, and Dorcas had brought a jug of hot water, soap and towel to the spare bedchamber. I dropped my sword, my satchel and my knapsack with my few remaining possessions on the end of the bed and stripped off my filthy garments with a feeling a joyous relief. I realised that if I had been able to sleep on the floor of Simon's lodgings, I would have been obliged to retain them, stench and lice and all. I was tempted to drop them out of the window onto the head of the Watch, whom I heard passing along the street below, but that would have been folly, in more ways than one. Instead, I bundled them into a heap and thrust it into the corner of the room furthest from the bed, in the hope that the livestock would stay there.

I washed every inch of my body with Sara's fine Castilian soap, and finished by plunging my head in the basin and scrubbing my fingers through my matted curls. Tomorrow I would need to borrow a comb. When I had finished, the water looked as if it had been drawn from a kennel running down one of London's filthiest alleys. I was ashamed that the servants would see it in the morning, but there was no avoiding that, unless I poured it out of the window. Once I was thoroughly dry, I pulled the shift over my head and it settled softly over my skin, which was still marked by bruises and sunburn, and the scabs left by the bites of fleas and lice. The touch of silk was like a caress on my poor misused body. As I washed, I had seen how my ribs stood out like the frets on a *viola da gamba*, and my hip bones poked like fingers through my flesh, for until we reached Plymouth I had starved along with the rest of our company.

Rikki was scratching earnestly as I stepped over to the window and opened the shutters. I feared he was also infested with fleas after his weeks as a stray. Outside, the rain had stopped and the moon, half-hidden in the final scraps of cloud, was dropping down to the west. Leaning out, I could see nothing moving below. I picked up the basin of filthy water and flung the contents out in a great arc into the dark, hearing the splash as it hit the ground below. Surely all the household would be abed now and would not notice, except perhaps Ruy, and his room looked out on the other side of the house.

The bed was soft, the linen scented with lavender, the feather bed and pillows surely filled with the finest goose down.

Ruy was never one to stint himself on the little luxuries of life. I was sinking rapidly into sleep when I was jerked awake by a heavy weight landing on my feet. Rikki had always slept on my bed at home. It would be difficult to make him understand that the dirt and fleas he now carried might not be welcomed amongst the Lopez bedding. He turned around several times, lay down, got up, then padded along the bed until he could stretch out against my chest. I put my arm around him and pressed my face against his thick fur. Holding him close, I finally let my grief break free.

The next morning I had feared I would have to force myself back into my filthy doublet and breeches, though my shirt and hose had fallen apart at last when I had peeled them off. Yet before I was fully awake there was a light tap on the door.

'Aye?' I called sleepily.

With sound instinct, Rikki jumped off the bed and stood wagging his tail just inside the door.

'I have brought you some clothes, Kit.'

Sara came in, her arms full.

'They are some of Ambrose's,' she said. 'They will be a little large, but better than those rags you were wearing last night.'

Ambrose was her eldest son, a grown man now and working for his grandfather, Sara's father, Dunstan Añes. They would certainly be too large, for he was broad in the shoulder and at least six inches taller than I, but they would be wonderful after the horrors of the bundle in the corner. I sat up.

'Sara, you are a marvel,' I said. 'Ambrose does not mind?'

'He is living at my father's house now, and does not need them. Besides, he would be glad to help.'

She laid the clothes on the end of the bed, then stirred the dirty bundle on the floor with the toe of her shoe.

'What shall we do with these?'

'Burn them!' I said with a shudder. 'Not even a beggar would welcome them.'

She picked them up fastidiously and held them well away from her.

'I'll give them to one of the men to burn. When you are dressed, come to my parlour. You and I and Anne will break our fast together. Ruy has already set off to deliver his letter in person to the Privy Council.'

'Anthony is not yet on holiday from Winchester?'

'He comes home next week.' She looked anxious.

I knew that the Queen had sent the younger Lopez son to Winchester at her own expense, for he was a promising boy. Like her father, the Queen chose to raise men to serve her from amongst the middling sort, preferring them to the sons of the great families, who were petty kings in their own lands. Men who owed everything to the monarch could be counted on for their loyalty. Lord Burghley had once been simple William Cecil, from a minor gentry family, like my own employer, Sir Francis Walsingham. Walter Raleigh, Francis Drake, John Norreys – so many of our distinguished men had risen by reason of their own abilities rather than their ancient lineage.

'Anthony is happy at school?'

'He missed his home and family at first, but now he has made friends and the masters think well of him.' She smiled a little sadly. I knew she must be thinking that Ruy's grandiose schemes for the Portuguese expedition might destroy the prospects of his children.

I climbed out of bed, reluctant to leave it after the first truly comfortable night I had spent in months.

'These clothes of Ambrose's will be loose,' I said, 'but I will manage well enough with them. I surely cannot wear his shoes!'

She laughed, for Ambrose was often teased about the size of his feet, which his sister Anne claimed would rival those of the African oliphant.

'You shall have a pair of my plain house shoes. They are near enough like to a man's shoe. I'll bring them to the parlour.'

After she had gone, I dressed quickly. The clothes were indeed loose, but they were clean and comfortable, and made of good worsted cloth, the hose knitted of a fine silky yarn, better than any I had worn since those long ago days in Coimbra. I ran my fingers through my hair and realised again I would need to borrow a comb, for it was densely matted. All this Rikki watched with interest. Looking at him I realised that one of my first tasks would be to bathe him, if he was to be allowed to stay in this respectable house, for he was far from respectable himself at the moment.

Satisfied that I had done the best I could with my appearance, I made my way downstairs to join Sara and Anne in the parlour. Anne was of an age with me and had become, over the years, a kind of sister, though she still believed me to be a boy, just as her father did. Until now, Sara had kept my secret well. I hoped I could maintain the fiction while I lived cheek by jowl with the rest of the family.

The next two weeks I spent in a curious kind of limbo. Until I had respectable clothes which fitted me, I was confined to the house, and while I lived here I tried to make myself as unobtrusive as I could. I wanted to avoid Ruy, but this was clearly impossible, and matters were not helped when he encountered me the first morning bathing Rikki in the paved court behind the kitchen premises. We were both thoroughly wet, although Rikki was now clean and – as far as I could tell – free from fleas.

'What is this?' Ruy had come to stroll about his garden, of which he was particularly proud, having plans to emulate some of the great gardens of London. There was insufficient room for a sizeable garden here in Wood Street, and before the voyage he had been talking of moving to a larger house.

Now he frowned at the dog. 'I did not know you had brought this cur with you, Christoval.'

'I left him with my father while we were away,' I said stiffly. 'When I returned to discover my father dead and my home and all our possessions seized, I found Rikki turned out into the streets. As I was.'

At this, a faint look of embarrassment passed over his face, but did not linger.

'What does Mistress Lopez say to this?'

'Sara says that she is happy for him to stay as long as I do. He is well trained. He will be no trouble. And I trust *I* shall not trouble you for long.'

I could not keep the bitterness out of my voice, for I owed my present predicament largely to Ruy. It was he who had persuaded my father to invest in the expedition and to send me – as Ruy claimed – to 'keep an eye' on that investment. As if anything I could have done would have hindered the disaster. Had I remained at home, I could have cared for my father, perhaps even have prevented his death. I could have dealt with our creditors, for the thousand pounds my father had invested would have paid them off with ample to spare. Even had my father died, it was likely I could have kept my place as assistant physician at St Bartholomew's Hospital, for the governors had good reason to think well of me. Instead, all was lost because of this man.

He ignored my words now, turning on his heel and strolling away down the garden. I dried Rikki on an old towel the cook had given me. I wished I could walk out of the house there and then, but I could not.

Since I could not leave the house at present to look for work, it seemed the most useful thing I could do would be to write up a full account of the entire Portuguese affair as I had witnessed it, from the time the raw recruits had run amok in Plymouth to the wasted siege of Coruña, and the disastrous decision to divide the army from the fleet at Peniche. I would recount in detail the horrors of the overland march from Peniche to Lisbon, with the men sickening and dying with every yard we covered. The *soi-disant* siege of Lisbon had been nothing but a despairing encampment before the walls, where more men had died. And then the final betrayal. Drake had loaded up all our food and sailed off to the Azores, while the remaining army had been left to starve and die on the return journey. On our return to Plymouth we had discovered that Drake had lied and sailed straight home.

The report was intended for Walsingham, for I had promised him to present all the facts when I returned, but writing out the entire account and sparing none of the leaders – Drake,

20

Norreys, Dom Antonio, Ruy Lopez and the errant Earl of Essex –
I was able to work off some of my anger, although I kept the tone
as factual and distanced as I was able.

Since I thought he might wish to share this report with the
Privy Council, I also wrote a second separate report intended for
him alone, setting out how I had fared on the two missions he had
set me to carry out. The first – the rescue of the agent Titus
Allanby from Coruña – had been successful, as he would know
already, since Allanby had returned to England directly from
Coruña. The other, to ensure that his agent Hunter was freed from
prison in Lisbon, had proved impossible, since we had never set
foot in the city.

Writing these reports occupied several days, during the
time when my new clothes were being ordered and made. Sara
herself sewed me undergarments, a night shift and some new silk
shirts, with some assistance from Anne. Even back in Coimbra I
had not been very skilled with a needle, and since taking on my
masculine disguise I had never had one in my hand, except to
stitch wounds. Several pairs of hose were ordered from the
stocking-knitter who supplied the whole Lopez family, and a
Marrano tailor came to the house to measure me for breeches and
doublets. Sara was more nervous than I that he might detect my
sex, but I was accustomed to deceiving tailors and the session
passed off without trouble.

The day came when I could don an entire suit of clothes at
last, and I was outfitted in all but shoes.

'I know a family of leather-workers in Eastcheap,' I told
Sara. 'If you will permit me to wear your shoes long enough to
go there to be measured and fitted, I should like to give them the
business.'

'Of course. Is this the lad who had the leg amputated, after
the fall of Sluys?'

'Aye. William Baker. He works with his brother-in-law,
Jake Winterly. He was more fortunate than most injured soldiers,
that he had a home and occupation to go to.'

I frowned, thinking of all the soldiers and sailors turned
ashore at Plymouth after the recent expedition, with nothing in

return for all their suffering but a paltry five shillings and a licence to beg their way home to their villages.

'Before I left in the spring,' I said, 'William was learning the craft of cobbling with the shoe-maker in the shop next door. He's sweet on the man's daughter, I suspect.' Thinking of William, my heart lifted, for he was one man close to death whom I had managed to save.

It felt strange to walk out of the front door of the Lopez house into Wood Street, free at last to make my way across London. My confinement had been comfortable and as pleasant as Sara and Anne could make it, but it had felt like a prison nevertheless. Anthony was now home from school and asked to come with me, but I persuaded him to stay at home. I wanted to be on my own for a while. The Lopezes had been more than kind, but I could not live on their charity for ever. Once I was decently shod, I would take my reports to Sir Francis Walsingham at his house in Seething Lane and discover whether there might be work for me again as a code-breaker with Thomas Phelippes.

August heat had ripened the stench of the London streets, which struck like a blow after a long period surrounded by the sweet herbs and well scrubbed rooms of the Lopez home. It brought to my mind the stark contrast between the confined quarters on shipboard and the fresh scents of the forest of Buçaco when I had ridden to find my sister Isabel. Was it really no more than three months earlier? I pushed thoughts of Isabel from my mind. I must have the courage to face a future alone in this great stinking City, for I knew nowhere else that I might find work and a livelihood.

When I stepped inside the leatherwork shop, William's sister, Bess Winterly, greeted me at the door with exclamations of pleasure.

'Dr Alvarez! You are returned alive and well from that terrible voyage! Come in, come in.'

She bustled about, pulling forward a stool for me and holding aside the curtain which divided the shop from the working premises.

'Jake! Will! See who is here!'

Young Will, son of Bess and Jake, came through from the workshop with a half-finished belt in his hand.

'Will,' I said, clapping him on the shoulder, 'I swear you have grown six inches since I saw you last.'

He blushed with pleasure. 'Not six inches, surely, master, but I do b'leeve as I'm taller by an inch or two.'

Jake arrived, wiping neat's-foot oil from his fingers with a rag before he shook my hand, grinning.

'But where is William?' I asked, with a momentary stab of fear. Had the gangrene returned?

Bess and Jake exchanged a glance, smiling.

'Our William?' Bess said, pouring me the mug of ale they always insisted on giving me. 'Our William is quite taken with the shoe-making trade.'

Young Will snorted. 'My uncle is quite taken with Liza Cordiner, you mean, Mother.'

Jake sat down beside me and poured himself a mug of ale. 'Matters have gone well for us, Dr Alvarez, since we saw you in the spring. Ned Cordiner, who owns the shop next door, has decided to retire from business and join his sister on her farm in Essex. Her husband died of the sweating sickness four months ago and she finds it hard to run the farm alone while her children are so small. He has sold us the business and we will join the two premises together.'

'And,' Bess interposed, 'what is best of all, our William is to marry Liza, and they will manage the shoe-making business. She has assisted her father for years, and William has taken to the craft as if he had been born to it.'

'That is good news indeed,' I said.

Good news in many ways, I thought. The Winterlys had taken William in when he was invalided out of the army, but I had seen their cramped home above the leather shop. When William married, he and his wife would have the living quarters next door, and the increase in business would help them all.

'Indeed, it is shoes I have come in search of,' I said. 'Will they able to fit me out? My own were ruined and I am wearing borrowed gear.'

Their eyes all went to my feet. It was clear they recognised women's shoes, but were too discreet to comment.

Young Will insisted on accompanying me to the shop next door, which proclaimed its trade with an enormous cavalryman's boot painted gold and hung outside for a sign. Jake had explained that Ned Cordiner had already left for Essex, but that Liza was fully skilled enough to make me any shoes or boots I might require. William was still learning the trade, but could manage the easier tasks.

I had not encountered a woman shoe-maker who undertook the entire work herself instead of merely assisting, but Liza Cordiner soon showed herself confident and skilled. She was perhaps a year or two older than William, not beautiful but with a sweet face and neat person. When she turned her eyes to William, they glowed. Here was one woman, it seemed, who cared not a fig that he had lost a leg and would only walk with a crutch for the rest of his life.

'I need both a pair of house shoes and some light summer boots,' I explained, as I removed Sara's borrowed shoes. I had already explained my losses and answered William's questions about the expedition. Young Will had been shooed back to his work in his parents' shop.

Liza began to measure my feet with callipers and a tailor's tape, while William made notes in a leather-bound record book. As she worked, Liza gave me one or two puzzled glances. I realised that a cobbler must be able to judge a great deal from this close examination of feet and I knew mine were too slender and fine-boned to pass easily for a man's. A padded doublet and breeches did much to disguise my sex, but there was nothing I could do about the shape of my feet. However, she said nothing, though I wondered whether she might share her suspicions with William when I was gone. I had no fear that William was a tattle-mouth, but the fewer people who knew my secret, the safer it would be for me.

'Will you have the house shoes made first, master?' Liza said when she had finished measuring. 'Or the boots?'

'The boots,' I said. I knew that I could continue to wear Sara's shoes for the moment about the house, but I needed the boots for my visit to Walsingham.

'If you will come over here,' Dr Alvarez,' William said, 'I can show you the skins we have in stock. Or if you would prefer something else, we can get it for you.'

They had an abundant supply of suitable leather, and I was more interested in speed than in some special skin, so I chose a tough but supple cow-hide the colour of ripe horse-chestnuts.

'They will be ready for fitting in three days' time,' Liza said, making a note in the record book.

I offered to pay something in advance, for Sara had given me money, but they would not take it.

'No, no,' William said. 'Not until you are satisfied with them.'

We discussed their plans for the future before I left. The banns for their marriage had already been called once in their parish church, and it would take place in three weeks' time.

'We would be honoured if you would attend, Dr Alvarez,' William said. 'And we will have cakes and ale in the Fighting Cockerel afterwards.'

I accepted heartily. It would be a pleasant change from the strained atmosphere in the Lopez household. 'Just before Bartholomew Fair?' I said.

'Aye. We'll be busy then. Jake always takes a booth. We're building up stock for the Fair now.'

'It's important for all craftsmen, I know. I haven't visited the Fair these two-three years.'

I had been busy about others affairs, I thought. But perhaps I would take the chance this year, having so much idle time on my hands. Perhaps Anne Lopez and I could get up a party.

When I left the shoe-maker's shop, I strolled slowly back in the direction of Wood Street. There was nothing to make me hurry, so I took my time, glancing at the goods displayed on the shopmen's drop-down counters, firmly ignoring the street vendors who plied me with trinkets and, for some reason, with spectacles. The spectacles made me think again of Phelippes. Surely he would be glad of my services again? Three days or a little more before I could go seeking work. This enforced idleness did not suit me.

As I turned along Cheapside, I thought I saw a familiar figure coming toward me. Still some way off, a man was pushing his way impatiently through the pedestrians dawdling along the streets, slow to get out of the way of horsemen or carts. My heart gave a nervous jerk. At this distance I could not be sure, but it looked like Robert Poley. The last I had heard of him, some months ago now, he was carrying despatches for Walsingham to the Low Countries and spent most of his time out of England. It would be my misfortune if he was back in London again now and busy about the Seething Lane office.

I didn't wait to meet him face to face. Instead I dodged into a narrow alleyway until I was certain he must have passed. When I gained the street again, the man was well past the mouth of the alley. The shape of the back, the style of the walk – it could be Robert Poley, but I wasn't sure. I made my way back to Wood Street in a sober frame of mind. I knew that Poley held a winning hand as far as I was concerned. By threatening to reveal my disguise, he could force me to fall in with whatever scheme he had in hand. So far he had only coerced me, against my will, into Walsingham's service. I smiled wryly. There was some irony in the fact that, despite my initial reluctance, I had taken to the work of code-breaking and – although I was reluctant to admit it – I had even enjoyed some of my more dangerous tasks. In retrospect, at any rate, if not at the time. And now I would be going to see Walsingham and Phelippes as my only hope for employment.

However, that did not mean Poley could not use his knowledge to blackmail me in other ways. I hoped I was mistaken. That the man in the crowd had not been Poley. That I had let my imagination deceive me.

After three days I returned to the cobblers at the sign of the golden cavalry boot. Liza fitted my new boots, carefully examining them from every angle and making me walk up and down in them until she was satisfied. They were the most comfortable footwear I had possessed for a long time.

'They are excellent, Mistress Cordiner,' I said. 'You made them entirely yourself?'

She blushed a little. 'William cut all the pieces. I stitched them and William hammered in the studs on the soles.'

'You work well together, then.' I grinned at William, who smiled back. I had never seen him look so happy. It was difficult to remember him as he had once been, in such a state of despair that he had wanted only to die.

'The boots are ready to take now?' I said.

'They need a further polish,' Liza said. 'We can do it now, while you wait, or you can come back tomorrow. The shoes will be ready by the end of the week.'

'I'll wait,' I said. I was impatient to feel myself fully clothed and shod.

Within half an hour the boots were ready and Sara's shoes wrapped in a sheet of brown paper for me to carry away. I stepped out of the shop into a bright day, determined to think nothing of Poley or the possibility that my services might not be needed at Seething Lane. Tomorrow I would take my reports to Walsingham.

Chapter Three

The following morning I rose early. It had been a restless night. What if Walsingham did not need me? My only other hope for employment was as an assistant physician in one of London's two hospitals. I only knew St Bartholomew's and the woman living in our house in Duck Lane had said there were no positions there now. She might have been lying, though I thought not. Despite my anger at her indifference to what had happened to my father and to me, she had seemed an honest woman. Because of my services in the past, I knew that the governors of the hospital respected me, but money was always short and they could not authorise employing an extra physician if one was not needed.

The other hospital, St Thomas's, lay south of the river, outside the City of London itself, in the borough of Southwark. I had been there just once. When the sailors and soldiers from our fleet which defeated the Armada were struck down by typhoid and the bloody flux, my father and I had cared for several ships' crews docked at Deptford. When the worst of the epidemic was over, we had transferred the last few convalescent patients to St Thomas's, the nearer hospital, before we returned to our own work at St Bartholomew's. I had seen very little of the southern hospital, though I knew they often took on desperate cases. There might be a vacancy there. However, the summer this year had been remarkably free of the plague and other diseases of the warmer weather, so it was likely they too had no need of extra physicians. No doubt, like St Bartholomew's, they never had money enough.

If I was not needed in Walsingham's service, I would approach St Thomas's. Even if Sir Francis could offer me some code-breaking work I might do so, for I did not want my medical proficiency to grow rusty. Since childhood I had always admired and loved my father's medical skills, honed by his studies of Arab medicine. As a girl in Portugal, I could never have hoped to become a physician. The great advantage of my boy's disguise had meant that from the age of fourteen I had become my father's assistant, learning his profession both in practice at his side and through the studies his set me at home. I would not, could not, sacrifice all that and what it meant to me.

I decided to take Rikki with me to Seething Lane, but not into Sir Francis's office. After I had rescued the dog in the Low Countries – or more truthfully, after he had rescued me – I had brought him home and in time taken him with me on my days in Phelippes's office. He was used to lying quietly in a corner while we worked, and I certainly felt safer on the nights when I walked home in the dark, having his large protective presence by my side. More than once he had bared his teeth and seen off a potential cutpurse or attacker.

Rikki would not be welcome around the house by Ruy on this of all days. While I was out collecting my boots the previous day, Ruy had heard that he had lost his sumach and aniseed monopoly and the Privy Council looked coldly on all his excuses and appeals. The Queen, however, who had always valued him and treated his family kindly, had sent word that she would not dismiss him. It was his nature always to rage at any insult or setback, while an instance of good fortune was regarded as merely his due. Today he was stamping about the house, swearing at the servants and snapping at Sara when she pointed out the blessing of the Queen's continued patronage. All he could think about was his treatment by the Privy Council.

Soon he would need to concentrate solely on his medical practice once more, particularly after the loss of income from the monopoly, and leave off meddling in affairs of state. He would again be scurrying between the courts at Greenwich, Hampton Court, and Whitehall, or attending the Queen on her progresses, then riding out to Eton to treat Dom Antonio, who was held there little better than a prisoner (for he had tried to escape to the Continent), and riding back again to treat my Lord Essex at Essex House. In the meantime, however, all he could think of was the insult and drop in income through losing his monopoly. It was better for both Rikki and me to be out of the house.

So I would take Rikki with me once again to Seething Lane. However, I thought I would make a better case if I went alone to see Sir Francis. I could leave the dog with the stable lad Harry, who was fond of him. It would also give me the chance to look in on Hector, the ugly piebald I often rode on Walsingham's business. It seemed a long time since I had last had the chance to do so.

I donned my new clothes, strapped on my sword, and begged a couple of small apples from the cook to give to Hector. While I had been waiting for my boots to be polished by Liza Cordiner, I had gone next door and bought a new collar and lead for Rikki from Bess Winterly. His old ones had vanished along with all my other possessions. I was running up more debts to Sara, who brushed aside my promises to repay her, but I was keeping careful note of everything I spent. I would never let myself fall into debt as my father had done, but would repay her every penny and groat. For a moment I thought longingly of replacing my father's lost medical books, but it would be long before I possessed the chinks to do that, even if I could find any copies amongst the booksellers in Paul's Churchyard.

The evening before I had sent a note round to Seething Lane, asking if Sir Francis could see me, and a servant had brought back a reply before I went to bed, saying that he would be free after he had returned from his morning visit to the Queen, at ten of the clock. Sir Francis was Her Majesty's Principal Secretary, which meant he carried a great burden of duties in addition to organising and directing his secret service of agents and code-breakers. When I had last seen him, he had looked even more ill than usual. It was never spoken of, and I could not be sure what ailed him, but I knew he was often in pain. I suspect it might be some disease of the kidneys or liver. Dr Nuñez was his physician and would, of course, maintain the strictest silence on the condition of his distinguished patient.

As I walked through the hot and busy streets, where everyone seemed to be going about their daily occupations as usual, I thought how deceptive was this appearance of calm. The three greatest figures in the realm, on whom rested the peace and security of England, were all of them growing old or ill. The Queen seemed indomitable, but she could not live for ever. She had no child and would not speak of appointing an heir, though Lord Stanley's mother might be regarded as the nearest thing to one, by the provisions of King Henry's will. Lord Burghley, on whom the Queen had depended since she was no more than a girl, was becoming old and frail. Sir Francis had constant bouts of illness, which the weight of his responsibilities must frequently aggravate.

And always Spanish King Philip circled like a waiting shark, preparing to make another attack. A year had passed since his great invading fleet had swept up the Channel, and although our recent expedition had done a little damage to his remaining navy, he had almost limitless resources drawn from the gold and silver mines of the New World. It would not take him long to rebuild and re-equip his ships. What then? The state of England was like a three-legged stool, held steady by those three mighty figures. If one failed, would the whole country collapse into impotence and ruin?

As usual when I walked across London, I ignored most of the street vendors, but when a pamphlet seller cried, 'My Lord Essex's tale of heroism! Read all about My Lord's adventures against the stinking Spanish! Only a farthing!'

He waved a crudely printed pamphlet in my face. On my journey back from Plymouth I had heard that Essex was putting about stories of his fictitious heroic exploits during the Portuguese expedition. It might be wise to see what this latest version said, before I saw Walsingham and presented my reports. Though I begrudged the farthing.

Walking on towards Tower Ward, I quickly read the pamphlet, growing more annoyed with every sentence.

Something I found inexplicable, as one who had been in Essex's company for most of the Portuguese venture, was the heroic light in which he was now viewed by the Court and

31

populace alike. He had taken advantage of his early return, before the rest of us, to spread about his story of the expedition, in which his achievements and gallant behaviour outshone the bumbling mistakes of everyone else. Within days of his return, his friends and followers were publishing these encomiums in verse and prose, detailing the mythic (and truly imaginary) deeds of this great man. He had much to gain from such a portrait, as did those who hung about him like leeches. These same eulogies were repeated, in even more extravagant terms, in the present pamphlet. When I had read it, I tore it up in disgust and threw it in the gutter. Yet who would have listened to me? Somehow, he had the skill to persuade people that what was, was not, and that what was not, was.

I could only hope that Walsingham, who well knew both me and the Earl, would balance my report against these fly-blown attempts to ennoble the absurd follies of this arrogant and often dangerous nobleman.

On reaching Seething Lane, I entered as usual through the stableyard, from which I could reach both Walsingham's and Phelippes's offices by the backstairs. The stable lad Harry was crossing the yard, carrying a bucket of feed for the horses. He set it down with a clatter and seized my hand, pumping it up and down enthusiastically. My position here at Walsingham's house was always ambiguous. I might be a gentleman, entitled to work on almost equal terms with Thomas Phelippes, but the grooms and stable lads saw me as one of themselves, knowing my affection for the ugly Hector.

'So you survived the mad attempt to put that Portingall fellow on the throne,' he said. 'I'm that glad to see you! I never thought it would succeed, even with Drake leading it.'

I did not try to disillusion him with my harsher opinions of Drake. The piratical captain was a hero amongst the young lads of London, who dreamed of one day sailing the seas with him in search of booty from the Spanish treasure ships. It amused me that he spoke of 'Portingalls' as an alien species. Not long ago I would have been labelled as one of them, but it seemed I had earned my right to be regarded as an Englishman, at least here in the stableyard, and that was an opinion worth valuing.

'And here's Rikki,' he said, squatting down and fondling the dog's ears. 'How are you, old fellow? Has your master been starving you? You've lost weight.'

He gave me an accusing look.

'You should have seen him when I first returned,' I said defensively. 'My father died and Rikki was turned out on to the street. He was but skin and bone when I found him. He's recovering now.'

Harry stood up, his face grave. 'I'm sorry to hear that, Master Alvarez. Your father was a fine physician. I know some who have been treated by him at Barts, and all have praised him.' He reached out and tentatively touched my arm. I felt my eyes begin to prick. I had not expected this show of sympathy.

'I thank you, Harry. Now, I have a meeting with Sir Francis shortly. May I leave Rikki with you? And I've just time to see Hector. Is he well?'

'Well enough. Fretting at being so long kept in the stable. Will you be taking him out, do you think?'

'That I cannot say. Probably not. I have come to report on the expedition, but I do not know if Sir Francis has any work for me.'

Rikki went off quite happily with Harry as he carried the oats round the stalls and I let myself into Hector's loose box. He whickered a greeting and nuzzled into my shoulder. I put my arm round his neck as I palmed the apples for him. As always when I was with Hector I felt an intense longing to own him. He was just one of Walsingham's horses, but he felt as though he was mine. It was sheer folly. Even if I had the riches to buy him, even if Walsingham would sell him, how could I pay for his livery? He had been bred on Walsingham's country estate at Barn Elms and for all I knew, Sir Francis cared for him as much as I did. He was the cleverest horse I had ever known and the fleetest of foot, despite his ugly coat, which drew the eye away from his beautiful proportions and the fine modelling of his head. He was part Arab and had all the qualities of the breed. He was favourite amongst the stable staff here and at Barn Elms, so I probably had plenty of rivals in wanting to own him. I gave him a final rub between the ears and let myself out of the loose box. It was time to see Sir Francis.

I made my way up the stairs and along the corridor with its familiar gloomy family portraits. In answer to my knock, Sir Francis called me in and greeted me warmly, shaking my hand and bowing. He drew up two chairs beside the empty fireplace and motioned me to one of them.

'You've been visiting Hector?' he asked.

I was startled at this indication of clairvoyance, then realised that the front of my doublet was covered with grey and white hairs. Hector must be shedding in the hot weather. Embarrassed, I brushed myself down.

'Aye. I always bring him an apple or two whenever I come. He's served me well in the past. Got me out of one or two scrapes as well, thanks to his speed.'

'I remember.' He smiled, and I realised he was not chiding me.

I drew the two reports out of my satchel and handed them to him.

'As I promised, I have written an account of the Portuguese expedition for you, Sir Francis. One is a general account of every stage of the venture, from the time we arrived at Plymouth in the spring until we returned there last month. I have tried to set out everything as accurately as I could, avoiding nothing. It does not make pretty reading.' I paused. I might as well prepare him, I thought. 'Matters were not well managed,' I said bluntly. 'The other is a brief summary of the two particular missions you set me, one successful, one not.'

'In that,' he said grimly, 'you proved more successful than the expedition itself.'

'There was a terrible loss of life.' I should have kept my tongue behind my teeth, but the words burst out.

He looked at me sadly and nodded.

'Aye. There was.'

Then he put on his spectacles, and read both reports at once, while I sat there, growing more and more nervous, as he turned over the pages, frowning as he read. At last he laid his spectacles on the small table at his elbow, rubbed his eyes, and sighed. His face looked even more gaunt than when I had last seen him, before we sailed from London. The dark patches under his eyes were black as ink, and he wore a little velvet cap, like a night-cap, from which a few thin strands of grey hair straggled like unravelled wool. His hands, clasped on top of my reports, were bony as a skeleton, and they trembled uncontrollably.

'Yes, Kit,' he said at last, glancing down at the reports lying on his lap. 'You have done well to set all this down. I have heard parts of the story from some of the leaders, but each man blames the others. As an outsider, you have dealt fairly with them all. Nothing can be done now to recover the disaster, but perhaps we can gain some wisdom from it.'

'I fear . . .' I said.

'Aye, Kit? You may speak freely.'

'I fear the matter may not yet be finished. As you say, Sir Francis, the various leaders blame each other. Their quarrels will not be over today or tomorrow. A great many people have lost their investments, from Her Majesty herself down to smaller investors than my father. The vast numbers of men dead – there will be thousands of women widowed, even more thousands of children orphaned. Of the men who survived, many were wounded or left much weakened by sickness, especially those on the ships left without food.' I drew a long breath, recalling that nightmare journey of starvation and death.

'When we reached Plymouth, those who were able to walk were given nothing but five shillings and a licence to beg until they reached home.' I reached out my hands to plead with him, 'Sir Francis, these men were promised great riches if they joined the expedition! They were not all worthy men. Some were cowards. Some were scoundrels. Some were no more than idle. But their sufferings were terrible. They deserve justice. And I think they will not all go quietly home until they get it.'

He studied me closely, with a curious expression on his face.

'I think you are turned lawyer, Kit.'

Then he must have seen something in my face.

'Nay, I do not mock you. You care for these men and their fate, and I respect you. I too fear the aftermath of this ill-managed

35

affair. You are quite likely right, that we may see some claims for better recompense from the survivors, even for the widows of those who died, but I do not know where it is to be found. As you say, many have lost great sums. The public purse is empty. I would gladly see the men better rewarded, but we have no means to do it.'

He poured himself a glass of wine with one of those shaking hands, and a drop fell on my report. He made an impatient noise, angry at his weakness, and with a fine silk handkerchief dabbed up the spilt wine.

'Come, let us turn to other matters. Will you take a glass, Kit?'

'Thank you, sir.' I was relieved. I did not think he would offer me wine if he was displeased with me.

We sipped our wine in silence for a minute. Then he said, 'And you, Kit, what will you do now? I hear that your father died while you were away.'

Was there nothing this man did not know?

'He did, sir. I have lost my father, my home and my employment at St Bartholomew's. My father had invested all his savings in the venture, so when he died all our possessions were seized by his creditors.' I could not keep the bitterness out of my voice. 'Even these clothes you see me wearing I owe to the kindness of a friend.'

I drew a deep breath.

'The woman who is now living in our house has told me that there are no positions free at St Bartholomew's. I thought I might write to the governors of St Thomas's hospital, to see if they would take me, but there may be nothing there either.'

'Hmm. I might be able to do something for you there. You have not attended university, I remember.'

'No, my father could not afford it. And I have no money now. I was trained simply at my father's side.'

'Do I not recall that the governors of St Bartholomew's once offered you the chance of a place at Oxford, in gratitude for your treatment of Sir Jonathan Langley? But you turned down the chance.'

'There were family problems, Sir Francis, at the time. I do not feel I could go a-begging now.'

I felt a chill. Much as I would have welcomed the chance to study at Oxford and qualify as an officially recognised physician, there was no possibility I could hide my sex, sharing rooms with fellow students for several years.

'Without a degree,' he said, 'you will never be elected a Fellow of the Royal College of Physicians. You will have to stay an assistant all your life.'

'I know that. But I have no choice.'

'Although sometimes there are special circumstances . . .' He looked thoughtful. 'Well, we shall see what can be done. And whenever Thomas Phelippes has need of your code-breaking skills, we will send for you. Will that help you to earn a living?'

'Yes,' I said. 'Thank you.' I had never thought I would be grateful to be working for the spymaster, but who can predict how our lives will shape themselves?

'Go and see Thomas now. He may have work for you, or be able to tell you when there might be need of your skills. We know your aptitude for deciphering codes, and your fluency in languages is also useful to us.'

He got to his feet, easing himself out of the chair by gripping the arms. I rose as well.

'I will make enquiries at both Bartholomew's and Thomas's and write to you when I have any news.'

I bowed. 'I thank you for your kindness, Sir Francis.' I hesitated. It was not quite my place, but we had come gradually to be on closer terms than in the past.

'Your family, sir, are they well?'

'My wife, God be thanked, is in excellent health. My daughter Frances is out of the official mourning for her husband, of course, but his loss grieved her deeply. She had known Sir Philip since she was a tiny child. Little Elizabeth grows well and never stops chattering!' He gave a faint smile, then shook his head. 'The younger child died.'

'I am sorry for it,' I said. Frances Walsingham was little older than I and had been carrying her second child when her husband died in the Flemish wars.

'Aye, well.' He sighed. 'What kind of a world is this to bring a child into? War and plague and treachery at every turn.'

I had never heard him so downcast.

'I believe we are strong,' I said hesitantly. 'With yourself and My Lord Burghley to guide and protect Her Majesty, England is in safe hands.'

'Only by keeping a constant vigil, Kit, and we grow old.'

Unconsciously he was echoing my very thoughts earlier in the day. He laid his hand on my shoulder.

'We shall not always be here, and then it will be for the next generation to assume the care of the nation.' He paused, and his glance shifted to the open windows, through which faint sounds drifted from the busy Customs House and quays.

'As for Frances and little Elizabeth . . . it is time to be looking for a new husband for my daughter and a father for her child.'

As I walked along the corridor to Phelippes's room, I wondered about those last words. Would Frances Walsingham have any choice in the matter? The alliances of great families must take more into account than the personal feelings of their individual members. Sir Francis had nearly beggared himself, paying off the debts of his son-in-law, Sir Philip Sydney, and giving him a funeral fit for a monarch. There would be little enough left of his estate to leave to Frances, his only child. How ill was he? If he thought death was approaching, he would want her safely married to a man who could give her position and financial security. It was said that the Queen had been angered at the original marriage, between Frances Walsingham and Philip Sydney, but then she often took against marriages she had not arranged herself. Sir Francis would want a man of similar rank for his daughter's second husband. I wondered who he had in mind.

'Kit!' Phelippes rose from his chair, seeming glad to see me. He was not a demonstrative man, but he smiled warmly and welcomed me in to the familiar office where I had spent so many hours poring over obscure coded letters in the last three years. I looked around. There were my own table and chair. On the wall behind, the shelf where I kept my keys to the various codes, my spare quills and ink, and the seal Arthur Gregory had made for me last year.

'Have you come back to work for us?' Phelippes said. 'You cannot have enjoyed your little adventure away from us.'

I felt that 'little adventure' would not be my own description of the horrors we had endured, but perhaps the whole disaster had little reality for Phelippes, cooped up here with his documents.

'Sir Francis said I should speak to you about whether you had work for me. I am no longer employed at St Bartholomew's.'

Once again I explained what had happened to my father. And as with Sir Francis, I did not mention where I was living at present. I had no tangible reason for this. Merely I felt that the less mention there was of Ruy Lopez at the moment, the better for all concerned, particularly me.

'Well,' Phelippes said, 'as you see, matters are under control at the moment.'

He tapped a neat stack of papers with the end of his quill. Indeed, the room was not sinking under its usual load of documents waiting for decipherment.

'However, I am expecting another consignment shortly,' he went on. 'There are one or two new stirrings amongst the Spaniards, some new despatches . . . ah . . . diverted . . . as they came through France. I expect I could use some assistance in the next week or two. How can I reach you?'

Still reluctant to mention my address, I said, 'Suppose I call here in a week's time? Then perhaps you will know better what you may need.'

'That will do very well. Take a holiday.'

I grimaced. 'I have had too much holiday since I've been back in London. However, I've a wedding to attend this month, and perhaps I'll look in at Bartholomew Fair.'

'Bartholomew Fair?' He gave a reminiscent smile. 'I haven't been there since I was a young lad. My mother used to take me with my little sister. There was a woman who sold the most wonderful gilded gingerbread. I was a greedy rascal and ate mine up at once, but my sister used to treasure hers – a castle, a knight in armour, a mermaid. She could not bear to eat them, but kept them until they turned soft or the mice found them.'

I was astonished. Thomas Phelippes had never mentioned his family to me before. It was hard to imagine him as a small boy, gobbling up his gingerbread while walking through the Fair.

'Does your sister still hoard her gingerbread?' I was emboldened to ask.

He shook his head sadly. 'Nay, she died of a raging fever when she was just twelve years old. We never went to Bartholomew Fair again.'

'I'm so sorry, Thomas,' I said. I seemed to hear of nothing but the death of children today.

'It was many years ago.' He sighed. 'I never valued her as I should until it was too late. But the Fair – only a few weeks away. A happy time for cutpurses and confidence tricksters.'

'Perhaps,' I said, 'but a good time, as well, for the common people to enjoy themselves before the end of summer. And important for all the cloth merchants. Their booths are so numerous they block the way into the hospital. And now that the Spanish have been chased out of the Channel, at least for a time, there will be merchants there from the Continent. It should prove profitable for the guilds of London.'

'You are right. The legitimate business of the Fair was always the trade in cloth, and after the losses in the Portuguese expedition, there will be many hoping to make a good profit. And the other trades too, metalwork, jewellery.'

'Leatherwork,' I said. 'I know a family of leatherworkers who have taken a stall for the first time. Last year, with the invasion, no one could think of trade, but this year it is another matter.'

I glanced towards the door to Arthur Gregory's small cubicle.

'Is Arthur not about?' I said.

'Gone to fetch some special fine-grained wood he needs for his seals,' Phelippes said. 'He will be sorry to have missed you.'

He asked me about the expedition, but he was mainly interested in the escape of Titus Allanby, one of Walsingham's own agents.

40

'It was unfortunate that you were not able to secure the release of Hunter from the prison in Lisbon,' he said.

'There were many things which were much more unfortunate than that,' I said grimly. 'Besides, Hunter seems to be accommodated in a fair degree of comfort, and to have valuable sources of information about the Spanish. Is he not of more use to Sir Francis where he is?'

'Perhaps, perhaps.'

I left soon afterwards and collected Rikki from the stableyard.

'Will you be coming back to us then, Master Alvarez?' Harry asked.

'It seems Master Phelippes will have some work for me shortly, so you will be seeing me again. Thank you for looking after Rikki.'

'He's a good lad. I gave him a bone to chew.'

Rikki loped across the yard to me, the bone still firmly clenched in his jaws.

I laughed. 'Very well, you may bring it with you, but do not expect me to carry it.'

I set off on the walk back to Wood Street. The sun was high in the sky now, beating down with relentless August heat. Although it was nowhere near what we had endured in Portugal, it was enough to bring the stench of the City streets to a full ripeness. Very cold weather in winter brought many deaths from chest diseases and even from the very cold itself, but very hot weather brought its own dangers, above all the plague. There had not been a serious outbreak since 1582, the year my father and I arrived in England, but there were some cases every summer, often in the crowded slums near the docks, for the disease somehow seemed to arrive with foreign ships, though no one knew how. It was best to avoid such places when the weather was hot.

As I neared the Conduit in Cheapside, I caught sight of a familiar face in the crowd.

'Peter!' I called. 'Peter Lambert!'

He turned and pushed his way through the throng to reach me, and grabbed both my hands.

'Dr Alvarez! I heard you were come home, despite all the losses.'

'Am I no longer Kit to you, Peter?'

I laughed. Peter and I were of an age and had often worked together at St Bartholomew's, he as assistant apothecary, I as assistant physician.

'Kit, then,' he said, looking at me critically. 'You've lost weight.'

'We all lost weight, those who managed not to die of wounds or disease or starvation. Are you not at work?'

'I've been running errands, ordering new stocks for the hospital. Some have been allowed to get too low.' He made a face, as if he could say more.

'Have you time for a beer and something to eat?'

'Aye, why not? We must all eat. There's a decent inn back there a step or two.'

We made our way to the small inn he had pointed out, Rikki following behind, still carrying his bone. When we were seated in the small garden at the back, with mugs of beer and a couple of pies and Rikki under the table, Peter took a swig, then set down his mug and looked at me seriously.

'That was a bad business about your father.'

I nodded. I had been able to speak of it fairly calmly to Walsingham and Phelippes, but Peter knew my father and I found my eyes filling. I turned aside in the hope he would not see.

'This fellow Temperley,' Peter said with contempt, 'he's a relic from the last century. You'd think Dr Stephens a modern revolutionary to hear Temperley carry on. After working with your father, I know that many of those old ideas of medicine have been proved wrong. Temperley thinks bleeding and cupping and purging are the cure for everything, from a woman's morning sickness to the bloody flux to . . .to . . . I don't know!...plague and lightning strike! Most of the time he will not even look at the patients, just requires me to bring a phial of their urine, holds it up to the light, then tells his brother – that's his assistant, one who's cut from the same cloth – tells him how much to bleed the patient.'

I'd never seen Peter so angry. He drained half his beer in one swallow.

'You heard me say we were running short of supplies? Temperley never restocks, has no use for curative herbs. We'd almost run out of your father's salves and other medicines. I asked Master Winger if I could order what we needed, and he gave me leave. He's as unhappy as I, but what can an apothecary do, when the physician will not act?'

'What of Dr Stephens?' I asked. He was my father's older colleague, who often argued with him, being suspicious of modern trends, but I believed that secretly he recognised their effectiveness.

'Oh, he is growing old and lets Temperley take the lead. I think he will retire soon. He only wants the quiet life.'

I picked up my pie and began to eat. It was somewhat greasy, compared with the fare in the Lopez house, but the flavour was good.

'So the patients are not being well treated?'

'Far fewer are recovering than used to,' he said glumly.

There was a pause, then he gave me an odd look, almost conspiratorial.

'May I tell you something in confidence, Kit?'

'Of course.'

'I have not worked beside you and your father these last years without learning something. I have been using your wound salves and burn salves myself, unknown to Dr Temperley. I have had some success, at least when he has not thoroughly weakened a patient with too much bleeding.'

I grinned. 'So you are turned physician?'

'I could not claim that, but I want to help those poor folk. That's why we have run low on some of our supplies. I do remember how to make up some of your cures, but not all of them, so I'm glad to run into you today. I heard you were staying with Dr Lopez and planned to visit you, to ask if you could remind me of those I have forgotten. That is, if you do not think you should keep them secret.'

'Of course not. I would want to help the patients as well, even though I am told there is no place for me at Barts. You must

43

be careful, though, Peter. Dr Temperley could make trouble for you.'

'I know. I am careful.'

'The Temperleys are living in our home in Duck Lane. They bought some of our goods when the creditors seized them. But it seems Dr Temperley thought the books of Arabic medicine were full of demonic symbols.'

Peter snorted. 'The man is a fool.'

'Not a fool, if he has qualified in medicine at Oxford, but clearly a man blinkered by his own old-fashioned opinions.'

'What will you do now, Kit, if you are not coming back to Barts?'

'I've just been to see what work they have for me in Walsingham's office. And I might find work at St Thomas's.'

'Don't they just take the hopeless and dying?'

There was a slightly patronising tone in his voice, for Barts looked down on Thomas's.

'They are all sick folk,' I said. 'They all need our help.'

We finished our pies and ordered more beer and a platter of cheese.

'Do you remember William Baker?' I said. 'Who lost a leg after Sluys?'

He shuddered. 'Not likely to forget, am I? I attended the amputation.'

'Well, things have turned out well for him. He's learning shoe-making as well as other leather work and he's marrying this month. I'm going to the wedding. I'm sure William would be glad to see you there too.'

He smiled. 'That's good news indeed. He endured it bravely. I remember that little nephew of his, taking his mother's cakes and sweetmeats round to the other patients.' He sighed. 'Can't see that happening now.'

'The wedding is just before Bartholomew Fair,' I said. 'I've been thinking of getting up a party to go. Would you join us?'

'Gladly. We can hardly avoid it, right on our doorstep, occupying the whole of Smithfield and making more noise than all the cows, sheep, and pigs together. Aye, let's set aside our troubles and visit the Fair.'

Chapter Four

*A*t the end of a week, I made my way to Seething Lane
again, and this time I took Rikki into Phelippes's office
with me. Phelippes stood up at once and I saw that he had been
running his hand through his hair from behind, so that it stood up
like a cock's comb, a habit of his when worried or harassed.

'Ah, good, Kit,' he said. 'I was about to send Cassie out to
search for you amongst those player friends of yours. I must have
some way to reach you. These despatches have arrived sooner
than we expected and I need your help.'

Arthur Gregory was sitting at my table and now got to his
feet with an expression of relief.

'I'm delighted to see you, Kit,' he said, smiling warmly,
'and sorry to have missed you last week. I am even more relieved
than Thomas that you are coming back to work! You know how
slow I am at this deciphering. Leave me to my tools and my
seals. Every man to his own talents.'

I laughed. 'Come, Arthur! You are no slouch at
deciphering. You just take greater pleasure in your art. And who
can blame you?'

Who indeed? For Arthur's forged seals were works of tiny
perfection, even more beautifully made than the originals, which
he recreated from copying their imprints on wax. How he
managed to carve these tiny images, *in reverse*, was a source of
wonder to me. As I had remarked more than once to Phelippes, it
was fortunate that Arthur was an honest man, for he could have

made a great fortune as an unscrupulous forger. Instead, he dedicated his skills to Walsingham's service.

It was often necessary for us to open intercepted letters passing between foreign spies and their masters, decipher and translate them, then seal them again and send them on their way. Without Arthur's skills in first lifting the seals without damaging the paper, then resealing them using one of his forged seals to imprint the wax, all Phelippes's and my work would have gone for naught. The tampering with the letters would have been noticed at once.

Arthur was a quiet, modest man, but he was a true artist, and I sometimes wondered whether Phelippes and Sir Francis gave him all the credit he was due.

Now, however, he was very happy to take me through the despatch he had been working on, pointing out those parts he had been unable to decipher.

'It is in French,' he said, 'and destined for the embassy here. It was diverted through the network managed in France by Dr Nuñez's cousin, but originated with Mendoza. It is essential that we send it on its way as soon as possible. Here is my crude first attempt.'

He handed me a sheet of paper with a large number of crossings out.

'It's a new code?' I asked.

'A variation on one you cracked last year,' Phelippes said. 'It seems either they think it is secure, or else they were in too much of a hurry to devise a new one. It shouldn't give you much trouble. I am working on a batch from Rome.'

Mendoza was Philip of Spain's principal agent based in Paris. He had once been the Spanish ambassador in London, ordered to leave the country five years ago when he was discovered to have been involved in a plot to assassinate the Queen, a conspiracy led by the Duke of Guise, cousin of Scottish Mary. Ever since, Mendoza had lurked just across the Channel, like some poisonous spider, spinning his web of intrigue intended to ruin England.

Arthur cleared away his rough sheets and threw them on the fire. Even in summer there was always a small fire burning in

Phelippes's office, so that we could burn everything that did not go into the secure files kept in locked chests either here or – in the case of the most important papers – in Sir Francis's own office.

Arthur went back to his own cubbyhole, where we could soon hear the sound of his tiny tools carving a new seal. I went over to the window and pushed it open a little wider, so that the air from outside might counteract the heat of the fire. Phelippes grunted and placed a weight down on the pile of papers on his table to stop them blowing about. He rarely seemed to feel the heat. I removed my doublet, hung it on the back of my chair, and sat down to work in my shirt sleeves. Sara had made my new shirts with plenty of fabric, so that they bloused out generously, and I had no fear of being seen without my doublet, at least not by Phelippes, who was short sighted and anyway barely took notice of anything but the documents he was working on.

For an hour or so we worked in silence. Rikki had curled up under my desk, resting his head on my feet. After a while they began to feel a little numb, but it was so pleasant to have his companionship, I endured it. There was no sound in the room but his occasional sigh, the scratching of our quills, and faint noises from Arthur's room. The window here, like the one in Sir Francis's office, faced the quays, and we could hear the distant creak of the cranes, the occasional shouts of the seamen and dockers, and now and then a faint thump as some crate hit deck or quay.

Finally Phelippes laid down his pen, sanded his ink, and shook the excess into the bin beside his table. He laid the sheet down on his finished pile of documents.

I took the opportunity to pose a question which had arisen from my own work.

'Who is David?'

He ran his hands through his hair again.

'We don't know. It could simply be another identity for a known spy, but I don't think so.'

'No,' I said, holding up the document I had been deciphering. 'I don't recognise the hand. It's a skilled hand. A swift one. He doesn't labour over the coding as some do. He writes it as easily as the alphabet.'

'Aye.' Phelippes allowed himself a tight smile. 'Like yourself, do you think?'

He had often teased me about my pride in writing quickly in code.

'Perhaps. Even when it is deciphered, the meaning of all this is very obscure. He seems to be referring to a trip – to England, perhaps? And a "project". I do not like the sound of that. A "project" usually means trouble. Another attempt on Her Majesty's life, do you suppose?'

He gave me a sombre look. 'That could well be the meaning. Can you make anything of it?'

'Not really. I think there must have been other letters before this, which would have made the meaning clearer. There are no others?'

'None from this source.'

'Although it is written in French,' I said slowly, 'I think the writer is Spanish. Just by a few turns in the language, and one spelling mistake.'

'Well, it came from someone in Mendoza's service, that much we know, so the writer may be Spanish. But if it is addressed to the French embassy, that is no doubt why it is written in French.'

'Aye.'

The relationship between France and Spain in recent years was constantly volatile. Both were Catholic countries, both hated Protestant England. However, France was riven by internal conflict, where those Huguenots who had survived the Bartholomew's Day Massacre of 1572 formed a strong opposition to the Catholic court. The French were also more than a little uneasy at King Philip's ambition to rule the entire world. *Non sufficit orbis.* Moreover, his armies' exploits in the Low Countries came dangerously near to France's borders. The two nations would join forces when it suited them, but could turn on each other at times. The third player in the forces ranged against us was the Pope. According to Papal decree, our Queen was a bastard, a heretic, and an excommunicant. The Pope had granted a blessing and pardon in advance on any man who assassinated her.

It was little wonder that rumours of a world of tension and suspicion at the English Court were widespread throughout London, or that Sir Francis looked so grey and drawn with worry. On his shoulders rested the safety of the Queen in the face of all this danger. Even Phelippes, Gregory and I played our part in it.

For the moment, we could do nothing but keep watch for more messages from this new agent 'David'. Something about the confidence of his writing worried me, that and the hint that there had been earlier despatches, concerned with a project and a planned visit to England.

As I was donning my doublet before leaving that afternoon, I turned to Phelippes.

'That despatch from the new agent, David – it refers to a visit to England.'

'Aye.'

'I wondered . . . Everyone is saying that this year Bartholomew Fair is to be larger than for some time. Many foreign merchants are expected to come. Do you not think it might prove easy for an agent from France or Spain to slip into the country, under cover of the Fair? The customs officers at all the ports cannot be sure to scrutinise everyone who comes.'

'A good point, Kit. I'll give orders for extra vigilance at the ports. And I will make sure the constables and officers patrolling the Fair keep their eyes open. Do you still plan to attend?'

'Aye. I think I will go with a party of friends. I will also keep my eyes open. Though I suspect any secret business will be carried on well out of sight.'

'No harm in being watchful.'

'I will do my best.'

However, I doubted my ability to recognise a foreign agent amongst all the hurly-burly of the Fair. Agents are chosen for their skill at disguise, at blending in with ordinary folk. Despite the lurid descriptions in the penny chapbooks hawked in the streets for the entertainment of the common people, dangerous foreign spies did not dress in flamboyant clothes, wear masks, or grow extravagant facial hair. They were more likely to resemble the humble shopman who sold you new laces for your shirt, or the street vendor carrying a tray of pasties or ribbons.

'Before you go, Kit,' Phelippes said.

'Aye?'

'Where can I reach you, if need be?'

Reluctantly, I gave him the address of the Lopez house in Wood Street.

The marriage of William Baker and Liza Cordiner took place at their parish church, St Clement's in Clement's Lane, just round the corner from Eastcheap, and was attended by a sizeable crowd. The marriage itself was held, as the custom is, at the church door, then everyone followed bride, groom and priest inside for the service of blessing on the marriage. I went to the wedding in company with Peter Lambert. When I asked William if Peter might attend he grinned with pleasure.

'Indeed! I shall not forget how he gripped my hand while the sawbones cut through my leg. I near broke his fingers. Bring him, by all means.'

All William's family were there, and Liza's father, come back from Essex for the occasion, with a large family I took to be her aunt and cousins. It seemed nearly every shopkeeper from Eastcheap was there, leaving their premises – trustfully! – to their apprentices. Amongst the throng I noticed a sprinkling of soldiers, friends from William's army days, some of whom I had cared for after the disaster of Sluys, including the very young boy who had been carried off by his scolding, diminutive grand-dam. There were a few of the better sort as well. One man I knew as the landlord of many of the premises rented by the Eastcheap traders, though I believed Jake Winterly owned his shop. Also, to my surprise, I saw Dr Stephens from St Bartholomew's. I poked Peter in the ribs with my elbow while the priest was delivering his sermon, and nodded toward Dr Stephens. He put his mouth close to my ear.

'I told him I was coming,' he whispered, 'and he said he would come too. I think he takes some credit for William's recovery, though we know that it was you who saw that he must have an amputation, and who cared for him day and night till he recovered. And found his family.'

I made a face and shrugged. It will always be thus. The greater men will always take the credit for a success but shed the blame for any failure on those of lower rank. It was the Portuguese expedition all over again. Essex would claim imaginary credit, while the common soldiers perished or were turned away empty handed. As for my own success in bringing William through both his physical injury and his state of despair? Well, I was gone from Bartholomew Hospital now, so I was of no account.

The service was mercifully short. Some of these parishes in the heart of the City have a Puritan tendency, and their sermons are known to be interminable. It seemed this parish priest was a firm adherent to the Queen's own moderate stance on religion. The service, like the church, displayed none of the flamboyance of those secretly inclined to the old faith, nor had it stripped away all beauty and grace in favour of the aridity of Geneva.

Less than an hour made the young couple man and wife, properly blessed and preached over, and saw our cheerful company making its way a few hundred yards along Eastcheap to the Fighting Cockerel inn. This was an old building, sagging a little on its timber frame and beginning to sink into the Thames clay, so that you must step down through the front door into the main parlour. The room was somewhat dark, for the tiny ancient windows admitted little light, and the ceiling, once white-washed, had taken on the colour of caramel from the smoke of many pipes. It is surprising how men even of the small shop-keeping class can find the chinks to buy the new smoking weed from the New World, but they say that once you have taken up the habit, you cannot leave off. Two old men sat here now, with mugs of beer before them and pipes in their mouths, so that their heads emerged from a smoky cloud like a species of humanoid dragon. Surely it must spoil the flavour of the beer?

However, the marriage feast was not to be held here. The inn had somehow managed to retain its garden at the rear, despite all the greed for building land in London. It was a fine, sunny summer day, and we were to take our refreshment out of doors.

Trestle tables were set out in the shade of some apple trees which looked as crooked and loaded with years as was the building. Fresh white tablecloths covered what were probably rough boards, and the inn servants were now laying out platters and bowls of good, substantial fare, not the delicate and exotic titbits served at Sir Walter Raleigh's evening meetings at Durham House, but slices of beef and pork, chunks of pease pudding, purple and white carrots seethed in butter, vast two pound loaves fresh and warm from the baker's oven, pats of butter yellow as primroses, two great cheeses nearly as big as wagon wheels. There were more refined dishes to follow, probably made by Bess Winterly and her gossips – bowls of flummery, plum tarts, dried apple pies, candied orange slices, and round-bellied jugs of cream. For a moment I felt queasy, and the ground shifted under me, remembering how we had starved on board ship, not many weeks before, but Peter dragged me forward and we joined the rest of that happy, jostling crowd, filling our wooden platters to overflowing, and finding a couple of stools beneath a pear tree where we could turn serious attention to the meal.

The crowd milled around the tables, then resolved itself into small groups. Glancing up, I saw Dr Stephens approaching us. We both stood and bowed. Peter offered his stool to the elderly physician, while I fetched another from beside the inn door. Once we were all seated, Dr Stephens turned to me.

'I was sorry to hear that you had lost your father, Christoval. He was a good man, though we did not always see eye-to-eye.'

I thanked him, recalling with a rueful smile, how often they had bickered over the treatment of a patient, though I knew that they had always respected one another.

'And I have now lost my place at Bartholomew's,' I said. This was stating something he knew as well as I did, but I was curious to see how he would respond.

'Aye, well,' he said, looking a trifle uncomfortable. 'You have no degree in medicine, you are not a Fellow of the Royal College. Your position was as your father's assistant. Indeed, it was not even certain whether you would return from Portugal. It was necessary for the governors to make other appointments quickly. I could not carry on alone, with none but my own assistant. In fact, I had already reduced my hours at the hospital.'

I longed to ask how things had been managed while my father was in his last illness, but this was not the time.

'And how do you find the new physician?' I asked. 'Dr –' I glanced at Peter.

'Dr Temperley,' he supplied.

'A sound man,' Dr Stephens said, with a certain air of complacency. 'A sound man. Oxford, you know. A university man, and a Fellow, as I am, of the Royal College.' He stroked his beard, with the air of a man well content with himself. 'Dr Temperley has been practising in a provincial hospital – Norwich, I believe – but has now made the move to London.'

I felt the stirrings of anger beginning to bubble up in me. My father had been the senior professor at the university of Coimbra, with a reputation that drew students from all over Europe to study under him, until the Inquisition drove us from our home. His skill in both conventional and Arabic medicine far surpassed that of Stephens, and no doubt of this Temperley fellow as well, still mired as they were in the out-dated theories of centuries past. Perhaps it was as well that I could not do as Walsingham had suggested, and study for a degree. I should probably find myself thrown out of the university on my ear for my unconventional views. I do not always find it easy to keep my tongue behind my teeth.

As if he suspected what was going through my mind, Peter touched me lightly on the elbow and began to talk about the wedding and the fine crop of apples and pears growing here in this little orchard behind the inn. I swallowed hard and managed to join in, as if there were no more important matter in the world.

When he had eaten his fill, Dr Stephens got to his feet somewhat stiffly and said he must be going.

'And what will you do now, Christoval?' he said, as though it had only just occurred to him that I might still have my living to earn, even though I was cast out from St Bartholomew's. 'Do you still find work in the office of Sir Francis Walsingham?'

Everyone at the hospital had known that I worked there as a code-breaker, for whenever there was a glut of work in

Phelippes's office, Sir Francis would arrange for me to be released from my duties at the hospital. This, perhaps, had annoyed Dr Stephens in the past, and he was hinting at it now. What neither he nor anyone else at St Bartholomew's knew was that I had undertaken work of a very different, and often dangerous, nature for Walsingham.

'Aye,' I said. 'I have been doing some work for Sir Francis since I returned. However, I do not intend to abandon my work as a physician. Sir Francis is hoping to help me find a position, either back at St Bartholomew's or else at St Thomas's. I hope to hear something before the end of summer.'

Dr Stephens looked somewhat disconcerted at this. Having happily seen his hospital slip back into its old traditional ways, he would probably not welcome me again with my advanced foreign notions.

'Ah, indeed,' he said. 'Well, I wish you every success.'

He bowed to us and walked away.

'Do you really think you might come back to Barts?' Peter asked. 'It would be like old times.'

Not quite, I thought, without my father's guidance.

'Nay.' I laughed. 'I said that only to ruffle his comfortable feathers a little. The governors have filled all the places, I believe. Sir Francis thinks there might be a place at St Thomas's. I am waiting to hear.'

The crowd of guests was beginning to thin and the heat had turned sultry, as though there might be a storm in the offing.

'Come,' I said. 'We haven't given William and Liza our gift yet.'

Peter and I had shared the cost of two fine glass goblets as a marriage gift, and I had been carrying them all day, carefully wrapped in cloth, in my satchel. I would be glad to be rid of them before they broke. And their cost was yet another debt I owed to Sara. We made our way over to where the couple were sitting on a bench under an arch of roses, looking shy and very self conscious. I unwrapped the pair of glasses which, to my relief, were still intact.

William struggled to stand, leaning on his crutch, but I laid my hand on his shoulder to keep him seated.

'No need to rise for friends,' I said. 'Peter and I thought these might come in useful when you broach a bottle of French wine.'

We all laughed. Such a likelihood was small.

'Or,' I added, judiciously, 'for the excellent ale I am sure Liza makes.'

'Nay,' she said, blushing, 'I am a poor ale wife. Even Bess rarely makes ale nowadays. We City wives are too occupied with business.' As she said the word 'wives', she blushed even deeper, and William smiled at her like one besotted.

Others were coming with congratulations and gifts, so we both kissed the bride and made our way out of the inn. Before we parted, we stood a moment in Eastcheap, where the heat seemed to rise up from the ground as if it were a bake stone.

'A storm before morning, I reckon,' Peter said.

'Aye. It will clear the air. But let us hope it does not spoil the Fair. Only four days to go.'

'These summer storms don't last long, as a rule. Are you still planning a party to visit the Fair?'

'Aye. You. Me. Anne Lopez and her brother Ambrose. He is walking out with the daughter of one of his grandfather's colleagues, so she may come as well.'

'Five of us, then.'

'Would you like to bring someone else?'

He avoided my eye and shuffled his feet.

'Peter!' I said with a laugh. 'Who is she?'

'Well,' he said, hesitating, 'there is a daughter of one of the senior apothecaries. Master Winger, do you remember? Mistress Helen Winger. I have spoken to her a few times, but I've never asked her to walk out. She might think it too forward of me. Or her father might.'

'But he could have no objection to this,' I said. 'A large party. Ambrose is older than we are and the grandson of the Queen's Purveyor of Groceries and Spices. Very respectable. Mention that.'

He laughed. 'Very well, I will. Aye, I will. There can be no harm in a large party strolling about the Fair together. It will do excellently.'

'It will do perfectly,' I said. 'I will send you a note when everything is arranged – where and when we should meet. You still have a room at the hospital?'

'Aye. My little attic up under the roof.'

It was hard to credit it now, seeing Peter as a competent young apothecary, but he had come originally to St Bartholomew's as an orphan, to work as a servant. One of the older apothecaries had realised how clever and promising the boy was and taken him under his wing. Peter had worked hard to reach his present position. He would soon be fully qualified. I hoped the girl he had set his eye on was good enough for him. He was an old friend and it would be a fine thing to see him properly established at last.

We walked together through the City to Cheapside, until I turned north to Wood Street and Peter continued west toward Newgate and Smithfield. As we parted, I heard the first far off rumble of thunder.

It rained for two days and three nights, a cold downpour, the rain sheeting down the windows solid as a river, the streets awash with all the refuse afloat from gutters and kennels. Sara loaned me a hooded cloak of her own, which reminded me that I should need one myself before winter came, as well as a physician's cap and gown if Sir Francis managed to find me a place at St Thomas's. I had carried both cloak and gown with me on the expedition, but they were long gone, torn into strips to make bandages for the wounded.

Each morning I made my way, head down, across the City to Seething Lane, and despite the cloak I was soaked through by the time I arrived. For once I was glad of the summer fire in Phelippes's office, standing and steaming before it, like a ruff steaming with a crimping iron. I was glad, too, of my new boots, which kept out every bit of wet. I would recommend Liza's cordwainer's skills to anyone who valued a fine pair.

There had been no more trace of the new agent, David, though Sir Francis had authorised increased vigilance at the ports. This had led to the discovery of two barrels containing smuggled papist books. A merchant and several sailors were now kicking their heels in the Marshalsea prison, awaiting trial. I felt somewhat guilty, in case my suggestion of watching the ports had resulted in their arrest. I understood why the Queen and Privy Council were anxious to arrest the Catholic priests who flooded into the country from the training seminary at Rheims. The men were prepared there not merely to minister to Catholic families in England, and celebrate the mass with them. They were also trained to make new converts and to foster rebellion against the State. Several had, in the past, been involved in plots to assassinate the Queen.

However, I did not feel as strongly about Catholic books as some did. It seemed to me that what people read in the privacy of their own homes was not the business of the Privy Council. This was not, however, an opinion shared by the great men, including the one I worked for. To them, a papist book was as dangerous as a papist sword. Perhaps they were right. At least on this subject I was wise enough to keep my peace. I could understand Sir Francis's strong feelings. He had been trapped in a house in Paris with his young family while all around the slaughter of Protestants filled the streets with blood. I knew it had marked him for life. He had even, in a moment of unusual intimacy, shared his feelings with me.

If David or any other spy had entered the country with the crowds coming to the fair, he had passed unnoticed. It could be that the name 'David' concealed some other identity. Many of Sir Francis's own intelligencers assumed false names, sometimes a whole handful of them. If David was indeed a man known under some respectable true name, possibly even owning an official passport which allowed him to travel freely, then he could come and go as he pleased. No official at a port would detain him.

During those dark, damp days, Phelippes and I worked our way through the large bundle of letters and despatches, which contained little out of the ordinary. They brought us up to date on the movement of Spanish and French agents, and contained some names of new young men arriving at the seminary in Rheims. The letters from Rome were from our own intelligencers, who managed to stay well informed of the activities of the Pope and the College of Cardinals, thanks to some informers amongst the papal servants. There was even one brief despatch from the agent we knew only as 'Hunter', still held in the Lisbon prison, but apparently unharmed after our blundering expedition, and still able (we knew not how), to smuggle his letters out to us through a network of allies and friends.

'How I hate this rain!' I exclaimed to Phelippes, in the afternoon of the second day of storm. 'I was glad of it at first, for everything was hot and dry and dirty, but we have surely had enough by now. It is as dark as night.'

We had both been obliged to light candles to see our work. Only the best beeswax were good enough, and I was conscious of the cost.

Phelippes looked up vaguely. In the general way of things, I do not think he took much notice of the weather, unless it had some effect on the working of the service.

'Aye, it is dark.' He seemed surprised. 'What o'clock is it?'

He had removed his glasses, as usual, for close work, and could not see across the room to the mantel clock Sir Francis provided for us.

'Not yet three o' the clock. If the rain continues as heavily as this, the whole of Smithfield will turn to mud and the Fair will be quite ruined.'

Now that I had decided to go, I was somewhat put out. I should be sorry to miss the entertainment. When I lived secluded with my father, I had rarely had the chance to enjoy simple pleasures, except for occasional visits from my mathematics tutor, Master Harriot, who came to Duck Lane sometimes to make music with us. It was to Harriot that I owed several visits to the group which met in the turret room of Raleigh's home, Durham House, to discuss matters of exploration, new discoveries, and natural science. My friendship with Simon Hetherington had introduced me to the haphazard world of the players, but I had ventured neither to Durham House nor to the company of players since my return to London.

Now that I was beginning to grope my way toward a new life, without my father and without my employment at the hospital, I still felt somewhat at sea, and the idea of belonging to a party of young people, making a visit to the Fair like any other group of Londoners, gave me a tentative sense of belonging, of finding my feet in this new life. I should be sorry if it fell through.

I woke once during that night and sat up, listening, not sure what had roused me. Then I realised that the rain, which had been lashing against my window, driven by a strong east wind, was no longer so noisy. I had been woken by silence. I climbed out of bed and padded across to the window. The boards were still cold under my bare feet, but perhaps not as cold as they had been in the unseasonable weather of the last few days.

I opened the shutters, then unlatched the window and pushed it open. The wind had dropped. The air which flowed in from outside was slightly warmer than the air inside the room. It was still raining, but it was a soft, warm, summer rain, not the cold bluster which had felt more like November than August. Although the wind had calmed here below, in the high airs the clouds still chased each other across the sky, playing tag with the moon, which gave enough light for me to see down into the street below. The kennel down the centre was running with water like a small stream and the cobbles shone slick with wet, like so many fragments of the moon itself, cast down upon the earth. If the rain continued to die away, there was every chance that the grounds of Smithfield would dry up enough for the booths and stalls to be erected today and tomorrow, ready for the Fair.

Leaving the shutters open, so the warmer air could flow into the room, I padded back to bed. Already the boards felt less cold. I pulled the feather bed up round my shoulders and turned on my side. Before I could put two thoughts together, I was asleep.

At breakfast, a note was delivered from Ambrose, addressed to both Anne and me. I handed it to Anne to open, since he was her brother. She read it quickly.

'Ambrose says he will come tomorrow afternoon, and the three of us can go to see the Fair being set up. Then he will stay the night here, so the following morning we can leave early, in good time for us to reach Newgate before the Lord Mayor arrives to open the Fair. Mistress Hawes will arrive later, in her father's carriage.' She gave a wicked grin. 'It seems that Mistress Hawes is not accustomed to having to walk through the dirty streets of London.'

'Hmm,' I said, 'I am not sure that bodes well. She will have to walk on her own two feet about the Fair, and I cannot say that the ground of Smithfield is the cleanest in London. They will shovel away the worst of the dirty straw and dung, but all the rest of the year it is a market for beasts. One cannot expect it to resemble Whitehall Palace! Have you met the lady?'

'Once only. She *is* rather fine. I think my brother is somewhat in awe of her.'

'I hope she may not put a damper on our holiday.'

'If she tries to, we will leave them to their own devices,' she said. 'You and I, and your friend Peter.'

'Peter may also bring a young lady, though I think he is a little shy of asking her.'

'We shall be three couples, then. You must be my beau!'

I laughed, for I knew she was only teasing. 'What would your affianced say to that?' I asked.

'Oh, we are not strictly affianced yet,' she said, reddening a little. 'Though, to be sure, Master Francisco Pinto de Brito is a match much more to my taste than that elderly banker in Lyons that my father was talking about last year.'

I was not sure whether the banker from Lyons was as elderly as Anne made out, but I knew how she had hated thought of being sent off to France, to marry some unknown man whom Ruy had picked merely to strengthen his own trading and political alliances. Anne's current prospect, Master Francisco Pinto de Brito, would be much more to her taste. She knew him and liked him, though I am not sure that she was in love with him. However, she longed fervently to remain in England and had been horrified at Ruy's plans to move the entire family to Portugal on completion of the successful restoration of Dom Antonio to the throne. Like her mother, Anne had been born in England and regarded herself as English, whatever her father might say. She did not even speak Portuguese, apart from a few simple words.

'Well,' I said, 'I will squire you to the Fair, but should we encounter Master Francisco, you must excuse me if I run away before he can draw his sword.'

She laughed, and I went off to pen a note to Peter. He would not be able to take time off to come with us for our preliminary look around the fairground, but would join us for the opening by the Lord Mayor. I suggested that we meet by the hospital gatekeeper's lodge before the ceremony, so that we would have time to find a good place to see and hear everything.

I borrowed some sealing wax from Sara and sealed my letter, stamping it with the seal Arthur Gregory had made for me before my visits to the Low Countries last year, which I had retrieved from Phelippes's office. I gave the kitchen boy a farthing to deliver it for me to Bartholomew Hospital. Leaving Sara's cloak behind, I set off for Walsingham's house under a warm sun, which was quickly drying the muddy streets.

Chapter Five

*A*s he had promised, Ambrose arrived shortly after noon the next day and joined us for a meal before we set out. I had not seen him since the spring, and in the meantime he had grown a beard, exquisitely trimmed to a neat point by some modish barber. His clothes too were of the latest fashion. I need not have worried about borrowing his old clothes to replace my rags during the previous month, while my own new ones were made. So fine a gentleman would not deign to wear such plain garments! Today he wore a doublet of tawny velvet, its sleeves puffed out with excessive padding and slashed so that the lining of purple satin could be pulled through. The buttons were gold – or perhaps gilt silver – embossed with the Tudor rose, blazoning forth his loyalty to the crown

Even his breeches were velvet, of a dark forest green, and his hose (which displayed a fine, shapely leg) were of white silk. I feared they might suffer in Smithfield, for – although the returned sun had done much to dry the streets – there is usually a goodly layer of mixed mud and dung paving the whole area where the Fair is held, which was unlikely to be fully hardened yet.

I hid my smile at all this finery, but Anne, with a sister's licence for frankness, did not.

''Sblood, Ambrose, you are got up for a day at court!' she said, as we rose from the table. 'What are you doing here in Wood Street? Do you mistake us for Whitehall or Hampton Court? Kit and I shall be obliged to follow humbly along behind, like your household servants.'

Ambrose looked half annoyed and half embarrassed.

'Just because you dress like a shopkeeper's daughter, my maid, that does not mean the rest of the family must do the same.'

Privately, I thought this unjust, for Anne was very suitably dressed in an overskirt and bodice of the finest wool, a rich blue, picking up the colour of her eyes, and her hair was neatly tucked into a net of lace sewn with pearls, while the embroidered underskirt which showed beneath the front opening in her skirt was of silk the colour of cream. Taking my advice, she was wearing stout boots.

I knew that brother and sister were very fond of each other, despite this exchange, and for a moment my heart ached, remembering those long-lost days when I too had a brother and sister to tease.

Ambrose drew himself up to his full height.

'You must know, little sister, that I *do* often have business at Whitehall and Hampton Court, and Greenwich Palace too, for our grandfather often sends me in his place these days. One must dress the part. I deal only with the senior members of Her Majesty's entourage, and one must not appear slovenly and underdressed.'

'Her *entourage*!' Anne said, drawing the word out. 'By Heaven, brother, where did you learn that long word? Are we to be permitted to walk with you at all, then?'

He laughed and tapped her lightly on the shoulder. 'Enough. Time we were off. Is your friend to meet us today, Kit?'

'Nay,' I said, 'he would not be able to leave his work, but he has arranged matters so that he can join us tomorrow, and the other days of the Fair, if we decide to return again.'

'Excellent,' Ambrose said. 'Well, let us be on our way.'

Young Anthony was waiting by the door as we left, and begged to come with us.

'Not today, Anthony,' Anne said. 'Mama has said she will take you and the little ones tomorrow when the Fair opens.'

'Will you bring me back some gingerbread?' Anthony was clearly sulking.

'The gingerbread stalls won't be open until tomorrow,' I said. 'Today the men will just be building the booths and setting up the stalls and tents.'

'Then why are you going?'

It was a fair question. We were going merely for amusement's sake, but we would not be the only ones. There is something magical about seeing a dull and familiar place – in the case of Smithfield, quite an ugly place – transformed into something strange and wonderful. When the Fair was over, it would vanish away again, like those palaces that disappear in the old tales, seen for a time as if in a dream, yet solid and real, only to fade away like a puff of smoke.

We set off down Wood Street until we reached the corner where I had parted with Peter after the wedding, then turned west along Cheapside. This led us to Newgate Street, then past Newgate Prison and under the gate in the City wall. Just inside the gate I saw the man who sold roast chestnuts in winter. Today he had a tray of candied plums. They looked a little withered, but we bought a paper cone of them, for he looked very forlorn, as if he were doing little business. He recognised me, for I often bought chestnuts from him.

'Thank 'ee, young master', he said, his grin showed the gaps between his teeth. 'Business a'nt good these days.'

'Never mind,' I said. 'Come the Fair tomorrow, you'll be doing a roaring trade.'

'I've no money to rent a stall,' he said glumly, 'nor even the sixpence for a licence to carry my tray round the fairground.'

'Here,' said Ambrose, opening his purse and handing the man a sixpence. 'That will buy you a licence for the whole Fair, and good luck to your trade.'

That was more like the younger Ambrose, I thought. The fine clothes were no more than dressing over the honest man beneath.

The chestnut seller seemed astonished, gazing at the coin on his palm as if he expected it to melt away. 'Why, I thank 'ee, sir,' he said, tugging at his cap in a kind of clumsy salute. 'That'll do finely. I be much obliged, sir.'

He would have gone on heaping thanks on us, but we smiled and took our leave. Ambrose looked truly embarrassed.

'It was but sixpence,' he muttered, as we turned up past the cookshops in Pie Corner.

'To a man like that,' I said, 'sixpence may make all the difference between life and death.'

'You exaggerate, Kit,' he said.

'Nay, I do not.'

I thought of how close I had been to such desperation myself, just a few weeks earlier, and how much I owed to Ambrose's mother. With my wages from my work at Seething Lane I was beginning to pay off my debt to her, but I had kept a little back to spend at the Fair.

Although there was still a day to go before the Fair began, the whole of Smithfield was a-buzz. It was as noisy as a market day, but instead of the mooing and baaing that usually deafened those making their way to Bartholomew's hospital or the church of St Bartholomew-the-Great, there was shouting, hammering, cursing, the rattle of carts, and the crash as loads of timber were dumped. Smithfield is probably one of the noisiest places in London, whether given over to the regular market, the annual Fair, or the occasional more sinister purpose – the burning of heretics.

I suppose the place has always been used for a livestock market, lying as it does just outside the City wall, but close enough for the convenient supply of meat. I've often wondered whether it was already here when the original Priory of St Bartholomew was built beside it, all those centuries ago. A priory, I suppose, is meant for a place of quiet contemplation and prayer, but it cannot have been very peaceful for the monks who dwelt here in such close proximity to the market. Though in truth they had always been an outward looking group, those monks of St Bartholomew, for hundreds of years maintaining their large hospital to relieve the suffering of the poor citizens of London, and their extensive giving of alms and care for widowed women and destitute orphans. All that had ended with King Harry's reforms.

For a time after the priory was dissolved, so I had been told, the fate of the very church itself lay in the balance, as the monastic buildings began to be demolished and the hospital lay abandoned. Part of the church was torn down and a cluster of small houses built in the priory grounds, using the salvaged stone from priory and church. The loss of help for the poor half a century ago from all the monastic institutions had led to the streets of London becoming filled with beggars and the sick, spreading disease and crime throughout the City.

A few good men had reopened the hospital, pleading for funds and medical services from any who would support it. It must have been a hard task and often thankless, but at length even the Privy Council had seen the advantage of providing help for those who could not afford the attentions of a private physician. Nowadays the hospital was organised and staffed on a permanent basis, although funds were always short. And the racket from Smithfield could still be heard in the wards on market days.

Along with the other sightseers, we picked our way through the crowds of workmen, who must have been mightily annoyed by us. From time to time one of them would shout at us to get out of the way. One fellow dropped a plank so close to Ambrose that he jumped back in alarm as the dust spattered his fine hose. I did not think it was entirely an accident. His finery might well have been seen as a provocation to these workmen, many of them in nothing but tunics of rough sacking, their legs and feet bare. In the summer heat and labouring hard, they would be warm enough, but what of the cold, when winter came? The weather-wise were forecasting a bitter winter to follow this hot summer, commenting on the thick clusters of berries and hips already beginning to form on the City's trees and bushes.

'God's provision for the birds,' they said. 'Sure sign of a bad winter.'

I could not but pity any man in a sacking tunic and no hose if they were to be proved right.

'Look,' said Anne, 'they are building the booths in the Cloth Fair.'

I followed her pointing finger and we began to walk toward the most important part of the Fair.

'Bartholomew Fair started originally simply as a cloth fair, did it not?' Anne said.

'Aye.' Ambrose nodded. 'It's one of the specialist fairs found all over Europe. Our father has had dealings with the spice fairs. There are wine fairs and beer fairs and cheese fairs and fairs for gold and silver work, but the great annual cloth fair in London is based on the importance of our fine English wool and woollen cloth, so the cloth merchants, and the Drapers' Company of London, still hold the most important place in the fairground.'

'But it has grown and changed over time,' I said. 'The people of London wanted more from their fair than cloth. So that is why the Fair now sells goods of every sort and serves as much for entertainment as for buying and selling.'

'It is the same in other countries,' Ambrose said. 'I was sent by our grandfather to the Frankfurt fair last year, and everything you can imagine was on sale there, including cloth from England. Just as foreign cloth merchants also come here with their goods – silks and damasks from Arab lands, French tapestries, even cotton cloth from North Africa. In Frankfurt there were musicians and jugglers and fortune-tellers too, just as we have here.'

'I have heard that these foreign traders pay a heavy tax,' Anne said, as we reached the most favoured area of the fairground, 'yet they occupy booths on the very fringes of the Cloth Fair.

The double street of the Cloth Fair, the area set aside for the cloth merchants, ran along one side of the church, on slightly higher ground than the muddy area of Smithfield, and here men were at work erecting the elegant booths. The best places were still reserved for our English merchants, although it must be said that even the booths for the foreigners were handsome affairs.

'Indeed,' Ambrose said with a grin. 'Our merchants want all the advantages for Londoners. I am certain they pay a high tax when they go to Frankfurt.'

'The booths are like little shops themselves!' Anne exclaimed in delight. 'They even have more than one room. I never noticed that before.'

Ambrose nodded. 'A drop down counter at the front, like the shops in Cheapside, to display their general goods, then the main shop in the front room, with shelves for the rest of the stock. Or in other shops, barrels, I suppose, for other sorts of goods. But here, shelves for the bolts of cloth.'

'And the room at the back?' she asked.

'For more expensive items, I'd wager, and the cash box, and a cot for the watchman who stays in the booth overnight.'

'People live here?'

'Just for the duration of the Fair. A merchant could not pack up his goods and move them away every night, could he? Nor would he dare leave them unguarded. One of his trusted journeymen will stay to guard them.'

'I suppose that is very true. So – men will be sleeping here tonight?'

'It would seem so,' I said. 'They cannot wait until tomorrow to set out their goods. All must be ready when the Lord Mayor opens the Fair in the morning.'

I had never given it any thought before, but the Fair was even more like the enchanted town of a fairy tale than I had imagined. Before dusk the place would be populated. Someone must also provide food and drink, although the stalls selling roast pig and ale and other victuals would not be free to serve until tomorrow. Some provision must be made for the dozens of watchmen tonight.

Thinking of this, I glanced over my shoulder to where a temporary street of stalls was growing before my eyes on the open area of Smithfield. Officers of the Fair were bustling about with plans in their hands, sharply directing the erection of the less grand stalls for ordinary traders, making sure that they lay along prescribed lines and were not put up higgledy-piggledy. The traders would each have rented a certain patch of ground and woe betide any man who tried to push his stall to the front or claim a better position than he had paid for.

There was a great deal of shouting and argument going on, most of it fairly good natured, though sometimes tempers flared.

'You will do as you're ordered, Nicholas Borecroft,' one of the officers shouted, his face puce with barely suppressed anger. 'You know and I know that you have rented the fourth place along the row, not that costlier pitch at the corner. You'll take down your stall *now*, or my men will take it down for you, and they'll not be over careful.'

The said Nicholas Borecroft was a large, fair haired young man with a wide grin and an insolent air. It was clear he knew he was in the wrong, but he set about dismantling his stall with maddening slowness, whistling a tune which I recognised from my days with the soldiers in Portugal, before they became too exhausted to sing or whistle. The song had words of a particularly scurrilous nature, deeply offensive to any man in authority. It was obvious that the officer recognised it too, but there was nothing he could do. You cannot forbid a man whistling, except perhaps in church.

Ambrose and Anne had walked further along the Cloth Fair while I was watching this little drama. The cloth traders' booths, which belonged to the Fair and were brought out afresh each year, were very fine, stoutly built of oak, with carved uprights and lintels, leather straps for raising and lowering the counters, shingled roofs, and strong locks on the doors. Some of the posts looked as beautiful as ancient church carvings. I wondered how old they really were. Borecroft's stall, which he probably owned himself, or rented for the time of the Fair, was a ramshackle and tottering framework of cheap unseasoned wood, with canvas for sides and roof, a length of dirty string to support the counter, and a flimsy door any strong shoulder could break down. If Borecroft's goods were of any value, he would need to keep a sharp watch on them. Probably he would spend the night here himself.

As I began to turn to follow the others along the Cloth Fair, I had an odd sensation that I was being watched. No one seemed to be looking at me from the main fairground, though I scanned it carefully. I turned right round and looked down the Cloth Fair. A little way along, four men were erecting one of the grander booths, under the supervision of an older man, one of the Fair's senior servants, for the labouring men did not appear to be very skilled at their work. I realised that one of the men had paused, with an end of a timber post in his hands, and was looking directly at me. As I caught his glance, he looked away and said something to his companions. Disconcerted, I began to follow Ambrose and Anne toward the far end of the Cloth Fair and as I passed the group of men, I felt sure they were discussing me. What was more, they looked somehow familiar.

I paid them no attention, but when I had joined the others, I still felt I was being watched. It sent a prickle down my back. There was sometimes a certain danger in the work I did. In the past I had carried out various secret missions for Sir Francis, but they had mostly been abroad, in the Low Countries, Spain, and Portugal. I had once briefly masqueraded as a tutor in a Catholic household, but these common workmen would have had no place there, nor could they have seen me during the pursuit of the Babington conspirators. I had had an encounter with fishermen on the coast of Sussex, but the night had been dark and I had not been seen clearly, I was sure. Why, then, had these men looked at me so intently, as though they knew who I was? And why did I have a vague sense that I had seen them before? It made me uneasy.

After we had strolled along the Cloth Fair we turned back to the main fairground. Passing the booth where the men had been working, I saw that it was now complete and they had gone. Still, I could not quite rid myself of that uncomfortable sense that they knew me and were watching me.

'I wish we might buy some gingerbread for Anthony,' Anne said. 'It is tiresome to have to wait until tomorrow.'

We were passing Nicholas Borecroft's stall, which was already re-erected, fragile as it was, and I saw that he was laying out his stock.

'Look,' I said, 'a toy man. Perhaps Anthony would prefer a toy, rather than a piece of gingerbread which he will gobble down in no time.'

'He is far too old for toys these days,' said Ambrose. 'He's a great schoolboy at Winchester now.'

'They are not all toys for little ones,' I said. 'Look, there are musical instruments and skittles. No one is too old for skittles. Or a pipe and drum.'

'Not a drum,' Anne said with a laugh. 'Mama would never forgive us. And it would drive our father mad!'

'Perhaps not a drum,' I conceded.

'Toys and trinkets for every age,' Nicholas Borecroft called out to us. He had clearly been listening to our conversation. 'Beads and baubles for lovely ladies too.'

He leered at Anne, holding up a string of cheap wooden beads, such as a girl of three might wear. She laughed.

'Nay, toy man,' she said, 'you may not sell today. You know the rules.'

'Then you must return tomorrow, fair maiden, and I will make you special price, just for the sight of your lovely eyes.'

I could see Ambrose draw himself up indignantly at this presumption, but Anne merely laughed again.

'I shall tell my mother to bring the younger children to visit your stall, toy man,' she said, 'and you may make your special price for her.'

He bowed, not a mite put out by Ambrose's glowering looks. 'I shall be glad to, my lady.'

We walked on, Ambrose muttering indignantly until Anne told him smartly that she was not offended. This was the Fair, where all ranks mingle.

'The fellow was only doing what all shopmen must do, enticing folk to buy his wares.'

'He should not have spoken to you so. It was unpardonable insolence.'

'Come, Ambrose.' She slipped her hand through his arm. 'I am not offended, so you must not be. You are grown too grand since you have been working for our grandfather. Forget your royal customers and let us see a little more of the preparations, then have a glass of wine at a respectable inn.'

After this, Ambrose relaxed and began to enjoy himself, like the boy I had known when we first came to London. The crowds were quite thick by now, getting in the way of the workmen and shopkeepers, who were trying to prepare for the opening the following day, some patiently, some less so.

'Look,' I said, 'there is a puppet show. I have not seen one, oh, not for many years.'

' "A grand performance by the miniature Commedia dell'Arte",' Ambrose read from the billboard propped up against the side of a large tent. 'Do you suppose they mean the real thing, with Pulcinella and Arlechino and Pantalone and Scarramuccia? I saw the Commedia when I visited Italy in the spring of last year, for Father's business.'

'They used to come to Coimbra,' I said unguardedly, 'the Italian Commedia dell'Arte travelling troupes.'

They both looked at me in surprise, for I rarely spoke of my childhood in Portugal, for fear I might let something slip.

'We should come to see them tomorrow,' I added hastily. 'To judge whether the puppet master performs the true Commedia.'

'I have never seen it,' Anne said.

'I do not understand how the puppet master can make the movements so real, and speak in so many different voices.' Ambrose was peeping through a gap in the canvas of the tent.

'There must be an assistant as well,' I said. 'One man could not handle more than one manikin at a time.'

I felt myself suddenly jostled and at once thought of the men who had been watching me. Then my hand went to the purse at my belt. It was as well it did, for I was just in time to snatch it away from a cutpurse.

'Stop, thief!' I cried, and Ambrose made a lunge for the fellow, a weasely lad of fifteen or so, but he slipped away through the crowd and was gone before we could catch him.

'Enough,' Anne said. 'We have seen how everything is being prepared. If there are thieves about, we'd best get away from the crowd.'

'Aye.' Ambrose linked arms with us both. 'Let us find that glass of wine you spoke of. You have your purse safe, Kit?'

'Aye, though the strings are cut.' I stuffed it down the front of my doublet and as I did so I noticed that my hand was bleeding.

'The wretch caught me with his knife!' I sucked the side of my hand. It was not a deep cut, but it smarted.

Anne looked at me anxiously. 'Are you badly hurt, Kit? Should we go straight home?'

'Nay, it's nothing. I'll salve it when we are back. I'd rather have that glass of wine.'

We pushed our way through the crowd, all of it seemingly moving in the opposite direction to us, until we reached the edge of the fairground.

'I have told Peter we will meet him tomorrow over there,' I said, nodding toward the gatehouse of the hospital. Stacked up beside it was a great heap of the hurdles which were used on market days to make pens for the beasts. Usually they were stored on the other side of Smithfield. The governors of the hospital would not be pleased to see them there. The Fair made access to the hospital difficult enough without this extra impediment. Some of the patients could barely keep on their feet, while the more serious cases had to be carried in.

'Can you walk a little further, Anne?' Ambrose asked, as we reached Pie Corner again. 'The inns hereabouts are not suitable for a lady, but if we go on toward Chancery Lane and the lawyers' quarter, there are some respectable houses.'

Ambrose, of course, had spent his two years at one of the Inns of Court, picking up a smattering of the law, which Ruy had thought would be useful to him in business. He would know the area well. We followed his lead away from the Smithfield area, with its smell of beasts and butchery, so long familiar to me. The streets grew pleasanter the further west we went, with fine modern houses, many with large gardens. As the City itself within the old walls grew more and more crowded and dirty and disease ridden, the wealthier merchants were moving out to this area where the air was cleaner and they were closer both to the Palace of Whitehall and the Law Courts at Westminster, where many had mercantile disputes to settle. I wondered whether this was where Ruy was planning to move when he spoke of a better house. A far cry indeed from the crooked houses in Duck Lane where my father and I had our home, and where Ruy and Sara had once lived briefly when they were first married, during the time Ruy himself had served at St Bartholomew's.

It was no more than a ten minutes' walk down Old Bailey to the bridge over the Fleet River, which was hardly more than a stinking sewer at this time of year, choked with dead dogs, a yearling pig and other unimaginable refuse. It would need the winter rains to scour it out and wash everything down to the Thames and out to sea. On the Fleet Bridge, the figures of Gog and Magog, ancient guardians of London, gazed out of their weather beaten faces, bearded with lichen and coifed with bird droppings. Along Fleet Street, Ambrose led us to a large modern inn, where we sat in a private parlour to be served with a jug of pale gold French wine and plates of marchpane shapes. The wine was almost as good as that I had sometimes drunk in Sir Francis's office.

'I must confess,' Anne said, 'I am a little tired. Pushing through those crowds was exhausting.'

'It will be worse tomorrow,' Ambrose said.

'Ah, but tomorrow there will be jugglers and magicians and the puppet show! And if we are tired we can sit and eat roast pig. Best Bartholomew pig!'

I kept my thoughts to myself. I had been brought up never to eat pig, and although in recent years I had been moving more and more away from my Marrano heritage, the thought of greasy pork sickened me. If the others wanted to eat the famous Bartholomew pig tomorrow, which would be roasted on spits and served with ale at temporary taverns throughout the Fair, I would need to make my excuses. I reflected that it was strange that the Lopez children had not been reared in the same tradition as I, but their families had lived long in England and were more thoroughly assimilated into English ways and an English diet than I was. Peter Lambert, a thorough Englishman and proud Londoner, would certainly want to eat roast Bartholomew pig.

To divert their thoughts from this, I mentioned the odd incident of the men who had watched me at Smithfield.

'And you think you know them?' Ambrose said.

74

'I cannot be sure.' I shrugged. 'Perhaps they were once patients in the hospital, though why should they all have been there together . . . Unless–' I paused, frowning.

'Yes?' Anne said.

'Could they have been some of the soldiers returned from the fall of Sluys? Discharged from the army now and working as labourers?' I shook my head. 'I cannot remember. William Baker would know.'

'The one-legged leather worker?' Anne said.

'Aye. He was one of those who fought at Sluys. It's no matter. I shall probably remember when I least expect it.'

When we had finished our wine and marchpane, Ambrose said he would treat us to a wherry, to save us the walk home. We hailed a tilt boat at Temple Stairs and were swiftly rowed on an ebb tide down to Queenhithe, a short walk from the Lopez house in Wood Street.

In the middle of that night I woke suddenly, remembering where I had seen those men before. They were soldiers, but not from Sluys. They had been on the Portuguese expedition. None were men I had known closely or physicked, indeed I believed they were amongst the heartier ones who had been chosen to sail with Drake on the mission to the Azores, a trick of that lying pirate to take all our provisions and sail straight back to Plymouth. These men had not been amongst the sick and dying I had cared for on the return journey. But they would have known me, one of the small group of Portuguese gentlemen, and also one of the few physicians on the expedition. Was it merely for that reason they had stared at me? I shivered, despite the warmth of the night. There had been something else in their look, a kind of desperate intensity.

The next morning, Bartholomew Eve, dawned with a promising brightness in the sky. The last of the storm clouds had quite blown away and any lingering dampness in Smithfield would have been dried out. On the other hand, it would probably become very hot amongst the crowds at the Fair by the middle of the day. We planned to go early, to watch the opening by the Lord Mayor, then stroll about the Fair and attend the puppet show. We would take some refreshment (not pig, if I could help it) and return no later than the middle of the day. That, at least, was our intention. But matters were brewing that would change everything.

Ambrose had spent the night in his parents' house, and the three of us met to break our fast before the rest of the family was stirring. Sara and the younger children would follow us later. Ruy, naturally, had more important matters to occupy him. He had mentioned the previous evening that he would be riding out to Eton to attend on Dom Antonio. I wondered whether he peppered his treatments with demands for the return of the gold he had loaned the would-be king of Portugal.

We set out promptly after a hasty meal of bread, cheese and ale, and made our way as before to Newgate. There was no sign of the chestnut seller, so I assumed he had already bought his licence and found a suitable pitch on the fairground, ready for the opening of the Fair. Crowds were already gathering here, awaiting the first stage of the morning's events. I suppose we had been standing some half an hour, and more people had crowded in behind us, though we had retained our places at the front, near the entrance to Newgate prison, when a shout from further back on Newgate Street alerted us to the arrival of the Lord Mayor.

A way was cleared along the street by uniformed City servants dressed in scarlet trimmed with gold braid, each bearing a sharp and wicked looking halberd. They formed up, lining the two sides of the street, tilting their halberds to form crosses, preventing anyone from slipping through. Then we heard the clatter of hooves and wheels on the cobbles as the Lord Mayor's open coach approached and drew to a halt in front of the prison. But for the halberdiers, I could have reached out and touched it, and a splendid affair it was – carved into the semblance of rearing dragons on either side, with a near life-size gilded wooden figure of St George brandishing his spear upright in front of the liveried servants perched on the rear foot-board of the coach.

The Lord Mayor himself was clad in an immense scarlet robe of velvet, heavily embroidered with gold thread, which must have been almost unbearably hot on this August day. On his head was a black velvet hat with white exotic plumes pinned in place with pearls the size of my thumbnail. The embroidery on the robe depicted the arms of London, the Tudor rose, and images of the Thames and the City, all intertwined with rose leaves and briars. About his neck the interlinked gold chain looked as though it weighed as much as a small child. The current mayor was Richard Martin, himself a goldsmith, so perhaps he had fashioned the chain with his own hands. Or perhaps it was passed down from one incumbent of the office to another. I did not know. When we had left London in the spring, the Lord Mayor then had been Martin Calthorp of the Drapers' Company, but he had died shortly afterwards and Richard Martin had assumed the office early. He looked stern and somewhat haughty, an effect marred by the beads of perspiration gathering on his brow.

As the coach drew up outside the entrance to the prison, the doors were opened by two prison guards and the governor of the prison stepped out. He too was grandly dressed in a long dark blue velvet robe and he too wore a heavy gold chain, though not so fine a one as the Lord Mayor's. He was followed by a servant bearing a silver tray, on which stood two heavily embossed silver cups and a flask, which I knew would contain sack. With great ceremony, the governor poured sack into the cups and handed one to the Lord Mayor, who stood up in the coach. The two men pledged each other and drank down the sack with a flourish.

No one had ever told me why this particular bit of the ceremony took place. It seemed very strange that the governor of a prison should have a part in it. What had that to do with a cloth fair, originally held for the benefit of London's cloth merchants? Nevertheless, the drinking of the cup of sack at the door of Newgate Prison took place every year. It always had been done, and always would be done in the future.

The two gentlemen finished their drinks, exchanged a few words which we could not hear, then the prison governor stepped back and the mayor resumed his seat. The driver of the coach gathered up his reins and clucked to the horses, who moved off through the City gate. Along with the rest of the crowd, we followed.

After we had left Smithfield the previous day, the rest of the Fair had been assembled, so that it now seemed almost a permanent part of the City, with streets of shops displaying the signs of their trades and their goods laid out on counters, taverns surrounded by tables and stools, roast pigs on spits turned by ragged scullions, tents with billboards announcing the pleasures to be found within – freak shows, astrologers, quack doctors. In the distance I saw a fountain of coloured balls rising into the air above the roofs of the stalls, where some juggler was practising his art. There were the shrieks of monkeys and parrots and other exotic creatures – 'See the wonders of the New World, only a ha'penny'. As we passed one of the larger tents, I smelled an unmistakable musky smell and heard a rumbling growl which I recognised. A bear. Would there be bear baiting? It seemed a dangerous thing, in the midst of the Fair.

We washed up at last near the gatehouse of the hospital, and there was Peter, with a lively young girl clutching his arm. He looked both pleased and self-conscious. Just beyond him was a platform which had not been there when we had left yesterday, on which there were several handsome cushioned chairs. This was where the Lord Mayor would sit to declare the Fair open and watch the first entertainment of the day.

'You have found us, then,' Peter said as we reached him. 'It was wise of Kit to suggest the one fixed point in all this hurly-burly.'

Peter already knew Anne Lopez, but I introduced Ambrose and the two men bowed formally.

'This is Mistress Helen Winger,' Peter said, colouring a little. 'You will know her father, Kit. Master Winger, head apothecary at Barts.'

'Indeed.' I bowed. 'I am delighted to meet you, Mistress Winger.'

On such occasions I could not help but reflect inwardly on the oddity of my position, as seemingly one of the gentlemen in the party, instead of one of the maidens.

'I understood from Kit that you would be bringing a lady, Master Lopez,' Peter said, looking about for the other member of our party.

'She will join us in a little while,' Ambrose explained. 'She thought it would be too hot and crowded at the opening. Mistress

Hawes will be here about nine o' the clock, coming in her father's coach.'

I saw that he could not forebear a little boasting, that the lady with whom he was walking out belonged to a family which possessed their own coach.

'Look,' said Anne, 'the Lord Mayor is here now.'

The mayor's coach had taken him to a side door of the hospital, where he would have been received by the governors and superintendent. All now climbed on to the platform and arranged themselves on the chairs.

Robert Martin's speech was mercifully brief, then he took up a large silver bell and rang it, to signal the opening. At once a group of wrestlers ran on to the cleared space before the platform. The Fair always opened with a display of wrestling before the Lord Mayor. Whether it was a sport enjoyed by every Lord Mayor, who can tell? I believe there is said to be some skill in it, but it has always seemed to me like men grunting and heaving more like wild animals than civilised human beings. In was not unknown for them to do each other serious injury. Even a dislocated shoulder was bad enough, but sometimes a man's back or neck might be broken. As a physician dedicated to the care and healing of the human body, I was revolted by such barbarity.

The men bowed. There were eight of them. They would wrestle in pairs until only two were left, and the last pair would fight for the purse of gold the Lord Major held on his knee. The wrestlers were naked from the waist up and wore nothing but tight leather breeches. Their skin gleamed with oil, intended to make them more difficult to grip, and the tussle more exciting to watch. Six of the men withdrew to the edge of the cleared space and the first pair squared up to each other, crouching and circling, watching for a chance to make the first move.

And so Bartholomew Fair began.

Chapter Six

The first wrestler moved in for the attack, hooking his leg around that of his opponent, seeking to throw him, but the second man somehow managed to slither away, and the first nearly lost his balance. They circled again. The crowd leaned in, faces eager, twisted, hoping to see a man hurt or even blood spilt.

I turned away in disgust. Behind the Lord Mayor's platform the gateway to Bartholomew Hospital rose in stately dignity, indifferent to this vulgar brawling in front of it. A sharp longing shot through me. Ever since I had started work there, soon after my fourteenth birthday, I had walked heedlessly through that gate very nearly every day, save Sundays and Holy Days, or when I was sent away from London on some task for Sir Francis. And now I could enter no longer. To stand here and feel myself shut out from the place where I had worked in such contentment, earnestly learning the profession of physician, hurt more than I could have believed possible. Until the time of the Fair I had avoided the hospital. Now I longed simply to walk through the door in my physician's gown, my satchel of medicines over my shoulder, and bid a good morrow to the gatekeeper, an old friend of mine and Rikki's, who used to spoil my dog with titbits from his own plate.

For a moment I felt my eyes blurring, but I must not weep. What would my companions think of me? Sir Francis might perhaps find me a place at St Thomas's Hospital, but it would never be the same as Bartholomew's, which felt to me like a second home, and where every corridor and ward held memories of my father.

I must put it behind me. Resolutely I concentrated on the wrestling. While my attention had been elsewhere, one of the men, slighter of build and younger than the other, must have taken a tumble, for his greasy torso was now coated with dust from the ground. That would make it easier for his opponent to grip him. And so it proved. The other man, a thickset, swarthy fellow with a broken nose, who looked as though he had survived many far less disciplined fights than this, suddenly ducked his head into the younger man's stomach and seized him around the thighs. With a grunt he heaved him over his own back and flung him to the ground, where he landed with the audible snap of a breaking bone.

The younger man let out a sharp cry and lay winded, then tried to scramble to his feet, only to fall back again. Even from where I stood, I could see that his right leg was broken. His opponent strode about the wrestling ground, his hands clasped above his head in victory. He passed quite close to us, the stench of his sweat and the oil – which I now identified as pig's grease – making me gag. The hair in his armpits was as black and thick as coiled wire.

Anne did not look as though she was enjoying this any more than I was, nor did Peter and his young friend. Like me, Peter was probably thinking more about the broken leg than the victory. A couple of hospital servants, who had been standing by in case of such accidents, were lifting the defeated man. Propping him up between them, they helped him hop one-legged to the hospital gateway. It was fortunate, I supposed, that medical help was so close at hand. The beaten wrestler was sweating with pain, but biting his lip to stop himself crying out and adding to his humiliation.

The next pair of wrestlers walked forward and bowed to the Lord Mayor.

It was then that my attention was drawn to something I had been half aware of for a few minutes already. From the direction of the entrance to the fairground on the south side of Smithfield, a noise seemed to be growing. Of course there had been a great deal of noise already. The crowds were thick in the fairground and not everyone had stayed to watch the wrestling. Once the

Lord Mayor had declared the Fair open, the chief officers of the Drapers' Company had made their way to the Cloth Fair, with their official yard measure made of silver carried ceremoniously before them. There they would check that every merchant was using a standard yard and not cheating his customers. Now that the Fair was under way, the shopmen could sell their wares, and many people had begun to stroll along the streets of stalls, looking for bargains, or for some fairing to take home as a memento of the Fair. Around the wrestling itself the crowd seethed, cheering and jeering the competitors in turn. Many would have made bets on the outcome of the various bouts.

What I had noticed was a different kind of noise. It sounded like – but surely could not be – marching feet. And yells of alarm. Had the London Trained Bands been turned out to search for some malefactor? There was always trouble at the Fair – cutpurses, theft from the booths, disputes between sellers and buyers, fights and drunken brawls – but it was far too early yet for a response from the militia.

Ambrose was the only one of our party who had been taking an interest in the wrestling, for he claimed that there was much skill in it, for anyone who understood the moves. I tapped him on the arm now to draw his attention away from the second pair who were just squaring up for their fight.

'Ambrose!' I said urgently. 'Listen! What do you think that is?'

He cocked his head. 'Many men walking together? Perhaps there is some planned procession? Nothing of concern, I think.'

He turned back to the wrestling.

'Did you hear it, Peter?' I asked.

Peter was talking softly to young Mistress Winger and hardly seemed to notice when I spoke to him. I shrugged. It must be nothing.

The second bout of wrestling was over even sooner than the first, as was the third. It seemed that in each case a much heavier, more experienced man had been matched against a younger one, less skilled and easily defeated. It was more than likely. Whoever organised the wrestling matches would want the final bouts to be the most impressive, between the strongest contestants. The less experienced men were probably there simply to provide opponents in the early rounds and were expected to lose. I hoped they would be well rewarded, for a badly broken leg – or worse – was a high price to pay for appearing before the Lord Mayor.

I wandered away from the wrestling and peered over the main concourse of the Fair. The toy man, Nicholas Borecroft, was doing a brisk business, but I saw that the puppeteer's tent was still tightly laced. I strained my ears for further sounds of marching feet, but I could hear nothing but the usual noise of the crowds, and the hawkers and shopmen shouting, 'What do ye lack? What do ye lack?'

By the time I returned to the wrestling, all the competitors had been eliminated but the last two, both large, heavy men, with bulging muscles and ugly, vicious faces. Anne was looking bored. I could see Peter and Mistress Winger walking slowly away in the direction of the Cloth Fair. Only Ambrose was watching the wrestling and even he had a slight twist of disgust to his mouth. I was glad I had not been there to see what had caused it.

'It will be over soon,' I murmured in Anne's ear. 'Then we can enjoy ourselves in the Fair!'

'I do not like the look of those last two men,' she said with a shudder. 'I'd not care to encounter them in the street.'

'Nor I.'

'In the last fight – you did not see it – that black-haired man tried to gouge out the eyes of his opponent. It was horrible.'

'It is a filthy sport.'

Yet irresistibly my eyes were drawn to the wrestling ground. Men in the crowd were still placing bets with each other on the final outcome of the matches.

'I'll wager you three shillings on Podraig the Irishman,' I heard from someone behind me. 'Those Irish giants are a wild breed, nothing can stop them. You saw how he twisted the last lad's arm behind his back till it burst from his shoulder.'

So that was why Ambrose had looked so disgusted. That and the attempt at eye gouging.

'Nay, I'll take your wager and raise you to five shillings,' said another voice. 'The Irishman is beginning to tire, He's

83

winded after the last bout. That great fellow from Cornwall has had time to rest the while. What's he called? Some uncouth name. Merion? Meredew?'

'I'll match you. Five shillings on the Irishman.'

'What are those servants doing, Kit?' Anne asked. 'Over there.'

Two men in the Lord Mayor's livery were pushing a large cage on wheels up to the far side of the platform.

'Rabbits,' I said.

'Rabbits?'

'When the wrestling is over, they let loose a whole pack of rabbits into the crowd. The young lads try to catch them, to take home to their mothers for the pot. And some lads not so young.'

'They just turn them loose in the crowd?'

'Aye.'

'It will cause chaos.'

'For a few minutes.'

'Poor creatures! They will be terrified.'

'Aye, but some will escape. If they are quick and clever. There's plenty of waste ground still in the old priory precincts, and hiding places amongst the rubble.' I smiled at her reassuringly. 'Many of them will escape. I remember soon after I started work at the hospital, I hadn't gone to the Fair, but of course we could not avoid hearing it, even within doors. One of the rabbits ran into the ward, then froze, shaking with fright, in a corner. If the cooks had caught it, we'd have had rabbit pie for dinner next day.'

'They didn't catch it?'

'Peter and I rescued it.' I laughed at the remembrance. 'We were both a little soft in the head, I think! It wasn't long since I had fled from Portugal and he had been an orphan living by begging on the streets. We had some fellow feeling for the poor creature. Peter grabbed it and hid it in his shirt. I led the way through a back passage I knew, to a door that opened into the old priory herb garden, and we let it go.'

She gave me a radiant smile. 'That's a good memory to have.' She paused. 'I didn't realise Peter had been a beggar.'

'He came from a decent family, but his parents both died of the sweating sickness within days of each other and he was left without home or family. Begging was his only means to stay alive. Luckily he found his way to Barts.'

And lucky, I thought, that I had been able, this very summer, to find my own way to Sara.

Anne looked at me soberly.

'Sometimes we forget how much sadness and suffering there is all around us, Kit.'

'Aye.'

Anne had been reared in the safe haven of a well-to-do home, but Ruy's unwise exploits might yet expose her to danger, I thought.

There was a yell from behind us. The vast bulk of the Irishman was still upright, but I could not at first see the Cornishman.

'He's been tossed into the crowd,' Ambrose said, pointing.

At the far side of the wrestling ground the crowd was milling around two men who were sitting in the dirt, looking stunned. In front of them the Cornishman lay without stirring. Before I stopped to think, I had darted around to him and knelt on the ground. I laid my fingers below his ear, although there was no point. I did not need to feel the lack of any heart beat to know that he was dead, for his neck was broken. I got to my feet, brushing the dust from my knees, and shook my head at the official who had hastened after me.

'I am a physician,' I said. 'His neck is broken. He is dead.'

Across the wrestling ring the Lord Mayor tossed the purse of gold to the Irishman, who tucked it inside his leather breeches. Then, even before the dead man could be decently carried away, the servants opened the cage and a flood of rabbits poured out into the crowd. Everywhere around me people were leaping and diving, trying to catch the poor creatures.

I struggled back to rejoin Anne and Ambrose and saw that the Lord Mayor's party had left the platform. They would probably visit the Cloth Fair and perhaps one or two of the grander booths. Since Robert Martin was a goldsmith, perhaps he would walk along the street of stalls selling gold and silver work, though there would be only small things on sale – gold hoops for ears, or simple bracelets. No one would risk anything of great value at the Fair. The official party would take a glass of wine with the governors of the hospital, then the Lord Mayor would be driven in his coach back to London.

I reached the Lopezes, but there was no sign of the other two, who must still be over by the Cloth Fair.

'It is nearly nine o' the clock,' Ambrose said. 'Mistress Hawes will be arriving. I said I would meet her at the entrance to the Fair. Will you come with me, or go to the Cloth Fair?'

Even as he spoke, the bells of the church clock began to toll out nine o'clock.

'I'll come with you, brother,' Anne said. 'I am eager to see the fair lady!'

'I will come too,' I said. 'We can find Peter later. I want to know what that disturbance was that we heard a few minutes ago.'

We began to push our way through the crowd, which was difficult, for the young lads were still chasing the rabbits. One gangling youth had caught two and struck them on the head. He was now carrying the bleeding bodies by the hind legs and looking about for more. An apprentice in a blue tunic tried to snatch them from him, but the youth punched him smartly on the nose and ran off. An official of the Fair shook his fist at the apprentice, instead of commiserating with him.

'No stealing, you dog's turd. You deserved that.'

The apprentice gave him two fingers, then spotted another rabbit and leapt after it. To my delight, the rabbit shot under the edge of a tent and the apprentice was frustrated.

As we drew nearer to the south end of the fairground, the crowd thinned out and I noticed an agitated bustle of Fair servants and constables.

'What's amiss?' Ambrose said, frowning.

Then through a gap in the cluster of officials, I saw an extraordinary sight.

Had we been in the Low Countries, as I had been once before, in the disputed territory between the Spanish forces and the United Provinces, I would have said that what confronted us was a line of battle. A vast number of men were drawn up in rank, blocking the southern entrance to Smithfield, and every one of them was armed. Some carried swords, some daggers, some no more than a cudgel, but a few had muskets and looked as though they knew how to handle them. They looked, in truth, like a professional army. My jaw dropped in astonishment and alarm.

During the long months of our abortive mission to Portugal, I had learned to estimate numbers, as the size of our army fell away. This army – as suddenly sprung from nowhere as the city of the Fair had sprung into being – must have numbered at least five hundred men. An army of five hundred men! Where had they come from?

Ambrose, who had been striding ahead to reach his young lady, saw them at the same moment as I did, and stopped dead. Anne clutched us each by the arm and whispered fearfully, 'Who are they? What do they want? Are they going to attack?'

No one appeared to know what was going to happen next. The armed men stood in a solid phalanx, the Fair officials scuttled about. They did not seem to think they were about to be attacked, but they were clearly very frightened. Who would not be, suddenly confronted on the happy occasion of the opening of the Fair, by a grim-faced army, their weapons all too visible to everyone?

'What is happening?' Ambrose grabbed a passing constable by the elbow and made him stop,

'They are demanding to speak to the Lord Mayor,' he gasped. 'We've sent to fetch him.'

'But who are they?' I asked.

'Men from the Portuguese expedition,' he said, his eyes rolling like those of a frightened horse. 'Trained soldiers, all of them, and armed, as you can see. They say they were promised great booty if they enlisted with the expedition. Instead, they suffered enormous hardship, then were turned ashore with nothing but a handful of coin.'

'And so they were,' I said.

He squinted at me suspiciously.

'And what do you know of it?'

His tone was unpardonably rude, but the situation was truly alarming.

'I was with the expedition, as a physician.' This was partly true, and it was none of his business to know anything more. 'Why are they here? What do they want?'

'They say that if they do not receive proper and full recompense for their service for England and the Queen, then they will wreck the Fair and pay themselves by looting its goods.'

'And why do they want to speak to the Lord Mayor?' Ambrose asked. 'Neither he nor the Common Council would have the means to pay them.'

'Aye,' I said. 'There must be five hundred men there.'

We all looked across at the soldiers. Their disciplined silence was more frightening than any clamour would have been.

'They want the Lord Mayor, as the leading citizen of London, to plead their case with the Queen,' the man said. 'They believe there was treasure taken on the expedition.'

'Aye,' I muttered, under my breath. 'There was. From Coruña, and from the treasure ship Drake captured. There is treasure which could be used to pay them. Yet . . . I wonder.'

Remembering how the common soldiers and sailors had fared under the command of Norreys and especially Drake, I had little hope of it. But an attack on the Fair would lead to much injury and death. The situation was fraught with danger and I feared that the Lord Mayor, a successful craftsman and merchant, would have little skill in dealing with a formidable force of armed and angry soldiers. I looked at them again. As I searched their faces more closely, I caught sight of the men who had watched me the day before, now standing in the front ranks. One carried a musket and looked prepared to use it. So this cast a new light on why they had been working to set up the Fair. They would have been scouting the layout of the ground, how the streets of stalls were arranged, where the richest pickings were to be found.

And there behind the men I recognised from the previous day were two men I had last seen stumbling ashore from the death ship in which I myself had travelled back to Plymouth. They had been sick and ragged then, and looked not much better now. Like many of the men blocking the entrance to Smithfield, they lacked shoes, and their clothes were no better than a beggar's. Hunger had carved away the flesh of their faces, so that the cheekbones stood out sharply, and their eyes were sunk deep in their sockets. Although most of this rag tail army were young men, their hollowed cheeks showed where teeth had rotted and fallen away, giving them the look of ancient grandfathers. My heart twisted with the pity of it. They might be threatening the innocent fairgoers and the small stallholders and shopkeepers, but they had a righteous case. Their treatment had been disgraceful and they deserved justice.

For some time there was a stand-off, there at the entrance to the Fair, and Ambrose became more and more agitated. It was impossible to see past the ranks of soldiers, so we could not tell whether Mistress Hawes had arrived as she had said she would.

'You must not worry, brother,' Anne said, patting his arm. 'As soon as she saw what was afoot, I am sure she will have told the coachman to drive her home again.'

'I wish I might be sure.' Ambrose groaned, and wiped his face with his hand. Trapped there in the crowd, confronted by the angry soldiers, we were growing hotter and hotter. His face was running with sweat.

At last a bustle and noise behind us made us turn. The mayor's halberdiers were clearing a way through the crowd, followed by the Lord Mayor himself, on foot, accompanied by some of his officials. He reached the front of the crowd, face to face with the soldiers. Everyone fell silent.

'What insolence and treason is this?' he demanded in a voice of authority and scorn. Perhaps I had been wrong about him. A man does not rise to be Lord Mayor without some skill in handling men.

'How dare you meddle with the opening of Bartholomew Fair, laid down by statute to take place this day? You come here – armed and in force – with your insolent demands! This is more than a breach of the peace.' He shook his fist at them. 'This is an act of treachery and treason against Her Majesty the Queen!'

At these words, some of the men eyed each other, worried expressions on their faces, but they remained steady and resolute.

One of the men carrying a musket stepped forward. He kept it pointing downward, but everyone could see his powder horn and his belt of shot. A slow match smouldered beside the stock of the gun.

'We have already told these fellows of our demands.'

He made a contemptuous gesture with his free hand toward the Fair officials. I realised from his manner of speaking that he came from the West Country, probably Devon. That meant he was most likely one of the sailors, who had been recruited from that part of the country, Drake's own homeland. All these men, soldiers and sailors alike, had been put ashore in Plymouth. Instead of going home to their villages, they must have walked all those miles, perhaps as much as three hundred, to reach here. They were well organised. And where had they managed to get hold of their weapons? Any man may obtain a club, but swords and firearms are not so easily come by. Nor are gunpowder and bullets.

'You say you have not been well enough recompensed for your late service?' The Lord Mayor's tone was disdainful. 'You have received what your masters felt you deserved. It is not for you to question their decision.'

I thought at once: That is a mistake. These men have survived much and will not take kindly to being treated like street urchins or common servants.

'We were promised a goodly reward for our service,' the soldier said. He kept his tone even, but I saw a flash of anger in his eyes. 'Four months we served in terrible conditions, dying of disease, starvation and unbearable heat, while a parcel of gentlemen squabbled over an ill-conceived and poorly commanded expedition.'

The man clearly had some education, and every word he said was true.

'You say this,' the mayor responded, curling his lip, 'but we have no evidence of its truth. Neither evidence of any promise made to the men of the expedition, nor evidence that you were even amongst those men. You are just some rabble out to make trouble. You have no proof that you ever left these shores.'

As if on a signal, all the men reached inside their shirts and pulled out pieces of paper. Folded and dirty as they were, I knew what I was seeing. The licences to beg that Sir John Norreys had issued to each dismissed soldier and sailor, so that they had the right to beg from parish to parish as they made their way on foot to their several homes. Each would bear the declaration of who they were and the signature of Sir John Norreys. No one could ask for better proof of their service on the Portuguese expedition.

'What is this?' The mayor's tone was still contemptuous, but I thought he sounded less certain of himself.

'Proof that we are men of the Portuguese expedition,' the man with the musket said proudly.

One of the mayor's officials stepped forward and took the paper from his hand. After quickly scrutinising it, he nodded to the mayor.

'Aye,' he said. 'Signed by Sir John Norreys.' He handed the paper back.

'It may be a forgery.' The mayor was beginning to bluster now and the soldiers' leader did not even bother to respond.

For some minutes there was no further exchange. The Lord Mayor was consulting with his officials and in the crowd of fairgoers which had gathered, there was some muttering which suggested a certain sympathy with the soldiers, mixed with dismay that the Fair might be overthrown by force. The soldiers continued to stand in silence, having tucked away their papers. It was the silence and their firm stance that made them all the more formidable.

At last the Lord Mayor stepped forward, until he stood just a few yards from the soldier with the musket. That took some courage, I thought, for the least mistaken reaction might bring that musket up and pointing at his chest.

'Why do you come to me? What is it that I can do to address your grievances?' His tone was more conciliatory now. Perhaps the evidence of the papers and the discipline of the men had forced on him the realisation that he was not dealing with an ungoverned rabble.

'We would ask you,' the soldier said with dignity, 'to speak on our behalf to the Queen or Privy Council. We do not make outrageous demands, but many of us are craftsmen or fishermen or farmers or small merchants who lost all we would have earned, had we stayed at home instead of answering the call to avenge England against our ancient enemy of Spain. Queen and Council made the call, and we answered.'

His eyes turned toward me, and I realised he too must recognise me.

'There are many who were there who will bear witness to all we suffered. I see one such standing there.' He raised his hand and pointed at me. The Lord Mayor glanced at me and frowned, but he quickly turned back.

'All we ask is recompense for what we lost by enlisting,' the man said, 'and something to compensate for our injuries and illness. Besides, there are the many widows and orphans left by the great losses we endured. Many are reduced to beggary. They too deserve some share in the treasure that was taken, for there *was* treasure taken. Not what was promised when we were urged to undertake the expedition, but treasure none the less. We do not ask the Common Council of London, or any other parish in the land, to undertake such a financial burden. Give us our rightful share of what was seized on the expedition and we will gladly disperse and go our ways.'

It was a fine speech and I heard some cheers from the crowd. The common folk of London would gladly support a claim on the treasure which would otherwise find its way into the pockets of the rich and powerful. Particularly if it meant the saving of their Fair.

The Lord Mayor turned aside again and held a low-voiced consultation with his officers. Finally he turned back to the soldiers.

'Very well, I will see what I am able to do for you, but I do not hold out great hopes. We will need to have further consultation as to numbers of claimants and the sums of money you have in mind.'

I was surprised that he had taken such a conciliatory stance, but perhaps he was merely buying time, in order to avoid a more serious confrontation now.

'Let you choose four of your number to consult with us, four of your leaders who can speak for all. You can return with us to London now and tomorrow we will talk of this further.'

The soldier who had spoken began to turn away, signalling to some of the others who were standing in the front line to come and join him.

'You must leave your weapons behind,' the Lord Mayor said sharply. 'You may not carry weapons into conference with us.'

'That is understood,' the soldier said. He snuffed out his slow match and handed his musket, powder horn and bandolier of bullets to a soldier standing behind him. The other men he had chosen also laid aside their arms, and the four men stepped forward to join the Lord Mayor's party.

'As for the rest of you.' The mayor had to raise his voice above the burst of talking amongst the crowd. 'You other men. You must disperse at once and you must not enter the City. Is that understood?'

The men did not answer, but at a command from one of the other leaders standing in the front line, they wheeled about and marched off down Pie Corner. I thought that if they had been so well disciplined on our expedition, we might have fared better despite the follies and mistakes of our leaders.

As they marched away, I caught sight of another man I recognised, although I had never known his name. On that terrible march from Peniche to Lisbon, under a gruelling sun, with little food or water, we had been attacked one night when we were encamped, by a party of Spanish soldiers. As usual I had been sleeping away from the main body of men, anxious that I should not betray myself or my sex in my sleep. This man had come to find me and hustled me and my horse away from the attacking Spanish. Earlier he had also helped the man I had treated for snake bite, who later died in my arms aboard ship. The last time I had seen him, he was boarding one of the ships chosen to sail on Drake's deceitful voyage – not to the Azores but home to England. He caught my eye even as I recognised him, and raised a hand in a kind of half salute.

'Well!' said Ambrose, letting out his breath in a great gust. 'I think we have escaped quite a nasty encounter.'

'The Lord Mayor managed matters better than I would have expected,' I said. 'At least he is prepared to consult with the men.'

'Probably merely delaying matters,' Ambrose said, 'and protecting the Fair. It would not look well for him if it were to be ransacked during his term in office.'

Anne looked distressed. 'Do you not think he means to help them, then?'

He shrugged. 'I think it was politic to seem to do so.'

'I wonder where the men will go,' I said, as the dust kicked up by their marching feet settled again and the crowd of fairgoers began to drift back toward the stalls and entertainments awaiting them in the Fair. All the traders and performers must have heaved a mighty sigh of relief.

'And I wonder whether they will disperse, as they have been told,' Ambrose said. 'It seems unlikely, for how would they learn the outcome of the consultations?'

'Nay, I am sure they will stay together.' I bit my thumbnail, as I am ashamed to say I am apt to do when I am worried. 'They will have to find some large area, large enough to hold them all. They must have gathered together before they marched on Smithfield. Probably when they are out of sight they will turn aside to the fields north of here, out near the old Charterhouse and beyond. Finsbury Fields, perhaps. They're likely to return there.'

'You are right, Kit. In this hot weather, it will be no hardship to sleep out of doors.'

'No hardship for these men at all,' I said drily, 'after what they endured in Portugal.'

'Do you think the Fair will carry on now?' Anne said. 'Should we go back? Mama said she would come after all the hurly-burly of the opening was over. She won't know of all this disturbance and I promised to meet her here.'

Ambrose shook his head. 'I am not going back into Smithfield now. I must discover what has happened to Mistress Hawes. If I find her, I will seek you out. We said we would watch the puppet show of the Commedia dell'Arte, did we not? Why do you not both go back and find Peter Lambert and the young lady, and if I return, I will meet you at the puppet show. I think it was not to take place until the afternoon.'

It was agreed between us that this arrangement was the best we could think of for the moment. Ambrose set off down Pie Corner in the wake of the vanished army, while Anne and I turned back to the Fair.

'Well,' she said, slipping her arm through mine as we passed again down one of the alleys of stalls, 'that was not what I expected at the first day of the Fair. I used to come with Mama when I was small, but we always came after the opening, so I never saw that dreadful wrestling or the madcap running about after rabbits!'

'And certainly none of us have ever seen the Fair threatened by a massed group of armed men,' I said, 'bent on looting it if they did not get justice.'

'Do you think they would truly have broken down the Fair and stolen the goods?'

I looked at her soberly. 'They have been very badly treated, Anne. I am not as surprised as some that this has happened. I was there. I saw how they suffered. Indeed, I even told Sir Francis that I thought the matter might not be finished with, that there might be more trouble. I cannot say that I wanted to be proved right.'

'But it will be settled now, won't it?' She looked at me hopefully. Anne and I were of an age, but sometimes I felt twenty years older.

'Let us hope so,' I said, for I did not want to spoil the pleasure of her visit to the Fair. 'Look, there is your friend the toy man. Nicholas Borecroft, he's called, and he's an impudent rascal. Shall we buy something for Anthony? A drum?'

She laughed, her sunny good humour quite restored.

'Don't tease, Kit! We might buy him a pipe, or one of those little fiddles, or a Jew's harp. Something that will not make too much noise.'

'And I want to buy some gingerbread for friends,' I said. I had a plan to surprise Phelippes and Gregory. 'Then we will go in search of Peter.'

Chapter Seven

*A*nne and I began to make our way back into the fairground, jostled on every side by the crowd which had gathered out of curiosity to see what was afoot with the extempore army and the Lord Mayor. Now that free spectacle of their confrontation was over, everyone was hungry and thirsty and eager to spend their chinks in the taverns or on little penny dogs of crude pottery or toy dragons or hobby horses. The cunning men who had their premises every day in Cow Lane had set up shop in tents at the Fair, offering to cast your horoscope or read your future in your palm. Anne was tempted, but I managed to persuade her against having her fortune told. Such antics I find both deceitful and alarming.

'Better not to know your future, I think,' I said, 'for surely it must hold sorrow as well as joy. Our natures being more inclined to melancholy than to happiness, if we are foretold sorrow, that is what we will dwell on.'

'Perhaps you are right.' She gave me a smile in which there was more than a little pity. She knew something of what my life had already held, though not everything. Like all the rest of her family, save Sara, she thought me a boy. I gave her a cheerful smile in return. I do not care to be pitied.

'Buy any ballad! Buy my new ballads!'

The shout came so close to my ear I jumped.

'Buy a ballad for your pretty wench, sir?' The ballad singer was swarthy of complexion and his speech had an Italian lilt.

I shook my head, but a gaggle of girls coming up behind us gathered around him, begging him to sing something for them, so that they might know whether they would like to buy the music and words. At once he flourished one of the sheets from his satchel under their noses and began to sing. More people stopped to listen. In truth, he had the elements of a fine voice, though I thought he had used it too much in fairs and in hawking his ballads on the street, for it was beginning to wear thin on the high notes. Anne insisted on buying a copy of the song for a penny, though it was in Italian, of which she knew not a word.

'You can turn it into English for me, Kit, so that I may understand it,' she said as we walked away. She was humming the tune, for she could read the notes.

'What if I were to tell you that it is a scurrilous song, common amongst drunken oafs in taverns, roistering late at night?'

Her face fell in dismay. 'Oh, no! Have I wasted my money?'

I laughed. 'No. It tells of a shepherd singing about his lady love. She is drawn to another, but he begs her to return to him. It is perfectly respectable, though somewhat sickly in its sentiments.'

'Oh, you are cruel!' she exclaimed, punching me lightly in the ribs. 'For a moment I believed you.'

A coster monger was walking toward us, with a large heavy tray hanging from his neck. The way was so narrow here that it was nigh impossible to sidle past him, which was what he no doubt intended.

'Buy any pears!' he cried, drowning out the ballad singer. 'Pears, costards and pears! Buy my fine, my very fine pears!'

'I don't see any costard apples,' Anne whispered to me. 'And the pears are very small.'

'And probably unripe,' I said. 'An unripe pear is like chewing on wood.'

Fortunately the group of girls overtook us and crowded round the coster monger. They seemed determined to buy a little of everything.

'This way,' I said, drawing Anne after me through a gap between two stalls and into the next row of shops. 'I think if we follow this lane along to the end it will bring us to the Cloth Fair and we may be able to find Peter and Mistress Winger.'

She followed me willingly enough. The adjacent row contained some of the better quality of stalls – some selling embroidered gloves and silk handkerchiefs, some pewter plates and apostle spoons, some lengths of cushion lace to trim ladies gowns. Anne lingered over these stalls, while I looked about for a gingerbread woman. A little further along there was a tooth drawer whose stall displayed a huge pair of forceps as its sign, enough to make your jaw ache at the sight of it. Beyond it a man sat on a stool with his right foot in another man's lap, having his corns cut away with a small, sharp knife. I hoped the fellow knew what he was about and would not cut so deep that he did his client an injury. There was a man selling mouse traps from a wheel barrow.

'Buy your mouse traps here, goodwives! No more thieving from your pantries. The best mouse traps, invented by a scholar in Leipzig!'

He did not appear to be doing much business. Little wonder, for the gimcrack mouse traps looked as though they had been glued together on his kitchen table out of scraps of cast off wood.

Anne caught up with me.

'I have bought some lace,' she said, opening the paper to show me. 'It's very fine work and I beat the man down on price.'

'Good.' I grinned at her. 'Now help me find a gingerbread woman.'

'Look.' She pointed to some children walking towards us. They each held a gingerbread figure in their hands. Like Phelippes and his sister, some were biting into them already, while others cradled them protectively, intending clearly to take them home uneaten.

'They must have come from a gingerbread stall,' she said. 'If we go further along this way, we'll surely find it.'

We passed the corn cutter and the mouse trap man, and soon I began to smell the warm spicy scent of gingerbread. It was a large stall, sturdily built, almost as solid as the best booths in the Cloth Fair. Laid out along the counter flap was a dazzling selection of gingerbreads in every shape imaginable – figures of famous people, horses, dragons, ships, castles, musical instruments, fairy tale creatures. A few at the front were plain gingerbread, at a farthing each, for the poorer children who could afford no more. The rest were covered with real gold leaf and glittered in the sunlight, despite being partially shaded by an awning of stripped green and white cloth. A buxom, motherly woman was drawing a large tin out of a portable oven, on which there were half a dozen freshly baked figures, which she lifted on to a metal grid at one end of a table to cool. At the other end of the table sat a younger woman, by her looks a daughter. Her face was screwed up in concentration as she used a soft brush to lift a whisper-thin sheet of gold foil on to a ginger horse and then brush it all over until the gold clung to every line and fold in the gingerbread. The older woman reached down a handful of moulds from a shelf and began pressing dough into them, to make the next batch. The wonderful scent of spice and baking biscuits made your mouth water with anticipation.

Anne and I examined the finished gingerbreads carefully.

'Mama will certainly buy some for Anthony and the little ones,' she said, 'but no one can have too much gingerbread.' She chose a selection of gilded animals and paid the woman, who came to the counter, wiping her hands on a voluminous apron.

'I will take these,' I said, handing her a large gilded castle and a ferocious dragon. 'And these.' I chose two of the plain gingerbreads, a ship and a smaller castle.

Anne raised her eyebrows at me as the gingerbread woman handed me my purchases wrapped in paper.

'Do you have a lady friend, Kit? You have kept her secret!'

I laughed and shook my head. 'The gilded ones are for my friends at Seething Lane.'

I told her Phelippes's tale of how he and his sister had been bought gingerbread when they were children.

'He's so serious and absorbed always in his work,' I said, 'I've bought him the castle to remind him of his childhood. The dragon is for Arthur Gregory, the quietest, mildest man you have ever met! And these,' I said, handing her one of the plain figures, the castle, 'are for us to eat now.'

We walked on, nibbling at our gingerbread, then turning the corner past the gingerbread stall, we found ourselves near the Lord Mayor's platform again. All the dignitaries had gone, but a group of gaudily dressed acrobats and jugglers were performing there, while a child went around with a pewter mug, asking for twopence for the show. It seemed a lot, but we paid our share and watched for a time as the men threw the woman about in the air, juggled with balls and knives, and finished by forming themselves into a human pyramid. The child with the mug was casually thrown straight up into the air, caught by the woman at the top, and then stood on her shoulders, waving the mug triumphantly in the air.

Anne closed her eyes. 'I cannot bear to watch. I am sure he will fall.'

'These acrobats' children are as agile as African monkeys,' I said. 'Come, there is your friend, the toy man, Master Borecroft.'

We walked past three stalls to reach the toy shop. Borecroft must have been doing good business, for he was unpacking more goods from boxes at the back of his stall. As he turned to lay them out on the counter, he noticed Anne and grinned at her.

'It is the fair maiden from yesterday,' he said, 'who scorned my wooden beads.'

'Trinkets for children,' Anne said, but not unkindly. Despite his impudent manner, Nicholas Borecroft's cheerful air forestalled any annoyance.

'And how may I serve you, my mistress and sir?' He gave an exaggerated bow, nicely shared between us. 'What do ye lack?' He made the standard shopman's cry into a parody.

'Something for the lady's young brother,' I said. 'A school boy. We thought a musical instrument, but nothing too noisy, or his father will not approve.'

'A pipe?' he said, disappearing below the counter and reappearing with a handful of pipes in wood and metal, which he laid out before us. 'Or . . .' he disappeared again. 'A pipe and tabor?'

He laid the small drum beside the pipes.

'Nothing too noisy!' I reminded him with a laugh.

'Ah, but this is the softest and sweetest of little drums.'

He tapped it lightly with his fingers, picking out a soft marching rhythm, which reminded me of the men who had just marched away down Pie Corner. By now they would have circled north and east to Finsbury Fields, I was sure.

'Every young lad loves to play at soldiers.' He lifted a metal pipe to his lips and played a few bars of a marching tune on it, fingering the holes with his right hand, while he continued to tap out the rhythm on the tabor with his left.

'A pretty trick,' I said, 'but not one a young boy could imitate, unless he had gone for a soldier.' I looked at him keenly, but he only grinned.

'Or of course,' he said, diving into one of the boxes, 'I have Jew's harps. Anyone can play this.' He thrust it into his mouth and demonstrated.

'And if you speak with it in your mouth,' he added, in a strange squeaky voice, 'you may go for a puppet master's assistant.'

He removed it. 'They use such instruments to change their voices.'

'So that is how it is done,' Anne said. 'My elder brother was wondering only yesterday, when we saw the puppet show over there.' She gestured across the way to the puppet show tent, still firmly laced up, still with the board outside announcing the Commedia dell'Arte at two of the clock that afternoon.

'The grand gentleman who was with you yesterday?' Borecroft asked, all innocence. 'That was your brother? And this, of course, is your lover.'

Anne coloured and I snapped, 'Don't be impertinent!'

'Kit is a friend of our family,' she said, in a colder tone than she had used before.

'My apologies,' the toy man said, though he did not look particularly apologetic.

'We'll buy a Jew's harp for Anthony, shall we?' I asked Anne, and she nodded.

'Not the one you have just had in your mouth,' I said austerely. 'I am a physician and do not like to risk spreading diseases.'

I was being somewhat rude in return, though I meant it seriously. The man took it good humouredly enough and fetched another Jew's harp from the box. Before we walked away, Anne turned to the man, smiling politely.

'The puppet show, have you seen it?'

'They have not performed yet, my lady.' He was back to his flowery manners again. 'I saw the puppeteers last night, when the hawkers came round with pies and ale. Foreign, they are. Four men and a woman. I'd say they were Italian or maybe Spanish.'

'Spanish?' I was alert at once. This was just what we had discussed at Seething Lane. Spanish spies or priests slipping in under cover of the Fair.

'Nay,' he said, leaning back against the one of the posts supporting his stall and crossing his arms. 'Nay. I do not think they really were Spanish. I heard them speaking together. I know little of either language, but I think more likely it was Italian. The Commedia is Italian, is it not? And the Italians are great masters of puppetry, so I've heard.'

I nodded. 'Most likely Italian,' I said indifferently. I did not want to draw attention either to myself or the puppeteers, before I found out more. I was worried by the suggestion that they might be Spanish. We would attend the afternoon's performance, and then I would be able to judge for myself from their speech. Even Italians might be dangerous. The papal state, after all, was in Italy, and the Pope sought the downfall of England and our Queen.

We thanked the toy man for showing us the musical instruments and as we walked away I heard a plaintive tune start up. Looking over my shoulder, I saw that he was playing one of the small fiddles. He had it tucked into his shoulder and his face wore an expression of exaggerated soulfulness. I could not suppress a snort of laughter.

'A character indeed,' Anne said. 'We will not forget him in a hurry.'

I nodded. 'We will not. Ah, look! I can see Peter over there. He's waving to us.'

When we reached him, Peter greeted us with relief. 'I feared you had gone home,' he said. 'We heard what happened with the soldiers. Where is Master Ambrose?'

'Gone to find what has become of Mistress Hawes,' Anne said. 'And you seem to have lost Mistress Winger.'

Peter laughed. 'We all seem to be losing each other in this maze. No, she is just there, buying a pair of gloves. And please, she would like you both to call her Helen, if you are agreeable.'

'Of course,' Anne said, with her usual warmth. 'I must see whether she has found a good glover.' And she walked away from us.

Peter raised his eyebrows at me. 'How can anyone think of gloves in this weather?' He took out a handkerchief and mopped his face.

'Only fine ladies who wish to protect their white skin from the sun,' I said, glancing down at my own hands, which were still well browned after weeks in the Portuguese heat.

'When they are finished, shall we find somewhere to lunch, out of the sun?' Peter said. 'I'm hungry enough to eat a horse. I was on duty from midnight so that I could have permission to come to the Fair today. I never even broke my fast this morning.'

'I agree,' I said, 'but I will not eat pig.'

'Of course,' he said. Peter had known me long enough not to be surprised. 'I'm told there is an eating place on the north side of the Fair, a fine big place, where they serve all kinds of roast meats, not just Bartholomew pig, but beef and lamb and rabbit. There are tables and chairs as good as any tavern, outside under an arbour of green boughs to keep out the heat, and a tapster to serve beer and small ale.'

'That sounds just what we need,' I said, suddenly realising I was hungry too, despite my piece of gingerbread. 'Especially the green boughs. The heat here in the fairground is enough to try anyone.'

Anne and Helen were concluding their business with the glover when I turned to Peter. 'Do you remember the puppet tent we told you that we saw yesterday?'

'Aye.'

'Have you heard anything about the people? One of the other stallholders said they were foreign. Italian or Spanish.'

'Spanish?' he said, in the very tone I had used myself. 'I would hope not. The officials of the Fair would be very wary of allowing any Spaniards into Smithfield, surely? It is barely a year since the Spanish navy launched their attack on us.'

'Probably it is nothing,' I said. 'The man is most likely mistaken. Or they are Italian. No great friends of ours, but not such enemies as the Spanish.' Although I trusted Peter implicitly, I did not want to start any hares running. 'I expect they are Italian. As the stallholder said, the Commedia is Italian and so are the best puppet masters.'

'Well, we shall see this afternoon, shall we not? You still want to attend the show?'

'Aye,' I said, 'I certainly want to attend the show. Come, I do believe the girls are finished at last. Let us find this tavern of yours and a table under green boughs. I shall be glad to get out of the sun and drink a large pot of cold ale.'

'It may not be cold.'

'Well, warm beer, then!'

Peter led the way to the large temporary tavern on the northern edge of the Fair. Although it was still early for the midday meal, most of the tables were already occupied, but we managed to find one under an arbour roofed with intertwined leafy branches, which offered an oasis of cool shade away from the heat and dust which thickened the air of Smithfield. The ground had dried out thoroughly after the storm earlier in the week and the passage of thousands of feet was kicking up a cloud of dust everywhere.

We laid claim to a trestle table and four joint stools, sitting down with relief. This tavern was a cut above the other eating stalls I had seen scattered about the fairground. There were even clean white cloths on the tables, and the food was being served on pewter plates, not rough wooden trenchers.

'You've done very well, finding this, Peter,' I said. 'It's as clean and wholesome as the best London inn.'

He smiled knowingly. 'It is run by a well established innkeeper, who was a patient at Barts while you were away. He told me then that he would be setting up here. He had even paid for his pitch two months in advance. And here he comes!'

A plump man in his fifties was approaching our table, his prominent belly swathed in an enormous apron as brilliantly white as the cloths on the tables. His hair was a sparse sprinkling of ginger bristles, and there were at least three layers of chin above his plain collar. I wondered how he managed to keep his apron so white amidst the greasy business of roasting meats and dirty dishes.

'Master Lambert!' He bowed deeply to Peter. 'What can I serve you, you and your friends? I shall make you a special price, for I have not forgotten your kindness when I was unfortunate enough to spend time in St Bartholomew's.

'I thank you, Master Chawtry.' Peter had reddened a little at this praise.

Helen Winger looked at him admiringly. 'My father says that you will make an excellent apothecary, Peter.'

Peter looked even more embarrassed and turned from the innkeeper to the rest of us. 'What will you eat?'

The other three all chose Bartholomew pig, for this annual treat is almost a ritual with Londoners. I asked for beef. The innkeeper said he would bring us a salad to start with, for the first roasts were just ready and only now being carved. Afterwards, there were custards, another Bartholomew favourite.

When he had returned to the tent I said, 'He seems too prosperous to have been a patient at Barts. He's not one of the London poor.'

'Oh, I daresay in the normal way of things he would have been attended by a private physician,' Peter said, 'but on a particularly hot day in June he collapsed at the very gatehouse of the hospital. You can see that he is a heavy man, with a rubicund complexion. He was carried in unconscious before anyone knew who he was.'

'Dr Stephens bled him,' I said gloomily. I could imagine the scene.

'Aye. He was sure Master Chawtry was suffering from an excess of choler. I know your father believed in bleeding only as a last resort, but he was already . . . he was dead by then.'

I nodded, keeping my face expressionless. 'So how did Master Chawtry fare, after the bleeding?'

'He was unconscious a good few hours, and when he woke at last, he was very weak, barely able to move. Could not even sit up in bed. I had not much work to do that day, and both Dr Stephens and the new physician had gone home by then. I stayed with him and gave him some of that cordial your father used in like cases. It's all finished now. Also he was very thirsty, so I gave him plenty of small ale. I hope I didn't do wrong?'

He looked at me anxiously.

'Not at all,' I said. 'In the circumstances, I'm sure that was the best thing to do.'

'Master Chawtry began to recover and gave me the credit for it. He refused further bleeding the next day, then his wife fetched him home the day after. I did very little, really.'

I frowned. 'Was Dr Stephens's assistant not there, or the new man's assistant?'

'Oh, they went home after the bleeding. They are most particular about their hours of work now.' Peter gave a somewhat sad smile. 'They make sure they do not work for longer than they are paid. Not like those endless hours when we cared for the soldiers from Sluys.'

'No, indeed.'

We had worked all night then, all of us. Even, I recalled, Dr Stephens.

However, the innkeeper looked none the worse for this episode of ill health, for he was now bustling about, directing a small army of lads and maids who were serving the customers. It would do him no harm, I thought, to lose some of that excess weight, but that is a danger of his profession. Who would ever trust a skinny innkeeper?

We ate our salad, which was surprisingly good, for your London salad is usually a miserable affair, then we tucked into generous plates of roast meat. The tavern even provided napkins and a finger bowl for rinsing our greasy fingers after picking up our meat.

The custards that followed were firm and creamy, without that layer of watery sludge you find at the bottom of most. They were decorated with candied rose and violet petals, as good a finish to the meal as you could find in a first class inn. After this abundance of good food and several mugs of ale, we were all a little sleepy, without much energy to wend our way back to the puppet show.

Anne yawned, covering her mouth with her hand and apologising. 'Too much sun and too much food,' she said.

'Aye, and too much ale,' I pointed out.

Helen looked at me severely. 'She has drunk less than you, sir.' Then she blushed at having spoken so frankly, but I laughed.

'You are right, but she does not have the head for it.'

'We did promise to meet Ambrose at the puppet show,' Anne said, 'though I hardly think I can move.'

'Well, we cannot sit here all day,' I said, trying to be brisk. 'They will want our places for other customers. Peter, can you call for the reckoning?'

The cost of the meal was modest. Clearly the innkeeper had done as he had promised, and given us a special price. Peter and I divided it between us, for on such occasions I must play the man. Luckily Sara had insisted on giving me enough coin to cover a meal for the two of us, judging that Ambrose would be too taken up with his young lady and might not stay with us.

'We have seen nothing of your mother, Anne,' I said. 'Did you make an arrangement to meet her?'

'No, we thought we should easily find each other, but never thought there would be such crowds. We have not come to the Fair for a few years and the last time it was wet. Not many people came. I did tell her about the puppets, though, and she thought that would amuse the children. We may find her there.'

The first person we saw as we approached the puppet tent was Ambrose, for with his height he stood out from the crowd. Beside him was a very elegant young woman whom we soon discovered to be Mistress Hawes. She presented me with a limp hand when we were introduced, and I went through the charade of raising it to my lips, as that was clearly what she expected. Ambrose had told us that she had spent a brief time in France when things were peaceful between our countries, and had picked up French manners. Amongst the middling sort in London we do not normally go in for such folderols.

It was not yet two o' the clock, and we stood together a little way from the tent, which was still tightly laced. No one was even trying to tempt the crowds in or to sell tickets, as most entertainers at the Fair will do. My attention wandered over to the toy stall and I saw that Nicholas Borecroft had shut up shop. The counter had been raised and secured in place, the door was closed and a padlock fixed through the catch. Then I saw the man himself, moving almost stealthily for such a large and boisterous fellow, heading toward the back of the puppet tent.

Then my heart gave a jerk. He was not alone. Another man was also sidling round between the stalls to reach the far end of the tent. It was – and this time I was certain my eyes did not deceive me – it was definitely Robert Poley. Robert Poley, whom Phelippes believed to be on a mission for Sir Francis abroad. Robert Poley whom I thought I had glimpsed in the street the other day. Robert Poley, whom Phelippes suspected, as I did, of possibly being a double agent. At the time of the Babington Plot, Poley had helped to catch the conspirators, but I knew that he had lied about his friendship with Anthony Babington. He had acted as a go-between, taking orders from Sir Francis but possibly also from the traitors. He had been intimate with them. Perhaps even sympathised with them, though I was certain that he was a man who would never act from principle, he would only ever do what served his own best interests.

When the conspirators were rounded up, three years ago now, Poley had been rounded up with them and taken to the Tower. Unlike them, he had never stood trial nor faced a brutal execution. Instead he lingered in the Tower – up to what mischief I could not be sure. He stayed there two years, then was quietly released. I had seen him briefly before leaving for Portugal, an occasion when he had taken the opportunity to remind me that he knew my secret and could expose me to terrible retribution whenever he wished. Since then he was supposed to be working abroad, in Denmark and the Low Countries. When I thought I had seen him in the street the other day, I had assumed I must be mistaken. But I was not. As he slipped behind the puppeteers' tent with the toy man, he was no more than a few yards away. I could not be mistaken this time. By great good fortune, he did not look my way.

'What is, Kit?' Peter said. 'You have gone quite white. Are you feeling the heat?'

I shook my head. 'No, no. I have just seen someone. Someone who should not be here. It's no matter. Nothing to worry about.'

But I was worried. Poley clearly had a meeting with the puppet masters who were foreign and possibly dangerous. Certainly dangerous, if they were Spanish. Perhaps dangerous, if they were Italian. Was he working here for Sir Francis? Surely Phelippes would not then have told me he was abroad. Phelippes was ever cautious, but I believed he was generally honest with me. If he had wished to conceal Poley's presence in London, he need have said nothing. No, I was sure Phelippes himself had believed that Poley was indeed out of the country.

And what of the toy man? His excessive attentions to us yesterday and today now began to seem sinister. Could he know that I worked for Sir Francis? Had someone drawn me to his notice?

I suddenly remembered the soldiers' leader pointing to me as a witness from the Portuguese expedition. Had the toy man been in the crowd? I hadn't seen him. But why should that matter? It could be of no interest to him that I had been on the expedition, and the soldier had not named me. Had Robert Poley warned him to look out for anyone from Walsingham's service? The two of them had seemed very confident in each other's presence as they made their way round to the back of the tent. It might mean nothing at all, but I could not help feeling uneasy.

I shook myself. I must not let the sight of Robert Poley always disturb me so. He was mere flesh and blood, like any other man, despite his ability constantly to turn up in an unexpected manner. I could deal with him. I was much more experienced now than I had been when he had first known me as a retiring girl of sixteen, staying close beside her father and rarely mixing with others. Since then I had entered a Catholic household, spied on smugglers, travelled abroad, broken into a murderers' warehouse in Amsterdam and passed myself off as a Spanish physician to enter the besieged citadel at Coruña. I told myself I was a fool to be afraid of Poley. I was a match for him now. Still, he needed watching. I must report this to Sir Francis tomorrow.

I was called from these disturbing thoughts by the sound of Anthony Lopez's voice calling to us. Sara had arrived with Anthony and the two little girls, Cecilia and Tabitha. Sara looked worried.

'I was not sure whether we should come,' she was telling Ambrose. 'We heard there had been a disturbance at the Fair. Armed men. The Lord Mayor challenged. I wasn't sure whether you were all safe, but there was no word from you and you did not return . . .' Her voice was reproving.

'I'm sorry, Mama.' Anne kissed her mother and took her hand. 'It was all over very quickly. The soldiers were well behaved. They made threats, but did nothing. Their leaders have gone off to confer with the mayor and Common Council, the other men went away without any trouble. I am sorry you have been worried.'

'Well, in the end I sent Camster to find out what had happened. When he returned he said everything seemed quiet and the Fair was carrying on as usual, so I told the children we would come after all.'

'I would have come by myself,' Anthony said boldly.

'And caused your mother even more worry?' I said. 'I am sorry too, Sara. We should have realised rumour would fly across London on the bird's wing. You probably knew of it before we did ourselves. Everything is quiet now.'

I turned to Anthony. 'Anne and I have bought you a Jew's harp, and you shall have it when we are home again.'

Tabitha tugged at my sleeve. 'Have you got something for me, Kit?'

It was remiss of us not to have bought toys for the girls. I smiled at her. 'That is the toy stall just over there. When he opens again, you and Cecilia shall choose something for yourselves.'

'But why is it closed?' Her face fell.

'I think the toy man is going to the puppet show, as we will, when it begins.'

'Oh,' said Cecilia, seizing Anne's hand and jumping up and down. 'I want to see the puppets. I've never seen a puppet show.'

'You have,' Anne said. 'Last year there was one at Holborn Bridge.'

Cecilia frowned. 'I don't remember. I was only three, remember.'

We all laughed at her pompous tone. For a moment she sounded almost like Ruy.

'It was a very poor affair,' Anthony said disparagingly. 'There was only one puppet man and they were those foolish half-puppets you put on your hand like a glove. And it was a very silly show. This will be much grander. Proper marionettes.'

'What's marionettes?' Tabitha asked.

'They look like proper manikins,' Anthony said, 'worked by strings, almost like real people. You'll see.'

'The Commedia dell'Arte,' Sara read from the billboard. 'That is ambitious.'

'We think they may be an Italian troupe,' I said, 'so perhaps it will be the real thing.'

At that moment a man and a woman ducked out of the entrance to the tent. As the man began to unlace the opening and fasten it back, the woman stepped toward us. She wore flamboyant clothes, brightly coloured like a gypsy's, and her hair, black as a crow's wing, was piled on top of her head, threaded through with scarlet and green ribbons, in a style that was decidedly foreign. She had a Mediterranean complexion, as I do myself, darker than the pale skinned English. There was something haughty in her air, as though she considered the task of selling tickets for a fair ground show to be beneath her, but I have seen the same proud look on the faces of the gypsy vagabonds we saw sometimes in Portugal, as if they looked down their long noses at timid people who lived in houses. I did not think this woman was dark enough in colouring for a gypsy, however, despite her exotic attire. There was a wallet for money at her belt and she held a sheaf of crudely printed playbills in her hand for tickets.

'Come and see the true Commedia dell'Arte!' she shouted in a strong accent, Italian, I was sure. 'Straight from appearing before the Duke Alfonso d'Este in his palace at Ferrara!'

I shivered. Duke Alfonso had a sinister reputation.

The woman came toward us, sweeping her skirts aside from the commoner folk and making directly for Ambrose, holding out the play bills to him. 'Twopence only, Signori, Signore. Threepence with a stool.' Ambrose drew out his purse.

The puppet show was about to begin.

Chapter Eight

*W*e filed into the tent, the strange woman making a great business of leading all those who had paid for stools to the front, close to the puppet stage. By now we were a large party, ten in all: Sara and the three children, Ambrose and Mistress Hawes, Peter and Helen Winger, Anne and me. We were not the only threepenny customers, but we nearly filled the first row. Those who had paid just twopence stood behind. With everyone packed into the tent, it was filled to its very seams. The air was hot and stuffy, and I began to hope that the performance would not last too long.

'It is a very large stage,' Anne whispered to me. 'I did not think it would be so big. When we saw the puppet show at Holborn Bridge last year, the stage was no more that a yard wide and high. But look at this!'

I nodded. I was surprised as well. The whole end wall of the tent was taken up with the stage, or at least what we could see of it. At the moment the stage itself was concealed behind red velvet curtains trimmed with gold braid and suspended from an elaborate lintel of gilded wood. This lintel, I imagined, would conceal the puppeteers as they manipulated the manikins. At the bottom of the stage there was more red velvet in swags, in the centre of which were the traditional two dramatic masks, representing tragedy and comedy. A glow from behind these swags showed that the stage was lit, probably by candle lamps. Unprotected candles would be dangerous near manikins of flimsy wood and paper.

Anne had noticed the lights as well. 'I am glad the stage will be lit,' she said. 'It is so dark in here.' She shivered. 'Somewhat unpleasant.'

'Aye.'

She was right. I too felt the puppeteers' tent was more sinister than playful, which was strange, for the Commedia dell'Arte, as I remembered it, from seeing a few performances on an open air makeshift stage in a square at Coimbra, is a rambunctious, wild celebration of jokes, music and dance. Perhaps it was because this Commedia was to be performed by puppets. There is something a little unpleasant about puppets – half human, speaking in voices not their own. I wondered what my friends amongst the professional players would think of this. I had seen nothing of them since my return to London. Did they regard this kind of performance as cousin to their own? Or were they hostile, seeing it as a foreign rival to their own playhouses?

The audience was becoming a little restive when at last music began to play behind the curtains, a fiddle and a tambourine. It struck me then that perhaps Nicholas Borecroft had not had some unlawful purpose in creeping round to the back of the tent. Clearly he was a skilled musician, for all his buffoonery. Perhaps the puppeteers had lost their musician and begged for his assistance. I recognised the tune he had played earlier on the fiddle, though now it was speeded up to a lively tempo, accompanied by the tap and jingle of a tambourine, beating out the rhythm.

Slowly the velvet curtains were drawn aside and the entire audience gasped.

A painted scene filled the whole of the back of the stage, very skilfully done, showing the view of London as it appears to a traveller approaching from the south. There was the Thames, with a scattering of wherries. There was St Paul's with its truncated tower – the spire which had been destroyed by lightning in 1561 had never been rebuilt. The Tower was shown exaggeratedly large, looming over the quays where great ocean going ships were anchored. Somewhere amongst the clustered houses to the left would be Sir Francis's house in Seething Lane. So well was the painting executed, I almost thought I could pick it out. The scene depicted the whole of the City, stretching from the Tower in the east, past Queenhithe and Baynard's Castle, to the Fleet River and Bridewell in the west.

This was extraordinary indeed. For the Commedia is purely Italian. If any scene should be shown, it would be an Italian one, though the travelling players rarely used any scenery at all. They would not have had this scene at Ferrara (if indeed they had ever been there, which I doubted). Why should they have gone to all this trouble and expense for a few performances at Bartholomew Fair?

While I was still pondering this, there came another cry from the audience, this time one almost of alarm, for the first marionettes had walked on to the stage. There was some cause for alarm, for certainly I had never seen marionettes like these. They were enormous, the size of a child of ten or twelve, and they moved so like true humans that I caught, from the corner of my eye, the sight of several people crossing themselves. These were no gimcrack puppets of thin sticks and paper. The faces were carved with exceptional skill and the clothes were sewn from fine silks and velvets. I did not believe the jewels were real – they were certainly glass or paste – but they flashed in the light from the candle lamps as brightly as real gems.

There were two marionettes, a man and a woman. The man wore a fine robe of dark purple, with a heavy gold chain about his neck and a cap upon his head. His grey beard hung down to his chest. I knew the stock characters of the Commedia.

'That is Pantalone,' I whispered to Anne. 'He's an old buffoon, a miser with money, leering after young women, foolish, always being tricked by the young lovers and the clever servants.'

'Who is the woman?'

I frowned. 'It must be La Ruffiana. She's the old woman who tries to thwart the lovers.'

'She doesn't look so very old. Or is she? She has red hair.'

In truth she had. A distinctive red wig. Everyone in London knew who had red hair like that.

The two marionettes began to speak, and indeed it almost seemed that they really were speaking, for their mouths moved.

They were, of course, speaking in Italian. I wondered whether any one in the audience besides me understood the language. As I listened, I began to turn cold. The two marionettes had their heads together. The grey-bearded man was giving advice to the old woman with the red hair, in a deferential tone, urging her to keep the young man, whose name seemed to be Papio, from marrying his lady love, a girl called Anglia. La Ruffiana was nodding her head in agreement.

The two marionettes moved to the side of the stage, the bearded man still whispering in the ear of the red-haired woman, when two more of the figures entered. There were no more gasps, for the audience was growing accustomed to these enormous figures now, but it was still unsettling, for they moved so realistically. They must be jointed almost like a human body. The two new figures were both male, both had large hook noses and sly grins on their faces. One wore a physician's long black robe and cap.

'Il Dottore,' I murmured.

'I guessed that,' Anne said with a grin.

I studied the other figure. He had Pulcinella's humped back as well as his large nose, but he was not dwarfish, as Pulcinella usually is. And curiously, he wore a sort of tattered crown made of gold paper, which was slipping down over one ear. From time to time he raised his hand to straighten it. Of course, he did not really straighten it, for it must have been fixed somehow so that it would not fall off. However clever these puppets, their hands could not function like human hands.

'Who is that?' Anne asked.

I shook my head and shrugged. It did not seem quite right for Pulcinella. These two new marionettes were talking about a voyage to seize back a kingdom. They approached the other pair and bowed low. I was right. The paper crown did not fall off.

I was beginning to sweat, gripping my hands together between my knees. Even if the rest of the audience could not understand the words, surely they must begin to understand what was going on here? The faces of the manikins were so skilfully done, they were unmistakable. My mouth had gone dry and I tried to swallow. Pinned down at the front of the audience, we were trapped if someone tipped off the City pursuivants. Simply watching this performance could be regarded as treason.

Grey-bearded Pantalone was Burghley.

The robed physician, Il Dottore, was Ruy Lopez, whose entire family was sitting in a row beside me. Soon they would recognise him.

Hook-nosed Pulchinella with his paper crown was Dom Antonio.

And the old woman, La Ruffiana, with the bright red wig was Gloriana. Her Most Sacred Majesty. Queen Elizabeth.

Was it intended as mere comedy? A light hearted entertainment? Even in comedy, such mockery was dangerous. Even to suggest that the Queen was old was virtually treason. Anyway, I did not think this was thoughtless comedy. Pantalone was urging La Ruffiana to part the lovers Papio and Anglia. The implication was all too clear. Papio was the Pope, Anglia was England. The fairly blatant message was that England loved the Pope. Was this a call – coming perhaps from the papacy itself – to those who supported Rome and the old religion to rise up against Pantalone and La Ruffiana – Burghley and the Queen?

My mind was in a whirl. We ought to leave. To be found here was tantamount to professing support for the situation described and warned against by Pantalone, that England was in love with the Pope. The fact that the dialogue was in Italian was no more than a thin veneer over the real purpose of this charade. Yet how could we struggle through the crowd and out of the tent without drawing attention, possibly dangerous attention, to ourselves?

Anne was looking at me curiously, for something must have shown on my face, but before I could reach any decision, there was a further development on the stage. Il Dottore and Pulcinella had been urging Pantalone and La Ruffiana to support the capture of the lost kingdom with soldiers and with gold. La Ruffiana appeared to hand a purse to Il Dottore. I was not quick enough to see how it was done. Oh, they were clever, very clever, these puppet masters.

Now two more figures strode on to the stage.

'Il Capitano and Scarramuccia,' I whispered. 'The swaggering soldier and the hero figure, though this Scarramuccia shows more bluster than heroics.'

I had recognised at once who they were supposed to be. Il Capitano was wearing armour made of real metal, which glinted in the candle light. The faces, like those of the other marionettes were skilfully carved. Anne may be innocent in many ways, but she is no fool. She was screwing up her eyes and leaning forward. Then she took a deep breath and murmured in my ear.

'Scarramuccia,' she said. 'It's Drake.'

'Aye,' I said, 'and Il Capitano is Sir John Norreys.'

No one, surely, could mistake them. I heard a few murmurs in the audience behind us. Il Capitano was striding about the stage, waving his sword about and shouting, 'To war! Come forward, lads, and riches shall be yours! Gold and rubies and emeralds! You shall drink fine French wines and dine on swans and live like noblemen, every one of you!' He was, of course, speaking Spanish, for Il Capitano always speaks Spanish, I don't know why. Perhaps the Italians don't like the excessive swagger of the Spanish, though they have plenty of swagger themselves.

All these references to the spoils of war promised to the soldiers were all too clearly a reference to the demands of the soldiers that very morning. Was it possible this was mere coincidence? I began to wonder whether something even more complicated was going on here.

A man sitting directly behind me in the second row of stools hissed to his neighbour, 'That's Norreys for sure. And the other is Drake. Why the devil can they not speak decent English instead of this foreign mumbo-jumbo?'

Scarramuccia now struck an heroic attitude at the front of the stage, holding his wooden sword aloft and addressing his remarks partly to the audience and partly to La Ruffiana. He repeated Il Capitano's promises in Italian, with even more exaggeration, then bowed to La Ruffiana.

'Your Majesty,' he said, 'you and I know what these promises are worth. We'll share the booty between us. Let the churls starve. Such men are of no account. I'll bring all the treasure straight back to you.'

119

I was sure that, if a marionette could wink, he would have winked. And although I was also sure that few if any of those in the audience could understand Italian, the meaning of 'Vostra Maestâ' was clear to everyone, particularly as it was spoken slowly and loudly. It was not a slip of the tongue. There was no more pretence as to who was represented by La Ruffiana.

The audience was beginning to stir and shift. There were worried murmurings, but also I could feel a sense of excitement building up. I did not dare look round openly, but I began to wonder just who was there in the tent behind us. Were they merely a casual audience, as at any entertainment in the Fair? Or were some selected, known for their treasonous views?

Cautiously, I stole a glance over my shoulder. It was hopeless to think of trying to make our way out, for there was not room enough for a cat to squeeze past the people packed in between us and the entrance. We would have to sit out the entire performance.

Suddenly there was the blast of a trumpet, which made me jump. It was followed by a wild swirl of music that reminded me of performances of the Commedia that I had seen as a child. Perhaps there would be no more of this dangerous stuff and the puppet show would revert to the true Commedia dell'Arte tradition. At first, I thought I was right. The next marionette rolled on to the stage in a kind of somersault, which in less skilled hands would surely have tangled all the strings and limbs together, but Arlecchino leapt nimbly to his feet, bowed first to La Ruffiana, then to the audience, and slapped his traditional two wooden sticks together with a loud clatter that drowned out the voices of the other puppets. He pranced and postured about the stage, a great foolish buffoon, interrupting any other marionette who tried to speak, swearing that he would accompany the four adventurers to the war and show them how to defeat the enemy, for he, and he alone, had the courage and the skill to do so. As he swaggered, we could see his excessively puffed out chest, a fat belly, and the magnificent quality of his clothes.

Usually, Arlecchino wears a cat mask as part of his traditional costume, but this marionette did not, for it would have concealed his face, which was such a remarkable likeness of the

Earl of Essex that I had to cover my mouth with my hand to stop myself laughing. There were a few titters from behind me as others recognised the licensed fool. La Ruffiana – or rather the Queen – shook her fist at Arlecchino, forbidding him to accompany the expedition, but he cavorted about, tossing rude asides to the audience, then withdrew to the back of the stage. Il Dottore, Pulcinella, Il Capitano, and Scarramuccia went off at the right hand side of the stage, which I supposed was meant to represent sailing down river. After waving them off, Burghley and the Queen – I mean Pantalone and La Ruffiana – strolled away in the opposite direction, towards Whitehall or Hampton Court.

When all the rest had left the stage, Arlecchino came forward and swore to the audience that he would follow the expedition whatever 'the old woman' said, and went prancing off downstream.

The stage was empty. The fiddle began to play again, a slow mournful melody, while somewhere at the back of the stage, someone let off fireworks with a bang, which made us all flinch.

'What is that?' Anne said.

'The sound of battle,' I said grimly. 'Now the expedition will return.'

She glanced around, then whispered, 'How do they dare?'

I shrugged. 'The sooner we can leave, the better, but we will have to see it out.'

I was wrong about the next scene. Instead of the adventurers returning, the lovers rushed on stage, Papio, the Inamorato, from the right, and Anglia, the Inamorata, from the left. She wore the sort of gown you might see on any respectable maiden of the middling sort and, of all the marionettes, she was the only one who was beautiful, with the long flowing golden hair of a young unmarried girl. Papio was a handsome lad, with dark curly hair, on which was perched a curious cap.

Anne gripped my arm. 'Look at his hat,' she breathed.

It was red and gold, and constructed in three distinct tiers, tapering toward the top and adorned with cheap jewels. A crude copy of the Pope's triple crown. I caught my breath as the marionettes embraced and murmured sweet words of love to each other, which the Italian language is particularly suited to convey. The lovers slipped away, hand in hand, as the melancholy music ushered in the adventurers. Arlecchino – Essex – returned first, boasting to the audience of his wondrous exploits, which had led to great victories over the Spanish, while every one else in the party was a bungling idiot. He was followed by Il Dottore and Pulchinella – Lopez and Dom Antonio – their heads hanging and their feet shuffling. Without a word, they followed Arlecchino off stage. Glancing aside at Anne, I realised from the grim set of her mouth that she had now realised who they represented.

Then came Il Capitano, limping a little, and blustering as he wandered off. There was a pause. Scarramuccia entered at last, staggering under a heavy chest which clearly contained treasure. He gave us a mocking bow, then turned as La Ruffiana appeared, now, astonishingly, with a crown upon her head, lest there should be any doubt in anyone's mind. Hand in hand, the two profiteers executed a clumsy dance as the music played faster and faster, till the curtains swung closed.

The show was over.

There followed a moment's stunned silence. Even the dullest person in that audience must have understood what they had just seen, even without being able to follow a word of the Italian dialogue. Then a great burst of cheering and clapping broke out from the standing audience, while those of us seated at the front on stools clapped dutifully as well. I suppose it must have occurred to others besides myself that someone might be watching us through a peephole in the curtains, to check on our reactions. All through the performance I had quite forgotten Robert Poley. Suddenly I remembered him again. He was part of this. But in what way, and to what end?

What was the purpose of this elaborate show, which must have demanded much money and effort to prepare? I was certain now that it was meant for more than simple comedy. There is some licence in the playhouse for a little good natured mockery of the great and famous, but never, ever, of the Queen. And this had been more than simple mockery. As we stood up and waited until the crowd had cleared enough for us to fight our way out of the tent, which had begun to feel as claustrophobic as a prison cell, I tried to reason out what it had all meant.

Part of the message was that, despite the policies of the Queen and Council, England was in love with popery and, given the chance, would go off with it, hand in hand like the lovers in the play. Anti-Semitism was blatant in the depiction of Ruy Lopez and Dom Antonio, with a hearty mixture of the ingrained English hatred of foreigners. The pompous idiocy of Essex had been shown with an unflinching accuracy, while Norreys simply seemed hopelessly incompetent. Burghley was a bumbling old fool. But the worst attack was on Drake and the Queen herself. Those promises to the common soldiers and sailors which were slyly betrayed – this was all too close to this very morning's confrontation between the makeshift army and the Lord Mayor. There *must* have been collusion, but what did that signify?

At last we were able to struggle through the last of the crowd and regain the open air. It was still hot, but at least I felt I could breathe again. By unspoken consent we made our way along the lane of shops to a booth selling small ale and found a couple of benches out of the way of the passing fairgoers. Ambrose came across to us with a lad carrying a tray of ale mugs. When the lad was gone, Ambrose sat down heavily and looked at his mother.

'Well?' he said.

She shook her head, giving a nod toward the younger children. She was right. Better not to worry them. I realised that all the adults had grasped the meaning of that sinister charade. Peter looked worried. His position depended on the favour of the governors of the hospital. He must hope he had not been seen coming out of the puppet show.

I looked back up the lane to where the puppeteers' tent stood at the end of the row. It was laced shut again, but it was not empty, for I could see the signs of elbows or shoulders bumping against the canvas from within. Some of the audience had clearly remained behind. I did not like the smell of this.

'Do you want to go home, Mama?' Ambrose asked.

'No, no!' Cecilia and Tabitha were dismayed, tugging at their mother's sleeves.

'We've only just come!' Anthony said, glaring at his elder brother. 'You came yesterday and again this morning. We have done nothing but watch those horrible puppets talking foreign gibberish. I want to see the Fair! Mama, there is supposed to be a bear who will catch apples if you throw them to him. And there is a fire eater and jugglers, and fortune tellers.'

'We want to go to the toy shop,' Tabitha said. 'Kit promised, didn't you, Kit?'

'Aye, I did.' I shifted my gaze from the puppeteers' tent to the toy stall. Even from here I could see that the counter had been lowered again, and a cluster of mothers and children had gathered in front of it.

'I think it is open now, Tabby,' I said. It would be interesting, I thought, to discover whether Nicholas Borecroft could be persuaded to say anything about the puppet show or his part in it. Did I dare mention that I had seen him with Robert Poley?

'I will take the girls to the toy shop if you wish, Sara,' I said.

'We'll all come.' Ambrose was already getting to his feet.

'Of course.' Mistress Hawes smiled condescending at the two little girls. 'The children must have some toys after sitting quietly through that horrid puppet show. It was horrid, wasn't it, Ambrose?'

'Ah, indeed.' Ambrose looked flustered. I wondered whether he suspected, as I now did, that Mistress Margaret Hawes had not, after all, grasped the meaning of what we had been watching. Her father might own a coach, but perhaps she was not very clever.

Sara had noticed Peter and Helen exchanging glances. 'The young people will not all want to come with the children. We need not stay together. There is something for everyone at the Fair.'

Indeed, I thought, you speak truly, Sara. Something for the decent citizens of London, but something also for those who may have treachery on their minds. I wondered who those people were, who had stayed behind in the tent.

Peter and Helen decided they would stroll amongst the shops and perhaps buy a fairing before Peter needed to return to his work at the hospital, so we bade them farewell. I thought Peter seems somewhat relieved to escape from our company. He had surely recognised who the marionette Il Dottore was meant to be. It could be embarrassing to be seen in the company of Ruy Lopez's family.

At the toy stall Cecilia and Tabitha were entranced with everything on display, and Nicholas Borecroft, I observed, went out of his way to charm them, and Sara too.

'Fair lady!' he cried. 'You cannot be the mother of this great tall young man!'

He waved his hand at Ambrose and pulled a comical face. I saw that Ambrose was prepared to be offended again, but, like Anne, Sara merely laughed.

'What have you to show my little girls, toy man?'

'I have babies of the fairest sort, madam, kept only for my best customers.'

He went through into the inner room of his stall and came back with a box covered all over with fancy paper, like the new wall paper Ruy had installed in some of his rooms. Cecilia and Tabitha were standing on tiptoe, trying to see over the counter as he reverently lifted out two dolls and laid them down under the girls' very noses. They had carved wooden heads and I wondered for a moment whether they had been made by the puppet masters, but I decided these simpering maidens were not the puppeteers' style of carving at all.

'Real hair, you see?' Borecroft ran his finger down a glued-on wig of brown hair, which had been tightly curled. It hardly looked very natural, but if it was not horse hair, it might well have been real hair. Poor girls of the streets will often sell their thick hair for the making of wigs intended for ladies of quality whose own hair has turned grey or grown thin. Better that than selling their bodies.

'These are babies of the best,' Borecroft said. 'French made. See their fine gowns!'

The dolls were indeed, beautifully dressed, wearing the latest fashions, down to farthingales and crisply pleated ruffs.

125

They reminded me of a doll I had once cherished as a child. The girls opened their eyes wide and looked at their mother with longing, but they were too well behaved to beg. Anne had picked up one of the dolls to examine it more closely and I suspected that she wished she were still young enough to have one. My attention wandered as Sara began to haggle with the toy man over the price. Anthony was experimentally tapping the tabor we had seen before, while Ambrose and Mistress Hawes had their heads together, probably wishing they too could wander off around the Fair on their own.

The deal for the dolls was finally struck. Cecilia and Tabitha each clutched a doll as if they could not believe their good fortune, and Anthony had persuaded his mother to buy him one of the simple pipes. While the Lopez family was discussing what to do next, I leaned over the counter to speak to the toy man.

'We heard you playing for the puppet show, Master Borecroft.'

He seemed surprised that I knew his name, but I did not enlighten him that I had heard the Fair official shout it out the previous day. On the other hand, he did not appear at all concerned at my mention of the puppet show.

'Last night,' he said, 'when we were buying pies from the hawkers who come round to sell to the shopkeepers and watchmen who spend the night here in Smithfield, I got talking to the puppeteers. They had heard me playing and asked if I could help them.'

He gave me a smile of such insincere blandness that I hardly knew what to believe.

'Do they not have their own musicians?' I said, equally blandly.

'Oh, they must all turn a hand to everything. But it seemed there were so many puppets in this show that they must all manipulate the manikins and would need to do without music. They said if I could provide some fiddle playing and a trumpet blast, I should have five shillings, so I could not refuse.'

'Indeed, you could not,' I said, thinking of the men turned ashore with five shillings to pay for months of suffering.

'Can I interest you in a toy, master?' He gave me that wide, innocent smile again.

'Nay, I thank you.' I made as if to turn away, then said casually. 'Did I not see another go with you to join the puppeteers? A stocky fellow, probably in his forties? Was he another musician? Or perhaps one of the puppet masters?'

He shook his head. 'You must be mistaken, master. No one was with me. It must have been simply someone passing in the crowd.'

'Aye, you are probably right.' I walked away, but I knew that he lied.

Our party decided to break up. Ambrose and his lady strolled off with, I thought, some relief. Anne decided to go with her mother and the younger children. Although they urged me to come with them, I said something about perhaps visiting old friends at the hospital, promising to make my own way back to Wood Street.

I did not, in fact, intend to go into the hospital, for I still felt the hurt of being excluded. My principal friend there had been Peter, though of course I knew the other apothecaries and the nursing sisters. One of the sewing women was a former patient of mine. But I could not bring myself to go where I felt I was no longer wanted.

Instead, I sauntered about the Fair like any other member of the crowd, all the time keeping a sharp look-out for Robert Poley, for I knew I had certainly seen him, and he had certainly been in company with Nicholas Borecroft, however much the toy man might deny it. Whether he had also been going to the puppeteers I could not be absolutely sure.

I dawdled past stalls selling goods of every kind, from comfits to fine linens, from lucky charms to books of piety. As I turned the corner from one lane of stalls to another, I very nearly ran into the man I always thought of as the chestnut seller, though today he carried his tray of crystallised plums and other comfits. He looked much more cheerful than when we had seen him yesterday.

'Oh, young master,' he said, beaming with real warmth, unlike the false smile of the toy man, 'you and your friends did me a good turn! I have earned more today at the Fair than even the best of my weeks at Newgate! I have had to fetch fresh stocks twice. My wife is busy making more comfits now, for me to sell tomorrow.'

'I am glad to hear it,' I said. 'Every Londoner has a sweet tooth. You should do well for every day of the Fair. I'll take a cone of mixed comfits, if you please.'

He overfilled my paper cone, which I tucked into the pocket of my doublet, and we parted in mutual satisfaction. I thought of asking him to keep a watch for Poley, but decided it was better not to advertise my interest in the man.

By chance I came upon the Winterlys' stall of leather goods.

'Jake!' I said, 'and young Will as well. I hope you are doing a good trade.'

Will beamed at me over the counter. 'We have sold five of my belts, Dr Alvarez, and Papa has sold a saddle, three satchels and I dunno how many purses.'

Jake laughed. 'Aye, we do good business in purses. So many are stolen at the Fair, you would think we were in league with the cutpurses.'

'Mine was nearly stolen yesterday,' I said. 'I grabbed it just in time.'

I held up my cut finger. 'And got this for my pains.'

They both made sympathetic noises, and we fell to discussing the threat from the armed soldiers.

'It would have been a sad loss to us,' Jake said, 'if they had run riot through the Fair and seized our goods.'

'Aye,' I said soberly, 'it would indeed.'

I bade them farewell and walked on, to find myself at the edge of a cleared space where two men – by their looks, brothers – were demonstrating sword swallowing and fire eating. There were gasps of horrified astonishment as one man seemed to thrust a long thin rapier down his throat, and when the other began to wave his flaming torch about, everyone surged back several paces. On the far side of the space I saw Anthony watching with his mouth open, and gave him a wave, but he was too absorbed to notice. I do not know how such things are done, but I am sure it is some kind of trickery.

I was growing somewhat footsore and weary, and began to think of heading back to Wood Street. I would not waste my limited money on a wherry, so I would have to walk. There had been no sign of Robert Poley and everything seemed quiet and deserted around the puppet tent.

As I turned away from the flame swallower, someone nearby called out, 'Dr Alvarez!'

I looked round. A solid built man was elbowing his way through the crowd toward me. His clothes were ragged and his feet were bare. Although he had a big frame, his flesh was shrunken with hunger and his eyes burned feverishly in his face. It was the man I had seen this morning amongst the makeshift army, the soldier who had once roused me and got me away from the attacking Spanish on the march from Peniche to Lisbon.

I raised my hand in acknowledgement of his shout and waited until he reached me.

'I saw you this morning,' I said, holding out my hand to him. 'That was a strange business.'

He shook my hand heartily and I felt how hard and callused his palm was.

'We meant every word. We have walked all those miles from Plymouth, most of us with no shoes to our feet, to ask for justice.'

'It seems a little cruel to seize your justice at the expense of poor shopmen and hawkers, who are men of your own kind,' I said, but I said it mildly.

'I am not sure we would have wrecked the Fair,' he said. 'Well, probably the wilder lads would have done so. But we needed some lever with the City authorities, and the Fair seemed as good a chance as any. We could not hope to get near the Privy Council direct, nor that pirate, Drake.'

'So although you sailed with Drake for the Azores, you do not admire him?'

'You know as well as I, Dr Alvarez, that we had no choice in the matter. We was picked out like beasts at market – "You who are fit will board this ship, you who are not will board that one".'

'True enough.'

'And then, not half a day after we had set out, our whole fleet turned north and scurried home.'

'With all the food, while we starved.'

'We did not know that at the time. It was only after all was turned ashore at Plymouth that the whole truth came out.' He smiled grimly. 'You can be reassured, I have starved along with the rest ever since.'

'I can see that. Have you eaten today?'

'Nay.'

'Come with me.'

I took him by the elbow and marched him away to the inn at the north side of Smithfield where we had eaten at midday. We found a table and the innkeeper looked startled to see me returned in such vagabond company. I ordered Bartholomew pig followed by custard for the soldier and ale for both of us. When he had eaten half his meat and drunk his ale, he slowed down and gave me a weak smile.

'My stomach is not accustomed to so much food. I think it has shrunk.'

'Best not to stuff yourself,' I said. 'I will ask for a paper so you can wrap the rest of the meat and eat it later.'

We both sat back and looked at each other. We shared so many bitter memories that it was difficult to speak of trivial matters with the Fair swirling around us.

'You know my name,' I said, 'you have known it many months, yet I have never known yours.'

'Adam Batecorte, at your service!' He raised his hand to his tattered woollen cap in a mock salute.'

'Well, Adam, I do not know how successful the meeting between your leaders and the Common Council may be. Will the Lord Mayor or his advisors agree to take your case further, to the Privy Council? Matters can be very delicate between City and Court, you know. And I do not think any of the men in power will take kindly to being threatened by armed men.'

He shrugged. 'We are desperate. And desperate men take desperate measures. There's more than five hundred of us, nearly five hundred and fifty. All of us destitute. Some have lost their positions with masters who, back in the spring, urged them to fight for England. Some have lost their own small farms or shops to unforgiving landlords. Some have even lost their families.'

He began to draw a spiral with his finger in a puddle of ale on the table.

'I am a blacksmith myself, by trade. I worked with my father in our smithy in a village a few miles north of Plymouth. When the country was preparing for the Spanish attack last year, we was kept busy making every kind of iron fitting for the ships at Plymouth. Then when the time came, my father said I should offer my services to the navy. My wife begged me not to go, but go I did.'

'You fought against the Armada?'

'Aye, I did, and that should have taught me a lesson, for it was months before we was paid, though we was paid in the end. And I was one of the lucky ones. I got ashore and home quickly and did not take the killing diseases.'

'So when the call came to enlist this year, you answered again?'

'More fool I. Once again my wife begged me not to go, but we was told it would be quick and well rewarded. Not as quick as the fight against the Armada, but much more profitable. We had some debts to our landlord, my father and I. The local lord of the manor. I thought I could earn enough to pay them off. Maybe even enough to buy the smithy and all for ourselves. So I went.'

I knew in my heart where this was going. 'What happened when you reached home?' I asked gently.

He passed his hand over his face and gave a great sigh.

'My father, my wife, the two little ones, turned out for unpaid debts. They found shelter in a ruined barn, but first the youngest took a fever, then the rest of them. All dead by the time I reached home, except my father, and he was dying. He told me what had happened. I stayed only long enough to bury him, then I went back to Plymouth. That was where I fell in with the lads who was coming together and planning the march on London.'

We were both silent for a long time. Then I said, 'I too found my father dead when I returned.' We looked at each other bleakly.

I shook my head and drank the last of my ale.

'Adam, I do not know whether this plan you and your fellows have made will succeed. There was certainly some treasure taken by Drake, both at Coruña and later, when he captured that ship from the New World off Cascais.'

'When he should have sailed up river to Lisbon, to assist us,' he said.

'Aye. The problem is, Drake always maintains that he is under licence directly from the Queen. Any treasure he takes belongs of right to her. He is then rewarded with a small portion.'

'Small?'

'That is what he says. We might not think it so small. I heard all this from Dr Nuñez, who had it from Sir John Norreys, who has often had to deal with Drake.'

'But,' he objected, 'this licence from the Queen – surely this is when Drake makes one of his raiding expeditions against the Spanish. The Portuguese expedition was quite other, an attempt to restore Dom Antonio to the throne.'

'One of the official tasks of the expedition was also to destroy Spanish ships and seize their treasure.'

'So Drake will claim it was just another of his freebooting enterprises?'

'I fear so.'

'In which case, our chances are slim.'

'That, also, I fear.'

He gave me a look of such utter despair that I nearly reached out and took his hand, but I forbore.

'Listen to me, Adam. We neither of us know how all of this will turn out. It may be that the Lord Mayor will have sympathy with your case and take it to the Privy Council, or to Drake himself. It may be that Drake will be shamed into giving up some of the booty. Or it maybe that the Privy Council will oblige him to do so. But there are many imponderables here.'

132

He had slumped down, rested his head on his hands, bowed over the remains of his meat, which was beginning to congeal in a puddle of fat.

'If nothing good comes of this and you find yourself turned away,' I said, 'will you come to me? It may be that I can find work for you.'

I was speaking with unwonted optimism out of pity for the man, I who had only my small amount of work at Seething Lane and no hospital appointment any longer.

'Thank you,' he said quietly, raising his head and looking at me. 'If things turn bad, I will do so. Where can I find you? At St Bartholomew's?'

I shook my head. 'I no longer work there. With my father's death I too lost my home, but friends have taken me in. Ask for Mistress Sara Lopez in Wood Street.'

'Lopez? Is that –'

'Aye. She is the wife of Ruy Lopez, but she is a good woman and a good friend. You will come to me?'

'I will come.' He reached across the table and shook my hand.

Chapter Nine

The following morning I was up and dressed early, and on my way to Seething Lane. Thomas Phelippes was surprised to see me, for I was not due to work that day. He was examining a new seal Arthur Gregory had just completed and they both looked up as I entered the office.

'Why are you here, Kit?' Phelippes said. 'I thought you were visiting the Fair this week.'

'I have been twice,' I said, 'first to watch the set up, then yesterday to the Fair itself.'

I set my satchel carefully on my table and drew out two packages wrapped in brown paper. They were large, about a foot across, and I was afraid they might be broken, but they seemed to be intact.

'I did not forget my friends.'

Arthur's mouth fell open as he unwrapped the gilded dragon and he flushed with pleasure.

'That is a kind thought, Kit,' he said. 'I shall take it home to share with my wife. She is expecting our first child, and she has been craving gingerbread, above all things!'

Phelippes had taken off his spectacles and was pinching the bridge of his nose.

'Indeed, it was kindly done, Kit,' he said, turning the castle so that it glinted in the light from the window behind him.

To my astonishment, and some discomfort, I saw that his eyes looked moist. None of us knew whether Thomas Phelippes had any family. He never spoke of any, and none of us would have asked. His mention of his sister who had died young was the

134

most personal thing I had ever heard him say. It came as a shock to me that perhaps no one had ever given him such a gift as this since he had come to manhood.

'There was a fine gingerbread stall at the Fair,' I said gruffly. 'And I thought of my friends.'

I realised I was repeating myself, and felt my colour rising. Here at Seething Lane we worked at our intelligencing for Sir Francis, and I do not think any of us had ever spoken of friendship before, yet I was aware for the first time that over the years these two men had truly become friends. Arthur was shy, but generous and warm-hearted. Phelippes was a much more difficult man – reserved, often suspicious, never one to show his feelings. In spite of that and our strict habit of work, I believed he liked me, even perhaps trusted me in a way he did not trust many of the agents.

Phelippes laid the gingerbread castle down on his desk, but I noticed it was placed carefully where he could look at it while he worked.

'Did you come all across London just to bring us these?' he asked, putting on his spectacles again, so he could see me better.

'Not only to bring these.'

I swung my chair out from behind my table and sat astride it, resting my arms on the back and my chin on my arms.

'A number of things happened at the Fair which I thought I should report.'

'If you mean the armed soldiers from the Portuguese expedition,' Phelippes said, 'then we know of that. It is in hand.'

I wondered briefly what 'in hand' might mean. I did not quite like the sound of it.

'I was sure you would have heard of that,' I said. 'No doubt all London knows by now. They have a genuine case of grievance, as I well understand. The best thing to do, for both peace and justice, would be to give them a fair share of the booty, and provide compensation for those who are still sick and wounded, and for the families of those who did not come home.'

Phelippes gave a grunt, which conveyed nothing.

'Nay, it was something else which disturbed me.' I drew breath, wondering how best to convey the sinister atmosphere at the puppet show.

'You recall that we were worried that the Fair might be used to smuggle in Catholic sympathisers and troublemakers under cover of the festivities? Well, there is a party of Italian puppeteers who may be what you were looking for.'

'Puppeteers?' Phelippes opened his eyes wide and smiled incredulously. 'I do not think puppets will be saying Mass or leading an attack on Her Majesty.'

Recalling those near life-size puppets, I could well imagine one of them saying Mass, but I shook my head.

'They are performing a version of the Commedia dell'Arte,' I went on patiently. 'The puppets are remarkable. This big.' I indicated with my hand the height of the puppets off the floor. 'So that when they speak, they do not seem like manikins, more like real people. The clothes are magnificent, indicating their rank and profession. The carved faces are so lifelike, there is no mistaking who they are meant to be.'

I saw that I had now caught his interest.

'Are you familiar with the Commedia?' I asked.

He nodded.

'So you will know the character type of each of the players – or in this case, puppets. The miser Il Pantalone is made to represent Lord Burghley, shown as a foolish old man.'

Phelippes raised his eyebrows and Gregory looked uncomfortable, but neither said anything.

'Pulcinella and Il Dottore are Dom Antonio and Ruy Lopez,' I went on in a level voice. 'Il Capitano is Sir John Norreys, while Scarramuccia plays the part of Drake, not as a hero but as a schemer.'

Phelippes and Gregory were both looking more and more puzzled at this. I drew a deep breath, and chose my words carefully.

'Arlecchino, the knavish fool with his slap-sticks, is the Earl of Essex, capering about, a blustering idiot. As you will understand, the whole play is a burlesque of the Portuguese expedition.'

136

'Defamatory,' Phelippes said slowly, 'but not necessarily dangerous, Kit.'

'I have not finished. There is a subplot of two lovers, Papio and Anglia.'

This time, he caught the reference at once, and began to twist a quill in his hand until he broke it.

'The lovers are shown as being united at the end,' I said. 'England and Popery.'

He opened his mouth to interrupt, but I held up my hand.

'There is one more puppet. La Ruffiana, the scurrilous old woman, who tries to thwart the lovers in the usual performance? You remember her? Here, she wears a red wig and her face–' I paused, nervous at what I must say next. 'Her face is that of the Queen.'

Both men drew in a sharp breath at this revelation.

'As well as the assertion that England is in love with the Pope, the piece ended with Scarramuccia and La Ruffiana – figuring Drake and Her Majesty – plotting to share the spoils of the expedition and cheat the common soldiers and sailors. I think the puppet show, as well as encouraging treason and popery, was linked with the soldiers' demands in the morning. Now, I believe many of the soldiers are simple men, making a rightful demand for compensation, but I also suspect that they are being used by others who have something else in mind, which might mean danger to Her Majesty.'

I had nearly finished, but I added, 'After the performance was ended, I saw that people had gathered in the puppeteers' tent, but it was tightly closed, so I could not see who they were, though I believe some had attended the performance.'

I lifted my chin from my arms and looked steadily at Phelippes.

'That is why I have come and why I think I should see Sir Francis at once.'

Phelippes sat back in his chair. He took off his spectacles and began to chew the piece which hooked over his ear. I had seen him do this before when he was seriously worried.

'Sir Francis is very ill, Kit. Worse than usual. He is confined to bed at his house in Barn Elms. His physician, Dr

Nuñez, has forbidden him even to work in bed, though we all know that Sir Francis does not always obey his doctors. This time, however, I understand he is in great pain.'

There was silence between us, and I was sure we were all thinking the same thing. These bouts of ill health were becoming more frequent. By the sheer strength of his iron will, Sir Francis worked through illness and pain that would have felled a lesser man, but how much longer could he survive? He demanded too much of his failing body. And what would become of all of us, of his carefully constructed intelligence service, and of England's safety, if this great man were to die?

'I am truly sorry to hear that,' I said. 'Dr Nuñez knows his physic and he knows Sir Francis. If Dr Nuñez says he must rest, then he *must* rest. He asks too much of himself.'

Phelippes nodded. 'And I was to tell you – he sent word in the note about his illness – that he has written to the governors of St Thomas's about a position for you, but he has not yet had a reply.'

I felt my eyes pricking. This was characteristic of the man, who could juggle so many claims on his time and attention, that he should remember my own need for a position, when he was suffering so much.

'There is something else,' I said. 'Where is Robert Poley at the moment?'

'Poley?' Phelippes looked surprised at what seemed to be a sudden change of subject. 'Poley is working on the Continent, probably in the Low Countries by now, or else France. He has a mission to contact Gifford in Paris, then either together or separately they are to go to Rheims and gather the latest intelligence on the activities of the seminary for English priests there. We have not had information from Rheims for some time. Both of them are well able to pass for Catholic sympathisers. They should be able to secure good intelligence.'

Well able indeed, I thought, remembering Poley's involvement with the Babington plotters and the time I had discovered him arriving with a priest at the Catholic Fitzgerald house.

'Well,' I said, 'I must tell you that Robert Poley is *not* in the Low Countries. Nor is he in Paris or Rheims. A few days ago I thought I saw him here in the streets of London, but he was some distance away and I could not be sure. However, yesterday I was as close to him as I am to that window.' I waved my arm. 'There could be no mistake. He was behaving furtively, sneaking round to the back of the tent of those same puppeteers, in company with a fairground toy man, one Nicholas Borecroft, who seems a little too disingenuous to be true.'

'Poley here in London?' Phelippes had gone red and then white.

'Aye. In Smithfield.'

'I have never trusted the man,' Arthur Gregory ventured cautiously. 'Is he loyal, or does he work for England's enemies?'

'Hmm,' said Phelippes, 'I too mistrust him. But he has done good work for us in the past. Catching the traitors in '86 was made all the more effective thanks to his efforts. And he has been able to divert to us letters addressed to the French embassy.'

'But,' I said, 'did he not try to negotiate with Sir Francis on behalf of the conspirators, saying that they – or at least Sir Anthony Babington himself – would turn their coats?'

'Aye. Though what the truth of it was, we'll never know.'

'Nay,' I said grimly, 'the truth of it went to the grave with Babington. For myself, I believe Robert Poley serves no master but his own interests. Pay him well enough and he will swear or do whatever any man of position asks him to do.'

'Perhaps. You may be right. But – Poley here in London? He has not reported here, nor brought any word of his missions abroad.'

'From the way he slipped away through the crowd,' I said, 'I suspect he did not wish to draw attention to himself.'

'Did he see you?'

'Nay. Fortunately he did not look in my direction.'

Phelippes ran his hand up the back of his head and through his hair, in that characteristic gesture of his.

'It seems to me–' Gregory said hesitantly.

'Aye, Arthur?' Phelippes put his spectacles back on and turned his gaze from me to the seal carver. 'Spit it out.'

'From what Kit says, these puppeteers are up to no good. Such a performance, why . . . it must have taken a great deal of work and expense to prepare it. Would they do such a thing for a few performances at the Fair?'

'That is what I thought,' I said.

'It seems to have been carefully planned,' Gregory went on, with greater certainty now, 'to incite both those with popish sympathies and the more troublesome of the armed soldiers. Should the two factions join forces, surely it could be dangerous? Now, it might be that Robert Poley has become friendly with them in order to find out their intentions and report back to you . . .'

'But in that case,' Phelippes finished for him, 'why did he not come to me first? Nay, I agree with you both. It has the smell of rotten fish about it.'

We chased the subject round and about for some time, but it did not become any clearer. At last Phelippes sighed and leaned back in his chair.

'We cannot trouble Sir Francis with this, in his present state of health. It may mean nothing. The Italians may intend no more than a little malicious mischief. Poley may simply be ferreting out some information he intends to sell to me. He has gone his own way before and sometimes it has been to our profit.'

'And the soldiers?' Gregory said.

'That is not our affair. The Lord Mayor and Common Council have it in hand. They will not want to make any promises on their own account. They will take it to the Privy Council. It could be decided swiftly, or it might drag on for months.'

'The soldiers will not like that,' I said.

Phelippes shrugged. 'Whatever way it goes, it is not our affair. This other matter may be, but we need to know more. In Sir Francis's absence, Kit, I am going to authorise you to find out whatever else you can. Go back to the Fair this afternoon. Do you think the puppeteers will give another performance today?'

'I would expect so. After so much expense, they will want to earn as much coin as they can from their audiences, whether or not they have another purpose in being here.'

'Good. See that you attend again, and keep your eyes open. Take notice of who stays behind. Watch out for Poley. And this toy man, what did you say his name was?'

'Nicholas Borecroft.'

Phelippes shook his head. 'I do not think we have heard of him before. Do you think he is one of these covert priests?'

'Nay.' I shook my head. 'I think he may be many things, but a priest? Nay, I do not think so. I cannot make him out.'

'Well, do your best to make him out,' Phelippes said somewhat sharply.

I could see that having this problem crop up while Sir Francis was ill had made him edgy.

'I wonder whether you should go alone.' Phelippes had picked up another quill and was tapping his teeth with the feather end of it. 'You would be less conspicuous if you went with a maid on your arm. Who did you say accompanied you yesterday?'

'We were a large party, as I said, but I suppose I was mostly with Anne Lopez.'

'Then take her with you again.'

'I do not think I could persuade her into that tent again. It was – unpleasant. And you must understand, her father was mocked. She will not want to repeat the experience of sitting through that.'

'Hmm. Very well. I still think you are better not alone.'

'I could accompany Kit,' Arthur Gregory offered. 'Not as good, perhaps as man and maid visiting the Fair, but often groups of friends will go.'

Phelippes nodded. 'Aye, that's a good plan. You both know Poley, so you can both look out for him. And two pairs of sharp eyes looking over the audience will be better than one. Well thought of, Arthur.'

I smiled at Arthur. 'We'll buy more gingerbread for your wife.'

'Do not forget. This is a serious business for Sir Francis.' Phelippes frowned a little, as though he thought my remark foolish.

'We must look like every other fairgoer,' I said firmly. 'If we stand about, spying on everyone, we will attract attention at once.'

'Very well.'

'I noticed yesterday,' I said, 'that as well as the performance at two o' the clock, there was to be another in the evening, at eight. If there are two shows today, do you want us to attend both?'

'Best if you do. It will give us a clearer picture of who is associating with these Italians and their treasonous plays. Keep your eyes open for troublesome soldiers as well. I have been told that they camped in Finsbury Fields for the night, but they are unlikely to stay there. I want to know what they are doing, where they are going, even if the Lord Mayor is dealing with their leaders and considering their demands.'

'Certainly,' I said. It struck me then that I had not mentioned my encounter with Adam Batecorte. I would not do so. The man had probably saved my life once. At least I could keep his whereabouts to myself now.

'I will stay late here in the office,' Phelippes said. 'If you have anything serious to report after you have attended the evening performance, come straight to me here. I will wait until midnight. If I hear nothing, I will assume you have nothing to report, and you can both come here tomorrow morning, when we will consider whether there is anything else which needs to be done.'

I nodded. 'Very well. Arthur?'

'Aye.' He looked a little troubled. 'My wife is somewhat near her time. I would not wish to be too late going home.'

'If there is anything urgent to report,' I said, 'it will not need both of us. You can go straight home to your wife after the second performance – if there is one. I can come on here by myself.'

I turned to Phelippes. 'Of course, there may be no evening performance. In that case, how long do you want us to stay?'

'Come back about seven o' the clock in that case,' he said. 'If you hang about the Fair too long with nothing to do, that might raise suspicions.'

And put us in some danger, I thought.

Phelippes handed me a purse. 'There is enough there for you to take a fast wherry back here from Smithfield. If you go wandering about the streets of London as late as that, you may be set upon.'

He glanced at my side. 'Keep your sword with you.'

'I will,' I said, somewhat fervently, and they both laughed.

Not that I could regard myself as a skilled swordsman even now, despite the training Sir Francis had arranged for me with Master Scannard at the Tower. I knew that I was quick, and that I was a good judge of an opponent's character and intentions from watching his eyes, but my wrist would never be as strong as a well-built man's. As far as skill was concerned, I was probably a fair match for an average swordsman, and Master Scannard always said that skill was what mattered most, but against a really skilled opponent, or one with sheer brute strength, I would have little chance in hand-to-hand combat.

These less than comforting thoughts accompanied me back to Wood Street. I would take an early meal there, then meet Arthur where we had arranged, by the Conduit in Cheapside, which would give us time to reach the Fair before the first performance of the puppet show. I found myself hoping that there would not be a later performance, for I did not care for the thought of being abroad so late at night, even with money to take a wherry back downriver. I began to work out the various possibilities in my head as I walked.

If there was to be no evening performance, we would take a wherry back to the upriver side of the Bridge at seven and report to Phelippes. I could then walk home no later than usual. If we had to stay late for the evening performance, then after reporting at Seething Lane, I could take a wherry back up river as far as Queenhithe, but I would then have to walk up from the landing through a rough and unsavoury part of the city all the way to Wood Street. At that time of night it would be dangerous. I wished I could take Rikki with me, for he was capable of scaring off any casual cutpurse or attacker, but I could not take him to the Fair. It would make me too conspicuous, for he was a large dog, and I would draw even more attention to myself if I tried to take him with me into the puppeteers' tent.

The only answer seemed to be to spend the night at Seething Lane. I had done so before, when we were hard pressed. I could do so again. I frowned. I was beginning to wish I had never troubled to take word of the puppet show to Phelippes. It might well turn out to be a great blow about nothing.

Arthur was already waiting by the Great Conduit when I arrived, a little before one by the clock of St Mary-le-Bow. Despite his concern for his wife, he seemed rather pleased than otherwise to be having this unexpected holiday from the toils of Seething Lane.

'We may be undertaking a serious mission for Master Phelippes,' he said, 'but there is no reason we should not enjoy the Fair, is there, Kit?'

'No reason at all,' I said, with a grin. 'And there is an excellent inn set up in Smithfield, where we may take supper. Phelippes has given me coin enough.'

We set off at a smart pace until we reached Newgate, where the crowds became so thick that no one could move faster than a donkey's pace. With the weather remaining fine, it seemed that even more citizens were taking time off from their lawful occupations to come to Smithfield. There was a large crowd of apprentices in front of us, in their blue tunics. From their noisy chatter is seemed they were apprenticed to master drapers, so I suppose they had some legitimate business here at the Cloth Fair, though I thought it unlikely they would be spending all their time fingering fine English broadcloth and Italian damask. There was certainly some talk amongst them of betting on the cock fights.

At last we were through the gate and on our way up Pie Corner to Smithfield. Music floated through the air towards us from the fair ground, for there must be some entertainment of dancing or singing afoot. There was also cheering from somewhere over to the left – sport of some kind, wrestling or bear baiting. I hoped the stand for the bear baiting was secure. The temporary structures on the Fair could never provide the same safety as the Southwark bear gardens. A few years ago an eager boy had leaned forward for a better view at the Smithfield bear baiting and fallen over the barrier. Before anyone could save him the bear had seized him and mauled him to death in front of his horror-struck parents. Since then the barriers had been made higher by law, but they were still flimsy.

'This way,' I said to Arthur.

By now I had a clear map of the temporary streets and booths in my head. One thing I have been blessed with is a good sense of direction.

'The Cloth Fair is over there,' I said, 'beside St Bartholomew-the-Great. That is all well guarded and respectable. There will be no malpractices there. Too many watchful eyes. The inn I mentioned is right at the north end. If we follow this lane of stalls along to the end, we'll come out beside the platform where the Lord Mayor opened the Fair. Since then it has been used by different groups to put on their shows.'

We sauntered along, like any other visitors to the fair ground, stopping to examine the stalls and exchange jests with the shopmen.

'At the end of this lane,' I said, 'is the gingerbread stall where I bought your dragon.'

'My wife was delighted,' Arthur said with a grin. 'I fear it may all be eaten by the time I reach home tonight.'

'Then we had better get another. Shall we buy our gingerbread now, which means we must carry it with us, or wait until later?'

'Let us buy it now. Later all the best pieces may be gone.'

The same mother and daughter were hard at work, as they had been the day before, and the display on the counter was undiminished. I bought several pieces of the plain ungilded gingerbread to share with the Lopez family, while Arthur bought another dragon and a love knot, both gilded. He reddened when he saw me grinning at the love knot.

'Well, Kit, I do love my wife! I am not ashamed of it. And she has been very much afraid with this child she is carrying. We have lost two already before they were born.'

'I am not laughing at you, Arthur. You are a very fortunate man. Look, I shall buy this gilded baby for her. Tell her she must not eat it until the new babe is safely born. It will be a good luck talisman for her.'

I handed over more coins from my own purse. I was carrying both Phelippes's purse and mine tucked into the breast of my doublet, after my experience with the cutpurse at my belt two days before. Arthur had also taken the hint and hidden his purse.

'Now,' I said, as we came out into the open space where the wrestling had taken place before the Lord Mayor, 'you can see along several lanes from here. The one ahead of us leads to the far end of the fair ground, where the inn is. Over to our right, as you can see, is St Bartholomew's Hospital, and further along the church and the Cloth Fair.'

The music we had heard must have come from here, for a group of musicians was packing up their instruments – fiddles, lutes, crumhorns, a psaltery and a simple type of portative organ. Two men were dismantling a temporary May pole on a stand and laying the pieces in a donkey cart along with the instruments. There were half a dozen women in blue gowns with full white sleeves, and half a dozen men in white shirts with waistcoats and breeches of the same blue.

'Dancers,' said Arthur. ''Tis a pity we missed them. You don't see so much dancing in the City any more. Some of those on the Common Council look on it with disfavour.'

'Puritans!' I said in disgust. 'They would banish all fun and joy from life.'

'I do not understand their doctrine,' Arthur said earnestly. He was still watching the musicians rather sadly. 'They say that, before ever we are born, some of us are destined to be saved, all the rest destined to end in the everlasting torments of Hell. How can that be? Does God not care how a man leads his life?'

I reflected that I had never heard Arthur say so much in all the years I had known him as I had heard him say today.

'It does call in question the worth of a man's good conduct,' I said. 'If a man is destined for Heaven, he need not bother how he leads his life. Let him misbehave how he will. And if he is destined for Hell, why should he be a good man on this earth? It seems to me a doctrine leading to chaos.'

As if summoned by our words, but more probably by the sound of music which had floated across Smithfield, a dark-visaged and angry man strode toward the platform, where the May pole was now dismantled and the last of the instruments, a couple of tambourines and a small drum, were being added to the cart. He carried a heavy staff with a brass handle and wore the gloomy dark grey clothes of those very Puritans we had been discussing. Instead of a ruff, he had a wide flat collar of a rather grubby white, and on his head he wore the distinctive tall hat of the Puritans. Anne had once said she believed they wore them to make themselves look taller and more important than the common folk they raged against.

'Sons and daughters of Beelzebub,' he shouted, 'you come here with your filthy mummeries, you lewd music and disgusting capers, and turn the minds of the people to lust and every kind of abomination.'

Quite a crowd was beginning to gather, and there were a few nervous titters, but I saw that most people looked grave or even frightened. The musicians paid no attention to him, but continued gathering up their belongings.

'Heed me, you scum!' The Puritan shouted, and swung his staff so that it clouted one of the men on the neck. It was a nasty blow. The man was not one of the dancers in blue, but must have been one of the musicians. He staggered slightly, but regained his balance and turned to faced the ranter.

'Go your ways,' he said, loudly but calmly. 'We do no one any harm: man, woman or child. Not like you with your talk of hell fire, frightening the very wits out of weak women and children. All of your kind, you are no more than bullies, though you think yourselves so godly.'

There was a gasp from the crowd. Few would dare defy the Puritans so boldly. They were widely disliked, but most people simply tried to avoid them.

'No harm, fellow? No harm!' The Puritan was incandescent with fury now, spittle flying from his mouth as he leaned toward the musician. 'You shall not go unpunished!'

At that he brought down his heavy staff on the pile of instruments in the donkey cart. There was a terrible splintering noise and the twang of snapped strings. Several of the musicians cried out and began to lift their broken instruments from the cart. One of the fiddles was smashed into fragments, most of the strings of the psaltery were broken, and the portable organ – surely their most valuable possession – looked damaged beyond repair.

'Constable!' The shout was taken up by several in the crowd, as the musician grabbed the Puritan's staff and snapped it over his knee. The cry echoed along the lane and I saw a Fair official and two constables nearly running toward the fracas. I took Arthur by the elbow and drew him to the back of the crowd.

'It will be a case for the Court of Pie Poudres,' I said.

'We should bear witness,' Arthur said. 'It was the Puritan started it all.'

'Aye, it was, but Phelippes would not want us to become involved. It will make us conspicuous and it will be impossible for us to do what he asks. It is near time for the puppet show.'

'You are right,' he said reluctantly, 'but I do not like to see that vile ranter go unpunished.'

'I do not think he will. There are plenty in the crowd who saw what happened. Such men are not loved. There will be enough there ready to see him punished.'

'Very well.' He was still doubtful.

'Look,' I said, 'that is the puppeteers' tent just across there, and they are getting ready to admit the audience. The toy man's stall is three pitches along and on the other side of the lane, do you see? And it is closed up. So I suppose that means he is playing their music again.'

There was no sign of Robert Poley.

We each bought a twopenny ticket and took our places amongst those standing behind the three rows of stools, near enough to see everything, but better placed to leave at the end than we had been yesterday, when we were trapped at the front of the audience. I was not sure whether the performance would be the same – I should look a fool if it was some harmless comedy today.

I was soon justified in having gone to Phelippes and brought Arthur with me today. I think he was not quite convinced

148

of all I had told them, for it had been difficult to convey the menace I had felt. I knew that Arthur had a little Italian. His Latin was good, and that is a great help in understanding Italian, which is, after all, just a modern dialect of Latin, even if the pronunciation has changed a good deal over the centuries. Arthur would be able to follow much of the dialogue, more than most of the audience, I suspected.

By the time Il Dottore and Pulcinella had made their entrance and begun to speak, he glanced at me and gave a slight nod. He believed me now.

I cannot swear that every word of the performance was the same, for I suspect that the puppeteers were speaking without a book, what my player friends would have called 'speaking at liberty' or 'ad lib', but the sense of the whole was the same – the folly of the country's leaders, the disaster of the recent expedition, and above all, the asserted love of England for popery and the corrupt scheming of Drake and the Queen.

I spent less time watching the stage this time, but covertly eyed the audience, trying to make out what sort of people were here. Some were clearly ordinary fairgoers – families with children, pairs of young lovers who welcomed the private darkness of the tent for reasons of their own – but there was a large group of men whose demeanour suggested that they were not here for entertainment. Some, I was almost certain, had come from amongst the makeshift army. As Phelippes had said, they were not likely to spend all their time in Finsbury Fields. For one thing, they must eat. If indeed they had between them no money at all, then they must steal to eat, and what better place than here, amongst the crowds and stalls?

When the performance was over, there was even warmer applause than there had been on the previous day, and as Arthur and I made our way out of the tent, I saw that some (though not all) of those I took to be soldiers had remained behind.

'Well?' I said, once we were out of earshot of the rest of the audience.

'You are right.' He looked worried. 'It is subversive and dangerous. I wonder what they really have in mind.'

'Did you take note of the faces?'

'Aye. A mixed lot. Many ordinary folk, but I think some were soldiers.'

'So do I. And there was one swarthy fellow who stood just inside the entrance. I do not think he was English.'

'I did not see him.'

'He was in the shadows. Difficult to see if you were watching the puppets. He was not. He was watching the audience, as I was.'

'What do you want to do now?'

'I think we must quarter the whole of Smithfield, searching for Poley, if we can do it without drawing attention to ourselves. I would also like you to take note of the toy man, Nicholas Borecroft. He may be quite innocent, and he may be telling the truth, that the Italians asked him at the last minute to play for them. Still, I would like to be sure. I have just seen him return to his stall, behind you. Don't turn round. I'll work my way along this lane and then into the next one. Perhaps you could buy something from his stall. Get a better look at him.'

Arthur looked blank. 'What can I buy?'

'He has everything in that stall. Why not a rattle for the new baby when it's born?'

His face cleared. 'A good plan. My wife will be pleased. She was *not* pleased that I was coming here with you and not with her.'

'It is much too hot and crowded for a woman near her time!'

'That is what I told her.' He grinned. 'That did not make her any less annoyed! By the way, did you see on their billboard, there is another performance at eight o' the clock tonight?'

'I saw,' I said gloomily. 'I hoped we need not stay. Well, I shall start looking for Poley. We might as well work the Fair separately. Shall we meet at the inn when St Bartholomew's strikes six? That gives us plenty of time to look for Poley, and time enough to eat before the second performance.'

He nodded his agreement and we separated.

For the best part of two and a half hours I worked my way back and forth across the fair ground, finishing at the Master

150

Chawtry's inn just as the church clock sounded out six o' the clock.

But I saw no sign of Robert Poley.

Chapter Ten

*O*nce again, we made a good meal at Master Chawtry's inn, though both Arthur and I were downcast at having made so little progress in our hunt for Poley. The inn felt different as night drew in. Flaming torches had been set up in stands all round the periphery, and every table held a branched candlestick. Their light made the surrounding darkness seem all the darker. A small wind had arisen, casting fluttering shadows from the leafy boughs, so that from the corner of my eye I thought I saw furtive movement. The underlit faces of the diners, the occasional burst of raucous laughter, gave the whole place the air of another stage, another playhouse, in which I was not sure what role I was supposed to fill.

'A fruitless search, eh, Kit?' Arthur dipped his fingers in the bowl of water in which a few sprigs of lavender floated, then dried them on the napkin over his shoulder.

'It seems so.' I was very tired, for I had slept badly the night before, worrying about the motives of the puppeteers, and now I seemed to have been wandering around the Fair for days, to no purpose.

'I could see nothing wrong with that toy man,' he said. 'He was courteous enough and seemed harmless. A gaggle of mothers with children came up behind me, so his attention was called away from me.'

I nodded. 'Probably he is telling the simple truth, that he was asked at the last minute to provide music. All the same.' I paused, rolling bits of bread into pellets and eating them, one by one. 'Just for that brief moment when I saw him with Poley, I got the impression they knew one another. Perhaps I was mistaken.'

'I do not think you were mistaken about the puppet masters,' he said, 'whether or not Poley and Borecroft have anything to do with it. There is certainly something afoot there. And I think you are also right, that some of the soldiers are also involved.'

It was reassuring that Arthur had gained the same impression as I, and I was glad he had accompanied me, for he could back up my report to Phelippes.

'Quite what is afoot, though,' I said, 'is the problem. No constable or pursuivant could arrest the Italians merely on such weak evidence as our impression of what their performance seemed to signify.'

'Oh, I think they might. The performance was scurrilous and the puppets themselves, especially the one of the Queen, must be near treasonable.'

'But what would be the point of arresting them, if we do not know what they intend?'

'No doubt some would say that Topcliffe would soon get it out of them, in the dungeons of the Tower.' He shuddered.

'No doubt. But how does it relate to the soldiers? Are they meaning to start an uprising, the two groups working together? If so, why did the soldiers stand quietly under discipline at the entrance to Smithfield and send four of their leaders to negotiate with the Lord Mayor and Common Council?'

'You said it yourself to Phelippes. Most of the men are peaceable by nature. All they are pursuing is compensation for their suffering and lost incomes. But some, either in the army group or outside it, are pursuing other aims.'

'I wish I could make sense of it,' I said, thumping my fist against my forehead in annoyance at myself. 'Come, it is nearly time for the next performance, and we have to walk almost the whole way across Smithfield.'

'It will soon be over, Kit,' he said, 'then we can take a wherry home to our beds.'

Or rather, back to Seething Lane, I thought, before ever we see our beds.

As we came out of the circle of light which marked the inn, the darkness seemed to hit our faces like a bag over the head. We paused at the top of the first alley of stalls, waiting for our eyes to adjust. The whole Fair seemed to have changed in character. The families had all gone home and the forms looming out of the dark and disappearing again were mostly groups of rowdy young men. Many of the stalls were still doing business and had a candle or two burning in order to light up the goods for sale. These intermittent pools of light left great stretches of blackness between them, which could easily conceal an attacker. The increasing wind stirred the canvas sides of tents and the awnings over stalls, so that there was a constant sense of stealthy sound and movement – movement which might hide the sudden thrust of a sword or dagger coming out of the dark.

Arthur and I hurried along, both conscious of this change in the atmosphere of the Fair. As we neared the puppet tent, I noticed that several of the nearby stalls were being closed up, though faint slivers of light showed around the doors and shutters, where the owners were preparing to spend the night watching over their goods. I shivered. I was glad I did not have to spend the night alone in a flimsy stall in Smithfield. The very air seemed filled with the remembrance of the dying cries of beasts slaughtered in the nearby Shambles, while the place itself, so gaudy and merry by day, was now haunted by the ghosts of those who had gone to the fire on this very soil for their faith, both Catholics and reformers.

We reached the platform, which was empty, except for a drunkard snoring under the edge of it. At the nearest corner of the lane leading down to the Fair entrance at Pie Corner, the gingerbread stall was closed and dark. If someone was spending the night there, they were already abed, but it had an air of emptiness about it. The women would have little there which was worth stealing, just their gold leaf and their moulds, and those could easily be carried home for the night. Unsurprisingly, the toy stall was also closed and dark. Few of the present fairgoers, a looming mass of young men, would be buying toys. Besides, Nicholas Borecroft would probably be playing again for the puppets.

A crowd of half a dozen roisterers, much the worse for drink, lurched toward us out of the lane of shops. My hand went to my sword hilt, but Arthur caught me by the arm and pulled me firmly back into the shadow of the platform.

'Best just keep out of sight,' he murmured in my ear, so softly I could barely hear the words.

I nodded, though he could hardly hope to see me in the dark.

Across the wrestling ground from the platform, a group was gathering outside the puppet tent, where candle lanterns had been mounted on tall posts on either side of the entrance. They lit up a crowd of different composition from the earlier ones. As I had expected, there were no families. There was a high proportion of rough-looking men, and – curiously – several finely dressed gentlemen, of a higher rank than anyone I had seen here before.

The flap of canvas over the entrance was pulled aside and tied back, the flamboyantly dressed woman appeared again, with her handful of cheap playbills. She seemed to be looking all about and studying the crowd waiting outside. Then she gave a nod. If she said anything, we were just too far away to hear. Then the men began to file inside, without paying.

Arthur and I looked at each other.

'I think,' he said carefully, 'that we were better not to go in there again.'

'I agree.' I could not keep the relief out of my voice. 'Though it is strange they should advertise a performance if it was meant only for their friends.'

'Perhaps it was a signal to their friends, when to meet.'

'Aye. And if anyone else turned up – like us – they would have been told that all the tickets were sold, or some other deceit. Listen, there is no music.'

We both strained our ears. All we could hear was a murmur of voices, too faint to make out distinctly. I wondered whether Nicholas Borecroft was there, or asleep in his stall. And what of Poley? He seemed to have vanished.

'Shall we catch a wherry back to the city?' Arthur asked hopefully.

I wanted very much to agree, but reluctantly shook my head.

'I think we should wait and see whether anything further happens,' I said. 'I don't suppose it will take as long as the performance would have done. If we stay here by the edge of the platform, we won't be noticed.'

We made ourselves as easy as we could, sitting on the lumpy ground beside the platform. It was dry but very stony, and did not make for comfortable sitting. The remaining shopmen at this end of the Fair soon closed up their stalls and no one was left roaming the lanes. Further over to the west, several of the pig roasts were still doing good business, serving roast pork and ale, and bursts of laughter and drunken shouting reached us over the dark and empty spaces between. There were lanterns on poles at the junctions of the lanes, and a dim glow from the area of the pig roasts, but otherwise it had grown very dark. I realised that clouds had built up, masking any light from the moon.

Beside me, Arthur shifted uncomfortably.

'My bum is as numb as a drunken sailor,' he muttered.

I grinned in the dark. I could not imagine Arthur saying such a thing in the formal atmosphere of Seething Lane.

'Is that rain?' I whispered.

'Aye.'

It was indeed. Just the beginnings of one of those fine mizzling rains that look like nothing but nevertheless relentlessly soak you to the very skin. We both huddled closer to the edge of the platform for shelter, and I heard the drunk on the far side groan and turn over, but he stayed where he was. I was on the very point of suggesting that we give up and catch that wherry home before we were truly sodden, when the tent flap opened opposite, and men began to slip out into the darkness. The very furtiveness of their movements was enough to reawaken my suspicions. We both sat up and leaned forward.

The men did not all leave in a crowd, but in twos and small groups, dispersing in different directions and mostly in silence.

One group of four men walked past us so close I could have put out my foot and tripped up the nearest one. They were whispering together and I heard only a few words, but one of them was 'Dowgate'.

At last it seemed that all those who had been in the tent had gone and the swarthy man I had noticed during the earlier performance came out to carry the two lanterns inside and lace up the tent door. Soon after, the lights in the tent went out. I stood up and jerked my head in the direction of the river, hoping Arthur could see me against the distance loom of light from the pig roasts. He got to his feet with a faint groan, dusted himself down, and we set off along the dark lane of stalls leading toward Pie Corner. The ground was uneven and once or twice we stumbled, but we reached the street at last. It was easier going here, and we hurried down to the river and Whitefriars Stairs, for the rain was getting heavier.

Fortunately, a few wherrymen were lingering here, sheltered in their hut, hoping for a fare from some of the roisterers still eating and drinking at the Fair. We found a boat with a canvas shelter and bade the wherryman take us down to the Bridge. He seemed glad of the fare. It was a strange, dreamlike journey. I had never before been on the river at night. The clouds covered moon and stars, so that we moved within the small circle of light cast by the wherryman's lantern, reflected back from the ripples made by his oars. All around us the waters of the Thames were black under the midnight sky. On the south shore of the river there were no lights to be seen, for it was long past the time when the bear pits closed. Even the brothels would have put up their shutters. On the City shore, a lighted window showed here and there amongst the wealthy houses along the Strand, but there was no movement on the river. It seemed as though we travelled alone through a deserted world.

When we reached Old Swan Stairs on the upriver side of the Bridge and I had paid the man from Phelippes's purse, with an extra twopence for his trouble so late at night, I urged Arthur to go home.

'There is no need for us both to see Phelippes,' I said. 'Go home to your wife. Here, I almost forgot.' I reached into my satchel. 'The gilded baby. Mind, she is not to eat it until after the babe arrives.'

He laughed. 'I thank you, Kit, and I will tell her so.'

'And I thank you for your company,' I said. 'I would not have liked to spend that last vigil alone.'

I saw that he shivered in the light of the torch mounted on the landing place.

'Nor would I.'

We parted then. He assured me he lived not far away, and I hurried off to Seething Lane. This was a better part of the city than Queenhithe, with lanterns hung before many of the substantial houses, but it was not far from the Legal Quays near the Tower, and the sailors there were a rough lot.

The watchman in the stableyard of Walsingham's house gave me a nod – he must have been warned I was coming – and unlocked the door for me. I ran up the backstairs, glad to be out of the rain. Phelippes was sitting at his table, working as usual at his papers, looking no different from that morning. I was glad to see there was a fire on the hearth and took my stand in front of it, where I steamed gently like a goodwife's cookpot.

'Well?' he said. 'What news?'

'A little news, but no Poley.'

I recounted everything we had seen and done, of which the most important was the gathering of men at both performances in the puppet tent, but especially the latter, and our complete failure to find any sign of Robert Poley.

'One last thing,' I said. 'When the men were leaving the puppeteers' tent, one group passed near us. I heard only one word of any importance. Dowgate.'

'Dowgate?' He looked at me thoughtfully. 'And what do we have in Dowgate?'

I searched my mind. 'London Stone?' I said.

'Aye.'

I pictured the street, one of the main thoroughfares in the centre of the city.

'Ah,' I said, 'the Herbar. The house Sir Francis Drake bought with the loot he seized in the midst of the naval battle against the Armada. When he was supposed to be leading our navy forward, but slipped away for a little freebooting of his own.'

'Careful what you say, Kit.'

Phelippes spoke automatically, but I felt he agreed with my view of the matter. I had not been present at that part of the naval battle, only later, off Gravelines, but I had heard what Drake had done after I came ashore. It had not made him popular with either commanders or sailors, deserting them like that. And now I thought about it, his actions then were all of a piece with the way he had behaved toward the rest of us on the recent expedition. The man was a greedy, self-serving pirate, though it did not do to say so publicly.

'You think something might be intended against Drake?' I moved a little away from the fire, for my legs were beginning to roast.

He laid down his quill and clasped his hands behind his head, tilting his chair on to its back legs.

'Let us think what we have. A crowd of angry soldiers and sailors, who feel they have been cheated out of their due reward for their services.'

'As they have,' I said.

'Don't interrupt. I know what you think, Kit.'

I closed my mouth. He was right. I had said it often enough.

'The moderate men among them will await the outcome of their leaders' meeting with the Common Council. In the meanwhile, the wilder spirits among them may not be willing to wait, but may wish to take matters into their own hands.'

He let his chair fall forward again.

'Add to this some travelling Italian performers, almost certainly papists, who have gone to a great deal of trouble to prepare a treasonous play, probably to incite covert Catholics *and* disaffected soldiers into action.'

'Would they have known about the disaffected soldiers?' I risked interrupting, for this seemed like an important point. 'The making of those puppets, the painting of the backcloth – that must have taken a long time.'

'You are right. But perhaps they did not learn about the march on London at the last moment. How long have you been back in England? Six weeks? Time enough for them to hear of this through their own spies and prepare accordingly.' He smiled grimly. 'We are not the only nation which employs spies.'

'True enough.'

'So if there has been a conspiracy from the start, if some amongst the soldiers are in league with these Italians, it begins to make sense. You said there were gentlemen present this evening. Did you recognise any of them?'

I shook my head. I had wondered for a fleeting moment whether Sir Damian Fitzgerald might have been there. It was his household I had joined briefly at Walsingham's orders three years before, but I had never believed him to be a papist conspirator of the more dangerous sort. He would hold secret Masses, hide priests, and pass letters, but I did not believe him capable of violent action. Moreover, he made great parade of his loyalty to the house of Tudor, even in the design of his new chimneys, with their Tudor roses. He had too much to lose.

'Nay, there was no one I recognised, but I would probably not know papist sympathisers. Arthur did not recognise anyone either.'

'Hmm. So what could be planned against Drake?'

'I can imagine the Spanish plotting to harm Drake, or *El Draque*, as they call him,' I said. 'Nothing would please them better than to put him out of action. His great fortune is built on what he has seized from their ships and towns. But, the Italians?'

'The Italians come from the very hornets' nest of popery,' he said sharply. 'As you have said, part of their performance was intended to encourage the papists. Perhaps there is a double purpose here. Harming Drake would also harm a well known enemy of all Catholics.'

'But does it make sense for the soldiers to harm Drake? They want him to hand over their share of the booty, not to kill or injure him.'

'That is the purpose of the more moderate soldiers, but these others – who knows? Men may be driven by anger and despair to act even against their own best interests.'

'Very well,' I said, 'if something is intended against Drake, or at any rate against his house, the Herbar, what are we to do?'

I was growing so tired I could barely speak. All I wanted to do was to go to sleep. 'And what of Poley?'

'Damn Poley!' he said. 'I don't know where he fits in. I'll need to put a watch on these puppeteers first thing tomorrow. And I'll send to the Common Council to discover what is happening about the soldiers.' He suddenly looked as tired as I. 'You had better go home, Kit.'

'I don't think I care to cross London alone as late as this,' I said. 'If you do not mind, I'll stay here until dawn.'

'Aye, that's probably wise,' he said.

He went to the door and shouted for a servant. A boy came, rubbing his eyes sleepily.

'Fetch a mattress for Master Alvarez,' Phelippes said, 'and put it in Master Gregory's room.'

When the boy had run off, he poured us each a cup of wine.

'Something to help you sleep,' he said.

I laughed. 'I do not think I will need any help.'

'You'll be quiet in Arthur's room. I still have work to do.'

I drank the wine gratefully, for it had been many hours since our meal at Chawtry's inn, but I forbore to say that he looked as though he needed sleep as well. With Sir Francis ill, there was a heavy burden on his shoulders.

The boy soon returned dragging a thin flock mattress, which he just managed to fit into the small amount of floor space in Arthur's tiny room, then he returned with a couple of blankets and a lumpy pillow. I lit the candle from my table at one of Phelippes's and bade him good night. Once shut into the cubbyhole I just managed to shed my shoes and sword and blow out my candle before falling on to the mattress and rolling myself in the blankets. I think I must have fallen asleep before my head touched that lumpy pillow.

When I woke next morning it was already light. I was stiff and uncomfortable, still in my doublet and hose, but I slipped on my shoes and picked up my sword before opening the door to Phelippes's office. He was not there, but Francis Mylles, Walsingham's senior secretary, was just coming in with a bundle of papers.

'Ah, Kit,' he said, 'I hope you slept well? I hear you were at the Fair till all hours last night.'

'Not for enjoyment,' I said. 'My head feels like an old bird's nest this morning.'

'I'll send for some food,' he said. 'Master Phelippes has gone to see the Common Council, but he has left word that you are to return to Smithfield when you have eaten, and continue your search.'

He looked at me enquiringly. Phelippes had clearly not mentioned that I was searching for Poley.

'I'll be glad of the food,' I said. 'Has Arthur Gregory come in yet?'

'Nay, he sent word that his wife is not well and asked that he be excused, unless there is urgent need of him.'

The food soon arrived. I pushed aside the papers on my table and tucked into the bread and cheese and cold meat hungrily. Afterwards I looked at myself in the small steel mirror Phelippes kept on the wall. I looked haggard and my hair was a tangled mess, so I ran my fingers through it, lacking a comb. I seemed to have lost my cap, but when I looked in Arthur's room I saw it, crushed in a ball beside the pillow. I pulled it into shape and straightened my hose, but there was little else I could do to improve my shop-soiled appearance. I would have liked to return to Wood Street to wash and change my hose, but I had better not. Phelippes had added more coin to the purse he had given me, so I walked down to Old Swan Stairs and took a wherry upriver to Smithfield.

As I followed the road back up to the Fair, I was glad that the rain had stopped, for I did not have even the protection of a light cloak, though my damp doublet had partially dried on me while I slept. The road was full of puddles, but they were beginning to shrink in the sun, and all around maids were shaking bedding out of windows and sweeping the steps of houses. The day was already turning warm again.

The way through to the centre of the Fair was familiar now. The gingerbread stall was open, the younger woman laying out the goods on the counter, while behind her the mother was lighting the fire in the portable oven. They both turned and smiled at me. I must already be recognised as a good customer. It would be better, I thought, if I were not too familiar a sight. I had no doubt Nicholas Borecroft would recognise me, but I did not want the puppet troupe to do so.

As I rounded the corner past the gingerbread stall, I saw that the platform was deserted. No group of performers was setting up as early as this, for they would not be able to attract enough of an audience to make it worthwhile. I wondered whether the toy man had opened yet. Children are often the first to arrive.

According to the original statutes which set up Bartholomew Fair centuries ago, it was licensed to last three days, and this was the third. However, over the years, and long before ever my father and I had come to England, the Fair had begun to extend quietly, to last more and more days. The city officials did nothing to stop it, for it brought business to London from the surrounding countryside, it attracted foreign dealers and their wares, and it stimulated brisk trade for all the local merchants and shopmen. So, although this was officially the last day, the Fair would probably continue for at least another week, which meant there should be time to find Poley, if he was lurking about in its shadow, and to fathom the intentions of the Italians.

I walked along to Nicholas Borecroft's stall, for I saw that the counter had been lowered. To my astonishment, I saw that the door was ajar and the stall empty of everything but a few wisps of straw blowing about, probably packing material for some of the more fragile items.

I simply stood and gaped, unable to believe my eyes. The third day of the Fair, with the weather sunny, would be excellent for business, and importunate children would be dragging their parents to all the toy stalls. Why was the stall here, but neither the toy man or his goods?

'Looking for Borecroft, are you, young master?'

The button maker, opening the adjacent stall, paused in laying out his goods and turned to me.

'Has he gone already?' I said, hastily thinking of some excuse. 'I was looking for a rattle for a new babe.'

'Gone already before I was awake. Must have packed up in the dark.'

'But he hasn't dismantled his stall.'

The man shrugged. 'Either he's coming back for it, or he's rented it and a'nt bothering to return it.'

'It would make a lot of noise, taking it down,' I suggested.

'Aye, perhaps he was thinking kindly of us sleepers,' he said sarcastically. 'Nay, he's done a flit. Probably hasn't paid his full rent for his pitch.'

'You don't like him.'

'Don't really know him. He a'nt done me no harm. Live and let be, that's the way at the Fair.' He gave me a curious look. 'Why are you asking? Does he owe you something?'

'Nay, I was just surprised to see him gone so soon.'

'He a'nt the only one to leave early.' He jerked a thumb over his shoulder. 'Those foreigners have gone as well.'

I spun round on my heel. There, where the large puppeteers' tent had stood, was an empty space. My heart began to pound. Phelippes would need to know this. Perhaps whatever they were plotting was already in train.

'They must have made a noise, taking all of that down,' I said. 'You cannot have slept through that.'

'Well, to tell truth, I was a little stained last night, drinking with the lads at the pig roast.' He grinned, showing blackened teeth, what was left of them. 'We was sprinkled with a cup or two before bed, and I slept sound. When I woke this morning, the strangers was loading the last of their clutter on to a mule cart.'

There was a wide dry patch, like an island in the damp ground.

'After the rain, then,' I said, pointing to it.

He shrugged. 'It was still raining when I got back, that I do recall. But I don't know when it stopped. I was away with Queen Mab by then.'

Once again he gave me a sharp look. He might be a drinker, but he was no fool. 'You're mighty curious. What are you after? Not working for the Fair officers, are you?'

I knew it would be clear from my clothes that I was not some menial, so I laughed. 'Just nosy,' I said. 'Wondering why everyone is closing down.'

'Not everyone. Those are the only two I've seen. 'Tis a pity, though, for the crowds at the puppet show brought me some custom.'

I took the hint, and bought half a dozen buttons I did not need. They were attractive enough, polished bone inlaid with a dome of black enamel. If I were ever to gain a hospital position once more, they would do for a new physician's gown.

Bidding the button maker goodbye, I began walking about the Fair at random, keeping my eyes open for Poley, but in a stew of thoughts, wondering what I should do. Phelippes had left clear instructions for me to continue the search, but the disappearance of both the toy man and the Italians changed the situation. The fact that both had departed at the same time made it all the more likely that Nicholas Borecroft was working with the puppeteers, though somehow I could not fit them together. He was not one of the soldiers and he did not seem like a covert papist, although I knew very well that it was often impossible to tell. Yet if his only connection with them had been as a casual musician, why had they both gone now? And where?

Either I must give up the search for Poley, which seemed more and more pointless, or I must send a message to Phelippes. It could well be that Poley had gone wherever the others had gone. Even to send a message from the Fair would be difficult. Perhaps I could draw on long-standing good will at the hospital, and persuade someone there to send a boy with a note.

I had reached the top of the fair ground, where Master Chawtry's servants were just setting up the tables and stools. I turned to head back along a parallel lane of stalls when there was a sudden movement as someone darted out from behind a stall and seized me by the arm. I made to grab my sword, but a desperate gasp stopped me.

'Don't. It's me, Dr Alvarez.' The words came out half choked.

It was Adam Batecorte. One whole side of his head was bloodied, his shirt was ripped off his shoulders, there was a slash across his back, and he was limping.

'Adam! What has happened?'

It could not be thieves, I thought. Threadbare as he had been when I had seen him before, no thief would have bothered to attack him.

'We are betrayed!'

'What do you mean? Wait! We must see to your hurts. The hospital is close by. Here, take my arm.'

He was limping, but he could still move fast and he kept looking over his shoulder as we hurried back in the direction of St Bartholomew's. Someone there would care for him. He wiped a ragged strip dangling from the sleeve of his shirt along the gash in the side of his head. I felt for my handkerchief, folded it into a pad and handed it to him.

'Press that against the wound,' I said, 'hard as you can bear. We're nearly there.'

I urged him under the gatehouse and nodded to the gatehouse keeper.

'An injured man, Rafe. I'm taking him in.'

'The physicians won't be here yet, Dr Alvarez. They work shorter hours now.'

'Then I'll see to him myself.' It might get me into trouble, but I did not care. It was more urgent to get treatment for Adam.

By good fortune I met Peter carrying a tray of bottles as we entered the hospital.

'This man needs help,' I said, 'and Rafe says the physicians are not here. Is there somewhere I can treat him?'

As usual, Peter could be relied upon. 'This way', he said. 'The small room where we sometimes put the sick mothers with new babies. There's no one there at the moment.'

When we reached to room, I sat Adam down on a stool and sent Peter for Coventry water, salves, needle and thread, and bandages.

'We was attacked,' Adam said, his voice still very weak. 'I thought I might find you at the Fair, then I was going to Wood Street, if I could get that far.'

'Later,' I said. 'Let's deal with this first.'

The slash across his back was fortunately not deep. It required no more than salving and bandaging. The gash in his head was worse and had to be stitched, then bandaged. Peter stayed with us, passing me what I needed. We had often worked together in the past and I had only to hold out my hand to him.

'You were limping,' I said to Adam at last. 'Is there damage to your foot or your leg?'

'Nay, I twisted my ankle, running from them, but it's nothing.'

I rinsed my bloodied hands in the basin Peter had brought and he handed me a towel, then I pulled up another stool.

'Now,' I said, 'what happened?' Seeing his dubious look, I added, 'Peter can be trusted.'

'It was before dawn,' Adam said. His voice was stronger now, for Peter had brought some spiced wine, which he gulped down thirstily.

'We was still camped out in the open, up on Finsbury Fields, and miserable it was, too, after the rain started last night. Some of the lads had rigged up a rough shelter with some canvas they nicked out of a farm, out beyond Finsbury, but it was crowded under there. We was scattered around. I found a bush of broom and crawled in under that, but it didn't give much shelter. I fell asleep finally and woke up to the most b'yer lady row. Horns blowing and yelling and muskets going off. I was that confused, I thought for a moment I was back that time we was attacked in Portugal.'

He took another swig of the wine.

'There was just a little light in the sky, before the sun comes up, you know. And it had stopped raining, so the sky was clear. I realised then that our whole camp was surrounded.'

'But who–' I said.

'The London Trained Bands. The militia. They wouldn't have stood a chance against us in the normal way, but we was taken by surprise, we was scattered all over the place, and there was officers on horseback.'

He ran his hand over his face.

167

'I crawled out from under my bush on the side away from the action. There was nobody nearby and I made a run for it. Nearly got away, but one of the officers spotted me and came galloping over. Slashed my head and then I fell and he got me across the back. He must have thought he'd done for me. He rode away and I crawled to the edge of the field and then I ran. I wanted to put as much distance between me and them as I could, so I kept running. I was already this side of the fields, so I ended up here.'

Peter and I looked at each other.

'But,' I said, 'your leaders were conferring with the Common Council.'

'Damn the Common Council! Those men who attacked, they were yelling that our men are thrown in Newgate and will be tried for treason, and so will we. All the more reason to get out of there.'

'Bastards!' said Peter.

'You'd better not stay here,' I said. 'It's the obvious place to look for the injured. I know where I can take you.'

I looked at Peter. 'William Baker?'

'Good idea.'

'I won't take you to Wood Street,' I said to Adam. 'Ruy Lopez is in serious trouble himself and – just possibly – he might want to ingratiate himself with the Privy Council by handing you over, for if it is to be a charge of treason, it will be a matter for the Privy Council. William Baker is a friend of both Peter's and mine, a soldier wounded at Sluys. I'm sure he'll take you in and hide you until it is safe.'

Peter frowned. 'He can't walk all the way to Eastcheap.'

'I've chinks enough for a wherry,' I said. 'I thank you for your help, Peter. Better not mention it to the hospital authorities. I'm not licensed to practice here any more.'

'More fool them,' he muttered. 'Don't worry. I'll clear this up and keep my mouth shut.'

'Perhaps a word to Rafe?'

'Aye, I'll speak to him.'

It was clearly painful for Adam even to walk as far as the river, and he settled in the wherry with a sigh of relief.

'Been in the wars, mate?' the wherryman said.

Adam gave him a weak grin. 'You could say that.'

'It's a disgrace,' the man said. 'Can't even walk the streets of London these days and be safe.'

He continued in this vein all the way down river, but we were both glad to sit and listen. After we landed, the walk to the shoe maker's shop was painfully slow, and I saw that Adam was sweating, his mouth grimly shut. It was William's new young wife who came out of the back room when we entered the shop. She went pale at the sight of us and her hand flew to her mouth.

'What has happened?'

'My friend has been attacked, Mistress Liza,' I said. 'I fear he may still be in some danger. Could you and William take him in until he is fit again?'

'Of course!' She lifted the curtain which covered the doorway to the inner room. 'William, Dr Alvarez is here.'

I heard the tapping of William's crutch and he appeared in the doorway, the upper part of a shoe in the hand not holding the crutch.

'A fellow soldier, William,' I said. I saw that Adam's eyes had widened as he realised William had lost a leg, then, embarrassed, he looked away. William was well accustomed to this by now and merely smiled.

'William and Liza can also be trusted,' I said to Adam, then I quickly repeated what he had told me of the attack on the soldiers.

William flushed with anger. 'It is always thus,' he said tightly, 'if I had not had Dr Alvarez's care and my family to come to, I too would have been starving in a gutter, or probably dead. How long will men continue to enlist, to fight for England, when we are treated so?'

Adam gave a shaky smile, and sank on to a stool.

'As long as men are hungry and gullible enough to believe the promises of the men who rule us.'

'Enough!' Liza said. 'You should be lying down, not talking of politics. Can you manage the stairs? We have a little room at the back, not much more than a storeroom, but there's a cot and blankets. Perhaps it will serve.'

'I thank you mistress,' he said, and got stiffly to his feet.

'I will come back to see you soon,' I said, as he followed Liza through the doorway.

'William?' I turned to him. 'Could young Will run with a message for me, to Seething Lane? I have information I must pass on.'

'Of course. Here.' He drew paper and quills out of a drawer at the back of the shop. 'And there is ink here, and wax. I will go next door and find Will.'

By the time he returned with his nephew, I had written a quick note to Phelippes, telling him everything I had discovered about the departure of Nicholas Borecroft and the Italian puppeteers, and that I had been unable to find Poley. I said nothing of my meeting with Adam, nor that I had heard about the betrayal of the soldiers. It would be best to pretend ignorance of that for the moment.

'Here you are, Will,' I said, stamping my seal on the soft wax and fanning the letter in the air for a moment to harden it. 'This must go to the house of Sir Francis Walsingham in Seething Lane. Do you know where Seething Lane is?'

'Aye, near the Tower.'

'That's right. Anyone there can tell you which is the house. Go in by the stableyard and up the backstairs. The letter is for Master Thomas Phelippes. If he is not there, give it to Master Francis Mylles. Do you understand?'

'Aye, Dr Alvarez. I can do that. I'm a very fast runner!'

'Good.' I smiled. 'Here's a groat for you, but don't run so fast you fall.'

He took the letter and jumped out of the door. William smiled at me.

'Don't worry. He's a good lad. He will see it safely delivered.'

I sat back with a sigh. 'I can see that. I'm beholden to you and your family, William.'

'No more than I am to you. Will you take a sup of ale?

I shook my head. 'I thank you, but no. I must go home and change my clothes. I slept in them last night and I feel like a booby set up to scare pigeons from the young wheat. I'll be at the Lopez house in Wood Street if I am needed.'

'Don't worry,' he said again, and glanced at the ceiling, where we could hear footsteps above. 'We'll keep him safe.'

'I know you will,' I said, and shook his hand.

Chapter Eleven

By the time I reached Wood Street it was well past midday and I realised how hungry I was. The whole house seemed very quiet and instead of ringing the hand bell for one of the servants I made my way to the back of the house and the kitchen. A furry shape threw itself at me and I grabbed the doorframe to save myself from being knocked over.

'Poor Rikki,' I said, fending off the worst of the wet licking. 'I'm afraid I've been neglecting you these last few days.'

'Aye.' Ned Somer, the cook, gave me a sour look. 'He's been under my feet the while. Master said he was to stay here, out the way, and he's for ever in front of me, tripping me up. I nearly sent a sambocade flying across the room last night.'

'I'm sorry.' I was contrite. 'I was sent off by Master Phelippes somewhere I couldn't take the dog and only got back to Sir Francis's house near midnight. I slept on the floor there. And all today I've been about his business.'

Somer sniffed, as if he did not believe me. I knew my dealings with Sir Francis's service were a mystery to the servants, and must remain that way. Even the Lopez family had very little idea of what I did, apart from code-breaking, and no one would have expected me to be roaming the streets of London in the middle of the night if that was what I was about.

'Is everyone out?' I asked. 'The house seems very quiet.'

'Master is off to the Privy Council again. Master Ambrose has gone back to his grandfather. The ladies have taken the children to visit Mistress Nuñez and will not be back until this evening.'

Trust the servants, I thought, to know everyone's business. In fact, Somer probably knew exactly what I had been doing for the last few days.

It was time to assert myself. 'I'll take some cold pie and ale in the small parlour,' I said, 'and some of those early apples.' I pointed to a bowl on a hanging shelf. There was a small orchard at the bottom of the garden and one of the trees, of an unknown variety, produced small apples the size and almost the colour of plums very early in the year. I ignored Somer's offended look and called Rikki to follow me.

Upstairs in my small room I found water and towels, which had probably been put out for me last night, when I had failed to come home. The water was cold now, but I washed with it anyway, stripping off my stale clothes and washing all over. Once I was dressed in clean clothes and had dragged a comb through the tangles in my hair, I felt almost human again.

Rikki followed me down to the parlour and we shared the pie and the slab of bread. From the way he wolfed it down I suspected Somer had not been feeding him. I ate one of the small apples and pocketed three more, in case I had the chance to look in on Hector in the stables. When I was finished, I went in search of Camster, the steward, who had oversight of all the servants and could be relied on to deliver a message accurately.

'I have to go back to Seething Lane, Camster,' I said. 'I will take the dog with me. Please tell Mistress Lopez that I am not sure whether I shall be back tonight. I may need to stay there overnight again.'

'Certainly, Dr Alvarez,' he said with a slight bow. Camster was always one to observe the formalities. 'Are you sure you wish to take the dog?'

'Aye, it will do him good to go outside. Beside, I think he is not popular in the kitchen.'

Camster permitted himself a small smile. 'Very good, Dr Alvarez. Your cloak?'

He reached it down from a peg in the hall panelling and placed round my shoulders. I thanked him, picked up my satchel from the table where I had left it when I came in, and fastened Rikki's lead to his collar.

We headed down Wood Street and turned left along Cheapside, walking briskly. Rikki seemed glad to be out of doors, though I had to restrain him from investigating every pile of rubbish in the road. By now, I hoped, Phelippes would have read my note and also found out from the Common Council just what was happening about the soldiers. What Adam reported was almost certainly true, I thought cynically. It did not surprise me that the authorities should pretend at first to negotiate, then afterwards break their word, imprisoning the soldiers' leaders and attacking the remaining men. I wondered whether the other soldiers who had been encamped at Finsbury Fields had also been carried off to prison, or had simply been frightened and beaten so severely that they would flee for their lives and abandon their demands. The outcome looked black for their leaders. A man on trial for treason may not defend himself. It would be a case of summary justice and a hanging at Tyburn.

The city suddenly looked a terrible place, dirty and dangerous. How could any man hope for justice here? Even in Walsingham's service I knew that tricks were played, false evidence manufactured, witnesses suborned. It was all done with the highest of motives, to maintain the safety of the country and the Queen, but that did not mean that it lacked its darker side. I reached Walsingham's house in a state of some melancholy.

I took Rikki with me up the backstairs to Phelippes's office. He was used to coming with me and ran ahead to the familiar door, which stood open. I could hear voices from inside.

'Ah, Kit,' Phelippes said as I entered, 'I was about to send someone to fetch you.'

'You had my message?'

'Aye. And a pretty mess it all seems. The Italians and this toy seller both gone in the night. Poley – if it was Poley – not seen again.'

'Good day to you, Kit.' The other man in the room was Nicholas Berden, one of the most trusted agents, with whom I had worked before, in the Low Countries.

'And to you, Nick.' I bowed. 'I thought you were leaving Sir Francis's service and moving to the country.' Like Titus

Allanby, the agent I had helped to escape from Coruña, Berden had begun to say that he had had a surfeit of intelligencing.

He shrugged and raised his eyebrows. 'Master Phelippes is very persuasive.'

'What news from the Common Council?' I turned to Phelippes. I would not mention yet that I had news from another quarter.

Phelippes pulled a face. 'The Common Council referred the matter of the soldiers' demands to the Privy Council, and the Privy Council decided that an example must be made of them – coming armed, as they did, and making threats of violence and disorder.'

'Threats only,' I said, without much hope.

'The leaders are to be tried for treason. The rest of the soldiers were rounded up and driven away from the city. Told if they were caught within fifty miles of London after tomorrow, they would be on a charge of treason as well.'

'I think this is a mistake,' I said, hoping that my face did not betray what I already knew. If Adam could be identified as one of the soldiers, he was in serious danger. I prayed William would keep him out of sight.

'Perhaps. But even you must understand their reasons, Kit. If the authorities once yield to the demands of an armed mob, where will it end? It will only encourage others to take the road to violence.'

'I do see that. None of this would have happened if the men had but been treated as they should have been from the start, when they first came ashore at Plymouth. I fear it will be found difficult to recruit men willingly to serve in the future, if there is the threat of another invasion.'

'Well, there is nothing we can do about it. It is out of our hands.' Phelippes waved dismissively. 'We need to turn our minds to what we *can* do. This supposed conspiracy. I have been telling Berden everything you have discovered. He, and some of the men he works with, are going to start a discreet search for these missing fellows.'

'Good,' I said. 'There is a woman too. Gaudily dressed. Something like the gypsies we used to see in Portugal. Am I to go with Nick?'

'Nay, I have another task for you. I received a letter from Sir Francis today. He is out of bed, sitting up now and doing some work.'

I shook my head. The man was incorrigible.

'I want you to ride over to Barn Elms first thing tomorrow and report all this to him in person. He can decide what he wants you to do and send any instructions for me back with you. If we just send him a letter, he will be here before we know it.'

'Shall I take a horse from the stables?'

Phelippes allowed himself a small smile.

'Aye. You can take that horse you are fond of. Horace.'

'Hector.'

He smiled more broadly. He knew very well the horse was called Hector.

'I will leave Rikki with the stable lads. He is somewhat unpopular in the Lopez household.'

'Do that.' He gave me a shrewd look. 'Do not become too close to Ruy Lopez, Kit. He is out of favour.'

'I know that. It is Sara Lopez who has long been a friend to my father and me, from the time I was a young child.'

'That is all very well, but take care.' He shuffled some papers on his desk. 'I will send some reports with you to Sir Francis. In the meantime, I need you to tell Berden everything you can about these people from the Fair.'

'Are you sure I should not go with Nick?' I said, although the thought of a country ride on Hector was very appealing. 'I will be able to recognise them.'

'Aye, and they will be able to recognise *you*. I do not want them to know that we are watching them, which they would soon realise if they saw you following them.'

'Of course,' I said, 'you are right.'

I spent some time describing to Nick Berden everything I could remember about the puppeteers and the toy man.

'Unfortunately,' I said, 'I only saw two of the puppeteers. The others never came out from the back of the stage, where they manipulated the manikins. There was the woman and a dark man, swarthy, with thick eyebrows that almost met over his nose.'

I did my best to describe these two, while Berden listened intently. He was very good at his job. If anyone could find these two, he would.

'I saw a good deal more of the toy seller, Borecroft,' I said. Indeed, I found I could describe him in fair detail, not only his appearances but his speech and mannerisms.

'Do you think he is a London man?'

I considered. 'There might have been something northern in his speech,' I said, aware of it for the first time, 'but I would say that was left over from his childhood, perhaps. Not recent. I'd guess he has lived in London a long time.'

'I do not think there is any particular quarter in town for the shops of toy men,' he said. 'Not like some trades.'

I shook my head. 'Nay. They are often street vendors, aren't they? With a tray round their neck, hawking one kind of toy – bird whistles or spinning tops. Most would be too poor to have a regular shop. Yet this fellow was not poor. And he had an immense stock, every kind of toy and cheap musical instrument you can imagine.'

'Then if he has a shop it's likely in Cheapside.'

'Aye.'

'That's the place to start, then.'

He got up from his stool.

'I'll be off, Master Phelippes. I need to find the lads I'll take with me, and we have a few hours left of the day.'

Phelippes nodded. 'If you have anything to report tonight, come back. Otherwise be here by seven o' the clock tomorrow morning.'

He turned to me. 'You as well, Kit. I'll have these reports ready for you by then and you can make an early start for Barn Elms.'

Berden and I left together, Rikki following at our heels. When we reached the yard, the stable lad Harry greeted Rikki as an old friend.

'May I leave the dog with you tomorrow, Harry?' I said. 'I've to ride over to Barn Elms early.'

'Of course, Dr Alvarez. And you'll need Hector saddled.'

'Aye, thank you.'

Berden and I parted at the gate. He headed towards the taverns around the docks, where no doubt he would pick up the men he needed, those nameless fellows who slipped in and out of Walsingham's service, but who knew the streets of London better than any City or crown official.

There was still some time to go before sunset, so I decided to return to William Baker's shop and see how my patient fared. I called Rikki, fastened his lead, and we set off.

On the whole, Adam Batecorte was better than I had expected. Although he still favoured his twisted ankle it was clearly not as troublesome as it had been earlier, and the sword slashes across his back looked no worse, but the great gash in the side of his head was still oozing blood mixed with some yellowish puss. As always I carried with me my physician's satchel, though its contents had not been replenished since my return to England. I had several of the things I needed to make a drying salve to hasten the healing of the wound, but I sent young Will to a nearby apothecary to fetch fresh woundwort and powdered lavender. From Mistress Liza I borrowed a pestle and mortar, and also honey, which is sovereign for healing.

When I had dressed the injury again, I decided to leave off the bandage.

'We will let the air reach it,' I said to Adam, sitting down across the kitchen table from him, and gratefully accepting a wooden cup of ale and a slice of seed cake from Liza.

'The air as well as the salve will help to dry it,' I explained, 'but you must be careful not to knock it, or allow any dirt in it. Leave off your cap.'

He nodded. 'It is feeling better already, Dr Alvarez.'

I doubted it, but I smiled anyway and took a large bite of my cake. Mistress Liza, it seemed, was a good cook. William had done well for himself. Both he and Liza had returned to the shop, where several customers had come in for fittings. Rikki settled down under the table with a bone Liza had found for him.

'Adam,' I said, 'there was an Italian puppet show at the Fair. Did you happen to see it?'

'Aye, but I had no chinks for a ticket.' He smiled grimly. 'Even if I had, I would have spent them on food, not on such foolery.'

'It was not exactly foolery.' I studied him seriously. I did not know him well, but everything I did know inclined me to trust him. 'Their performance was more than a little subversive, treasonous even.'

I saw that I had caught his interest.

'Papists, were they?'

'Aye. Certainly.'

'But not those ill begotten Spaniards.'

'Nay. Italians.'

'The Pope lives in Italy,' he said, 'like a spider at the centre of his web.'

'He does.'

He looked at me shrewdly. 'Another of these papist plots against the Queen, are you saying?'

'It may be. Certainly some of the performance was intended to encourage any Catholics in the audience to rebellious thoughts. But there were other strands to the story. It attacked the all leaders of the Portuguese expedition, and Lord Burghley.' I hesitated. How far should I go? 'And it defamed the Queen herself.'

He gave a low whistle and looked worried. 'Dangerous, then.'

'Aye. Dangerous indeed. There is something else.' I sipped my ale, and made up my mind to tell him everything, or almost everything. 'At the first performance, on the first day of the Fair, there was a mixed audience – families, groups of friends, but also a number of your fellow soldiers. Clearly they had coin enough to buy tickets.'

He looked surprised, but said nothing.

'There was also an evening performance. I was not there, that first day, so I have no idea who was in the audience.'

He nodded. He was listening intently now.

'I was worried by what I had seen, so I reported it to Master Phelippes in Walsingham's office.' At his look of astonishment, I realised he knew nothing of this side of my work. No need to go into great detail.

'As well as being a physician,' I explained, 'I sometimes work for Sir Francis as a code-breaker and translator. Master Phelippes was concerned at what I told him, and asked me to return and keep an eye on the Italians, together with another man from the service, Arthur Gregory.' I decided not to mention our search for Poley.

'And you saw more of the soldiers?'

'Aye. A large number at the first performance yesterday. In the evening, there was no performance. It was a meeting, rather, and all those who came were soldiers, together with a few gentlemen. And this morning, every trace of the puppeteers was gone.'

He shook his head. 'I do not like the sound of that. Certainly not all of our fellow soldiers stayed the whole while at Finsbury Fields. Everyone claimed to be penniless, and on the way here from Plymouth we lived by begging and foraging. Mayhap some were not telling the truth.'

'Do you think,' I said, 'that some of them had another purpose in coming to London? Not just to ask for compensation for their recent service?'

He lowered his gaze to his clasped hands, which rested on the table in front of him. For a long time, he said nothing, but at last he looked up, his eyes troubled.

'If our grievances had been heard, if something could have been done for us, and for those poor women left widowed and the children left orphaned . . . then I think we would have gone peacefully home. I think so.'

I noticed that his hands were trembling.

'I heard whispers, Dr Alvarez. I tried to pay them no mind, but now, after what you have said . . . I thought it was just talk, you see. Boasting and bragging. Something to make those fellows feel important. We'd had our faces ground in the mud, like, and some men needed to fight back more than others.'

I felt my heart beginning to beat more quickly.

'Certainly you managed to find arms.' I said.

'Aye, I had nothing more than a cudgel I cut from a branch myself, but some managed bows and even swords or muskets. Where they got them, I don't know, and I didn't ask questions.'

'Were there traitors amongst you, do you think?' I asked. 'Anyone who might have dealings with foreigners, or the Catholic-trained English priests who are smuggled into the country?'

He shrugged. 'Who could know, in all that number? I lost most of my friends before ever we came home to Plymouth. You remember the lad with the snake bite?'

'Aye.'

'He was my cousin.'

'He died on our ship,' I said.

Died in my arms, I remembered sadly.

'Aye, well. By the time we gathered for the march to London, I was on my own. Some of the lads were fine, but I kept to myself most of the time. That didn't stop me hearing things.'

'What things?'

He clenched his hands more tightly together. 'There was talk of gunpowder.'

'Gunpowder!' I was shaking myself now.

'Aye. It seems some of the men who was on Drake's ships – you remember we was provisioned and supplied to attack the Azores – well, before they went ashore, they stole some gunpowder. Thought they could sell it, in the first place. Then they had other ideas.'

'What other ideas?' I whispered. This was it, I thought.

'There was talk of making a stir. Something to force Queen and Council to sit up and take notice of our claims. An almighty bang at the gates of the city. Some even wanted to use it to make fireworks.' He gave a derisive laugh. 'Only no one knew how.'

'I suppose that would be fairly harmless,' I said.

'Not in the hands of those fools, it wouldn't,' he said. 'Mark you, they would probably blow themselves to the moon before they created a show like the royal Firemaster.'

He leaned forward and lowered his voices. 'Those who prevailed, though, did not think the gunpowder should be used merely for show. They argued there was enough to blow up a house, or to blast the way into the warehouse where Drake has the treasure hidden.'

'Do we know where that is?' I said. 'I had not thought it was common knowledge.'

In truth, I did know, for it was one of the many bits of information I had picked up, working in Phelippes's office. He thought it was essential that I should know all the locations in London which might fall prey to traitors.

'I think they only guessed where it is,' he said. 'But that plan was rejected, for they thought the warehouse would be too sturdy and too well guarded, though there were some who clung to the idea, thinking to get their hands on the treasure for themselves.'

'If not the warehouse,' I said, 'what then?'

'Some argued for one thing, some for another. The Earl of Essex is very unpopular after his foolish prancing about in Portugal. He has made himself even more of a laughing stock with these pamphlets and poems that are circulating, claiming he performed a host of heroic deeds, when we know – all of us who was there – that he caused a lot of lads to drown by getting them to leap into deep water wearing full armour. And his claim of an attack against the Spanish was no more than throwing a spear against the gates of Lisbon and shouting foolhardy threats. The Spaniards did nothing but laugh at him. We all remember that.'

'So you think they may attack My Lord of Essex?'

'Nay, I do not think they believe it is worth the waste of the gunpowder. They do not have much, only what a few men managed to carry off, hidden about their persons.'

'Not Essex, then,' I said. 'Norreys?'

'I doubt they even thought of Norreys. He's one of us, you see, a soldier himself. He made some wrong decisions, but they don't forget how badly his brother was injured and like to die. Is he recovered, do you know?'

'Not fully, I believe, but much better for decent food and regular care.' In my mind I ran through all of the men mocked by the puppeteers. 'Not Essex. Not Norreys. I suppose they may hold a grudge against Dom Antonio and Ruy Lopez.'

182

'Another pair of old fools,' he said frankly. 'Nay, we know they had no say in the way matters was carried on or how the men was paid off. They despise them, but see no profit in attacking them.'

'That leaves Drake,' I said slowly, 'or . . . Her Majesty.'

I went cold even uttering the words. Just how far did this conspiracy go? For it was becoming clear that it was a conspiracy, if these men had gunpowder, and if they knew how to use it.

He shook his head. 'I don't think even the most foolish and most angry amongst them would dare touch the Queen. They know she is to have the largest share of the booty, but she provided the most ships and the largest stake of the money. Besides, they are loyal to her.'

'Even if they conspire with foreigners?'

'Not all of them would be willing to do that.'

'So we are left with Drake.'

'So it would seem.'

I studied him carefully. 'Are you sure of this, Adam?'

He shook his head. 'I was not privy to their discussions, Dr Alvarez. I am telling you only what I learned from whispers and rumours passing round the camp. I was never part of this inner group who hold the gunpowder.'

'But by now,' I said, with some relief, 'they must have been rounded up by the militia who attacked you at Finsbury Fields. They will surely have confiscated the gunpowder. We need no longer worry.'

'Oh, no!' he said, 'I'm sorry. I thought I had made it clear. This group of men – these conspirators, I suppose you would call them – they went off yesterday. I thought they was going into the City, but perhaps they was the men you saw meeting at the puppet show last night. They took the gunpowder with them. And they did not come back.'

'They were not there when you were attacked?'

'They was not.'

I drew a deep breath. Putting together what Adam had heard rumoured about the camp and what Arthur and I had seen last night, it seemed very probable that the two groups of men were one and the same. Had they been warned of the attack on the soldiers' camp? Was there a sympathiser on the Common Council or the Privy Council? Or perhaps amongst the captains of the London Trained Bands?

'I do not like the sound of this,' I said.

'Nor I.' He regarded me soberly. 'For a time I thought it was all talk, but there are a few gunners amongst them. They'll know how to handle gunpowder. And now it seems they are conspiring with these foreigners who are up to no good.'

'Dowgate,' I said.

'What?'

'I heard one of them mention Dowgate last night,' I said. 'Drake's London house is in Dowgate.'

'Do you think that's what they have decided? To attack his home? Blow it up with the gunpowder?'

'It may be only one possibility,' I said. 'We do not know that they will reason as we have done. I wonder how much gunpowder they have in their possession, and how much it needs to blow up a house.'

He shook his head. 'I know nothing of gunnery.'

'Nor I. It might make no more than a bang to frighten people, but it might bring the house down, the other houses nearby. Many could be killed. Or it could start a fire. This is a fearful business.' I began to bite my thumbnail. 'And where do the Italian puppeteers come in? That I do not understand. Yet they must be part of it.'

I realised there was another side to this I had not mentioned, and told him about Nicholas Borecroft. 'Did this toy seller ever come to the camp? Could you have seen him with any of these plotters?'

He shook his head. 'I never saw such a man, but you must understand – five hundred men and more – it was a large camp, spread out wherever we could find some shelter. This man might have come without my seeing him.'

So I was no nearer understanding how Borecroft fitted into this muddled picture, or whether he did at all.

We talked around and around the matter for some time, but made no further progress. At last I saw that Adam was growing tired and pale.

'You must rest,' I said abruptly. 'Forgive me, I have tired you out. I will take what I know to those who may be able to act to prevent what could be a disaster. Thank you for your help.'

'You will tell me what happens, Dr Alvarez?' He looked at me anxiously.

'I will tell you all I can, when I can. There may be matters I am not permitted to discuss.'

He nodded, but continued to look worried.

I bade him farewell and went through to the shop. Rikki followed me, gripping his bone firmly, unwilling to be parted from it. William was stitching and Liza was fitting new shoes on a tiny child. His mother looked up and beamed at me.

'His first shoes!' she said proudly.

I thanked William and Liza and took my leave, wondering how many small children like this little lad might be killed or injured if the renegade soldiers managed to blow up Drake's house. I remembered the ruins of Coruña town, shattered by cannon fire as much from their own garrison in the citadel as from our puny artillery. There had been innocent civilians killed then, children amongst them, and homes shattered beyond repair. If the soldiers had a large quantity of gunpowder, the centre of London could end by resembling the ruins of Coruña. Despite the warmth of early evening, I shivered. If Adam was right, these men meant to use their gunpowder, though if their target was Drake's home, I could not see how it would profit them. Revenge, I suppose. But it would not benefit them financially, however powerful a gesture it might make against the authorities of City and court. And it would cause terrible panic throughout London. People would believe it was a plot by the Spanish or the French, or even the start of an invasion. Last year, when we knew the Armada fleet was bound to come at some point, rumours were rife for weeks beforehand that the Spanish army had already landed.

Of course, Adam might be mistaken. The soldiers might have reverted to their original plan of breaking into Drake's warehouse. I knew where it was, an anonymous building close beside the Legal Quays, under the shadow of the Tower, near to where he unloaded the treasure from his freebooting forays against the Spanish treasure fleet returning from the New World. Near enough to the Tower that there were always guards about. It must itself be strongly guarded. Drake was wealthy enough to afford his own private troop of guards. And now I thought about it, I realised that, although its location would not be generally known, many men must have unloaded his ships and moved the goods into store there. All it would have needed was for the soldiers to bribe one of the men who worked on the docks. Although, if they hoped to gain access to the warehouse, they would have to bribe the guards as well.

So there were two potential targets – the Herbar in Dowgate and the warehouse near the Tower. What I had overheard, that word 'Dowgate', might have been part of a discussion, not a final decision. And in all this, how did the puppeteers come into it, as I was sure they must do?

My feet were taking me automatically back to Seething Lane. Rikki kept wanting to stop and settle down again to his bone, but I tugged at his lead and would not allow him to linger.

I must tell Phelippes what I had discovered. There could be real danger for Berden and the other men searching for the puppeteers, if the Italians were in company with the soldiers. I had no understanding of how gunpowder worked, though I had seen it used in both cannon and muskets. Could you somehow light it and throw it? Use it as a weapon, hand to hand? I shook my head impatiently. Phelippes might know.

Although it was vital not to keep this new knowledge to myself, somehow I must protect Adam. I would need to tell Phelippes that the information had been passed to me, but not how I had come by it. He would want to know. He would want every detail. But somehow I must keep Adam and his whereabouts secret. It would not be easy.

The stable yard was deserted when I arrived, for the lads must be at their supper in the kitchen, though as always there was a watchman by the gate. Sir Francis Walsingham's house was too important, and held too many state secrets, ever to be left unguarded. The watchman nodded me through, grinning at the bone Rikki was carrying. Phelippes might not care for a greasy bone in his office, but I was too preoccupied with turning over this new development to care whether he was annoyed.

'Kit!' Phelippes looked up from his table, a candle, burnt down to a stub casting shadows up over his face so that it was oddly distorted. 'I did not expect you until the morning.'

'Has Berden been back?' I asked, taking a fresh candle from the box near the fire and lighting it from the dying end. I wedged it into a candlestick from the mantelpiece and carried it over to Phelippes's table, then pulled a chair forward and sat down.

'Nay, there's been no word from him.'

He took off his glasses and rubbed his eyes. 'Have you seen those men?'

'I have other news,' I said grimly. 'The renegade soldiers, the real troublemakers, have not fled. They had already left Finsbury Fields. They are in London.'

I drew a deep breath. 'And they have gunpowder.'

Chapter Twelve

'Gunpowder!' Phelippes's voice rose, as mine had done, when Adam had told me. 'Where would they obtain gunpowder? And where did you come by this information?'

He looked at me searchingly, pushing his papers impatiently to one side.

'They got it in Plymouth, it seems,' I said. 'They stole it from one of Drake's ships in harbour, when they were turned ashore. When our fleet left Cascais, all our provisions and military supplies were loaded on to the ships which were to go with Drake to attack the Azores. That included all our remaining shot and powder. Drake, as you know, made no attempt at the Azores. While we were encamped outside Lisbon and he failed to come to our aid, he learned from the crew of the New World ship he had seized that there was no treasure at present stored on the Azores. He failed to pass the information on to Norreys or any of the other leaders.'

Phelippes was becoming impatient and opened his mouth to urge me on, but I forestalled him.

'So instead of heading out to sea, of course he returned directly to England. The stores of gunpowder were still on board. When the soldiers were turned ashore, some of the bolder fellows managed to steal a quantity of gunpowder and carry it off, meaning to sell it and eke out their pitiful pay. Then, it seems, another plan was hatched.'

'Where have you heard this? Phelippes said.

188

'Just a moment.' I raised my hand to fend off his questions, thinking, even as I spoke, how I could steer him away from Adam.

'I expect if compensation for the soldiers had been forthcoming, a share in the spoils of war, that would have been an end to any other plot and the gunpowder would have been sold off to sportsmen or the like. Somehow the men with the gunpowder were warned about the attack on the camp at Finsbury Fields – something which ought to be looked into, I think. As a result, they were well away when the attack came, taking the gunpowder with them. In fact, it seems likely that they were indeed the same men that Arthur and I saw last night at the puppeteers' tent.'

'Do you have any idea what they intend?'

For the moment Phelippes was diverted from asking about the source of my knowledge.

'It seems likely that they intend to use the gunpowder for an attack on one of two buildings. Their chief quarrel is with Drake. One of their targets is his house, the Herbar in Dowgate, as we suspected last night. The other is his warehouse in Tower Ward.'

'We did not know last night that they had gunpowder.'

'Nay, we did not.'

'Anyone may know where the Herbar is,' he said. 'It is no secret. The warehouse is not so easily found.'

'I thought of that. We speak of these men all the time as soldiers, but some of them are sailors. They will know men who work on the docks. It would not be too difficult to find one who can tell them the location of Drake's warehouse.'

He nodded. 'You are probably right. I can understand why they would attack the warehouse. They would hope to gain access to the booty stored there. After all, the original threat of the men who marched on the Fair was that they would seize goods to pay themselves.'

'Aye, the intention behind the whole march was to repair their fortunes.' I paused, for I knew that it annoyed Phelippes when I asserted so warmly that the men had been ill treated. 'Some of the men must be truly desperate. Desperate enough, or daring enough, even to attack a guarded warehouse. It would not be easy, even if they bribed the guards. And I doubt whether they have the means to bribe them lavishly enough for the guards to risk their future employment by Drake.'

'So the most likely target is the Herbar.'

'I would think so. Though perhaps we should not rule out the warehouse.'

'Even so.' He took off his spectacles and passed his hand over his face. 'I cannot understand what they would gain from attacking Drake's house. They would not be so foolish as to think he keeps his booty there, surely?'

'They may think – and they are probably right – that Drake surrounds himself in his home with fine objects.' I thought of the house in Wood Street. 'After all, it is not unusual for self-made men to covet the luxuries of the landed gentry and the aristocracy. Ruy Lopez's house is stuffed with tapestries and rugs and gold and silver plate. Mostly bought from Drake, or obtained through his own spice trade. I expect there are such objects in the Herbar. Plenty to satisfy this small group of men. This is not the whole makeshift army needing to be paid.'

'Aye,' he conceded, 'you may be right. But an attack on a warehouse, probably at night . . . there would be few people about. The Herbar, on the other hand, is in the middle of one of the busier parts of London. There are fine houses tightly packed, all around. Even at night there will be people passing by, lanterns and torches hung at doorways, the Watch patrolling.'

'That is what has been worrying me,' I said grimly. 'I know nothing about the uses of gunpowder, except what I have seen when cannon or muskets are fired, but then it is used in very small quantities, is it not? From what I have heard, these men intend to use a large amount to blow up a building from within, but how would they do that?'

'Mining.' Phelippes said.

'Mining? What do you mean?'

'I do not mean mining for iron or coal,' he said, an edge of irritation to his voice. I think he was becoming truly worried now. 'When a besieging army attacks a castle or a town, they dig a mine under the fortifications. Then they place gunpowder there and set it alight. It explodes. As it does in a musket or a cannon, but on a much larger scale.'

'Of course, I have heard of that, but not how it is done. Why are they not blown up themselves?'

'I think they use a long fuse. A piece of string or rope, like the wick in a candle or the slow match on a musket. That way they can set it alight, then retreat to safety before the fire reaches the gunpowder.'

I shuddered. 'If that is what they plan in the Dowgate, dozens of people will be killed.'

'Aye,' he said soberly. 'They will. So we must prevent it.'

He put his spectacles back on and looked at me sternly. 'Now, Kit, you had better tell me how you discovered this plot.'

I decided to tell him the truth as far as I could, without endangering Adam.

'One of the soldiers found me at the Fair. He knew me already, from the expedition. Knew I am a physician. He had been badly injured when the camp was attacked. I treated his injuries and he told me about the gunpowder and what he knew of the plans to use it.'

'Why did you not bring him here for questioning?' Phelippes was looking even more annoyed now.

'This man saved my life in Portugal,' I said steadily, looking him boldly in the eye. 'It was the least I could do, to physic his wounds. He is one of the moderate soldiers and has nothing to do with this other plot himself. He is well away now. To bring him here would have been to put him in danger, after the attack on the camp. In undeserved danger,' I added emphatically. 'We owe him thanks for alerting us to the plot. We should not then risk his own life.'

He looked suspiciously at me. Perhaps he did not quite trust my assertion that Adam was well away, but he decided to leave the matter, at least for now.

'What I do not understand,' I said, 'is how the Italian puppeteers come into this.'

He shook his head in bafflement. 'Nor I. Nick Berden has sent in one message by a lad he uses as a runner. They have asked questions at all the inns in the centre of London where entertainments of this sort are sometimes arranged, but none of the innkeepers knew anything of a troupe of foreign puppeteers. Or if they did, they were saying nothing. One cannot be sure of their loyalty.'

'They might be performing at a private house,' I suggested. 'They might even have left London.'

'In which case,' he said, 'they are not involved with these plotters. Or of course they may be lying low somewhere. There are a few Italians living and trading in London. They may be housed amongst their compatriots. Berden is to report to me at nightfall. Tomorrow I will have him search out the homes of Italians in London.'

'And tomorrow I am still to go to Barn Elms?' I said.

'Aye. It is all the more important now to tell Sir Francis what we know.'

For the first time he seemed to notice Rikki.

'What is that dog doing!'

'Oh, I am sorry,' I said with a laugh. 'I am afraid he has made somewhat of a mess!'

Rikki had finally managed to shatter the bone and there were greasy fragments scattered all over the rush matting before the hearth. I knelt down and started to pick them up.

'Leave it, leave it be, Kit,' Phelippes said irritably. 'As you go out, send one of the servants to deal with it. Go and eat and get some sleep. I want you here at dawn, remember.'

I called to Rikki. He wagged his tail cheerfully at Phelippes, who waved him away in dismissal, and we left for the walk back to Wood Street.

The Thames was a soft pink in the early morning light as the sun began to lift its head somewhere above the Kentish marshes. I was dressed for riding, with stout boots and a cloak over my doublet, for despite the first signs of a bright day there was something of a cold wind also blowing off those Kent marshes.

I had brought another bone for Rikki, to keep him occupied while he stayed in the stables, and my pockets were full of more of the small plum-red apples, as well as the ones I had never had the chance to give to Hector the previous day. We had an

192

understanding, that whenever I visited him, I always brought apples, which could cause problems in the spring, when the winter store was finished and the new season's crop not ripe. I had tried dried apple rings, but their leathery texture had not met with his approval.

After I had left Rikki with Harry, who promised that Hector would soon be saddled and ready for me, I made my way to Phelippes's office, where I could almost swear he had spent the night. He handed me a thick packet of papers, which I stowed in my satchel.

'When he sees these,' I said, 'Sir Francis will be chafing to come back to London.'

'I am hoping that he will see that all is in hand, so that there is no need for him to return until he is well again.'

'Have you written to him about the gunpowder?' I asked.

'Only briefly. I have said that you will give him all the details.' He gave me a stern look. '*All* the details, including the source of your information.'

'Has Berden reported anything further?'

'Nothing about the Italians,' he said. 'However, he did find the toy shop of Nicholas Borecroft. It was in Cheapside, as we suspected.'

'Was he there?'

'Nay, the shop was closed and locked. The neighbours had not seen him for a week or more.'

I shook my head. 'I cannot see what part he has to play in all this.'

'Perhaps none at all. Perhaps he told you the truth, when he said he had merely been asked to play for the performance.'

I shrugged. 'Perhaps, but there is something strange about the man.' I slung the strap of my satchel over my shoulder. 'I'll go my ways, then. You will want me to come back here after I have seen Sir Francis?'

'Of course. Try to persuade him to stay in the country and rest.'

I smiled. 'If Dr Nuñez cannot do so, I doubt whether I can.'

As promised, Harry had Hector ready saddled and was about to put on his bridle.

'Just a moment,' I said, taking two apples out of my pocket.

I ran my hand down Hector's dappled neck and he nuzzled into my shoulder, with his beautiful Arab head. Most people failed to notice its exquisite modelling, seeing only what most considered his ugly colouring – irregular patches of black, white and grey, with no satisfying symmetry to them. Now that I knew him so well, loving his intelligence and speed, I had even become fond of this odd colouring. They say you should never judge a man by his clothes nor a book by its binding. I knew that Hector should not be judged by the colour of his coat.

'Two apples only for now, my lad,' I said. 'Perhaps more when we reach Barn Elms and you may take your leisure.'

When the apples had been crunched up in a few bites, Harry put on Hector's bridle and led him over to the mounting block for me. The one disadvantage for me was Hector's size, for I needed help in mounting. My friend Andrew Joplyn, the trooper, had given me a few lessons in leaping on to a horse from the rear, as the troopers will do when need arises. I had not practised it enough to be sure of myself, though I had attempted it a few times in the long trek across Portugal on a docile army horse. I feared Hector would not like it, and I had no wish to be kicked.

Even at this early hour the Bridge was crowded, which slowed our progress, but once we were across the river we were able to move a little faster along the streets of Southwark. The bear and bull baiting would not begin for hours yet, and the Winchester geese would be fast asleep in their tawdry beds, since most of their clients came a-visiting in the late afternoon or after dark. There was plenty of activity about the brick works, dye works, and tanneries, however, and the usual strong smells filled the air, the reason they were forbidden space inside the city.

It was an odd place, Southwark, both part and not part of London. The writ of the Common Council did not run here. It was like a separate village, yet people constantly passed back and forth across the Bridge, uniting it with the City. There was something faintly exotic about it, with its entertainments and bawdy houses, its strange foreign faces glimpsed here and there amongst the crowds. If Sir Francis did manage to find me a place at St Thomas's here in Southwark, would I find that strange too? Still, a hospital is a hospital, wherever it may be. Surely it would not be so very different from St Bartholomew's.

At last we were free of the final straggling outposts of Southwark, which were mostly more of those evil smelling industries and the clusters of hovels around them where most of their workers lived. The road opened out, between rich farm land, dotted here and there with small woods and copses. I gave Hector his head and he broke into a canter, then his lovely smooth gallop. The sun was higher now, bright on the ripening fields of wheat and barley, and reflected from the deep green of summer leaves on the trees, like so many small looking glasses. It was wonderful to have this interlude of beauty after the dirt and danger and stress of London. I took off my cap and shoved it into the saddle bag beside my satchel, so that I could feel the wind in my hair. It had been trimmed when first I returned to London, but by now it had grown again.

I was enjoying the gallop, the fresh country air, the sun, and the wind so much that I nearly missed the turn to Barn Elms. It was an anonymous road – no finger post or milestone here, for Sir Francis liked to maintain his privacy – but I had been here before.

As we branched off to the right, I glanced over my shoulder. In the opposite direction led the road to Sir Damian Fitzgerald's house, where I had briefly masqueraded as a tutor to his son and daughter. I wondered whether he had ever discovered that I worked for his neighbour, Sir Francis. If so, it would surely have made him more cautious about sheltering Catholic priests as they passed through from the ports of the south coast on their way to London. I also wondered, with a suppressed laugh, whether his daughter, who had once (mistakenly) made a play for me, had found herself a suitor. I supposed these Catholic families must have a web of suitable marriage partners for their sons and daughters. Neither Her Majesty nor Sir Francis cared to persecute them if they kept their heads down, attended the English church (as the Fitzgeralds did), and did not engage in treasonous activity. The Fitzgeralds had passed secret letters from France in the past, but I believed they no longer did so. Then I frowned at the remembrance of seeing Poley ride up to the house in company with a priest. We had forgotten about Poley, Phelippes and I, when we had been discussing the possible targets of the plot last night.

I was soon within the purlieus of Sir Francis's manor of Barn Elms, its surrounding farm lands looking trim and well cared for. The hay had already been cut and sheep were grazing in the stubble. I passed a field of wheat where the plump heads looked ready for cutting. If the good weather lasted, the labourers would probably start on it soon. The manor itself lay bright and inviting in the sun, the old stone house clothed with creeper, the trim stable yard, the outbuildings with brew house, bakery, and dairy. I could hear the clang of hammer on iron, for Sir Francis employed his own blacksmith.

Hector lifted his head and whickered a greeting as we drew up before the door. He had been foaled in these stables and surely knew that he was coming home. A boy ran out from the stable yard as I dismounted and lifted my satchel from the saddle bag. He was followed by a tall man with greying hair, whom I recognised – Sir Francis's steward here at Barn Elms, responsible for the running of the entire manor for its owner.

'Master Goodrich,' I said, bowing, 'it is good to see you again.'

He returned my bow. 'And you, Dr Alvarez. We were not expecting you.' He eyed my bulging satchel warily as the boy led Hector away to the stables.

'Master Phelippes was anxious for me to come to see Sir Francis myself,' I said, already beginning to feel guilty at breaking into this peaceful haven. 'How is he?'

'A little better today. He has been out of bed since yesterday, sitting quietly downstairs.' A look of sadness passed over his face. 'I fear that he still has much pain, but he will not let it defeat him.'

'Nay,' I said. 'He is one of the bravest men I know. It is all very well to be courageous for a short time in battle. It takes a much greater courage to endure pain day after day and not give way to it. I promise I will try not to tire him.'

He gave a brief nod. 'Well said. As a physician, you will be familiar with such things.'

'Never with pain so resolutely defied,' I said with all my heart.

'He is sitting in my lady's small parlour,' Goodrich said. 'Even in this weather he needs a fire, for he feels cold.'

'Is the Lady Ursula here at Barn Elms?' I asked.

'She is. And like Dr Nuñez, she tries to persuade Sir Francis to rest, as we all do, but we might save our breath.' He smiled, again with that touch of sadness. 'Lady Frances is here as well, and little Elizabeth. The child amuses Sir Francis, but I fear she tires him too.'

'Master Phelippes felt I should come.' I found I was apologising again. 'There is fresh news that he thought should not be kept from Sir Francis. As it was I who got wind of it, he thought it best I should come and tell him myself.'

We walked together to the door and he held it open for me. As we stepped inside and my eyes adjusted to the softer light, I saw a familiar figure bustling toward us.

'Mistress Oldcastle!' I bowed. 'I hope I find you well?'

The housekeeper stopped and her mouth dropped open. 'Why, it is the lad who came here soaked to the skin! Four years ago, was it?'

'Three,' I said, amused.

'Dr Alvarez is a physician,' Goodrich said reprovingly, 'and a code-breaker for the master.'

'Well,' said Mistress Oldcastle, not one whit abashed, 'I remember how he had to borrow my slippers and fell asleep in front of the parlour fire. You have grown into a fine young man. You were little more than a child then.'

I found myself blushing and wondered how I could put a stop to these reminiscences, but Goodrich came to my rescue.

'Dr Alvarez has business with Sir Francis and does not want to overtire him, so I will show him to the parlour. The master is still in the parlour?'

'Aye, I have just taken him a brandy posset. My lady is with him.'

'This way, Dr Alvarez.' Goodrich neatly side stepped the housekeeper and steered me toward a door I recognised, for it was where I had been welcomed – and had indeed fallen asleep – on my earlier visit to the house.

When Goodrich knocked and opened the door, the first person I saw was Lady Ursula, sitting on a low chair with her embroidery. I had encountered her a few times at Seething Lane, but for the most part she kept to the family's part of the house, well away from the offices from which Walsingham directed his secret service of intelligencers. She rose from her seat and I bowed. She dropped a slight curtsey – I was not of sufficient status to merit a deep one. I saw at once that she looked seriously annoyed.

'Are you here from Master Phelippes, sir?' she said sharply. 'We have sent instructions that my lord was not to be disturbed with business. He has been far too unwell.'

'That is enough, dear heart.' It was Sir Francis's voice, though weaker than I had ever heard it before. He was hidden from me by the half-open door. 'Who is it?'

'The Portingall boy.' she snapped. It was insulting, but perhaps she could be forgiven. She looked tired and worried.

'Kit Alvarez? Let him come in. Do you give us some time alone, Ursula. I am sure he would not have come unless it was important.'

She swept out of the door, her skirts brushing against me.

'That is what I am afraid of,' she said loudly, then in a quieter voice to me, 'Do not you dare to tire him.'

Goodrich closed the door behind them both and I stepped forward to the fireplace, where Sir Francis was seated in a large chair, padded around with cushions. He wore a long house gown of dark blue velvet, trimmed with narrow bands of coney fur at neck and cuffs. He was ever a modest dresser. On his feet were felt slippers, such as the very elderly wear. I was shocked by the sight of him. Even in the short time since I had seen him last in London, he seemed to have aged ten years. I knew that he was only fifty seven, yet he looked older than my father had done before I went away, when he was himself sick and aging, and ten years Walsingham's senior. Sir Francis's skin had taken on the dry yellowish pallor of a man suffering from some internal illness. Even his cheeks seemed more hollow, his eyes more sunken after this short time.

'You must forgive me for not rising, Kit,' he said, with a slight smile.

'Please, Sir Francis, you must not move. It is good that you have been able to leave your bed.' You should not have done, I thought.

'Sit down, Kit, and tell me all that has been happening in London. Thomas will not have sent you without good reason.'

'He thought not,' I said. 'He has prepared detailed reports of everything, so that you may know that all is in good hands. He has been working very hard.' I gave him a smile as I laid Phelippes's bundle of papers on the small table at Sir Francis's side, next to a silver posset cup, half finished. 'Truly, I think he has been sleeping in the office.'

He gave a hoarse laugh. 'That is Thomas Phelippes, through and through. The man is a marvel, but he is a worrier. He cannot leave well alone.'

And there speaks another, I thought.

'However,' he said, sitting up a little, and speaking more strongly, 'these reports could have been sent by any messenger. That he has sent you argues something else. Do sit down, Kit.'

Rather nervously I took the chair on the opposite side of the fireplace, where Lady Ursula had been sitting, first removing my cloak and laying it over the back. I found the room too warm for a summer's day, and stuffy after my brisk ride through the countryside.

'You had better finish your posset, sir,' I said, 'or Mistress Oldcastle will be waiting outside, ready to skin me.'

He laughed, sounding better now, and took up a long-handled silver spoon.

'Very well, I will eat it while you talk. Why have you been sent, Kit?'

'You have heard about the armed soldiers from the Portuguese expedition marching on Bartholomew Fair?' I said. I was certain Phelippes would previously have sent word of that.

'Aye.'

'Well, yesterday, some further information came out. I was told it by one of the soldiers, one I knew from the expedition. It is so serious that Master Phelippes thought you should know of it and send us your orders.'

'It must be serious, then, for I believe my wife and Dr Nuñez have put the fear of God and Hell fire in him.'

'Aye, it is serious. It involves stolen gunpowder.'

As concisely as I could, I told him all I knew about the theft of the gunpowder and the likely target for its use, omitting only Adam's present whereabouts.

'Master Phelippes and I have talked round and round the matter, sir, and think they must mean to attack either Sir Francis Drake's house, the Herbar, in Dowgate, or his warehouse near the docks, in Tower Ward. Nicholas Berden and his men are searching everywhere for the Italians, but had found no trace of them by the time I left London.'

I hesitated. Phelippes and I had not discussed this further, but I thought I should share my suspicions with Walsingham. 'There is also Robert Poley.'

'Poley?' He looked surprised. 'Poley is in Paris. Or by now he may be in Rheims, with Gifford.'

I shook my head. 'He is here in London, Sir Francis. I have seen him with my own eyes.'

I recounted what I had seen at Bartholomew Fair, Poley and Borecroft sneaking together round to the back of the puppeteers' tent, those same puppeteers who were somehow involved with the soldiers who possessed gunpowder.

He finished the posset and set the cup down on the table, then leaned forward, his hands clasped in his lap.

'I trust your eyesight, Kit, and you know Poley well. However, I do know that you dislike him, mistrust him. Might that have coloured how you saw him? Are you quite sure he was on friendly terms with this Borecroft? Or that Borecroft himself is part of what appears to be a dangerous conspiracy?'

'I don't know,' I said miserably. It was humiliating for Sir Francis to think that my judgement was warped by my dislike of Poley, but perhaps he was right. 'Those two men may have nothing to do with the conspiracy, or even with the Italians. I just thought that I should tell you everything I saw and heard.'

'Quite right, Kit,' he said kindly. 'Never omit the smallest detail, for you never know what may prove important in the end. Knowledge is power. Never forget that.'

He laid his hand on the packet of Phelippes's papers. 'I must quickly skim through these. Will you pass my spectacles? There, on the mantel shelf. Thomas has such impossibly small handwriting.'

I got up and handed him the spectacles. 'I know. I never knew such a small hand. It must be because he is short sighted. He often has his nose almost on the paper when he writes, but his sharp sight for things that are close to is a great asset in a code-breaker.'

'It is.' He put on his spectacles and began untying the ribbon which held them together. 'While I read these, go and find Mistress Oldcastle. Tell her I have said she is to give you something to eat, for you young lads cannot go hungry, and I'll be bound you have eaten little today. Are you still at Ruy Lopez's house?'

'I am, Sir Francis. Sara Lopez has been very kind to me, for apart from Master Phelippes's work I am still without employment.'

'I have something to tell you about that.' He was already studying the first document. 'Come back when you have eaten and we will discuss it.'

I found my way to the back of the house and the kitchen quarters, where Mistress Oldcastle was giving instructions to the cook about the evening's dinner. He was a big man, head and shoulders taller than she and almost as broad as he was tall, but he listened submissively, with his head bent. I gave the housekeeper Sir Francis's message somewhat nervously, but she merely nodded briskly.

'I will bring you something in the family dining parlour. Do you remember where that is?'

I nodded, for I had eaten there before, with Sir Francis and Master Goodrich. Before I was out of the door I could hear

Mistress Oldcastle giving orders to the cook for my meal. I was glad to escape.

The food, which arrived swiftly, was excellent – a thick pea soup, with bread fresh from the oven and still warm, followed by a beef and kidney pie in a rich wine gravy. To finish, one of the kitchen maids brought in a lemon syllabub, one of those I had heard being ordered for the family dinner. I ate alone, but just as I finished, Master Goodrich looked in on me.

'Sir Francis would like to see you now, Dr Alvarez.' His face was creased with concern. 'He has been getting dressed.'

I jumped to my feet, horrified. 'He is not planning to return to London!'

'I fear so. Why else would he dress?'

'Lady Ursula will have me in chains for this,' I said. 'Master Phelippes only asked me to bring the papers and make my report. He is anxious for Sir Francis to rest and regain his health.'

'The master has been restive for the last two days,' Goodrich said. 'Do not blame yourself. If he has made up his mind to return to London, nothing anyone can say, not even Lady Ursula, will stop him.'

I returned to the small parlour full of apprehension. Whatever Goodrich said, if Sir Francis insisted on returning to London after my visit and then fell seriously ill again, everyone would blame me. I would blame myself.

When I knocked and entered the parlour, I found Sir Francis dressed in his usual black doublet and hose, with a tiny ruff, his clothes always making a discreet criticism of the flamboyant outfits worn by courtiers like the Earl of Essex. He was sitting at the large table in the window, writing swiftly. Phelippes's packet had been tied up again. I knew that Sir Francis read at great speed, but it was astonishing that he could have been through all those reports in such a short time. He looked better, his face not quite so pale and sallow, and his whole demeanour without its former lethargy.

'Ah, Kit.' He took off his spectacles and smiled, motioning with them to another chair beside the table. He handed me a sheet of paper.

'You will see that I have received an answer from the governors of St Thomas's Hospital. They will be able to offer you a post.'

My heart leapt in sudden delight. I had thought the news he had spoken of might perhaps be this, but even so I hardly dared hope. It might merely have been another spying mission for the service.

'One of their senior physicians is losing his eyesight and must retire.' He smiled. 'He is past eighty, so it is little wonder. He leaves in two weeks' time, so you may start then. You are to visit before that, to discuss your duties. As you are not a fellow of the Royal College of Physicians, they cannot, of course, pay you the same salary.' He smiled sardonically. 'I have told them they will be getting a bargain, paying you at an assistant's rate!'

'Oh, Sir Francis,' I said, 'I cannot thank you enough! I have missed practising my profession.'

'Aye, I know you would always rather be mixing potions and salving old men's sores than working in a quiet office at Seething Lane.' He laughed. 'But indulge us for the next two weeks. We must nip this conspiracy in the bud, before it can grow into a poisonous plant.'

'Of course, sir, I will do everything I can.'

'Now, I am coming back to London with you.' I opened my mouth to protest, but he silenced me with a gesture. 'I will rest again once I am at Seething Lane, but I want to be close at hand to see this business finished. I am in much better health today, well enough to ride that far. Nay, do not look so distressed. You are not to blame.'

I feared that I was, but it was not my place to contradict him.

After that, matters moved swiftly. I scanned the letter from St Thomas's while Sir Francis finished his writing. It merely said what he had already told me. I was to call on Master Ailmer, the deputy superintendant, some time in the next few days, then report for duty in two weeks. I folded up the letter and tucked it inside my doublet, then followed Sir Francis out to the front of the house. Lady Ursula was there, and also his daughter Frances, the widowed Lady Sidney.

She smiled at me and walked over to where I stood, hesitating at the foot of the steps and hoping I could avoid Lady Ursula.

'Good day to you, Kit.'

I bowed. 'Good day, Lady Frances. I fear your mother will blame me for this.'

I saw that she no longer wore mourning, but dressed like the pretty young woman she was, despite her early bereavement.

'Do not distress yourself. We knew that as soon as my father was out of bed he would be impatient to get back to work. We will follow you to London in the coach, so that my mother can keep him under some restraint.'

'He has promised to rest, once he is there.'

She laughed. 'I think we know what such promises are worth. Look, here is my poppet.'

The child Elizabeth was running toward us, escaping from the care of her nursemaid. At the same moment, one of the stable lads led Hector and another horse toward us. He had not seen little Elizabeth. I made a sudden dive and snatched the child up, away from the horses' hooves.

'Careful, my lady,' I said. 'You must always be careful and quiet when there are horses about.'

Lady Frances had gone quite white, but the child was not at all perturbed.

'I know you,' she said. 'You're called Kit. That's a funny name.'

'It is a name my friends call me, instead of my right name, my lady, which is Christoval. I know someone who is also called Elizabeth like you, but her friends call her Liza.'

'Can I be your friend, and call you Kit?'

'Of course you may, my lady, I should be honoured.'

'And will you call me Liza, if you are my friend?'

'I think you look more like an Elizabeth, my lady. It is a very fine name.'

'It's the Queen's name. She is my godmother.'

'She is indeed, so you should be very proud to share her name.'

Lady Frances lifted the child out of my arms.

'Thank God you were so quick, Kit,' she said. 'I could not have reached her in time.'

'The stable boy should be more careful.' I was shocked myself at how close it had come to disaster.

'He shall be whipped for it,' she said fiercely.

'Perhaps it would be better to make him understand that he should keep a lookout for children. Better than hurting him and making him resentful. He's not much more than a child himself.'

She gave me a curious look. 'You sound like Philip. He was ever kind-hearted.'

'He was a very fine man,' I said, 'and much mourned.'

She nodded and I saw that her eyes were full of tears. I knew that it had been a marriage of love, for she had known Sir Philip Sidney from earliest childhood. They had even been together through the terrors of the Massacre at Paris when they were young. The Queen had disapproved of the match, since Sidney was the nephew of her beloved Earl of Leicester. She had not considered the daughter of Sir Francis Walsingham good enough for him. I suspected the child had been named to appease her. Well, it was all in the past now.

'I must go, my lady,' I said. 'I hope you have a safe journey to London. It is a fine day for it.'

'Aye.' She sighed. 'I shall be sorry to exchange summer in the country for the stinks and sickness of London in the hot weather.'

The disgraced stable lad gave me a leg up on to Hector, and I slung my satchel into the saddlebag and buckled it. Sir Francis mounted with some difficulty from the mounting block, and I saw him wince with pain, but he did not cry out. I wonder what it cost him to strive so hard to conceal how much he suffered. He was giving orders to the men who were to ride with us, a couple of grooms and half a dozen armed men. Even in broad daylight on the open roads of Surrey, the person of Her Majesty's Principal Secretary was vulnerable to attack.

He reached down for a moment and laid his hand on Lady Ursula's shoulder, but I did not hear what he said to her. Then he gave the signal and we all rode forward, down the lane through the manor, past the fields, and on to the road for London.

There would be no wild gallop on the return journey. We rode at walking pace to spare Sir Francis as much jarring as possible. If I had had the authority of Dr Nuñez, I would have ordered him to travel in the coach with the ladies. That way he could have been supported by cushions against the painful jolts of the journey, but I did not have the authority. Indeed, he would probably not have heeded even Dr Nuñez, for he would have felt shamed to arrive in London like a sad old man. He was one of the mightiest men in the kingdom and the least sign of weakness visible to the world would have cost him, and the kingdom of England, dear.

So slow was our journey that I began to feel chilled before we came in sight of the fringes of Southwark, and I was glad of my cloak. What had seemed nothing but a slightly cool breeze in the morning had whipped up into a cold wind by the time we were crossing the Bridge, sending icy fingers through the narrow gaps between the houses. It is nearly autumn, I thought, shivering. Then I remembered something which brought a smile to my face as we turned from the Bridge towards Seething Lane.

Simon would be returning from the Low Countries in the autumn!

Chapter Thirteen

$\mathcal{I}$t was nearly nightfall by the time we reached Sir Francis's house. He dismounted painfully outside the front door, staggering a little before he was able to stand steadily on his feet. One of the grooms had taken his horse by the reins and reached out to support him, but Sir Francis's brushed him aside, though politely and with a smile. Then he turned and made his way slowly up the steps to the door, followed by one of his retainers carrying two weighty satchels of papers. Before he reached the top, his secretary Francis Mylles opened the door and bowed him inside.

I rode round to the stable yard and slid down from Hector's back. I was tired myself, more tired by the slow ride back to London than the wild gallop of the morning. I seemed to have been in the saddle for hours, as I suppose I had been, and my legs and back were stiff. Harry came to take Hector, followed by Rikki, who greeted me in his usual exuberant manner. Fortunately, Hector was well used to him by now and merely sidled away to one side, to avoid being jumped on. I thought, I really must train Rikki not to jump up, particularly around horses.

'Can I leave Rikki with you a little longer, Harry?' I said. 'I need to see Master Phelippes before I go home, in case he has work for me.'

'Certainly, Dr Alvarez. Me and Rikki, we're just going to share a helping of pottage.'

I grinned. 'You spoil him!'

I made my way slowly up the backstairs, more conscious than before of the ache in my calf muscles. I hoped Phelippes would not keep me too long, for I would be glad to be early abed today.

Mylles met me at the top of the stairs. 'You are to go along to Sir Francis's office, Kit. They are all in there.'

There was a fire burning cheerfully on the hearth in Sir Francis's office. Realising how chilled I was, I went to stand near it. Phelippes and Sir Francis were seated on cushioned chairs. Nicholas Berden was standing, like me, near the fire. He looked exhausted.

'Ah, Kit,' said Phelippes, 'so you could not prevent Sir Francis from returning to London.'

I did not know how to answer this, but Sir Francis laughed.

'Do not tease the boy, Thomas. He would have had me stay at Barn Elms, like everyone else, but I can rest as well here as there.'

He turned to me. 'Thomas has been bringing me up to date on what has happened today, but perhaps Nick can tell you.'

I turned to Berden, raising my eyebrows in query.

'We found Borecroft,' he said. 'Or we nearly did. He has been back to his shop in Cheapside, and one of my lads came running to tell me, but he was gone out the back way by the time I got there.'

'Unfortunate,' I said.

'Aye. Unfortunate.' He smiled grimly. 'It seems he has a reason to make himself scarce. Just minutes after I got there, court officers acting for his creditors arrived. It seems he is considerably in debt.'

'Oh?' I was surprised. 'He seemed very prosperous, for a toy seller. He had a massive stock in his stall at the Fair.'

'That's *why* he's in debt. Overstretched himself. I had a word with another neighbour I hadn't spoken to before, who knows him quite well. Says he's a cheery fellow, always believes everything will turn out all right. A fine musician. A grand fellow with the children. Bit of a child himself. Can't manage money. That shop of his, the rent is much too high for the amount of business he does. Toys, you see, they're cheap. Even if you sell a lot, you're not going to make a fortune.'

'I suppose not,' I said, beginning to see where this was leading.

'So this Borecroft, he has grand ideas. He's going to be the greatest toy man in London. He's going to be the *king* of toy men! His father was a toy man before him, went about the streets with a tray round his neck, like a pie seller, and that's how this Borecroft started, but it wasn't good enough for him. So he rents this big shop, buys in a huge stock, runs up all these debts. He does plenty of business, mind. The children all love him. Just not enough business to meet his expenses. Too much money going out, not enough coming in.'

'I see.' I was beginning to feel sorry for Borecroft. After all, apart from flirting outrageously with Anne and Sara, I did not honestly know any real harm of him. Perhaps indeed he had agreed to play for the puppeteers simply because he needed the money.

'There's more,' Phelippes said.

I turned to him. 'You think he may be involved after all?'

'While he has been making these enquiries, Nick has spoken to the men who came to try to collect the debts. There is a fellow called Ingram Frizer.'

He exchanged a glance with Sir Francis.

'He's sometimes been useful to us,' Phelippes went on. 'He is not a regular intelligencer, but he moves in certain circles . . . He has occasionally passed us bits of information, for a consideration.'

I knew what that meant. Beyond the regular group of the service's trusted agents, there was a mass of rogues and vagabonds who could prove valuable in certain circumstances.

'How does Frizer come into it?' I said.

'His main business is getting foolish young men to borrow money on what seem to be good terms, but there is always a trick to it, and they end up owing ten times, a hundred times, what they borrowed.'

'And Borecroft borrowed from him?'

'He did. Borrowed heavily.' Phelippes paused before delivering the clinching blow. 'Frizer is a friend, and perhaps a business associate, of Robert Poley.'

Realisation broke through. 'You mean, you think Poley might have been putting some kind of pressure on Borecroft?' I said. 'Forcing him to pay back his debt to this Ingram Frizer, by making threats?'

'Possibly.' Phelippes glanced at Sir Francis again. 'We all know that Robert Poley often goes his own way, and his behaviour is not always–' he searched for the right word, 'not always, shall we say, desirable? But he can get results, and he has often been of great use in the past.'

'But this time he is certainly not working for Sir Francis, or you would know of it.' I was growing tired of the way we were tiptoeing around the subject. 'If Poley is not working for us, he is either working for himself or for someone else. What sort of threat could he have made against Borecroft? A threat of violence? Or do you think it was something different – not a threat of violence but a promise that his debt would be cancelled if he did something? Something which links him to the puppeteers and the soldiers with the gunpowder?'

'The whole thing baffles me,' Berden said. 'What use would a toy man be to a group of papist troublemakers or to soldiers planning to blow up a building? It makes no sense.'

'We can do no more tonight,' Phelippes said. He stole another glance at Sir Francis who had begun to look very tired. 'I have men watching both the Herbar and Drake's warehouse. I doubt anyone can interfere with either building without our being able to stop them. You, Kit, and Nick, go your ways for now and come back here first thing tomorrow.' He turned again to Sir Francis. 'You, sir, you must be tired after that long ride, when you are only just got up from your bed. Lady Ursula will not take it kindly if I keep you up late.'

Sir Francis levered himself out of his chair with a groan.

'You are right, Thomas. The rest of the family will be here soon. I had better look as though I am on my way to bed.'

'I think I can hear them coming now,' I said, for there was a clattering of hooves and the sound of wheels heading towards the stable yard, which could be heard even from here.

Nick Berden and I went down the stairs together, meeting servants on the way up, carrying bundles and chests. The stable yard was brightly lit with lanterns hung on all the walls, while Harry and the other stable lads hurried about, unharnessing the horses from the coach and the luggage cart, and leading them into the stables. I collected Rikki from the tack room where he had been shut to be out of the way.

As Berden and I headed west across the city, I said, 'What do you think is really afoot, Nick?' He was a shrewd and experienced man. He was as likely as anyone to guess what was being planned, but he still looked baffled.

'It's like some terrible conundrum, Kit.' He laughed ruefully. 'A pack of Italian papist puppet masters with a scurrilous play. An English toy man who seems harmless but may be in debt to one of the greatest rogues in London. Oh, aye. I know all about Ingram Frizer and his little schemes. A troop of disaffected armed soldiers in possession of a pack of gunpowder – we don't know how much. And a tricky spy who is probably as two-faced as that Roman god – what is he called?'

'Janus,' I said.

'Aye, Janus. A tricky bastard of a double agent I've never liked and wouldn't trust if I had him chained to the wall and gagged.'

'So you don't like Poley either.' It was a relief to find that my opinion was so widely shared.

'I do not. But what is the meaning of it all?'

I stood stock still as we came to the Cheapside Great Conduit.

'My mathematics tutor, Master Harriot, had some training in the law. I remember him saying to me that in trying to solve a crime at law, you should always ask "cui bono". He was talking about something else at the time, but I think it applies here.'

Three drunken young gallants pushed past us, singing some rude ditty. Once they were gone, Berden said, 'What does that mean, "cui bono"?'

'Well, "to whose good", in other words, "who benefits". If these people, or some of them, plan to blow up a building, how do they benefit? We don't know for sure that it is the Herbar, but suppose it is.'

He rubbed his chin with a rasping sound. He had three or four days' growth of stubble. 'The soldiers will benefit if they can steal some valuable goods. And they will get revenge on Drake for treating them shabbily.'

'Aye. And the Italians will cause terror and death in the heart of London, perhaps as a first step in a Catholic attack.'

'But then we come back to Poley and Borecroft,' he said. 'What does Poley gain?'

'I think he will do anything for a large enough payment. And he may be a true papist sympathiser, not just a fake one. There have been suspicions about that in the past.'

'So he could be in league with the Italians?'

'Aye, or paid by them.'

'That still leaves Borecroft,' he said, shaking his head. 'What could they want with him?'

'If Poley has some hold over him, through Frizer,' I said, 'he might be forced to do something for them, but I cannot imagine what.'

'It makes my head ache,' he said. 'We'll get no further tonight, Kit. I go down toward the river here. I will see you tomorrow.'

'Aye,' I said. 'Perhaps if we sleep on it, we will wake with an answer. Goodnight, Nick.'

I gave a tug on Rikki's lead, for he had fallen asleep on the Conduit steps, and we set off on the last part of our way to Wood Street. I had grown cold while we stood talking. It was not yet September, but that east wind carried the threat of autumn. Remembering the wheat standing tall in Sir Francis's fields, I hoped the farmers would be able to gather the harvest safely in, for famine was never distant in the crowded streets of London, which must depend on the work of men in fields far away. How many of the thousands lost in the folly of the Portuguese expedition should have been working at the harvest in the coming weeks? How many villages would have to depend on the labour of women and old men to bring in the crops before winter fell upon us all? I shivered.

When I reached the Lopez house I ran up the stairs to my room and quickly changed my breeches and hose, for I knew there would be a strong smell of horse about them after my long ride. Coming downstairs again I met Camster.

'Good evening, Dr Alvarez,' he said. 'The master has ridden out to Eton to see Dom Antonio, and the mistress is about to dine in the small family dining parlour with the children. Will you join them?'

'Aye,' I said with a smile. 'I am home in time to dine for once.'

I much preferred the smaller room for intimate family meals. The grand dining hall, with its vast table of imported wood from the Indies, had always intimidated me when I had come to dine here with my father. Ruy liked to impress guests with his dinner parties, but he was having to tread carefully these days.

In the smaller room I found Sara and Anne with the younger children just sitting down to eat.

'Ah good, Kit,' Sara said. 'I fear you have had little time for proper meals these last few days.'

'I had a meal midday at Barn Elms,' I said, and watched with amusement as Anthony's mouth fell open.

'You have been all the way to Surrey and back today?' Anne asked.

'Aye, and all my muscles are aching.' I pulled out a chair and sat down. 'Ambrose has gone back to his grandfather, then?'

'They are very busy with a large shipment of long pepper,' Sara said, 'which must be sent out to customers in Oxford and York and Bristol, as well as London.'

'We all of us had but a short holiday, then,' I said, 'to visit the Fair.'

'You seem to have had much business at Seething Lane ever since,' Anne said. 'I think you did not like those puppeteers.' She gave me a shrewd look. She had a quick understanding, Anne Lopez.

'I did not,' I said, as one of the maid servants carried in a steaming tureen of soup and began to serve us. 'But I am afraid I may not speak of it.'

Anne nodded, but when the girl had gone, closing the door softly behind her, she said, 'May you speak of it now?'

'Better not. Perhaps later, when . . . when things are settled.'

'Anne, do not tease Kit,' Sara said, frowning.

'She is not teasing,' I said. 'After what we all saw at that puppet show, Anne is right to be concerned. Later I am sure I can speak of it.'

Phelippes had not, in fact, forbidden me to speak of the concerns arising from what had occurred at the Fair, but it was understood by all of us at Seething Lane, without discussion, that we must avoid panic in the City at all costs. If the story of the gunpowder and suspicious foreigners were to spread abroad, that would be the inevitable outcome.

The maid servant returned to clear away the soup and was followed by Camster bearing a heavy platter holding two roast ducks, which he carved and served. The maid brought fresh bread rolls and a dish of summer salad.

Once we were eating again, I said, 'I can tell you some news, though. Good news.'

They looked at me expectantly.

'Sir Francis has found me a place at St Thomas's hospital. I am to replace a full physician who is retiring. Though,' I laughed, 'I am only to receive an assistant's salary. I start in two weeks' time.'

'That is wonderful news, Kit,' Sara said warmly. 'I know how much you want to be practising medicine again.'

'And I shall no longer be in your debt,' I said. 'I shall be able to pay my way now.'

'You know that does not matter, Kit,' Sara scolded, shaking a finger at me and laughing.

Anthony, however, was frowning. 'It does not seem fair,' he objected. 'You should be paid properly for the work you do.'

'Ah, but you see,' I said, 'I have not studied in the Faculty of Medicine at Oxford or Cambridge, or even at a university abroad, like your father and mine. I cannot become a fellow of the Royal College of Physicians. So the governors of St Thomas's are quite within their rights to limit my salary.'

'I still do not think it is fair,' he muttered.

'Well, make sure you study hard and attend university,' I said, 'then you will have no problem.'

'You sound like my schoolmasters.'

'Aye, I do!' I laughed. 'Who am I to lecture you? When do you go back to Winchester?'

'In two weeks. When you will be starting at St Thomas's.'

'Then we shall both be working hard. Will you be glad to go back?'

He made a face. 'The food is terrible. I wouldn't feed it to a pig. And some of the masters are too ready with a birch switch. But I like the lessons, and I've made some good friends.'

'I wish I might have gone to school,' Anne said wistfully. 'My father would not permit me to attend one of the new schools for gentlewomen. He said it was a waste of time, educating women.'

'Many men think that,' I said.

'But you do not?'

I smiled secretly down at my plate. 'Nay, I do not think that. But I was educated by my father, as you have been educated by your mother, and you have had the run of an excellent library here.' I sighed. 'What I regret most, amongst the things that my father's creditors seized before I reached home, was the books. And my lute.'

'If I know you,' Sara said, 'once you are earning again, you will be buying books.'

'You know me too well!' I smiled at her.

The rest of the evening passed in pleasant conversation. I remembered that I had not shared out the gingerbread I had bought at the Fair the day I had gone there with Arthur Gregory, so I fetched it from my room, to the children's delight. Later, after the two little girls had been taken away to bed, I played a game of chess with Anthony, while Sara and Anne embroidered. I beat him, but only just. He was beginning to master the game. I went to bed contented, thinking how pleasant it was to be part of a family again, at least when Ruy was not about, with his frenetic efforts to carry out some scheme or other. Yet I could not remain here for ever. Once I had paid back all the money Sara had loaned me and I was drawing my salary at the hospital, I must

215

find somewhere else to live. In the meantime, however, I was glad to shut out the world of Seething Lane and all its dangers, and pretend to be a normal person in a normal household, despite my disguise. This was the nearest thing to a family I had left to me now.

The next morning I was back again at Seething Lane, this time having left Rikki with Anne, who said that she planned to spend time sitting in the little summer house in the garden, reading, and Rikki could stay with her.

'You rightly pointed out to me last night,' she said, 'that once we have the gift of reading, we can educate ourselves. As a woman, I do not need a professional training in medicine or church or law. Though I would have liked to attend school, if only to make friends amongst girls of my own age.'

She looked sad again, for I knew she led a very restricted life, as Ruy Lopez's daughter. Though neither Portuguese nor even truly Jewish herself, she was set somewhat apart. Like her mother, she attended the secret synagogue held at Dr Nuñez's house from time to time, as a kind of duty to her ancestry. However, she went more happily to the Christian church in her parish, St Alban's, one of London's most ancient and holy churches. Although we hardly ever discussed religion, I thought that, like Sara, she regarded herself as English and Christian, despite the nod to the faith of her father's and maternal grandfather's birth. Ruy himself was a baptised Christian, as I was. What a tangle we lived in! Neither fish nor fowl.

Back with Phelippes and Berden, I turned my mind to other matters. At least here I knew what I was and how I must conduct myself. I was accepted as a young man, clever at cracking codes, fluent in several languages, and, perhaps somewhat to my surprise, one of the trusted inner group closest about Sir Francis. I felt some pride in this trust they accorded me, though I wondered whether it would be shattered if they discovered that I had been deceiving them all these years, that I was in fact no young man but a girl. They must never find out, for I valued their friendship and their respect too much. I felt a brief stab of pity for Anne, despite her wealth, her family, and her comfortable home.

Unlike her, I could go out into the world and find both friends and respect. I could even gain self respect through my work, here and as a physician.

'Arthur!' I said, as he came out of his small office. 'I am glad to see you back. How does your wife fare? I was worried.'

'Much better now,' he said with a smile. 'Quite well again. She had some severe stomach pains and was frightened that she was losing the babe, as she has done twice before, but it was a false alarm. All is well again.'

'I am relieved to hear it,' I said. 'It was unfortunate we had to stay away so late that night at the Fair.'

'Oh, it did not begin until after that, in the early hours of the morning. But she is quite well now, and has her appetite back.'

It was decided that I should go out with Nick this time, even at the risk of being recognised by the puppeteers or the soldiers or Borecroft. The more time that passed without our discovering their whereabouts, the more worried Phelippes was growing. Sir Francis was keeping to his bed today, after the strain of yesterday's ride, but Phelippes was reporting to him every hour, and Sir Francis himself thought I should help in the hunt.

'It is a mystery to me,' Berden said, as we set off from the stable yard, 'where they can all be lying hid. One man – like Poley or Borecroft who both know London – can easily lose himself amongst the streets and alleys, but surely some of these soldiers are country lads. They cannot know the City. And the others, the puppeteers, are foreign. It must be even more difficult for them, because as soon as they open their mouths they will be known for Italians, yet for all my lads who have been searching the City from end to end, there is no word of them.'

'Phelippes may be right,' I said. 'They may have gone to ground amongst the Italian community living here.'

'If so, they have been very thorough about it. We've kept a watch on all the known Italian merchants and have seen nothing.'

We made our way down to Thames Street. We would walk the length of it to Blackfriars, where the Fleet runs into the Thames just beyond the City wall, then work our way back through some of the narrow alleyways leading off Thames Street.

At various points there were inns where Berden's men would leave information for him, if they should have found anything.

The cold wind of the day before had died away and summer heat had returned. I began to feel hot and sticky as we trudged along, past fishermen's huts and tottering houses leaning together like old men. Many had been extended upward and outward in defiance of City regulations and looked ready to fall on our heads. I expect in the last century this might have been a fashionable part of the City, where the wealthy could have homes close to the heart of London yet overlooking the Thames, with their own steps down to the river and a boathouse for a private wherry or, if they were rich enough, a barge.

Now the area was thoroughly run down and the wealthy had moved outside the City to the west, where a string of mansions reached from the Inns of Court to Westminster. The river was not so foul there and the air was fresher. The old houses here had been divided up into many smaller lodgings. In some, whole families would live in a single room. We were restricting our search to the City, for the moment at least. Later, it might be necessary to extend it to the west.

'How many soldiers will there be, in this renegade group?' Berden asked.

I shook my head. 'I do not know. The man who told me about the gunpowder did not say. Perhaps he did not know.' I hesitated. 'I have no real reason for thinking this, but I felt it was not many.'

It occurred to me that I could visit Adam again and discover whether he knew, but I could not do so while I was with Nick Berden. He would feel obliged to tell Phelippes, who might have Adam fetched in for questioning.

'If it is a large group,' Berden said, 'it is even more baffling that they can remain hidden.'

'It is.' I could think of nothing more to say. Like Berden and Phelippes, I could not understand how the soldiers and the Italians had managed to disappear.

After I while I said ruefully, 'I hope I have not started a false hare. What if the soldiers have decided to go home after all? And the Italians left the country? And Poley pursuing Borecroft simply because of some debt to this man Ingram Frizer? I shall look a fool then, shall I not? Especially since Sir Francis has left Barn Elms all because of this.'

'You had to report it,' Berden said firmly. 'And Arthur was also sure there was something afoot. And so did this soldier who knew about the gunpowder.'

'I hope you are right,' I said, and sighed.

It was a fruitless morning. By noon we were both hot and tired and we had found no trace of those we sought. Word left by Berden's men at three taverns was just as negative. By now we had worked our way up to Cheapside, and went into the Three Bells for a pint and a pasty. I was feeling even more discouraged. And poor Nick had been doing this all the previous day as well. He did not seem unduly worried by our lack of success, but I suppose he was accustomed to these long, tedious searches. I was too impatient for this kind of work.

The afternoon was nearly as tiresome, but towards the end we had two pieces of good fortune. One of Nick's lads met us in Eastcheap and said he had caught a glimpse of Poley amongst the crowds in Three Needle Street, though he had lost him again, because of the press of people. So that meant at least that Poley was still in London.

The other bit of luck occurred when we were on our way back to Seething Lane, footsore and rather discouraged. At the corner of Lombard Street and Gracechurch Street, Nick pointed out to me a large merchant's house next to a grand shop selling fine cloth.

'That is one of the Italian merchants we have been keeping an eye on,' he said, 'Giancarlo di Firenze. He is a man of standing, an honorary member of our own Drapers' Company, for he has lived here more than twenty years. Phelippes has told me to be wary of him, for he has powerful friends. The house is as strong as a fortress, and so is the shop.'

'He will have been at the Cloth Fair, then,' I said.

'Almost certainly.'

And at that moment we had our first real piece of good fortune. A woman came out of the shop carrying a bundle, probably a bolt of cloth, and went up the steps of the house, where she was immediately admitted. She was dressed in the modest grey gown and white apron of a servant, but even so I knew her at once.

'That is the woman!' I whispered to Nick, though there was no need to whisper, there in the middle of a busy street. 'The woman who was with the puppeteers. She spoke the voice for La Ruffiana,' I said, suddenly thinking of the implications. 'The outrage against Her Majesty.'

'Are you sure? She did not look much as you described her.'

'She is clad very differently, but I got a good look at her face. I am sure it is the same woman.'

'Well!' He looked pleased. 'Something definite at last. That house is large enough to hide all that troupe of Italians. Or they may be scattered about, but at least one is here. Though the woman may be the least important.'

'Do not be too sure.' I remembered the imperious way the woman had looked over the men gathering for the meeting at the tent, as Arthur and I watched from the platform. 'I think she may be one of the leaders. Though from all I have heard, Italian women are readier to use poison than gunpowder!'

'More difficult to administer in a strange city,' he said, with a grim laugh.

All this time we had been walking on toward Seething Lane, quickening our steps now we had something at last to report.

When Phelippes heard that we had seen the Italian woman, he sprang up excitedly.

'The Italians will surely all be in that house!' he said.

'Do you want to arrest them now?' Berden asked.

Phelippes began to pace about the room, running his hand through his hair.

'I will speak to Sir Francis, but I think not. Our purpose will be to arrest them all, not just the Italians. We want those soldiers with their gunpowder as well, otherwise they might go ahead on their own.'

'Though how these Italians can be involved in a plot to blow up a building,' I said, 'I cannot imagine. It makes no sense. Subversive puppets and plays, yes, but surely not gunpowder?'

'I am as puzzled as you about how the puppeteers fit in, Kit,' he said, 'but no doubt it will all become clear in the end. Nay, unless Sir Francis orders it, we will not make any arrests yet, but Nick, you must draw away your men watching the other Italian houses and double the guard on this one. Take care you are not seen, for Master di Firenze is a powerful and influential man. Indeed, I am surprised that he should be involved in this. He has a very secure place in our merchant community. Why would he risk that? He has much to lose.'

'People will risk much for religion,' I said. 'If it is his religion that moves him. When we were sent to the auto-da-fé, there were those who went to the fire rather than repudiate their religion.'

Both men looked at me, suddenly shocked. I believe they had long forgotten that I had faced the Inquisition as a child. There was an awkward silence. Then Arthur spoke from the door of his room. I had not realised he had been listening.

'Kit is right,' he said. 'If the plan is to blow up a building in the centre of London, fanatical papists will think it justified that innocent people should die, in the cause of striking out against what they see as a godless, heretical country. Do not forget that in the eyes of such men, we are damned anyway, for we have rejected the traditional church, denied the authority of the Pope. They hardly see us as fellow Christians at all.'

'And are we any better?' I said, emboldened by hearing Arthur speak out like this. 'We believe all Catholics are in league with the Devil. There are many in positions of power, in the court, on the Privy Council, who would burn them all.'

'There is indeed intolerance on both sides,' Phelippes said in a soothing voice, for Arthur and I had both spoken passionately. 'What we need to concentrate on now is catching these conspirators.'

'I will stay with my men tonight,' Berden said, 'and keep a watch on that house. We can see whether any of the soldiers call there. That will settle the matter for once and all, whether the two groups are working together.'

'I think I should come with you,' I said, trying to keep my voice steady and determined, though inwardly I was shaking. I did not want to spend the night in the streets, keeping watch on a house full of dangerous conspirators, who might have the gunpowder in their possession. However, I had worked with Berden before and felt I would be as safe with him as with anyone in the circumstances. And after all, I had my sword. I thought – with an inward laugh – how little use I would be if it came to using it.

'That is an excellent idea,' Berden said. 'If anyone can identify the soldiers, it is Kit. He has seen them already, and he spotted that woman, which I would never have done.'

'I could also identify them,' Arthur said, coming forward into the room. 'Kit is an excellent code-breaker, and I know he has carried out several missions for Sir Francis, but he is still very young. I can come in his stead.'

Arthur, I realised, was trying to protect me from a possible dangerous encounter.

'Nay,' I said firmly. 'You must go home to your wife, Arthur. There is no one to worry about me.' I had not meant it to come out bitter, but I am afraid it did. 'Besides, I have been trained in sword craft by Master Scannard at the Tower, one of England's finest swordsmen. You cannot use a sword, I think.'

'Kit is right,' Berden said. 'You must go home to your wife, though I hope that there will be no need for skill with the sword! We will be watchful and discreet.'

'It is decided, then,' Phelippes said. 'The two of you will keep watch with Nick's men, mainly to see who comes and goes, particularly if there is any sign of the soldiers. Or Poley or Borecroft, come to that,' he added thoughtfully. 'If one of the soldiers does appear, Nick, see that he is followed, but do not draw attention to yourselves. We want to know where they are hiding out.'

Berden nodded. 'I have a good man for such work. I'll have him primed and ready to follow any soldier Kit identifies.'

'Let us hope, having discovered where the Italians are, we can also locate the soldiers,' Phelippes said. 'Then we can arrest both groups at the same time, so they have no chance to warn each other.'

'If the plan is to break into Drake's home or his warehouse,' I said hesitantly.

'Aye, Kit?'

'Why have they not done so already? They have had the gunpowder for some time. The meeting with the puppeteers was several days ago. The Italians are now in the city. So are Poley and Borecroft, if they are indeed involved. For all we know, the soldiers are here too. Why have they not acted? What are they waiting for?'

'This has been worrying me too, Kit,' Phelippes said. 'As far as the warehouse is concerned, it is unlikely that any new goods will be stored there in the next few months. Drake's credit is somewhat low after the failure of the latest expedition. He will find it difficult to obtain backers for another voyage against the Spanish treasure ships until men forget this latest disaster. They will forget, of course.' He gave a thin-lipped smile. 'Where there is possible profit, men can have remarkably short memories. That is why so many fall prey to fraudsters.'

'So they might as well have attacked the warehouse already?' I said.

He nodded. 'However, I have come by one piece of information which may have some significance. A large party of Drake's family is due to arrive in London from Devon any time soon. You may not know this, but Drake has a great many brothers and sisters, and although he has no children of his own, there are also a great many nephews and nieces. The source of my information did not know the reason for the visit, but it is not hard to conjecture. No doubt some of these family members are hoping that he will use his influence to find them places at court or in the London guilds.'

'They have not chosen the best time,' Berden said with a grin. 'As you say, he is somewhat out of favour at the moment.'

'Perhaps they do not realise that, dazzled by the fact that a kinsman of lowly status like themselves has risen to such eminence – a knighthood and a fortune to cause envy in even the greatest of aristocrats.'

We agreed, then, that the arrival of this party from Devon might have something to do with the seeming delay on the part of the conspirators, but everything appeared so tenuous, based on a few sightings, a few scraps of information. However, it was true that much of the work of the service began with nothing more than this. The sight of the woman going into the Italian merchant's house had given me some hope that our ideas were not all woven from mist.

By the time it was full dark, Berden and I were stationed in the deep porch of a house across the road from the Italian merchant's home. He had placed men at strategic points around the house, including two outside the garden wall at the back of the property. Also with the two of us was a skinny nondescript man who was introduced to me as Tom Lewen. This was the fellow Berden believed could follow anyone without being observed. If I should see one of the soldiers I recognised coming out of the house, Lewen would follow him and discover where he was lodged. It was not our task to accost him or arrest him, merely to discover where the soldiers could be found.

There was no reason why we should be lucky twice in one day. We might stand here all night and see nothing, for there might not be any need for the two groups to communicate. Before we had left Seething Lane, however, Phelippes had received word from his informer that the party from Devon would reach London the day after next. If the conspirators were waiting for them to arrive, they might also have heard the same news and need to confer together. It was a good enough reason for us to keep watch. Perhaps the plan was not simply to break in and steal valuables. Perhaps they wanted to kill as many of Drake's family as possible. I had no love for Drake myself, but such wanton killing horrified me.

We heard the bells from the church of St Edmund the Martyr strike midnight and I was becoming very tired of this uneventful waiting. At first I had stood beside the other two, but an hour or so earlier I had sat down cross legged on the wooden boards of the porch. In fact my head was nodding forward on to my chest when Berden poked me sharply in the ribs. I looked where he was pointing. The house, which had been in darkness, now showed the flickering of candles from two downstairs windows, and like all the wealthy houses in this part of London, a large lantern was hung beside the door. By the light of the lantern, I saw a man mount the steps. Before he could raise his hand to knock, the door was opened. The newcomer had his back to me, so I could not see his face, but the man who opened the door was clear enough in the light from the lantern. It was the swarthy fellow I had seen at the puppet show. He drew the other man quickly inside and closed the door.

'I could not see the new man,' I whispered to Berden, 'but the other is one of the Italians from the Fair.'

He nodded. 'We'll watch till he comes out. You ready, Tom?'

'Aye.'

It was the only word I had heard him speak.

I do not know how long we waited, for the time seemed to crawl by, slow as a slug, but at last the door opened again, and I could see the face of the man leaving. I was standing now and gripped Berden's arm.

'Aye,' I breathed. 'It is one of the soldiers that Arthur and I saw.'

He nodded to Lewen, who slipped out of the porch and slid away into the shadows.

The soldier looked about him carefully, then flung the hood of his cloak over his head. He ran swiftly down the steps and strode along Gracechurch Street. A portion of the shadow followed after him. I do not know whether Berden was holding his breath, but I know that I was. At last we would know where the soldiers and the gunpowder were hidden away.

Then there was a burst of shouting from the direction in which both men had disappeared, from the sound of it surely more than two men. A scream rang out, echoing from the walls of the surrounding houses. Berden and I burst from the porch and ran in the direction of the noise. Berden had drawn his sword already. I struggled to free mine from the scabbard as I ran.

The street ahead was empty.

A groan sounded from an alley to our right. In the dark, we fell over Lewen. I reached out and felt for him and my hand came away sticky.

More of Berden's men were running up now. One began striking at his flint until he was able to light a stump of candle. In its light we could see Lewen sprawled in the filth of the alley, blood pouring from his side.

'Hold that closer,' I snapped. 'I'm a physician.'

I knelt down beside the injured man.

'We need to staunch the bleeding,' I said, cursing myself for having left my satchel behind in Phelippes office.

I looked up at the other men standing around. Berden had disappeared.

'Help me tear a strip off his shirt to use as a bandage.' I said.

Two of the men knelt on the other side of Lewen and between us we managed to rip off a portion of his shirt tail. I wrapped it tightly round his body and knotted it off.

'Carry him back to Seething Lane,' I said. 'As quickly as you can. I'll follow. Jesu, where is Berden?'

'Here.' He loomed up out of the dark. 'There must have been more of that soldier's fellows waiting for him here in the alley. When they saw Lewen, they went for him. Has he said anything?'

I shook my head. 'He's unconscious. He's already lost a lot of blood. I will need to see to him at once. We need to go back.'

We turned to follow the others.

'Damnation!' Berden said.

Chapter Fourteen

When Berden and I reached Sir Francis's house, the men had already carried Lewen up to Phelippes's office, where he was now lying on a flock mattress in front of the fire, probably the same mattress I had slept on the other night. Someone had stirred up the fire, which I was glad of, for I feared that Lewen might be chilled from shock and loss of blood.

The room was crowded with men, all staring down helplessly at Lewen, even Sir Francis, who must have been roused from his bed by the disturbance, and was sitting in one of the chairs, clad in his dark blue house gown and looking almost as pale as Lewen.

I fetched my satchel from where it hung on the back of my chair and knelt down beside the injured man. While we had been quartering the city earlier in the day, I had taken the opportunity to replace some of the simple medicines I normally carried with me, together with needles and thread and fresh bandages. It seemed I would need them sooner than I had expected.

The temporary bandage was already saturated with blood and more was seeping through it, staining the mattress. I asked two of Berden's men to raise Lewen's shoulders so that I could cut it away and peel back what was left of his shirt to reveal the wound. It was a deep thrust, probably from a dagger or worse, for it was wide enough to have been a sword.

'How bad is it?' Berden had knelt down beside me.

'Nasty. I will need water,' I said, without looking up. I heard Phelippes call for a servant. A bowl of water came quickly. The whole household must have been roused.

I tore off a clean end of the discarded bandage and used it to wipe away the blood and dirt from the wound. It had been filthy in the alley where he had lain. I hoped no noxious substance had already entered the wound. The blood was flowing a little less freely now. I probed gently around it, and nodded.

'He's had the luck of the Devil,' I said. 'The blade hit a rib. Otherwise it would have penetrated his lung. I will need to stitch this.'

One of the men holding Lewen's shoulders gulped and turned somewhat green. I took pity on him.

'You need not watch,' I said. 'Lay him down and turn him on his right side, so I can reach this better. Then I won't need your help any more.'

They did as I asked, then drew back. I glanced along my shoulder at Berden.

'I won't need your men any longer, unless you do.'

He shook his head. 'We were all too far away to see what happened. Back you go, lads. Keep a watch on that house and report any activity, but for Jesu's sake, keep out of sight!'

I heard the men leaving, but I was occupied in cutting lengths of thread and threading a suturing needle.

'Can I help?' Berden said.

'Just hold him steady for me. If he wakes, you will need to hold him down, for this will hurt.'

I began to put in the stitches as swiftly as possible. I had been nearly asleep before the soldier arrived at the Italian's house, but now I was as wide awake as if it were midday. Luckily the wound was fairly narrow, despite being deep, for Lewen began to stir as I put in the last stitch. I cut the thread, then salved the wound generously.

'I will need to bandage this now,' I said. 'Can you lift his upper body, so I can reach round his chest?'

By the time I was stitching the end of the bandage in place to hold it firm, Lewen's eyelids were flickering and he gave a sharp moan.

'I have some poppy syrup here to ease the pain,' I said. 'I need some wine to mix it in.'

A hand passed me a cup of strong red wine. It was Phelippes. Berden propped the man up against his shoulder and I held the cup to his lips. He drank thirstily, then we laid him back on the mattress. His eyes were open now.

'Can you tell us what happened, Tom?' Berden asked.

'I'm sorry, Master Berden,' the man whispered. 'I've never been caught like that before.'

'Not your fault, Tom. We should have reckoned there might be more of them hanging about, even if only one went to the house.'

'I've lost you the chance to find where they're lodging.'

The poor fellow seemed more concerned about that than about his injury.

'Don't worry about that, we'll find them. How many were waiting in the alley?'

'I couldn't rightly see. It was dark as the Devil's pit, sir. But I think there was five or six.'

I sat back on my heels. 'Then you were lucky to get away alive,' I said. 'No blame to you.'

'Is that the doctor?' His eyes were shut and his voice was growing weaker.

'Aye, and you're a lucky fellow,' I said. 'You'll be sore and weak for a while, but you'll heal. They just missed your lung.'

I hoped I spoke the truth. I had not liked the filth in that alley.

'Thanks, doctor,' he whispered.

'Get some rest now,' I said. 'I have given you something to ease the pain.'

He was already drifting into sleep. Berden and I got to our feet and I threw the soiled bandage on to the fire, where it flared suddenly, then crumbled.

'Probably poor Lewen's only shirt,' Berden said ruefully.

'We'll get him a new one.' It was Sir Francis who spoke. 'I do not often see what you and your men must endure, Nick. It is a salutary lesson for me. Thomas and I sit here in our safe offices and send you out against these dangerous men. I am ashamed that this fellow has been so badly injured in my service.'

I looked up from repacking my satchel. 'The best thing you can do for him is to keep him here till he is recovered. He should not be moved tonight. What I have given him will help him sleep. Let him rest there near the fire, with a couple of blankets over him. Tomorrow perhaps he can be moved to a bed in the servants' quarters. What he needs is rest and feeding up.' I had been shocked at the man's emaciated body when we had lifted his shirt to reveal the wound. 'Of course, he should have a new shirt as well. Better, he should have two, to change about, so he does not wear soiled linen near that wound while it heals.'

Walsingham looked at me with amusement. 'He shall have everything you order, doctor.'

I coloured, realising I had spoken to him as authoritatively as I would speak to the family of one of my pauper patients at St Bartholomew's, but before I could apologise, Sir Francis got to his feet, raising himself by pushing on the arms of the chair.

'We are very fortunate to have you with us, Kit,' he said softly. 'I think you saved that man's life tonight.'

When he was gone, Phelippes, Berden and I looked at each other. Berden sighed.

'I am sorry. We bungled that. I am afraid we have lost the chance of finding the soldiers' hiding place. They have been warned off now.'

'Do you think that they understood that Lewen was following them?' I asked. 'There was no reason they should think he was – well – official. He does not look it. They may have thought he was just a street pad or cutpurse.'

'That is one reason why he is generally so useful,' Berden said gloomily. 'Not this time, though.'

'I think Kit may be right,' Phelippes said. 'There would be no reason to connect your man with this office. Still, we must keep up the watch on that house, in case we have another opportunity. Now you'd both best be off. It will be morning soon.'

I shook my head. 'You go, Berden, you've hardly slept these last few days. If you don't mind, sir, I'll stay with my patient. I want to be here when he wakes.'

So I spent another night at the office, though this time I slept in a chair.

When I woke to the first light coming through the window behind Phelippes's desk, I found I was alone in the room with the injured man. I walked over and looked down at him. He was still lying on his right side and the bandage was only slightly stained with blood, but not seriously. I took it as a sign that the worst of the bleeding had stopped. He appeared to be sleeping normally, but I laid my hand carefully on his brow, not to wake him. There was no sign of a fever. The risk from the filth of the alley, however, could not be reckoned over yet. Still, we had brought him to warmth and care as swiftly as possible. I hoped that, despite his undernourished body, he was resilient, as the street lads of London often are. He could not be more than twenty, scarcely older than I was. I suspected he was one of those who had grown up in the gutters of the City, and who had survived by stealing and begging. Those who did reach adulthood made small men like Lewen, but tough, for all that. Falling in with Berden and proving of use to him must have given him some hope in life.

The door opened and Phelippes came in, followed by one of the men servants carrying a tray.

'How is the poor fellow this morning?' Phelippes asked.

'He has had a good night and the wound has stopped bleeding. As I said last night – or was it this morning? – what he needs now is rest and good food.'

'From what Berden has told me about this fellow before, this is probably the first time he has slept on a mattress. He lives in the streets.'

'I thought he had that look about him,' I said. 'Is that breakfast? I am starving!'

'Aye. I had them bring enough for three, but had we better let him sleep?'

'For the moment.'

I cleared a space on my table for the servant to lay out the food – hot porridge, fresh bread, butter, cheeses, sliced ham and hot spiced ale.

When he was gone, I grinned at Phelippes. 'The Walsingham family is fond of porridge, I believe.'

He wrinkled his nose. 'It is not my favourite food. Fare for invalids and children. Is there any honey?'

'Aye.' I pushed the pot towards him. 'You may smother it with this.'

We both pulled up chairs and tucked in. Despite his complaints, Phelippes ate his porridge. For myself, I had come to quite like the stuff since coming to England. When I was a half starved waif, Sara had fed me up on it. I was glad of the spiced ale too. There was a nip in the air this morning and the fire had died down, though the servant had thrown on a couple of logs before leaving us.

'What do you want me to do today?' I asked, after I had eaten several slices of ham and some of the bread (which was very good). 'Shall I go back with Nick to watch the Italian merchant's house?'

'Nay, there are enough there already, now that Nick has called in his other men. Besides, I don't want you there in daylight, in case you are recognised.'

'I understand.'

'I went to speak to Sir Francis before I sent for breakfast. He has suggested that this morning would be a good time for you to go to St Thomas's to report to the deputy superintendent, as you were requested to do.'

He looked at me critically.

'You had better go home and change first. You'll hardly be a credit to Sir Francis, looking like that.'

I had not thought about my clothes, but now, looking down at myself, I realised that I had knelt in the dirt of the alleyway and my hose were smeared with unnameable filth. There were bloodstains on the sleeves of my shirt and on the bottom edge of my doublet. Blood stains are the very devil to wash out, unless you deal with them quickly, as I knew all too well from long experience. Joan was always moaning at my father and me about them. I hoped there was a servant in the Lopez household who could deal with these. In the past Ruy's clothes must sometimes have been stained, though these days his doctoring consisted more of administering soothing potions and listening to his rich patients' worries, rather than the messy business of physicking wounds and injuries. It was probably years since anyone had vomited over him.

'Aye,' I said with a grin, 'I would not wish to give my new employers the wrong impression. Clean and smart, that's the look I must aim for.'

'To save time, Sir Francis says you should ride home and then over to Southwark. You may take that horse. Horace.'

'Hector,' I said automatically, rising to the bait as usual. 'I will just wait until Lewen wakes, then I'll go my ways.'

'You should be back here by the afternoon. We may know better what is happening by then.'

'If there is any sign of the soldiers around the merchant's house, it will mean they think that their encounter with Lewen was just some street attack.'

'Aye.' He rubbed his chin. Like Berden, he had developed a growth of stubble. 'I wonder whether they will go back to see if there is a body in the alley.'

'They might. They may be worrying about it.'

'It is curious,' he said, 'how often a criminal cannot keep away from the scene of some misdeed or crime.'

'Aye,' I said, 'and if they do come back, they could be followed again.'

'Much more difficult in the daylight.'

At that moment Lewen yawned, groaned, started to turn over, and yelped with pain. I went to see to him.

An hour later I was once again riding Hector over the Bridge to Southwark, feeling a good deal more nervous than when I was on my way to Barn Elms. I was freshly dressed from head to heel, and Sara had even found an old physician's gown and cap of Ruy's for me to wear. I swallowed my pride and wore them. Ruy might consider them old, but they seemed perfectly sound to me, being made of sturdy wool cloth of a very fine weave. Even when he had occupied a humble position at St Bartholomew's, as did my father later, he had dressed well. Now, of course, his physician's gown was of best black velvet, for he could hardly attend on such clients as the Queen, Dom Antonio and the Earl of Essex in anything of poorer quality. When in court, one must dress appropriately. Or so he told us.

St Thomas's hospital lay a little south of the Southwark end of the Bridge, and as I dismounted at the gatehouse, I recalled what I could of its history, in case I should be quizzed about it, expected to know where it was I would be working. Like St Bartholomew's, it was very ancient, originally part of a monastic foundation established to care for the sick and homeless poor. No one knew what its original name had been, but the monastery had been named for Thomas à Becket after he was canonised, and was run by an order of Augustinian monks and nuns. Some time in the last century, the Lord Mayor, Richard Whittington, had endowed a lying-in ward for unmarried mothers, an extraordinary idea at the time, and still remarkable, though given the proximity of the stews of Southwark, no doubt it was kept busy.

Then, when the monasteries were brought down by the Queen's father, this hospital, like Barts, was abandoned, and the poor of both London and Southwark were left to die uncared for in the gutter. A number of compassionate and wealthy citizens had tried to gain possession of both hospitals, but had been refused by Henry. His son, Edward, was more sympathetic and the hospitals were restored, with superintendents and governors, and local women replacing the nursing nuns. St Thomas's had, however, been rededicated to St Thomas the Apostle, since Becket's reputation for opposing the monarchy did not find favour with the Tudors.

I could see that St Thomas's was as busy as Barts, even in summer, and even in a year when we had been mostly spared the plague. There was a bustle of carts arriving with goods, servants and nursing sisters crossing the courtyard, and long lines of sick people making their way to a small door at one side, where I supposed the almoner must handle admissions. Some were able to walk, but others had been carried here on trestles by their friends. By and large, they looked even more threadbare and destitute than the poor folk who came to us at St Bartholomew's.

I managed to hail a groom, who took Hector in charge and pointed to the stables where I would find him when I had finished my business here. Only once had I been to St Thomas's before, that time my father and I had brought the last few convalescing sailors here, sailors we had been treating aboard ship at Deptford after the defeat of the Spanish Armada. As we had done then, I entered by the main door and looked about me, wondering where I would find the deputy superintendent. As at Barts, he would be the one responsible for the day-to-day organisation and running of the hospital. The role of superintendent was largely honorary, carrying a salary, which was useful for rewarding some friend of the governors. According to the letter Sir Francis had given me, the deputy's name was Roger Ailmer.

'Your pardon, mistress.' I accosted a large capable-seeming woman, who looked as though she might be one of those in charge of the sisters. 'I am looking for Master Ailmer.'

She sized me up quickly, taking note of my physician's robe and cap.

'This way, sir, I will take you to him myself.' She began walking briskly along a corridor and I followed. 'Would you be the new physician that's starting soon?'

'I am.' I bowed. 'Dr Christoval Alvarez.'

She dropped a brief businesslike curtsey. 'I am Mistress Alice Maynard, in charge of the women's wards.' She gave me a sharp look. 'We have a great many women patients, sir. Are you accustomed to treating women?'

'Indeed,' I said seriously. 'We had women patients also at St Bartholomew's. We arranged a separate lying-in ward for the women there.'

'Ah, but it is a new notion for you. *We* have had a fine lying-in ward for a hundred and seventy years.'

'Aye, I know. Endowed by Richard Whittington. He also paid for repairs to St Bartholomew's. By all accounts, he was a very good man.'

She rewarded me with a smile, as if I had passed some test.

'Here we are, Dr Alvarez. This is Superintendent Ailmer's office.'

She knocked on the door, then opened it. 'The new physician to see you, Superintendent.'

She stood aside for me to enter. I suppressed a smile. It seemed Ailmer had dispensed with the 'deputy' in front of his title. That seemed fair enough to me. It was he who did all the work, not the gentleman who could rightfully lay claim to the title.

'Ah, Master Alvarez.' He looked at me over his reading spectacles, but did not rise from his seat behind an imposing desk. 'Thank you, Mistress Maynard.'

As she closed the door behind her, he motioned me to a chair, then took off his spectacles and looked at me more carefully. He was a man of middle years, with a somewhat choleric countenance. I could not decide whether he was the type to be jovial, or one with a quick temper. I would need to watch my step.

'You are very young.'

There was no answer to that, so I merely bowed my head slightly. After last night, I did not feel very young.

'Some relative of Sir Francis, are you? Some place-seeker?'

'Nay, Master Ailmer.'

I was not going to give him his title if he did not give me mine. 'I am no relative of Sir Francis, though I have worked for him as a code-breaker for more than three years, in the service of the State.' No harm in mentioning that. He looked like a man who would take note.

'In addition I have worked at St Bartholomew's hospital for nearly six years, in all the wards and all types of physic. Earlier this year I served as a physician in Sir John Norreys's expedition to Portugal.'

'Lost your position at Barts, haven't you?'

I gritted my teeth, but kept my temper. 'I worked as assistant to my father, Dr Baltasar Alvarez, who was formerly the senior professor of medicine at the University of Coimbra.'

'Aye. I thought from the name you must be a Portingall.'

I ignored this gibe. 'When the expedition returned, I found that my father had died in my absence and the hospital had appointed a replacement, who brought his own assistant with him. However, I believe that the governors of St Bartholomew's will speak to my capabilities.'

'Aye, well, Sir Francis enclosed their recommendation with his letter.' He shuffled the papers on his desk, put his spectacles on again and studied one of them.

'Highly recommended! Well, we shall see. You understand that although the place that is coming vacant is that of a full physician, you will only be paid as an assistant. You do not possess a medical degree and are not a fellow of the Royal College of Physicians.'

'I understand.'

'We will be losing a much loved and highly respected physician, who has served here for many years, Dr Colet. Sadly, age is taking its toll of his eyesight and he fears he can no longer practice. His place here will be a difficult one to fill.'

'I will do my best, Superintendent.' No harm in giving the man his chosen title. I felt he was softening toward me.

'I am glad to hear it.' He stood up and offered me his hand, even smiling at last. 'Report for duty on the twelfth day of September. Come to me here and I will instruct you on which wards you will be covering.'

'Thank you, sir.'

I bowed myself out and hurried along the corridor before I let out my breath in a long gasp. I must have been holding it. The encounter with Ailmer had not been quite what I expected, but I felt I had weathered it. The atmosphere here seemed more formal than the relaxed mood of Barts, but perhaps that was because the deputy superintendent at my old hospital handled the business side of Barts, while having few encounters with the medical staff. I suspected Ailmer was the sort of man who would patrol the wards, sticking his finger into every pie. Well, I had wanted this position, and now I had got it.

Hector and I made our way quite slowly back to the Bridge and over it, through the midday crowds. I noticed a man selling toys from a tray round his neck, painted wooden monkeys which by some manoeuvre could be made to climb a stick. It was not Nicholas Borecroft. I wondered where he was now. I had begun to feel quite sorry for the man, who seemed merely a little misguided in his ambitions. After all, many men started in

London with little and made their fortunes, even becoming an alderman or Lord Mayor. Look at Whittington. They even sang rhymes about him to children. Unlike many rich men, Whittington had not neglected the poor, but had worked to improve the conditions of Londoners, during his life and after his death, through his bequests. You could hardly blame Borecroft for wanting to rise in life. These were the times of new men, self-made men, like Ruy. Even Sir Francis and Lord Burghley came from quite modest families. A few generations back, the Earl of Essex's family, the Devereux, had been yeoman farmers in Herefordshire.

Of course Borecroft was a fool to have got himself into debt to a man like this Ingram Frizer that Phelippes had spoken about. And Poley was somehow involved with Frizer. I could imagine that Poley might well have found gullible marks for Frizer, as a card sharper's cronies will do. Poley could be a charming companion when he chose to be, as he had been with poor Anthony Babington. He would charm naïve young men, persuade them into spending more than they should, then suggest Frizer as a source for loans. Once Frizer secured them, they would be wrapped in his sticky web like flies preserved for a spider's dinner. I shuddered.

The other side of Poley was his utter ruthlessness, which I had experienced myself. If he could get a hold over you, he would exploit it for all it was worth. Not so different from Frizer. No wonder they worked together. But why did Borecroft appear to be implicated in this conspiracy?

Back at Seething Lane I learned that Sir Francis was out of bed again, so I went first to his office to report on my meeting with Deputy Superintendent Ailmer. I summarised our conversation briefly.

'He was trying to justify paying you the lower salary,' Sir Francis suggested, when he heard of the cutting things Ailmer had said.

'There was no need for it. I was prepared to accept those terms. What options do I have?'

'You know, Kit, the Royal College will sometimes accept fellows under certain special conditions. We will need to look into it.'

I stared at him in surprise, though I remembered that he had once mentioned this before. 'I thought one must have a degree in medicine,' I said. 'They are even reluctant to accept degrees from foreign universities. The fellows must vote on each individual case.'

'I'm not sure what the special conditions are, so do not get your hopes up! Now, you had better go along to Thomas and hear what the latest news is.'

There was indeed news in Phelippes office.

'The party from Devon spent last night some fifteen miles from London,' he said. 'They are expected to reach the Herbar this evening, if they are not delayed. However, there are women and children in the party, so they do not travel fast.'

He was looking tired and I wondered whether he had slept last night while I was dozing in the chair, or whether he had worked the night through.

'Surely we must take some kind of action,' I said. 'Or else warn them to stay at an inn instead of at the Herbar.'

I took off my gown and cap and hung them on a peg behind the door. Something suddenly struck me, which we had not discussed before.

'Where is Drake himself? I do not think we have mentioned him. Is he even in London?'

'He has ridden out to meet the family group. He spent last night at the same inn. And I agree. I am going to send a rider to warn them that something may be intended against the Herbar.'

'Do you think Drake will listen?'

I knew that Drake did not indulge in such foolhardy heroics as the Earl of Essex, but he was arrogant and full of pride. He would always believe he could take on any enemy and for the most part he won. But not always. I wondered whether Phelippes thought the same.

'He may not. We must–'

Before he could finish saying what we must do, we both heard running footsteps coming along the corridor from the backstairs and Berden burst into the room. He was out of breath and clutched at his side.

'What is it?' Phelippes jumped to his feet. 'Has something happened?'

'Nay, not yet,' Berden gasped, still hardly able to speak, 'but we know now!'

'Know what!' Phelippes was angry at this prevarication.

'Borecroft. Why they wanted Borecroft.'

Berden went to the side table and helped himself to a cup of wine, unasked. He gulped it down like water and poured himself another.

'Nick,' I said, 'Master Phelippes will have an apoplexy if you do not spit it out!'

Phelippes grinned, shook his head and sat down again.

'Very well, Nick,' Phelippes said. 'Tell us what you have found out.'

'Borecroft, it's an unusual name, isn't it?' Berden said, and I saw Phelippes grit his teeth, but he said nothing. Berden seized a stool and sat down.

'So I thought I would make some enquiries, see if I could get word of any other Borecrofts in London. While my lads have been watching the Herbar and the Italian's house, I've been seeking out all my sources, trying to discover whether there might be another Borecroft where our Borecroft was hiding out. I thought, if I can find him, I'll pull him in for questioning. He is the weak link in all this. He would probably be more afraid of you and Sir Francis than of those rats Frizer and Poley.'

'And did you find another Borecroft?' Phelippes asked, with what I thought was admirable patience.

'I did. At last. He has an older brother, one Oliver Borecroft. Not a toy man. Not a shop man or merchant at all. Guess what his occupation is?'

'Nick,' Phelippes said grimly, 'stop playing games with us.'

I had been watched Berden closely and I could see he was almost beside himself with glee. He could not bear not to savour his moment.

'Oliver Borecroft,' he said slowly, 'is a cook. A gentleman's cook. He is, in fact, the cook at the Herbar. Nicholas Borecroft is living with his brother at the Herbar.'

Phelippes and I simply gaped at him.

'You know that he is *living* at the Herbar?' I said at last.

He nodded. 'Oh, never fear. I did not walk up to the door and ask to see him. Once I discovered that his brother worked there, I made some discreet, very discreet, enquiries amongst the victuallers who supply the house, above all, of course, the kitchen. I was thinking then of how I might find an opportunity to speak to the cook, but quite by chance one of the butchers just happened to mention that the cook had his brother staying with him. He thought it a great joke. He knew the toy man was hiding from his creditors. 'Who would think of looking for him in the home of England's piratical sea captain?' was the way he put it.'

'But he is not merely hiding from his creditors,' Phelippes said slowly.

'Nay. Whenever the conspirators want to enter the house, all he has to do is open the door for them. In they walk, free as you please.'

'A Trojan horse,' I said quietly.

'Aye, exactly.' Berden nodded at me. 'A Trojan horse.'

'The attack could happen any time now.' Phelippes was on his feet again. 'It could happen tonight. Nick, will you go to Sir Francis and ask him if he will step along here? I will write to warn Drake's party, but it will be best if Sir Francis signs and seals it himself. They will be more likely to take heed, particularly Drake himself. Then we will need a fast and reliable messenger.'

'I'll see to it.'

Berden went out, having fully recovered his breath now, and Phelippes sat down to write his letter. I leaned back in my chair, aware that my heart was pounding, as if I too had been running. Everything was coming to a head now. I just hoped we could catch the conspirators before they carried out whatever was their plan.

It was only minutes before Sir Francis arrived to sign the letter and stamp the sealing wax with his insignia. One of the armed men who had accompanied us from Barn Elms came in, and Phelippes explained the route the Devon party was likely to take to London.

'If they are not on that road, you must search until you find them,' Sir Francis said. 'It may indeed be a matter of saving lives.'

The man took the letter, bowed, and ran off.

'And now?' Sir Francis said.

'Now we must be ready to forestall these villains,' Phelippes said. 'Berden, some of your men had better stay watching the Italian merchant's house, but I want you to move the rest to the Dowgate. Discreetly, mind. I not only want to stop this outrage but catch the men behind it. I will come myself, so I can be on hand.'

'I think I should come as well,' I said.

They all turned to me in surprise. I think they had forgotten I was there.

'You must remember the gunpowder,' I said. 'If it explodes, people will be hurt. I may be needed.'

Sir Francis nodded. 'Kit is right. There could be injuries, even if the gunpowder does not explode. Remember, we are dealing with men who are not only desperate, they are soldiers. However skilled Nick's men are at hunting out information and tracking people down, they are not trained in arms.'

'Some are skilled at fighting in the streets,' Berden said with a grim laugh, 'but you are right, Sir Francis, they are not accustomed to fighting soldiers.'

'It is too late to call out the militia,' Phelippes said. 'Besides, that would probably just drive them into cover. The London Trained Bands are not known for the subtlety of their manoeuvres.'

'It will be up to us then,' Nick said. 'Strategy against strength. We could do with that dog of your, Kit. He's a good fighter.'

I was thankful Rikki was not with me. He had taken a sword slash for me once, but he would have no chance against a musket.

'Very well.' Phelippes slung on his cloak and walked to the door. He looked absurd, his spectacles shining in the light of the sinking sun, his slightly stooped back more suited to a seat behind a desk than at the head of a ramshackle army of vagabonds.

Nick and I bowed to Sir Francis and followed him out of the door.

Chapter Fifteen

*B*erden, Phelippes and I made our way on foot to Dowgate. It was growing dark and the shops along the streets were ceasing business for the day, the apprentices putting up the shutters while their masters stood by, ready to lock up the premises securely for the night. A few street traders were still crying their wares, their voices hoarse at the end of the day, hoping to dispose of the last of their stock rather than carry it home till the morrow. Suddenly a man loomed up out of a dark alleyway, making us all start.

'Buy my fish, my fine fresh cockles, buy my oysters, fresh from the river!' he leered at us, waving a dead fish by its tail under Phelippes's nose

From the stench that surrounded him, his goods were far from fresh, and Phelippes backed away, dismissing him angrily with a wave.

The fishmonger spat on the ground at Phelippes's feet and went off in the direction of Billingsgate, cursing under his breath, as we turned into Candlewick Street.

'Who would eat oysters from the Thames!' I exclaimed. 'It is no more than an open sewer. A man who falls overboard into the Thames might as well jump into a plague pit.' I shuddered at the thought of that filthy stew of offal and dung closing over my head. 'You should never eat Thames oysters, not from near London. Kent oysters, from Whitstable or further away, are the only ones safe to eat.'

'Some poor folk,' Berden said, 'have no choice but to eat Thames fish and Thames oysters. Though even Kent oysters may turn bad.'

'True enough,' I said. 'I first met Robert Poley through a matter of bad oysters.' And that was where all of this had begun, I thought.

'The Thames grows more polluted every year,' Phelippes said. 'With the city drawing in more and more people, we shall soon drown in our own filth.'

'More of it should be buried,' I said, 'instead of dumping everything in the river. It is not only the soil from privies and chamber pots. The butchers from the Shambles throw their leavings in the river, whatever the stray dogs do not steal.'

'Middens and cesspits are become more valuable,' Berden said with a grin.

I stared at him. 'Valuable!'

'Aye, did you not know? They use the muck from cesspits in some way to make gunpowder.'

'Now there's a fine irony,' I said. 'Perhaps that is the answer to London's problems. Turn it into a mine for gunpowder.'

We all laughed nervously, for the strain of the forthcoming encounter was beginning to tell on us.

At last we reached Dowgate, but stopped short of the Herbar, at the corner where Berden's men had been told to meet us. Lined with substantial houses, the Dowgate was a prosperous street, with only occasional shops here and there. Those few to be seen were of some considerable quality – milliners and glovers, swordsmiths (but not their forges) and a few bake houses selling dainty pastries and suckets. Every house had a lantern hung before its door now that it was past dusk, though city regulations did not require it at this time of year. The householders here would want to discourage undesirable prowlers. There were several stout hitching posts for horses at intervals along the street, and near the Herbar a well-built stone horse trough. It seemed the inhabitants ensured excellent conditions for their own and their visitors' horses as well.

Berden deployed his men quietly, sending four of them down an alley running alongside the Herbar, so they could keep watch on the garden at the back of the house. The rest he placed along the Dowgate in both directions, both down towards Thames Street and the river, and up to Walbrook. We ourselves found a corner beside a jutting wing of a house directly opposite the front door of Drake's house.

'The kitchen door opens into that alleyway,' Berden murmured softly, pointing to where his men had disappeared into the dark. 'That is where the deliveries are made. Our fellows could gain entrance either there or here at the front.'

'Do you suppose they plan to wait till the party from Devon is here?' I said. 'If so, they will probably keep a watch for them, and if they do not come, delay any action until another day.'

'We don't know for sure that they mean to attack Drake's family,' Phelippes said reasonably. 'They may prefer to attack while the house is empty except for a few servants, grab what valuables they can, then flee.'

'They could have done that any day since the meeting at the Fair,' I objected.

Berden shook his head.

'Nicholas Borecroft only moved in here yesterday,' he said. 'Probably they were waiting for that, to make it easier for them to gain entrance.'

I nodded, but doubted whether he could see me in the dark. What he said made sense.

'But still,' I said, 'now that Nicholas Borecroft is lodging in the house with his brother – and if we are right, he is there as a Trojan horse, to let them in – what is the purpose of the gunpowder? There are too many strands to this plot. I am not sure we have made it out, even now.'

Phelippes grunted. 'Well, we shall have to wait and see.'

He shifted uncomfortably. He was even less at ease with this long wait than I was, but Berden seemed quite relaxed, managing to remain quiet and still, like a skilled hunter waiting for his prey.

Time stretched on. There were no more passersby, neither small tradesmen hawking their wares nor ordinary citizens on their way home to supper. One by one, the candles and lanterns inside the houses along the street began to go out as the inhabitants made their way to bed. In the Herbar there had been lights in two of the ground floor windows at the front when we arrived, and a light shone across the alleyway, probably from a window in the kitchen premises. Now one of the downstairs lights went out and we could see a light moving upwards – someone, probably one of the servants, climbing the stairs to the attic bedrooms.

Somewhere, a church clock struck eleven.

Then we all tensed, for the clatter of a horse's hooves suddenly rang out on the cobbles, approached rapidly from our left, coming up from Thames Street. We drew back further into the corner. It would not do for Sir Francis Walsingham's senior agent to be reported to the Watch for lurking in the street after dark.

The rider halted before the Herbar, threw his reins loosely over a hitching post, and ran up to the front door. There was nothing at all furtive about his approach. He banged on the door and called out. 'Message for the steward!'

The door was opened almost at once. We could see a lantern and just make out a tall man in Drake's livery holding it up. The rider handed over a letter, the men exchanged a few words, then the door was closed again. The rider mounted his horse and rode away up into the city.

'Of course,' Phelippes breathed softly. 'Drake will have sent word that he and his party will not be coming tonight. The steward and housekeeper were probably waiting up for them. Watch. We'll see them going to bed now.'

He was right. More lights moved upstairs and soon went out. Only the dim glow showing in the alleyway remained.

'I wonder how many servants there are in the house,' I said. 'If the plan is to blow the place up, do the conspirators not care that they are likely to die?'

Beside me, I felt Berden shrug. There was, of course, no answer to that.

I began to get cramp in my right calf and had to bend down and rub it. How long would we stay? Nothing at all might happen tonight. The same church clock struck midnight. I seemed to be hearing that sound every night lately.

Phelippes stirred again in discomfort. If the vigil was to be called off, it was Phelippes who would have to make the decision. I suspected he was reluctant to do so simply on the grounds that he was tired and bored. It would make him look weak, and that would do him no favours with the men he employed. However, nothing seemed to be happening. We could hardly stand here all night.

Perhaps we had read the signs quite wrongly. There might be no plan of attack, for all the scraps and rumours that we had were but straws in the wind, no real evidence. Or it might be that the target was the warehouse, not the Herbar. Nick still had two men watching the warehouse, but they had seen nothing unusual about the place in all the time they had been there. Or perhaps the target was the Herbar, but for a different night. Or perhaps the conspirators intended their gunpowder for someone or somewhere else altogether – Essex, or Goldsmiths Hall, or even the Queen herself! We might have our noses down on quite the wrong trail. Except that Borecroft had been seen with Poley and the puppeteers, the puppeteers had been seen with the soldiers who had the gunpowder, and now we knew that Borecroft was here. Surely we could not be mistaken? That trail must lead to the Herbar.

Phelippes was whispering to Berden. 'I think we will stay until two o' the clock. If nothing has happened by then, we will abandon this for now, just leaving a few of your men to keep watch. All is so quiet, I cannot believe anything is afoot tonight.'

By now my eyes had adjusted well to the dim light cast by the lanterns hanging from the house fronts and I saw Berden nod in agreement.

'Very well.'

I lifted my cramped leg and wriggled my toes. A little less than two hours to wait. I could manage that.

Then I saw that the faint loom of light in the alleyway had grown, and at the same time I heard the creak of a door. I grabbed Berden's arm and jerked my head in the direction of the light. He nodded. He had noticed it too. I held my breath. Was something happening at last, or was it just some servant going to visit a privy in the garden?

I thought at first that the light had gone dim again, then realised that it was blocked by the figure of a man, who was not heading to the garden but out into the street directly opposite us. He paused a moment, looking up and down Dowgate, then began to head up the street in the same direction as the messenger, walking fast at first, but quickly breaking into a kind of shambling run.

Berden was tense beside me.

'That is the cook,' he said. 'Oliver Borecroft. Where is he off to at this time of night? Meeting the conspirators? But why him, not his brother?'

A shape detached itself from the shadows and slipped after the cook. One of Berden's men.

'I could see the likeness to Nicholas Borecroft,' I said. 'This man is plumper, but his face is similar, and he has the same curly fair hair, though his hair is beginning to recede.'

'It seems something is toward after all,' Phelippes said, leaning forward eagerly. He had clearly forgotten his tiredness.

The light in the alley remained bright. The door must be open, adding to the light from the window. A candle or a lantern in the kitchen, probably. But it remained quiet. No one was stirring in the house, no one approached from outside.

'Has he gone to fetch the others?' Phelippes sounded impatient.

I suppose he hoped that the cook would bring the soldiers back with him now and they could be seized at last, after leading us such a dance.

'What will your man do?' I asked Berden.

'Keep the cook in sight, but not approach him. I've warned them all that we want to round the conspirators up, all of them. No point in stopping the cook. He'll just be the messenger boy.'

'An odd person to choose,' I said. 'He's too fat to run fast. But everything about this whole affair is odd.'

I thought I could hear some furtive noises from the house and strained my ears to hear better. There was the creak of rusty hinges, then a brief silence, then the sound of running footsteps

249

as Nicholas Borecroft suddenly burst from the alley, his hair tangled and his eyes wild. Berden put his fingers in between his lips and whistled loudly. As he rushed across the street, his men sprang out from their hiding places up and down Dowgate.

Phelippes and I followed Berden, though I was limping a little from the cramp in my leg. Berden had Nicholas Borecroft gripped firmly with his arm twisted up behind his back, and to my astonishment Borecroft was sobbing.

'I didn't want to do it!' he cried. 'I didn't want to do it!'

Berden was shaking him, but could get no more sense out of him. He slapped Borecroft across the face, but he only sobbed the louder.

'Do what, you turd!' Berden shouted, but Borecroft merely became more hysterical and incoherent.

All this noise was rousing the inhabitants of the neighbouring houses. Lights began to appear in upstairs rooms, windows were thrown open and dimly seen figures leaned out.

I was suddenly seized by a terrible notion. Borecroft had *already* done something. I was certain of it. His brother had fled, not because he was fetching others but because he wanted to get away from the house.

I pushed past Phelippes and Berden and all the men crowding round them and limped down the alley. Berden's four watchers coming up from the garden nearly collided with me, but I dodged them and reached the open door.

It led, as we had expected, directly into the kitchen. Everything seemed orderly within. There was a huge fireplace, empty now, with a complicated spit mechanism and hooks for stewpots. A row of shining pans, neatly arranged by size, hung on one wall. Shelves reached all the way up another wall, filled with every kind of fancy mould for elegant desserts, jars of expensive spices (all neatly labelled), bottles of essences, three sizes of mortars, and the most enormous block of sugar I had ever seen.

There were two doors opposite me. One stood half ajar and seemed to lead to a larder with stone shelves for keeping meat and fish cold. The other was closed and probably led to the main part of the house. Nothing seemed amiss.

Then I noticed that a hatch in the floor was open, the trap door laid back against the wall below the shelves. That must be where the sound of rusty hinges had come from. There were three candles lit on the huge scrubbed table of pale wood which stood in the middle of the room. I picked up one and carried it over to the hatch.

It was black as shipwright's pitch down there. A cellar of some sort, reached by a ladder. Then I saw that it was not entirely black. A tiny gleam like the eye of a cat winked in the darkness. My hands were shaking, but I must see what was down there. Whatever Borecroft had done, it must have something to do with opening the hatch.

I could still hear the shouting from the street, but as I climbed below the level of the floor, the sound was cut off. All I could hear now was a faint fizzing noise. Could there be a cat down here, hissing at me? But I had seen only one eye, not two. When I reached the floor, I raised my candle and looked around me. There were rows of barrels here. This would be where they kept the beer and ale. Against the far wall there were racks of bottles, French wine by their shape. No doubt part of Drake's loot. He was not above a little piracy against the French as well as the Spanish.

Nothing. It all seemed perfectly normal. I turned to climb back up the ladder, then my heart gave a sudden jerk. A face was looking up at me from the floor. My hand was now shaking so much I nearly dropped the candle, but as I brought its light nearer, I saw that it was not a human face, though I recognised it.

Scarramuccia leered up at me from the damp stones of the cellar.

Nearly life size, the puppet who had represented Drake in the show at the Fair was easily mistaken for a body in the half light. Yet he was not quite his same dapper self. Gone was his wooden sword, his strings had been cut off, and instead of his elegant shape he had now developed a huge belly, more grotesque even than Arlecchino's.

I stared at him. This at last was evidence of the connection between the puppeteers, Borecroft, and the Herbar. But why had

251

the puppet been tampered with like this? And above all, why was he here in the cellar of Drake's home?

My attention was caught again by the hissing sound. Perhaps a cat was trapped down here. He would be frightened by this figure, which looked human but was not. I turned slowly, so as not to scare the animal. There in the shadows was the tiny glow I had taken to be a cat's eye. I walked over to it. It was not a cat, and the hissing noise seemed to come from the same place. I bent to look at it closer, aware that the candle was nearly done and the last of the melted wax was running down over my fingers.

Lying at my feet was a piece of thin rope, the end of it burning with a small yellow light. Rope does not normally hiss when it burns. This rope must have been soaked in something. I followed it along with my eye, realising at the same time that it was burning quite fast. The rope led to Scarramuccia. It had been sewed to his back, like a mocking monkey's tale.

I gasped as I remembered the discussion I had had with Phelippes about gunpowder and the mining of castles. Scarramuccia was a mine, his belly stuffed with gunpowder, and there was no more than two feet of his fuse left. I yelped as the end of the candle fell over and landed on the floor. Suddenly I had nothing but the light coming from the hatch to see by, but even with that small amount I saw that the dying candle had hit the fuse and started another spark, this time barely a foot from the puppet.

As soon as the spark reached Scarramuccia, he would explode. I must get out of here. Then I remember the servants in their beds upstairs, the men in the street, the neighbours hanging out of their windows. I stamped on the burning fuse again and again, but I could not put it out. Whatever the fuse had been treated with, it would not go out that easily. There was only one thing to do. I grabbed the macabre figure around the chest and hoisted it over my shoulder. It was as heavy as a well grown child. I needed a hand to climb the ladder, but the puppet kept slipping and in the end I had to steady it with one hand and keep letting go of the ladder with the other to stop it sliding down my back.

The burning fuse was licking at my hand now, but I bit down on my lip and climbed through to the kitchen. The door was still open. No one had followed me inside. I could still hear the shouting from out in the street. I yelped with pain as the fuse burned into my hand, but I thought if I could clamp my hand around it, it might go out. You can snuff out a candle by pinching its wick, could I not do the same with this?

Sobbing with pain as I closed my left hand round the burning portion of the wick which was nearest to the puppet, I stumbled out of the door and along the alley.

'Out of the way,' I shouted, 'out of the way.' I pushed through the crowd, elbowing them away from me relentlessly.

I nearly fell into the horse trough, but managed somehow to heave Scarramuccia off my shoulder and fling him into the water. I held the figure down by the chest with both hands, its face staring up at me as if I were drowning a real man. Drake at the bottom of the ocean. At last I saw the two burning sections of the fuse fade and go out. The pain in my hand seemed to shoot right up my arm, so I kept it down in the water to cool, leaning against the edge of the trough, feeling sick.

Berden was beside me, staring down at the drowned puppet. A dirty cloud was rising from that awful paunch, staining the water. I snatched my hand out of the trough in horror, and looked blankly at the reddened and blistered skin.

'What in Jesu's name?' he said.

'The puppet,' I said. 'The gunpowder is in the puppet. I managed to reach it before the wick set it alight.'

Then I slid to the ground and the world went black.

I cannot have been unconscious long, for when I came to myself the men were still crowded round Nicholas Borecroft, whose sobs had turned into gasping hiccoughs. Phelippes was leaning over me in concern, his spectacles catching the light from the doorway of the nearest house. Beyond him Berden was hanging over the horse trough, trying to fish out Scarramuccia without soaking the sleeves of his doublet. He shouted to one of his men to bring a stick.

Outside the Herbar, I could hear Borecroft saying over and over again, 'Thank God! Thank God it didn't go off! I didn't want to do it. I didn't want to do it, but I had no choice.'

I sat there, feeling very tired and wishing dully that the pain in my hand would stop. The sleeves of my doublet and shirt were soaking wet up to my armpits. I wondered what they would do to Borecroft. I knew vaguely that I ought to get up and fetch my satchel, which I had dropped when Borecroft came running out of the house. I must salve my hand, though the best ingredients were probably to be found back in that kitchen.

'Kit?' Phelippes put his hand on my shoulder. Nervously, I thought. 'Are you all right? That was a brave thing you did.'

'The gunpowder,' I said muzzily. 'It won't explode now, will it?'

'Nay, it will not,' Berden said, holding up the dripping puppet. 'But we had better warn people not to let their horses drink from that trough until it has been drained.' He ran his free hand over his eyes. 'Jesu, Kit, I thought you had run mad, rushing out of the house carrying that puppet. What a monstrous thing.'

'And what a monstrous deed.' I could barely hear my own voice. I glanced over my shoulder at the Herbar. A scared group of servants was standing in front of it in their night shifts, some with cloaks, others barely decent.

'They likely owe their lives to you.' Berden jerked his head toward the servants.

I nodded vaguely. At the moment, I could hardly think. At least the explosion had been stopped.

'We must do something for that hand of yours,' Phelippes said. 'Tell us what is best to do?'

I tried to rouse myself, but I still did not trust my legs to hold me.

'If someone could look in that kitchen,' I said. 'I need white of egg beaten together with honey, then the whole pounded with a little grease – any animal grease will do. It will make a paste. It needs to be done quickly, to save the skin.'

I looked at my burnt and blistered palm clinically, as if it belonged to someone else, one of my patients. I tried to struggle to my feet, but Phelippes pressed down on my shoulder.

'Stay there,' he said. 'I will see to it.'

I wish I could have seen Phelippes in that immaculate kitchen. I do not imagine he had ever separated an egg in his life. It must have taken him several attempts. Too tired to tell him the amounts, or how to work the ingredients together, I continued to sit on the ground, leaning back against the trough with my eyes closed. As water began to soak through my breeches and hose, I realised I must have splashed a good deal of it on to the ground. I supported my left wrist in my sound right hand as if it were a fragile piece of glass. If my hand were to be permanently damaged, I would not be able to continue to practice as a physician.

Someone touched me lightly on the shoulder and I opened my eyes to see Phelippes anxiously holding out a fine porcelain bowl toward me. Something else Drake must have looted on one of his voyages and much too fine to use for mixing up a paste for burns. I hoped Phelippes had not broken anything.

'Will this do?' He held out the bowl to me.

'Thank you. Egg white, honey and grease?'

'Aye. I found some bacon grease, will that do?'

'Fine,' I said. Though I will not eat pig, I have no objection to its medical uses.

I balanced the bowl on my knees. The mixture looked as it should, so I scooped some up and spread it over my burned and blistered palm. Despite my best efforts, I gasped at the pain.

'Does it not soothe the burn?' Phelippes was frowning worriedly.

'It will in the end. Just touching it at the moment hurts. Thank you again. I do not think I could have done it myself, with only one hand.'

I got up slowly, still feeling somewhat dizzy.

'What is happening?' I asked. 'Has Borecroft told you anything of use?'

'Aye, he has told us where the soldiers are lying low. He can't talk fast enough. He's terrified of them and terrified of us. We'll have no trouble with him. Nick has sent one of his men to rouse the constables and another to fetch the militia. They will surround the house, and also the house of the merchant di Firenze. We should soon have them all in hold.'

'And what about Poley?'

He shook his head.

'Borecroft does not know what has become of Poley.'

I have only a confused recollection of the next few hours. Somehow we were back at Seething Lane and I was sitting by a hastily lit fire in Phelippes's office, shivering in my wet clothes. Phelippes had offered me a change, but I had, of necessity, refused. I could hardly strip in front of him.

'I will dry out by the fire.'

I remembered saying that.

Sir Francis came in, followed by a servant with a flagon of the rich red wine he obtained from France. Then a maid servant, hurriedly and untidily dressed, brought bread and cheese. I was glad of the wine, for it helped a little with the cold which had seized me, which I knew was the effect of shock. I did not think I could eat anything, but when Sir Francis himself set down a plate of bread and cheese beside me, I found I was hungry after all. When I had finished both wine and food, I looked around.

'Where is Nick?'

'Dealing with Borecroft,' Sir Francis said.

'I hope he will not deal too harshly with him,' I said. 'I think he was merely a tool of other people, forced to act by their hold over him.'

Phelippes looked grim. 'You can thank him for that burned hand of yours.'

'They do not need to deal harshly with him, to get him to talk,' Sir Francis said, with a short bark of laughter. 'The difficulty will be to stop him talking. When I looked in he was telling them everything he knew.'

'He's here?' I said. 'In this house?' I remembered that, back at the time of the Babington conspiracy, Walsingham had made arrangements to interrogate some of the men involved here at Seething Lane.

'Who is questioning him?'

'Berden and one of the sheriffs, Richard Saltenstall,' Phelippes said. 'I stayed for a while myself, but they have it in hand. Francis Mylles is acting as clerk. We want to keep the whole affair as quiet as possible. No need to start a panic.'

I wondered how it would be possible to keep it quiet, when all the inhabitants of Dowgate must know about the attempted explosion, even if they knew nothing else.

'Have the renegade soldiers been rounded up? And the Italians?'

'Aye, we have the soldiers held in Newgate,' Phelippes said. 'The Italians are more difficult.'

'But why? We already knew where they were.'

Sir Francis answered me. 'Giancarlo di Firenze is refusing to let the constables enter his property. He has powerful friends on the Common Council and has appealed for protection to the Italian ambassador. We may have trouble there, but I hope we may arrest them in the end.'

'Do you think that was all the gunpowder the soldiers had?' I asked. 'The gunpowder that was in the puppet? There is not any more that could still be used?'

'Berden and his men searched their lodging house very thoroughly,' Phelippes said. 'That seems to have been all of it.'

'It would have caused a terrible explosion,' Sir Francis said seriously, 'had you not prevented it. Many lives lost. Homes destroyed.'

'I wonder,' I said. 'Borecroft had placed it in a far corner of a stone built cellar. It would certainly have caused damage, but not nearly as much as it would have if he had left it in the middle of the house. I suspect he was trying to minimise the harm done. He was probably told to cause the maximum damage. Putting the puppet in the cellar was the only way he could do what he was forced to do, while hoping for the least hurt.'

'You may be right,' Sir Francis said.

'I hope that will be remembered when he is punished.'

Of course he would be punished. It was an act of terror and violence, even if it had been carried out unwillingly. I could not get out of my mind the contrast between the cheerful impish toy man of the Fair and the gibbering wreck in Dowgate. The thought that he might receive the savage sentence of being hanged, drawn and quartered sickened me.

'I have sent a message to the inn at Westminster where Drake's party have been spending the night,' Sir Francis said. 'I wanted him to have an accurate account of what happened before he reached home and heard some garbled version from the servants.'

Phelippes nodded his agreement. 'They only witnessed the aftermath,' he said.

I was too tired to care.

Not long after this, the sun rose and Phelippes extinguished the candles. Though I had refused dry clothes, I was anxious to go back to Wood Street and change.

'Am I needed any longer?' I asked.

'Nay,' Sir Francis said. 'Go home and rest, and look after that hand of yours. I do not want to see you here again until it is recovered.'

'You'd best take this,' Phelippes said, holding something out.

It was the porcelain bowl with the rest of the salve in it.

'That is Sir Francis Drake's property,' I said. 'It is the sort of valuable piece the spice traders sometimes bring back. Ruy Lopez has one that he treasures. They come from China. I cannot take that.'

'Take it, Kit,' Sir Francis said. 'You have saved Drake a great deal more than one little bowl. And I shall tell him so.'

Thus it was that I arrived back at the Lopez house on stumbling feet, wet through, barely able to keep my satchel from sliding off my shoulder, and carrying in my good hand a bowl that was probably worth more than my entire year's salary would be from St Thomas's.

Sara took one look at me and sent me to bed. She arrived in my room shortly after I was under the covers, carrying a hot stone wrapped in a piece of old blanket for my feet and a cup of brandy posset like the one I had seen Sir Francis eating at Barn Elms. She was followed into the room by the insinuating shape of Rikki. As soon as the door closed behind Sara, Rikki jumped up on the bed, licked my nose and settled himself comfortably at my side.

When I had finished the posset I slid down into the bed and put an arm over Rikki's warm, shaggy side. To my shame, tears started up in my eyes, for my mind kept playing over and over that moment in the cellar when I had stared at the lit fuse and the grotesque puppet staring back up at me. Besides, my hand was very painful.

By the time I next woke, it was dark. I must have slept for the entire day. Rikki was asleep, but I realised that I had heard a light tap on the door.

'Aye?' I called.

Anne put her head round the edge of the door.

'Good, you are awake. Mama is going to send you some supper to have in bed.'

She came across and rubbed Rikki behind the ears.

'How bad is your hand?'

I held out my left hand, palm up, for her to see, and she gave a gasp.

'Oh, Kit, that looks terrible!'

'It was treated quickly,' I said, 'and I have healthy skin. I think it will heal. Would you pass me that bowl? I'll salve it again.'

She picked up the bowl and sniffed it. 'It smells very odd. Almost like something you might eat, though I'm not sure I would like it.'

I laughed, and tried not to wince as I spread a fresh layer on my hand. 'Egg white, honey and bacon grease.'

'Ugh!' she said.

Rikki must have smelled the bacon grease, for he woke and became very interested first in the bowl, then in my hand, so that I had to push him gently away.

'I'll see that your supper is sent up,' Anne said. 'Will you be able to manage?'

'As long as I do not need to cut anything up,' I said.

'I will tell them.'

For the next three days the family treated me as an invalid, though I was out of bed the next morning. It was time for Anthony to return to school, so Ruy rode with him down to Winchester, and we were a house full of women, though we might not appear so. Then a summons came from Sir Francis. I was to present myself at Seething Lane at two o' the clock the next day.

'Wear your physician's gown,' the note said cryptically. 'I hope your hand is healing.'

When I presented myself at Sir Francis's office at the appointed time, I found with him not only Phelippes but a familiar figure I had not seen since our arrival in Plymouth all those months ago.

'My lord,' I said, bowing deeply to Sir Francis Drake. Had he come to ask for the return of his valuable bowl? It was sitting on a joint stool beside my bed now, washed clean.

'Dr Alvarez.' He inclined his head slightly. 'I remember how you and Dr Nuñez laboured to save Norreys's brother at Coruña.'

'Do you know how he fares, sir?'

'Quite recovered now, I understand.'

I lifted my eyes and looked Drake fully in the face for the first time.

How to regard such a man? Undoubtedly a gifted seaman, probably one of the best then living. A man who had risen entirely through his own efforts from very humble beginnings to become perhaps the richest man in England. An intrepid adventurer and implacable enemy of the Spanish. A favourite of the Queen, whose exploits filled her coffers with treasure and humiliated her foes. In the eyes of many, England's greatest hero.

Yet he could act with tremendous cruelty, not only to his enemies but to his own men and his officers. He would brook no criticism, listen to no advice. He was also a lying, treacherous brute.

I kept my eyes steady on his, but it took some effort.

'I see you are a bold fellow, Dr Alvarez,' he said, with a sharp laugh, quickly cut off. 'As Walsingham here tells me you are. Let me see your hand.'

I held out my left hand. It was bandaged now.

'Take off the bandages.'

I glanced to one side at Sir Francis, who gave the merest of nods, so with some difficulty I unwound the bandage. I would need help to replace it. My palm was still an unpleasant sight. The blisters from the burn had burst and some were oozing a yellow pus, which clung to the bandage. Removing it was painful, but I would not cry out before this man who would not tolerate weakness.

Drake seized my wrist and examined my hand. Only then did he smile and relax.

'Well, Dr Alvarez, it seems I am greatly in your debt. I understand that it was you who first discovered this conspiracy and later it was you who carried the gunpowder out of my house before it could explode. It was a brave action. Braver than I would have expected from a civilian, and a young one at that.' There was a note of contempt in his voice, in spite of his praise.

I bowed, unable to think of anything to say.

'I believe in rewarding bravery. Hold out your other hand. I hope you are right handed?'

'I am, sir,' I said, somewhat baffled by this.

He reached into the breast of his doublet and drew out something which he dropped into my hand. I barely caught it before it slipped to the ground. It was a heavy purse of coin. I took an involuntary step backward and opened my mouth to refuse, but I caught Sir Francis's eye. He gave me a warning look and shook his head, fortunately out of the line of Drake's sight.

'I, I thank you, sir,' I stumbled out the words, 'but there is no need . . .'

He made a dismissive gesture with his hand. 'The matter is finished. And the details, I am sure you understand, are not to be made public.'

I flushed. Was I being bribed to keep my mouth shut? I wanted to shout out to this arrogant, untrustworthy man, that he had no right to speak to me in that tone, but who was I, a humble Marrano physician, to answer back to one of Her Majesty's courtiers?

'Come, Kit,' Phelippes said, springing to my rescue and speaking for the first time. He had probably read the expression on my face correctly. 'I have a new cipher I want you to look at.'

We both bowed ourselves out and walked along the corridor without speaking. Once inside Phelippes office, I let out my breath like a minor explosion in itself.

'That man!' I said. 'That man, who betrayed us! When I remember all the men who died on the voyage back from Portugal . . .'

'Sit down, Kit,' Phelippes said, 'and let me help you put that bandage back.'

'You are become quite the physician,' I said, doing as I was told. 'He thought I was a fraud, even though Sir Francis, *our* Sir Francis, told him otherwise.'

'He is not worth you anger, Kit.'

He made quite a neat job of fixing my bandage back in place.

'Where is this cipher you want me to look at?'

'There is no cipher. I thought I should get you away before you exploded and we were all in trouble.'

I laughed weakly. 'Ever the diplomat. But I cannot accept his money, like some grubby fawning servant. He was trying to bribe me, as if I would babble!'

'You cannot refuse it. Do you not see that? What would be the consequences? Take it and rest content. Did you not say that you needed money to buy your own physician's cap and gown, so you need not wear those borrowed from Ruy Lopez? Spend it on that.'

'Aye,' I agreed reluctantly. 'I do need them before I start at St Thomas's.'

I looked at him suddenly in alarm. 'Jesu, I've forgotten the date, with spending time in bed and mooning about the house! What is the date?'

'The ninth of September.'

I took off my cap and ran my hand through my hair, breathing a sigh of relief.

'I thought I had missed it. I am to report at St Thomas's on the twelfth of September. Three days still from now.'

I looked down at my bandaged hand.

'If they will have me.'

Chapter Sixteen

*J*took Phelippes's advice. There was a great deal of money in the purse, though perhaps not quite as much as the value of the porcelain bowl. Sir Francis was sure no questions would be asked about that, and if there should be, he assured me that he would deal with it. I took the purse to one of the best robe-makers with premises near the Royal College of Physicians and demanded that he have both gown and cap ready for me by the eleventh of September. I handed over the buttons I had bought at the Fair. I must have impressed him, for he scrambled to finished the work in time.

Ever since facing up to Drake, despite not following my inclination to refuse the money, I had a new sense of confidence. My suspicions, first aroused at the Fair, had been proved right. I had been taken seriously by Sir Francis, Phelippes and Berden, all of them men I greatly respected. By acting on those suspicions, however confused and baffled we had been, we had prevented a disaster. I was beginning to feel that I had earned my place within that inner group. My only worry now was that the deputy superintendent at St Thomas's would take one look at my injured hand and refuse me my position there. My hand was getting slowly better, but it would not be fully healed before I had to report for duty.

While I waited for my gown to be finished, I decided to pay a call on William Baker and his wife, to discover how Adam Batecorte was faring. I had already sent a message to ask whether his injuries were healing and had received a reassuring answer, but I would be happier if I could see him for myself.

I had now learned more details of what had happened in the action against the soldiers who had marched against the Fair all the way from Plymouth on their blistered and bleeding feet, the men who had waited quietly for justice, encamped in Finsbury Fields. I felt that Adam should be told all that I now knew.

The Bakers welcomed me into their shop in Eastcheap, for once quiet and empty of customers. Liza was sitting close to the window, stitching the upper of a lady's elegant dance shoe to the sole, while Adam was carefully drawing round a pattern on to calf skin with a piece of chalk, watched by William..

'Excellent! We will have Adam a shoemaker before we are done,' William said cheerfully. 'He's very neat fingered. He's a born craftsman.'

Adam grinned and shook his head.

'I've never worked at any craft but smithing and soldiering,' he said. 'I was born on my grandfather's farm, but there were too many of us to make a living there. My eldest brother has it now. Then I worked with my father at the smithy. I can trace out a pattern, but I could never stitch as neatly as that.' He gave a nod toward Liza.

'It comes with practice,' she said, biting off her thread. 'You did not learn to handle a sword or a blacksmith's hammer overnight, nor did Dr Alvarez learn his physic without much study. Every trade demands time and patience.'

'Wisely said.' I smiled at her. I was more than ever glad that William had found this haven after the horror of losing his leg.

'Now,' I said, 'may I borrow your apprentice for a short while, and examine his injuries?'

'Certainly,' William said. 'Go through into the back. You can be private there, in case a customer should come in.'

Once we were in the back room, Adam removed his shirt and I saw that the sword slashes were healing well, though they would leave scars.

'And what of this nasty gash in your head, Adam?' I said, tilting his head to the light. 'I can see that it looks clean, but have you been troubled by any recurring pain or dizziness?'

'Not at all, doctor. It was very sore at first, then it began to itch as it healed and I had to remind myself not to scratch it. But now it is only a little tender if I touch it.'

'It is time to take the stitches out.' I removed the small scissors from my satchel and snipped through the threads.

He slipped his shirt on again and tied the strings.

'It looks as though you have been in the wars yourself.' He gestured toward my bandaged hand.

'A burn, quite a severe one,' I said, 'but it is getting better. I hope it will not bar me from work, for I have a new position.' I told him about starting at St Thomas's on the twelfth.

'Well, if they need any recommendations from patients, William and I will speak for you,' he said.

I laughed. 'I will remember that! And what of you, Adam? When you are fully recovered, will you return to the West Country? Or do you think you might like to take up the shoe-making craft, as William suggests?'

He sat down across the kitchen table from me.

'They have been more than kind to me, William and Liza, but they have no room for another pair of hands in the business. With William and his wife, and Bess and her husband, and even young Will coming along, they have more than enough people for the business to support. Even if they should decide to take on an apprentice, I am far too old. They would want a young lad to train up.'

He began to trace circles on the table with his finger.

'I feel no desire to go back to the West Country. Too many sad memories. I will try to find work of some kind here in London.' He looked up at me, somewhat desolately. 'I am strong. There must be employment for a strong labouring man, working on the docks, perhaps, or for a builder. I have not been outside much, for fear they were still looking for us soldiers, but from what little I have seen, there is a lot of building work going on in London.'

'Aye, there is,' I said. 'I will ask around for you. I think you are safe to go outside now, for I do not believe they are still looking for soldiers. I will tell you what I know for myself and what I have heard from others about the outcome of your march on Bartholomew Fair.'

I hesitated, for what I had to tell was not a pretty story, but Adam deserved the truth.

'The Lord Mayor was so terrified by the march you made on the Fair,' I said, 'that, after he reported the situation to the Common Council and the Privy Council, he himself called out two thousand of the London Trained Bands. Those were the men who attacked the camp and injured you.'

'Aye,' he said, 'I thought they were the London militia.'

'It seems they rounded up most of the men after some vicious scuffles, but without too many casualties on the part of the militia. They probably inflicted far more injuries than they received.'

'Our veterans were still weak from our time in Portugal and the starvation journey home,' he said.

I nodded my agreement. 'Most of them have now been driven out of London,' I said, 'with a warning that if they return they will be imprisoned. If any remain, they have gone into hiding. I believe the City authorities feel they have won that particular skirmish.'

His face grew sad. I do not suppose he still had any hope that the soldiers' demands might be met, even in part. Instead his fellows had been defeated and disgraced, after those soothing promises of discussions by the Lord Mayor.

'What has happened to the soldiers who had the gunpowder?' he asked. 'Have they been taken, or are they still at loose in London?'

'They have been taken, the men and the gunpowder,' I said grimly, and could not forebear glancing at my burned hand.

Adam caught my glance and his eyes widened.

'How did you burn your hand, doctor?'

'I will tell you the whole story some day,' I promised, 'but for the moment it is not to be spoken about. Those men will certainly suffer punishment.'

He looked thoughtful at that, but did not press me further. He had a quick wit, Adam, as I had realised on more than one occasion.

'What has become of our leaders?' he asked. 'Our leaders who went unarmed to consult with the Lord Mayor and Common Council? We heard they had been thrown in prison.'

This was news I was reluctant to deliver, but it must be done.

'To set an example, they say, your leaders who were invited so courteously to consult with the Lord Mayor–' I found it difficult to go on.

'Tell me,' he said grimly. 'I know it must be bad news.'

'They have been hanged at Tyburn without trial,' I said. 'They went to the hanging with great courage, holding their heads high. I was told that as the noose was put round his neck, one of them cried out to the watching crowd, "This is the pay you give soldiers for going to the wars!" And then they hanged him.'

Adam covered his face with his hands and we sat in silence.

I believed, as I had said to Sir Francis, that this treatment of the men would have serious consequences the next time the State wanted the citizens of England to rally to the defence of country and Queen. More immediately, however, now that his fellows had fled from London, what was Adam to do, once he was well enough to leave the Bakers' home?

After a time, I said, 'They were brave men, Adam, and they were treated abominably. The Lord Mayor broke his word.'

He looked up at me, with a stricken face.

'Why do great men always feel they can betray the lesser? Drake betrayed us thrice over – by abandoning us at Lisbon, by stealing the food from half the army, and by refusing to pay us, keeping the booty for himself. Now the Lord Mayor and Council betray us.'

'I suppose that is how they become powerful,' I said slowly, 'by climbing over the bodies of other men. You cannot expect compassion from them. As they say, a rich man does not become rich by giving alms to the poor. If you want help, go to a poor man.'

He sighed deeply.

'But Adam, we must look to the future. I start at St Thomas's shortly. I will see whether there might be work there. When I visited, I found the whole place teeming with people.

There are workshops there, all kinds of businesses, left over from the days when it was a monastery. I will enquire whether there is anyone needing a strong reliable man.' I grinned at him. 'One who is also neat fingered.'

After I left the Bakers' shop, I decided to go for a longer walk. Sir Francis had said that he did not want me back at Seething Lane until my hand was healed, and after I began work at St Thomas's I would have little time to myself. It was a beautiful September day. Under a sky of that bright pale blue one sees at this time of the year, the occasional trees which managed to survive in London were beginning to take on their autumn tints. There was a little sharpness in the air, a reminder that colder weather would come soon, but it also managed to allay the stink that usually arose from the London streets.

I found my steps automatically turning to the places I had known so well and where I had lived since coming to England. Just inside Newgate I saw that the chestnut seller had set up his little portable brazier again and was roasting his nuts. He had a full sack on the ground by his feet and was slitting each nut swiftly before laying it on the grid iron. I stopped to greet him.

'Why do you do that?' I asked.

'If you don't slit 'em, master, they can explode. Don't know why. Tricky things, chestnuts. So I allus slits 'em.'

He reached forward with a kind of iron paddle, shuffled the roasting chestnuts on to it, then flipped them neatly over.

'And how well did you do at the Fair?' I said.

He beamed. 'That gentleman's sixpence made my fortune. I sold my comfits so fast my wife had to stay up all night, every night of the Fair, making more. I made a tidy sum, which will help see us through the winter.'

'I am glad to hear it.'

'It was a good thing those ragamuffin soldiers wasn't allowed to break up the Fair, or honest men would have lost everything.'

'They were badly treated,' I said. 'They were honest men too, and should have been paid for their service and their suffering.'

'But why make other poor men suffer?' He shook his head. 'Don't seem right to me.'

'I wonder whether they would have carried out that threat,' I said. 'I think they only wanted to force the authorities to pay them what they were owed.'

'Well,' he said, shovelling the cooked chestnuts on to the side plate of his brazier and laying out a fresh batch, 'I don't suppose we'll ever know, master.'

'I don't suppose we will. I'll have two pokes of chestnuts, please.'

As usual, I handed one of the paper twists of nuts through the grid of Newgate prison, where the destitute prisoners with no one to bring them food stretched out their hands to the passersby. I wondered whether any of those grubby hands belonged to the soldiers who had planned the attack on Drake's house.

Through Newgate itself, then up Pie Corner. The fair ground was empty of all the stalls and tents and booths, the acrobats and pig women, the fortune tellers and gingerbread bakers. Litter blew about the wide space, but soon there would be no sign that the magical town had ever been here. Like the fairy palace in some ancient tale it had vanished away for another year. Already the men who worked at Smithfield were putting up the pens for the beast market next day.

I crossed toward the hospital and stood looking at it with fondness, but sadly. It was there that I had learned my profession, and there that I had worked for so many hours with my father. It had been hard work, and sometimes distressing, but I had been happy there. A familiar figure emerged from the gatehouse and came toward me.

'Kit!' It was Peter Lambert, grinning from ear to ear. 'Have you come to see us?'

'Nay,' I said, backing away a little, as if I had somehow been caught out. 'I am free for a few days, so I am enjoying the fine weather taking a walk.'

He looked puzzled at this, for I was not known for idling away my time taking walks, like a gentleman of leisure.

270

'I start at St Thomas's on the twelfth,' I said, by way of explanation. 'Come to say farewell to the old place.' I nodded toward the hospital.

'Well, I hope you will not forget us,' he said. Then he smiled again, rather shyly. 'I have been meaning to write to you. I have some news.'

'You will take your final apothecary exams soon?'

'That too. Early next year. What I was going to tell you–' he coloured, 'the fact is, I have asked Helen Winger to marry me, and she has agreed.'

'You are affianced!' I seized his hand in my good one and shook it warmly. 'That is splendid news, Peter.'

'We cannot marry until I am fully trained,' he said, 'and have a salary enough to wed and support a wife. We will need to rent our own home. I cannot go on living in my room in the hospital. It will be some time next summer. The governors say that they will keep me on here.'

'You have done so well for yourself, Peter,' I said. 'I am truly glad for you. Such changes in life for both of us! Shall we go and drink to your good fortune at the tavern?'

'I wish I could, but it will need to be later,' he said regretfully. 'I am sent with a potion for a patient who went home yesterday. An old man, and stubborn. He *would* go home, though we wanted to keep him a few more days.'

I laughed. 'Not like some we have known, eh? The ones who like the warmth and the food and the nursing care so much that they want to move in. Do you remember that fellow we could hardly get rid of, when we needed the bed for the soldiers from Sluys?'

'I do.' He grinned at the memory. 'He had a shrew of a wife. Found it much more peaceful here.'

He turned away, then seemed to notice my bandaged hand for the first time.

'You have injured yourself!'

'A burn,' I said. 'I'm recovering!'

When Peter was gone, I followed the familiar way back from the hospital to Duck Lane. I had walked it so often with my father, I could almost imagine he was walking beside me still. I would take one last look at my old home, then never come here again. I felt I was closing one door after another on the past.

The woman I had seen before, the day I returned to London, was coming toward me from the other end of the lane, with a basket over her arm. Mistress Temperley, the wife of the new physician who had taken my father's place. She had her little boy with her, but not the baby. I supposed the reliable maid must be minding the house and the baby. She caught sight of me in my gentleman's doublet and dropped a courtesy. Her face showed no sign of recognition. I inclined my head, and watched her go into my home. My old home.

I turned my back on it and walked away.

I asked the servants to wake me before dawn on the twelfth. It was a long walk to St Thomas's from Wood Street and I did not want to risk being late. I donned my new cap and gown, which I felt looked impressive, but I had no stomach for breakfast. The previous evening Sara had helped me put a smaller bandage on my left hand and I felt it no longer looked too serious. I was leaving Rikki with Anne again, but I would need to find some permanent arrangement. The gatekeeper at Barts had always been fond of Rikki, but there was no knowing what the gatekeeper at Thomas's would be like. He might hate dogs.

It was strange to be walking through the City so early in the morning. The streets were almost deserted except for the homeless beggars still asleep, huddled for shelter in the doorways of shops. Soon they would be woken and kicked out by the apprentices. At least it was not yet cold. I did not know how they could survive in the cold of full winter.

The night soil men had finished their work and the street traders were not yet abroad. London seemed remarkably peaceful with so few people about. I saw a young shepherd herding a flock of sheep along Cheapside. They would be destined for the market at Smithfield. A couple of women were gossiping beside the Great Conduit, their buckets forgotten at their feet. They turned to stare at me as I passed in my finery, then, like Mistress Temperley, they curtsied. I inclined my head, suppressing a smile. Clothes maketh the man, it seemed.

Carts were rumbling down Gracechurch Street, come from the market gardens in Shoreditch and further afield. They were loaded with every kind of vegetable: cabbages, onions, leeks, carrots. There were cages of squawking chickens and ducks, baskets of eggs, and here and there a few rabbits hanging upside down from the tailboard of the cart. The farmers must have left home even earlier than I. Some would be heading to Newgate market, others would be going the same way as I, over the Bridge to Southwark to the markets there, where disputes sometimes broke out between these farmers from the north of the City and the farmers with smallholdings on the fringes of Southwark, who regarded the southern markets as rightfully theirs. I quickened my pace to get ahead of the carts before they reached the Bridge.

Even the Bridge was quiet this morning. A few people were passing on foot toward me, those who lived in Southwark but worked in the City. There were no pedlars or entertainers here yet. Overhead, maids were throwing open shutters and shaking out bedding. No need to dodge the contents of piss pots here, as one must in the London streets. The maids would simply tip them into the river, adding to the filth.

I had learned to avoid looking at the spiked heads over the gate at the southern end of the Bridge, though I had never quite forgotten how they had haunted my childhood nightmares. Today I had other worries. I slowed my pace now I was in Southwark, for after walking fast I was flushed and hot, in no state to arrive at the hospital. In any case, I was early. Instead I ambled along, looking about me at the unfamiliar streets with a new eye. I would be spending most of my time here now, and I would get to know the back streets and crowded alleys – and their inhabitants – as I had known the poor districts around St Bartholomew's. Both districts were poverty stricken, but this was probably a rougher area. The men and women who worked in the stinking industries banned from London lived here, as did the prostitutes of every sort, and those who were employed at the bear baiting and bull baiting. Although the Rose playhouse had been built here two years before to avoid the restrictions of the Common Council, it had to rub along with these coarser forms of entertainment. Although the Queen was said to love a play – and

Simon had appeared before her even when he was one of St Paul's boy players – the playhouses and their actors were still regarded by many as hardly better than vagabonds. The Puritans, those godly people, like the man I had seen ranting at the Fair, thought them creatures born of the Devil.

It was time. I made my way under the gate and into the great doorway of St Thomas's, still with the fine carving surrounding it from its monastic days, although empty niches on either side showed where statues of saints had been removed. Perhaps one had been St Thomas à Becket. No Tudor monarch would wish to have him presiding over a public building, a man who had dared to stand up to his king.

I knew my way now to Superintendent Ailmer's office, and strode along the corridor as though I already had every right to be there. Perhaps I had, but I would not be quite sure of myself until I was formally given my duties. Mistress Maynard was coming out of the room as I approached and rewarded me with a curtsey and a smile. I bowed in return.

'Dr Alvarez,' she said, 'I am glad to see you. Dr Colet left two days ago and we have had an outbreak of vomiting amongst the young children of the parish. I hope to see you on the wards as soon as you have seen the Superintendent.'

This was promising. If they were short handed, there was unlikely to be any question over my appointment.

Her eyes went to my bandage. 'You have hurt your hand?'

'It is nothing,' I lied. 'Besides, I am right handed.'

I knocked on Ailmer's door as she hurried away further along the corridor and turned to ascend a staircase.

'Come.' The Superintendent's voice was abrupt, but in fact he looked relieved to see me. I had decided that, in the interests of harmony, I would give him the title he was not quite entitled to.

'Good morning, Superintendent,' I said.

'Good morning, Dr Alvarez. I will not keep you long. Initially I have assigned you to take charge of the unmarried mothers' ward and the children's ward. We have many children at St Thomas's. These people breed like rabbits.'

Perhaps seeing the look of distaste on my face, he altered his tone, adding hastily, 'It is a young population. Young families. Not many live to a great age who work in the tanneries and brickworks. We have many cases of congestion of the lungs. Many young people from the country settle here as well. They cannot afford the London rents, even if they work in the City.'

'I have seen them crossing the Bridge of a morning,' I said.

'Aye. And then there are the Strangers,' he said, using the common London term for anyone not English born. 'We have some strange folk hereabouts. Sailors, some of them, with dark skins, or yellow skins and slit eyes, speaking gobbledegook.'

Ailmer, I decided, was not a tolerant man, but that did not mean he could not manage a hospital. He was clearly busy and distracted. He had not even asked me to sit down.

'Come,' he said, rising from his chair, 'I will show you the way to the two wards I am putting under your care. You will, of course, be required to assist in the other wards when you are needed, but you will be responsible for the smooth running of these two.'

Suddenly he caught sight of my bandaged hand.

'What is that? Are you injured?'

'A burn,' I said. 'It is nearly healed. It will be no impediment.'

He led me up the staircase where I had seen Mistress Maynard disappear. The lying-in ward was large, airy and well appointed. Silently I congratulated Mayor Whittington on his gift to unmarried mothers. What an extraordinary man he must have been, and a good deal more tolerant than Ailmer. Almost every bed was occupied. Most of the women looked pale and thin, hardly the bouncing whores common gossip spoke of when they mentioned the Winchester geese. Some were nursing newborn babes, some had yet to give birth, some were trying to sleep, despite a rich cacophony of infant wails.

'The children's ward is next door,' Ailmer said. 'Ah, Mistress Maynard! Will you take Dr Alvarez to the children's ward? I have a great deal of paperwork awaiting me. Later, introduce him to the almoner and show him the apothecaries' room.'

He turned to me. 'Mistress Maynard and John Haddon, the almoner, should be able to tell you everything you need to know. If there is anything else, you may come to me.'

It was clear from his tone that he hoped this would not be necessary.

'Shall we see the children's ward, then, Mistress Maynard?' I said. 'An outbreak of vomiting, you said. How have you been treating them?'

So began my work at St Thomas's hospital, Southwark. It some ways it was no different to my previous work at St Bartholomew's, but in other ways it was. The lying-in ward for unmarried women was, I believe, unique in the world, and it was always busy, for the prostitutes of the Southwark stews were forever getting pregnant. In other towns and cities, such women would have done anything to rid themselves of an unwanted child, but the enlightened practice here meant that the pregnancies usually went full term, the woman were better cared for and better fed than ever before in their lives, and the babies had some hope of a future. An unusual situation, to say the least.

Then there were the different practices regarding admission here, for St Bartholomew's turned away all patients whom two doctors judged to be incurable. Of those desperate cases refused treatment, some managed to drag themselves across the river to St Thomas's, which turned none away. This had been the practice here as long as anyone could remember. All were to be admitted, save those with leprosy, who were despatched to the Lazar House of St Mary and St Leonard, which was situated here in Southwark, without St George's Bar. Yet there were few lepers nowadays, compared with what we were told of the problem a century or more ago.

As a result of St Thomas's policy of admitting every sick person, in addition to the poor who lived south of the river we also treated the incurable cases from the City itself, which had been rejected by St Bartholomew's. This meant that all we could do for many of them was to ease their suffering, keeping them clean and warm and fed until they died, but my fellow physicians took some pride in the challenge of these seemingly hopeless patients, and occasionally succeeded in curing them. I found I soon shared in their keen desire to treat these cases. There was a mostly friendly rivalry between the two hospitals, and I found my loyalties sometimes severely tested.

In my second week, I approached the gatekeeper, Tom Read, for I had noticed that he had a dog, an ancient wolfhound, stiff in his joints, which spent his days sleeping in the gatekeeper's small room in the gatehouse.

'Goodman Read,' I said, 'I see you are a lover of dogs.'

'Aye.' He looked at me suspiciously. 'Superintendent says I may keep Swifty here. I have permission. He helps to guard the gate.'

'Indeed,' I said. The wolfhound lay snoring at his feet, and I had never seen him move whenever anyone went in or out at the gate. I crouched down and rubbed the old fellow behind the ears.

'I have a dog, Rikki, he's called. He was a stray, but he saved my life in the Low Countries.'

Tom looked interested. 'What sort of a dog would he be, doctor?'

I laughed. 'Nothing in particular. Not like this fine Irish wolfhound. Over there they use them as working dogs, to pull little carts.'

'That's a strange thing for a dog, that is.'

I saw I had caught his interest. 'I need somewhere safe to leave him while I am at work in the hospital,' I said. 'With someone who cares for dogs. Would you be willing, Goodman Read? There'd be a groat a week in it for you, and he would be company for your lad.'

To my relief, he agreed, so from the next day Rikki accompanied me to St Thomas's every morning. He was eager to befriend the wolfhound, but the old dog merely sniffed him and went back to sleep. Tom, however, seemed pleased with the company. I suppose he must often feel bored and lonely on his own when there was no activity about the gate.

Tom was useful in another way. I remembered my promise to Adam, and asked Tom whether he knew of anyone needing a strong honest worker in any of the businesses which continued to flourish in the old monastic grounds. Principal among them were a printing works and a stained glass foundry.

'Aye,' he said. 'There's a man from the glass works got in trouble with the law and the constables hauled him away. Your man could try there.'

And Tom was right. I sent word to Adam and visited the glass works myself, to recommend him. Before the end of September, Adam had started work as a labourer. It looked hot and exhausting work to me, but the windows they produced were almost miraculous in their beauty and colour. Although the monasteries had all been destroyed half a century ago, cathedrals and parish churches still had their stained glass windows which often needed repair, and sometimes a benefactor would donate a new one. There were hundreds of parish churches in London, Westminster and Southwark, so the glass-makers were never short of work.

Altogether I soon settled in to my new hospital and my new work. Then October brought two changes.

Normally I left the house before anyone else was astir, but one morning Sara was waiting for me, her face shining.

'You were so late home last night, Kit, that I could not tell you our news, but I wanted to see you before you left this morning.'

'I can see from your face that it is good news,' I said with a smile.

'Ruy has been partially forgiven by the Privy Council for his part in organising the Portuguese expedition and – so they say – losing them so much money. He has not received his import monopoly again. That has already been awarded to someone else. But instead he has been given two estates in the Midlands from which he can draw the income. He understands that there is extensive woodland of mature timber. That will be very profitable, now that so many new ships are being built to strengthen the navy.'

I took both of her hands in mine. 'I am so glad, Sara. It will be an end to your financial worries, after Ruy lost the monopoly. And his rich patients have not deserted him, for he is an excellent doctor. And the Queen still sponsors Anthony at Winchester. Everything is now looking fine and prosperous for the future.'

After all her kindness to me, I was relieved that all now seemed more hopeful for her. I saw there were tears in her eyes.

'You are a dear friend, Kit. I wish I could see you settled, and in your proper self.'

I laughed. 'I do very well, Sara. I am a hard working but contented physician at an excellent hospital, with occasional work for Sir Francis Walsingham. I lack nothing.' Nothing, I thought, but a family.

And the other change? Simon came home from the Low Countries.

He was waiting for me one evening by the gatehouse as I came out of St Thomas's on my way home to Wood Street. At the sight of him I felt almost giddy with pleasure, and tried hard not to grin like a fool.

'I am sorry to hear all your sad news, Kit,' he said, linking his arm with mine and giving it a friendly squeeze. 'I have been talking to Sara Lopez. Your father gone and your home gone, and the Portuguese voyage a disaster.'

I shrugged.

'It is all behind me now.' So much had happened since my return in the spring, I could hardly remember the person I had been then, sitting in desolation beside the Rose theatre. I did not tell him how glad I was to see him, or how the firm grip of his arm gave me a stirring of pleasure deep in my belly.

'And Walsingham himself finding you a position at St Thomas's!'

'It was kind of him. It is very different from St Bartholomew's, but I am enjoying my work there, especially with the new mothers and the children.'

'Have I not heard that they have a special ward for the Winchester geese to give birth?'

'There is a ward for unmarried mothers,' I said severely, 'but they are not all prostitutes. Some are the victims of rape. Some have been betrayed by the men who had falsely promised to marry them.' I did not want to fall out with Simon over this, when he was so soon back in England, but I had become very protective of my women patients.

'What becomes of the babies?'

'Some of the mothers keep their children, however difficult it may be for them. They are not all bad women, you know. A few babies are adopted, perhaps by women who have lost a child or have not been blessed with one. The rest go to Christ's Hospital, where they are cared for and taught a trade.'

I remember suddenly – something I too often forgot – that Simon himself had been orphaned young. He had been fortunate to gain a place at St Paul's school, where his talent for singing and acting had been fostered.

'Tell me about your adventures in the Low Countries,' I said. 'Your time there will have been very different from mine, I am sure.'

He laughed. 'Aye. I certainly did no breaking and entering, nor finding dead bodies. We travelled about, giving public performances at inns and private ones at the houses of noblemen, but the whole tale would take too long now. We will dine together one day this week and I will tell you all.'

'We'll dine together, will we?'

'Aye. Now, listen, Kit. Why do you spend so long every day crossing the City and the river between Wood Street and St Thomas's? You should be living here in Southwark.'

'I live free in Wood Street,' I said.

'But the time you must waste! There is a room for rent at my lodgings – the tenant moved out while I was away. Take it, and save the walk twice a day.'

He was persuasive, and at last I agreed to see the room. I knew I could not stay for ever with Sara, and after paying off my debt to her I still had some of Drake's money as well as my salary from the hospital. I was now in a position to rent a room of my own, if it should prove not too expensive.

'Why are you living in Southwark, Simon? Is Burbage's company not still appearing at the Theatre in Shoreditch?'

'I took the room when I was on loan to Master Henslowe at the Rose, and I find it cheap and comfortable. The walk straight across the Bridge and up Fish Street and Gracechurch to

Bishopsgate is not far, not nearly as far as you have to come from Wood Street. Besides, all the best rooms in Shoreditch around the Curtain and the Theatre are taken by players who earn more than I do and can pay a higher rent.'

We walked a short way from the hospital along Bankside to a house between Winchester Palace and the bear pits. It was a large house, three storeys high and fronting on the river. Simon introduced me to the landlord, who seemed respectable, unlike many in both the City and Southwark. And he did not mind Rikki, who was on his best behaviour. The landlord led us up a well swept staircase and unlocked the door of a room at the front of the house. It was surprisingly clean and pleasant, though fairly small and very simply furnished after the luxury of the Lopez house, but its very simplicity appealed to me. Ruy's flamboyant taste rather overpowered me. After a little wrangling, I agreed terms with the landlord, and by the end of the week Rikki and I had moved in.

The room was high up under the roof, just below the garret, but the window looked out over the river and gave me a view across the water-borne traffic to St Paul's on the rising ground beyond. The landlord had lime-washed the walls after the last tenant had left and the fresh scent of it still lingered. The small fireplace had a trivet and a hook for a cooking pot, so I would be able to make myself simple meals. The only furniture consisted of a low cot, a table, a carved chest for my clothes, and a couple of joint stools.

I decided that as soon as I could afford it, I would buy two chairs from the street market in Southwark, where secondhand goods were sold, and then I might invite a friend to dine with me at my own table. I laughed at myself for taking such pleasure in my small domestic arrangements. I laid my few clothes and my knapsack in the chest and knocked some pegs into the wall to hang my satchel of medicines, my cloak and my physician's gown. My two precious books I laid side by side on the table, both somewhat tattered now after their rough journeys in my knapsack: the *Testament* given to me by our old rector, David Dee, at St Bartholomew-the-Great and the privately printed copy of Sidney's poems that Simon had given me for my seventeenth birthday. Beside them I set the porcelain bowl I had come by rather illegitimately from Drake's kitchen. Perhaps I would fill it with pot pourri, like any proud housewife.

One evening soon after I had moved into my new lodgings, Simon met me again at the hospital gatehouse.

'We are all meeting for a celebration dinner tonight,' he said, 'and you are to come too. You can bring Rikki.'

'We?' I said.

'All my fellows from Burbage's company. Some of us have been away in the Low Countries, some of the others were touring the provinces of England – even as far as Cornwall. The rest have been working in London. Now we are all back together again, and we are meeting to dine at the Lion.'

The Lion Inn was close to our lodgings, so we made our way along Bankside and found most of the other players already gathered there.

'Can this be Kit, this fine fellow in a silk gown?' It was Guy Bingham, musician and comic. I punched him on the shoulder.

'It is not silk, you ass! How could I afford silk? My old gown was torn up to make bandages on the Portuguese expedition.'

He flashed me a quick look of sympathy, then patted the bench beside him.

'We have missed you, Kit. Where have you been hiding all summer?'

'Oh,' I said vaguely, 'I had some work with Walsingham. And now I have started at a new post in St Thomas's.'

'I know.' It was Christopher Haigh, who played most of the romantic young leads. 'We went looking for you there, but we could not find you.'

Richard Burbage gave me an elaborate bow and pulled a stool up to the table. Already he was gaining a reputation for his performance in dramatic roles, though he was not much older than I. His brother Cuthbert helped their father with the business of the players' company, but Richard lived only for the stage.

Amongst the others seated around the long table there was another young man, perhaps a little older than Richard, whom I did not know. He must be new to Lord Strange's Men. He was introduced to me simply as Will. He said very little, but I noticed that he watched and listened intently.

Then there was a roar for the inn keeper as the door swung open, and the magnificent figure of James Burbage strode in. As always he seemed to take up the space of any two normal men, not because he was large, but because he crackled with energy.

'Aha!' he cried, slapping me on the shoulder, so that I nearly pitched forward into the tankard of beer someone had just set down before me. 'Our missing companion, our *medicus magnificus*, our rival to Guy on the lute! You have returned to us, Christoval Alvarez!'

'It seems that I have, Master Burbage,' I said, raising my rescued beer to pledge him.

Rikki settled at my feet with a sigh. He was more at home under an inn table than in the elegant surroundings of the Lopez house.

'What can you give us to eat, Master Innkeeper?' Burbage roared, throwing himself down on my other side and nearly knocking me into my beer again. 'Roast unicorn? Larks' tongues in wine? Stags hunted by moonlight, by the goddess Diana herself?'

'Roast beef and onions, sir,' said the inn keeper, po-faced, who looked as though he knew Burbage of old.

Simon winked at me across the table.

I leaned back, avoiding Burbage's elbow, and stretched out my legs, careful not to disturb Rikki.

This – after all – this was my family.

Historical Note

The disaffected soldiers from the Portuguese expedition did in fact march on Bartholomew Fair in the summer of 1589, threatening to attack the fair and pay themselves by seizing goods from the stalls unless the authorities agreed to recompense them fairly for their service against Spain. They were fobbed off with false promises, driven away from the city by the armed London Trained Bands (the local militia), and four of their leaders were treacherously hanged. However, the theft of gunpowder and its use is my own addition to the story.

That same summer, Sir Francis Walsingham grew progressively more ill, but – as always – continued his demanding work, making no concessions to his physical condition.

The sources are inconsistent on the subject of the children of Sara and Ruy Lopez. They agree that five out of the nine survived. Ambrose, Anne and Anthony are documented, but some sources state that there were two other boys, others that there were two other girls. I have opted for the latter.

Richard (Dick) Whittington (1354-1423), Lord Mayor of London, established a lying-in ward for unmarried mothers at St Thomas's Hospital in Southwark some hundred and seventy years before the time of this story. It was only one of many public works he financed to improve the lives of Londoners, particularly the poor, which were carried out both during his lifetime and through bequests in his will. Even today, nearly six hundred years later, there is a Whittington Charity, providing help to the needy.

The Author

Ann Swinfen spent her childhood partly in England and partly on the east coast of America. She was educated at Somerville College, Oxford, where she read Classics and Mathematics and married a fellow undergraduate, the historian David Swinfen. While bringing up their five children and studying for a postgraduate MSc in Mathematics and a BA and PhD in English Literature, she had a variety of jobs, including university lecturer, translator, freelance journalist and software designer. She served for nine years on the governing council of the Open University and for five years worked as a manager and editor in the technical author division of an international computer company, but gave up her full-time job to concentrate on her writing, while continuing part-time university teaching. In 1995 she founded Dundee Book Events, a voluntary organisation promoting books and authors to the general public.

Her first three novels, *The Anniversary*, *The Travellers*, and *A Running Tide*, all with a contemporary setting but also an historical resonance, were published by Random House, with translations into Dutch and German. *The Testament of Mariam* marks something of a departure. Set in the first century, it recounts, from an unusual perspective, one of the most famous and yet ambiguous stories in human history. At the same time it explores life under a foreign occupying force, in lands still torn by conflict to this day. Her second historical novel, *Flood*, is set in the fenlands of East Anglia during the seventeenth century, where the local people fought desperately to save their land from greedy and unscrupulous speculators.

Currently she is working on a late sixteenth century series, featuring a young Marrano physician who is recruited as a code-breaker and spy in Walsingham's secret service. The first book in the series is *The Secret World of Christoval Alvarez*, the second is *The Enterprise of England*, the third is *The Portuguese Affair* and the fourth is *Bartholomew Fair*.

She now lives in Broughty Ferry, on the northeast coast of Scotland, with her husband, formerly vice-principal of the University of Dundee, a cocker spaniel, and a rescue kitten.
www.annswinfen.com

Made in the USA
Columbia, SC
15 October 2017